The shining splendor of our Zebra Lovegram logo on the cover of this book reflects the glittering excellence of the story inside. Look for the Zebra Lovegram whenever you buy a historical romance. It's a trademark that guarantees the very best in quality and reading entertainment.

Wild, Wonderful Love

Tonight, she did not want him to stop kissing her. Tonight she wanted to know the power this man possessed, the power that affected her so totally. Her mood was a wild and reckless one, and she wanted to give way to this feeling. Never had she expected to see him again, but he had appeared, and that had changed everything for her.

"Oh, Tiffany, I pray you won't hate me tomorrow, but tonight you're going to love me as you've never loved any other man," he moaned as he lowered the bodice of her gown.

She felt his hot, searing lips making a trail down her throat until they came to rest on the rosy tip of her breast. There was a magic he played that she'd never known before and her body arched with the new sensations. She knew nothing of this world of ecstasy he was drawing her into.

Caught up in a whirlwind of passion, nothing mattered to Tiffany except that Chad keep making wild, wonderful love to her.

THE BEST IN HISTORICAL ROMANCES

TIME-KEPT PROMISES (2422, $3.95)
by Constance O'Day Flannery
Sean O'Mara froze when he saw his wife Christina standing before him. She had vanished and the news had been written about in all of the papers—he had even been charged with her murder! But now he had living proof of his innocence, and Sean was not about to let her get away. No matter that the woman was claiming to be someone named Kristine; she still caused his blood to boil.

PASSION'S PRISONER (2573, $3.95)
by Casey Stewart
When Cassandra Lansing put on men's clothing and entered the Rawlings saloon she didn't expect to lose anything—in fact she was sure that she would win back her prized horse Rapscallion that her grandfather lost in a card game. She almost got a smug satisfaction at the thought of fooling the gamblers into believing that she was a man. But once she caught a glimpse of the virile Josh Rawlings, Cassandra wanted to be the woman in his embrace!

ANGEL HEART (2426, $3.95)
by Victoria Thompson
Ever since Angelica's father died, Harlan Snyder had been angling to get his hands on her ranch, the Diamond R. And now, just when she had an important government contract to fulfill, she couldn't find a single cowhand to hire—all because of Snyder's threats. It was only a matter of time before the legendary gunfighter Kid Collins turned up on her doorstep, badly wounded. Angelica assessed his firmly muscled physique and stared into his startling blue eyes. Beneath all that blood and dirt he was the handsomest man she had ever seen, and the one person who could help beat Snyder at his own game.

Available wherever paperbacks are sold, or order direct from the Publisher. Send cover price plus 50¢ per copy for mailing and handling to Zebra Books, Dept. 2887, 475 Park Avenue South, New York, N.Y. 10016. Residents of New York, New Jersey and Pennsylvania must include sales tax. DO NOT SEND CASH.

DECEPTIVE DESIRES

WANDA OWEN

ZEBRA BOOKS
KENSINGTON PUBLISHING CORP.

ZEBRA BOOKS

are published by

Kensington Publishing Corp.
475 Park Avenue South
New York, NY 10016

Copyright © 1990 by Wanda Owen

All rights reserved. No part of this book may be reproduced
in any form or by any means without the prior written
consent of the Publisher, excepting brief quotes used in
reviews.

First printing: February, 1990

Printed in the United States of America

This book is dedicated to all the readers who had urged me to write a sequel to Moonlight Splendor. *Your letters are always very important to me. So it was my pleasure to write this book about the daughter of Pierre and Charmaine Renaud. I'll hope you love Tiffany as much as you liked her parents.*

Let me hear from you!

Prologue

No place was as beautiful as Paris in the springtime, Tiffany Renaud thought as she traveled down one of the grand boulevards lined with trees burgeoning with pink and white blossoms. A brief shower of rain earlier in the afternoon seemed to have enhanced the sweet fragrance permeating the air.

She urged the driver of her father's fine barouche to move more slowly as they approached her house. Her mother sat beside her on the rich leather seat, a smile on her face, thinking to herself what a domineering young lady her daughter was becoming.

"You don't mind, do you, Maman?" Tiffany asked, "It's still so early."

"Of course not, cherie," Madame Renaud assured her. It was hard to refuse her beautiful Tiffany anything. After all, she'd had to bear three sons before she finally got the daughter she'd yearned for so desperately. But it had been worth the wait. Madame Renaud had never seen such a beautiful baby as Tiffany was with her hair as black as a raven's wing, just like her father's. It had delighted her that Tiffany had her own violet-blue eyes even though she did not have her silver-blonde hair.

Everything about Tiffany seemed to be special. She

sought to make her appearance into the world on the Renauds' eighth wedding anniversary. Madame Renaud could not have imagined a more precious gift. She knew that her devoted husband loved her dearly for giving him such fine sons, but there was a special glow in his dark eyes the first moment he saw his baby daughter.

It was inevitable that Tiffany would be spoiled and pampered by her doting father, three protective older brothers, and a worshipping grandfather. She grew up expecting and getting adoration from any man she encountered.

Tiffany had been denied nothing that wealth could buy. Her grandfather was one of the richest industrialists in France and now her father was in charge of the vast operations which extended beyond the boundaries of the country.

It had been an interesting afternoon for Madame Renaud this magnificent May day. Her daughter had accompanied her to the concert in the park where they'd joined friends of the Renaud family.

Being a worldly-wise, perceptive lady, Madame Renaud had observed an interesting scene there in the park this afternoon. She knew why Tiffany was so light-hearted now. She had caught the eye of an arrogant stranger strolling in the park. Madame Renaud had to confess she understood why such a striking young man would catch Tiffany's eye and interest her.

There was a different air about him that whetted Tiffany's fickle heart and curiosity when his piercing, cold gray eyes devoured her as he leaned against a tree. Madame Renaud had known that rugged, reckless breed of a man years earlier, and she knew the excitement such a man could arouse in a young lady of Tiffany's age.

A smug smile etched her face as she thought about those glorious years of her own past. Now, it would seem her own daughter was about to enter that time in her life.

8

She wondered what Tiffany would think if she knew about those times when her mother had known the heights of wild, wonderful ecstasy, as well as the pain and heartache of such an overwhelming love.

Something told Madame Renaud that the young man Tiffany had seen in the park this afternoon would not bow to her as all her other suitors had done. No, this young, handsome devil would bend *her* to *his* will!

She could not wait to get home to tell her husband about this little happening. They had agreed that sooner or later Tiffany would meet a man who did not immediately succumb to her charms. They'd wondered how their daughter would react when that happened.

Who was it, Madame Renaud wondered, that this young man reminded her of? It was someone from her own past, but couldn't remember! Was her past somehow to play a part in her beautiful daughter's future?

But that was a crazy thought, she told herself. *How could that be?*

Part I

Springtime In Paris

Chapter 1

Pierre Renaud took great pride in his lovely wife. With her silver-blonde hair and sapphire blue eyes, she was considered one of the loveliest ladies in Paris. Their daughter, Tiffany, was constantly praised for her stunning beauty, too. Two such beauties were a handful at times though.

Sitting now in their lavishly furnished dining room, tranquil and pleasantly decorated in soft shades of blue and ivory, he gazed at the two lovely ladies sharing his evening meal. God, they were beautiful, with the candlelight reflecting on their faces! Yet, how different the two of them were!

A smile came to his face as he thought of so many things which had brought about this moment—this time of his life. He swore he had to be the luckiest man in the whole wide world. Few men could boast that they were still as much in love with their wives as he still was after all these years. Never once had he thought about taking a mistress as so many of his friends had done. His wife made their home his castle wherever they might be. Whether they were spending time on their country estate or here in Paris, he always looked forward to coming home after his busy days at the office.

The vast Renaud empire required them to travel a great deal, and a part of the autumn months was spent at their townhouse in London.

While he sat there enjoying his pleasant, private musings, his wife's voice called his attention. "We wish you could have been with us this afternoon. It was beautiful in the park and the music was absolutely wonderful. Papa would have enjoyed it, wouldn't he, Tiffany?"

"Oh . . . oh, yes he would have," Tiffany replied after a moment of hesitation, for her thoughts were elsewhere. The splendor of this spring day and the brief, but exciting sight of that interesting stranger in the park confirmed her belief that there was always romance in the air in springtime Paris.

Already, she was anticipating telling her best friend, Denise, about the imposing young man with silver-gray eyes. How was she going to describe him? He was older than any of her other suitors and there was an air of boldness about him. She sensed a rugged, devil-may-care attitude when he gave her that crooked grin as his eyes danced slowly over her from the top of her head down to her dainty feet.

Tiffany wanted to meet him again. Her romantic heart told her that he was waiting for her. His intense, piercing eyes had promised her this as they locked into hers.

Madame Renaud could see that Tiffany was preoccupied. She had no interest whatsoever as her parents discussed what had happened at the office. She had not absorbed the announcement that her father had fired his bookkeeper and offered the job to her oldest brother, Charles. Tiffany could not have cared less about all this.

"Oh, Pierre, I think that is wonderful. It was time he came into the business. Was he pleased?" his wife anxiously asked him.

"He was more thrilled than I expected him to be,

14

cherie. It was the right move on my part. Besides, Charles will have the Renauds' interest in mind. I think some figures on the books have not been quite accurate for many months now and a few weeks ago when I heard the rumors that Albert had taken a mistress, I began to realize why his salary was not adequate. You know, I've always been generous with him, cherie."

"Of course you have, Pierre. You had not mentioned any of this to me. I had no idea of this suspicion."

"Why should I worry your pretty head about this? I knew that sooner or later the truth would come out, and I think it has. Anyway, I let him go today and I must tell you he was a very angry young man. But I'll not support his dallying around when he has a fine wife and two lovely babes."

"Good for you, Pierre!" Madame declared, the warmth of her love and admiration reflecting in her voice as her hand reached out to touch her husband's. He took it and raised it to his lips, giving it a gentle caress.

Tiffany gazed up to see this tender moment shared by her parents, thinking how divine the two of them were. She was glad that her parents seemed to share such a devotion and love. This was what she wanted with the man she would someday fall in love with. The shocking tales her friend Denise told her about her parents had stunned her. She found it hard to believe that the nice, quiet Madame Adrian had a young lover the same age as Denise's older brother and that her father chased the young servant girls, especially if they were pretty. Denise swore she had seen him fondling them in the darkened hallways of their home. Tiffany was appalled, for she could never imagine her own father doing such a despicable act as that.

Her mother's soft voice broke into Tiffany's private musings. "Isn't that wonderful, Tiffany . . . isn't that perfect that Charles shall be working with your father?"

She gave her mother a nod, agreeing wholeheartedly. Of all her brothers, Charles was very special, for he had pampered her all her life. That was not to say that Phillipe and Jacques had not been doting older brothers; but Jacques was interested in the sea and Phillipe had taken a wife and was completely engrossed in his farm outside Cherbourg where he raised his goats and grew vegetables.

"I think this is wonderful! Papa, I know you must be very pleased, too." Tiffany gave her father one of those sweet smiles which could melt his heart.

"Ah, Tiffany, I am a very happy man tonight. I am indeed lucky to have such a wonderful family. I have your mother to thank for all this. She gave me fine sons and a beautiful daughter." His dark eyes were warm with love. Tiffany knew that she could never do anything to disappoint him or dash that fierce pride he had in his family. There was a certain responsibility in being the daughter of Pierre Renaud.

"Grand-père will be thrilled, too, won't he, Papa?"

"Grand-père will be overjoyed, I can tell you, Tiffany," Monsieur Renaud chuckled. Nothing would please the elderly Etienne Renaud more than knowing his grandson had joined the Renaud empire.

"Then it is a grand day for the Renaud family, I would say," Tiffany declared, smiling at her parents in that special way of hers.

Madame Renaud decided then and there, as she sat at the table observing her seventeen-year-old daughter, exactly why she'd chosen the name of Tiffany. Tiffany was an exquisite silk, a raiment always worn by kings and queens. Ah, yes, this was her daughter, with her long glossy black hair that looked like luxurious black satin. Her gardenia-soft skin was as soft as the tiffany silk of her own wedding gown.

The two doting parents watched Tiffany rise up from

her chair and ask to be excused. "I am due at Denise's tomorrow at noon. I must get to bed early if I am to get there on time."

Madame Renaud gave a soft gale of laughter. "Knowing how long it takes you to attend to your toilette, ma petite, I would say you should."

Tiffany smiled; her mother knew her so well! It was an established fact around the Renaud household that she was not an early riser like her father and her brothers. That was another thing she and her mother shared besides their lovely deep blue eyes: they both liked to sleep late in the morning.

"Goodnight, ma chèrie—sleep well and sweet dreams," her mother softly remarked. Recalling her own special interludes of daydreaming at Tiffany's age, Madame knew she would lie there in her bed and think about that handsome man she'd encountered today. Ah, how wonderful it was to be young and in love with love. There was nothing like the romantic daydreams of a young girl. Nothing was more exhilarating or exciting!

She watched her daughter as she left the table and she surveyed the loveliness of her blossoming figure molded into her pretty silk gown of pale pink. She smiled as she watched the long cascade of jet-black curls bob around her shoulders and back. There was no denying the sensuous sway of her firm, rounded hips and her tiny waist. Was it any wonder that Tiffany excited and challenged the eyes of every young man she met?

Her husband's deep voice called to her and Madame Renaud turned in his direction. "What did you say, mon cher?"

"You looked so thoughtful as you watched Tiffany leave the room. I was just wondering what you were thinking."

"Ah, Pierre—do you remember our first meeting?"

His eyes glowed brightly and he smiled. For a moment

17

he did not speak but allowed his eyes to play over her lovely face. "I do. Obviously, you do, too. I pray you'll never forget, Charmaine."

"How could I? I have a harvest of that love, Pierre Renaud. I have three sons and a daughter to prove that I have loved you since the moment we first met."

A deep, throaty laugh erupted as Pierre declared, "God grant that you keep feeling just the same, ma petite Charmaine. Do you think our daughter shall find such a man as I?"

"I think she saw such a man as you today, my husband and I can tell you he appealed to her just as you appealed to me."

"She what?" Pierre said, sitting up straight in his chair.

"She saw such a man today in the park, Pierre, and I could tell, as only a mother can tell when her daughter is excited and curious about a man. I must tell you that he was a man who could catch the eye of any woman. He was an impressive man, like you, Pierre." She realized that she'd given her husband quite a jolt.

For a moment, Pierre said nothing to his wife. Slowly, his eyes turned in her direction. "I remember as if it were yesterday the first dark night we met, ma petite, and I damned well knew I'd have you for my own. So if he is such a man as I, then this is slightly disturbing news you tell me."

His wife gave an amused laugh. "Why, my darling? After all, Tiffany is bound to fall in love sometime."

"But she is so young," he said pointedly.

A sly smile etched his wife's face as she gently corrected him, "No younger than I was when you stole your first kiss up there on the cliffs . . . remember?"

What could he say? She was right, of course. To this day she was still just as enchanting to him as she'd been that night with the silvery moonbeams dancing on her

18

face and hair. He could not deny that he'd been a rather reckless rogue.

"It's—it's damned different when you're a father," he said.

"And a mother, too, Pierre."

The two of them exchanged warm, intimate smiles and Pierre suggested that they take a moonlight stroll through their gardens. Holding hands, they slowly walked out of the candlelit dining room and down the long carpeted hallway toward the front door.

While her parents strolled the pathways of the gardens to enjoy the pleasant serenity of the night, Tiffany lay propped against the mountain of pillows on her canopied bed, thinking about the divine afternoon in the park. She'd loved every minute of attention and adoration paid to her by the various young Frenchmen coming to her side, complimenting her about how lovely she looked in her exquisite gown of lavender and her wide-brimmed hat of the same color with its garland of pink and lavender flowers edging the crown. Madame Delose had designed the hat especially for this gown.

She knew that her little maid had been puzzled that she'd dismissed her so swiftly tonight but she wanted to be alone. In fact, she'd not wanted Magdelaine to lay out the gown that she'd wear for her luncheon with Denise.

She wanted to daydream about the handsome stranger whose every feature was etched in her memory. She wondered what it would feel like if his sensuous lips kissed her. She had watched his magnificent hand leisurely stroke the cheroot he was holding. How would it feel if his hand caressed her, ever so slow and gentle?

She remembered the powerful frame of his fine muscled body in the fawn-colored pants molded to his thighs and legs and the broad shoulders draped and covered by the bottle-green frock coat. He wore no hat like the other young Frenchmen did. She took notice of

19

that immediately and the fact that the thick left side of his chocolate brown hair had an unruly wave falling over his forehead. His long, slender fingers kept pushing it back away from his face.

Lying there on her bed, a smug, impish smile played on her beautiful face as she thought how she might meet this magnificent stranger. Never for a minute did she doubt that it was bound to happen. After all, she'd never been denied anything she wanted and she wanted most desperately to see this man again.

She hoped that her mother was not at her side the next time they chanced to meet. Somehow, she must see that this did not happen.

Being the clever little manipulator her older brothers always said she was, she knew she could easily manage that!

Already, an idea had ignited in her pretty head; tomorrow she would pursue it!

Chapter 2

It was a boisterous crowd in the small cabaret situated on the dark side street of the city. Albert Charboneau was a bitter, vindictive man as he sat with two of his friends, sipping wine and venting his wrath against Pierre Renaud for firing him from his job. His whole world had tumbled down today!

As his two friends, Lucien and Paul, listened, Albert boasted about his plans to make his former employer pay and pay dearly for firing him, leaving him in a miserable predicament. "I'll fix him as he's fixed me and I'll do it through that feisty little daughter of his who is the apple of his eye. Watch me! In fact, join me if you wish while I take my pleasure with her. You two could have a little pleasure, too."

The three of them broke into a lusty gale of laughter. Lucien prodded his companion, "How in the hell do you propose to accomplish that? She must be always escorted around Paris, Albert."

His spectacled friend, Paul, cautioned him, "You know you're asking for big trouble, don't you, Albert? You don't rile a family like the Renauds without paying a hell of a price. You better think about this before you go any farther with this crazy scheme."

"Crazy, is it? Did you ever have a nagging wife and two kids to support? Cecile warned me earlier tonight that she might just have to go back to work in the tavern if I couldn't keep her as I've been doing for the last six months. Damn! Renaud has put my whole life in devastation. I am now without wages. Yes, I shall make him pay for what he's done to me. Do you know how impossible it will be for me to get a job after being fired by the respected Pierre Renaud?"

"Then you might be forced to take a more meager position, Albert," Paul told him.

A disgusted smirk broke on Albert's face as he barked out at his easygoing friend, "Maybe that is what you would do, Paul, but never will I bow to that. No, I'll have my revenge and Renaud will rue the day he did what he did today to Albert Charboneau. I worked hard and long for Renaud."

Lucien could attest to that; he'd known Albert for over ten years, and all this time he'd worked for the Renaud Company. He would also agree that Albert had worked long, long hours after everyone else had gone to their homes, but he knew that over the last several years, Albert had helped himself to extra funds so he might woo and win the voluptuous Cecile and set her up in an apartment as his mistress. His salary could not cover all this extra expense.

Lucien asked how taking his revenge on Renaud's daughter was going to put extra money in his purse. Albert quickly responded, "At first, it won't, Lucien. But later it will. You'll see. That is all I can tell you at this time. I will invite you to accompany me if you like when I take my pleasure with her, for I know you to be a randy fellow." He turned his attention to Paul. "I know this would not appeal to you, Paul, with your gentle soul. That is why I have not included you."

"No, Albert. I'd—I'd wish to have no part of this plan

you're proposing." Paul was a little sickened by this whole evening. It was not like the evenings the three of them usually shared. Suddenly, there was a sour taste in his mouth and he wished not to have any more of the wine he'd been drinking. He wished only to leave the cabaret and go to his furnished room and read until it was time to retire.

He'd never been a womanizer like Albert and Lucien and now, as he sat there listening to the two of them talk, he wondered how he'd ever been drawn into this comradeship in the first place.

He fidgeted for another few minutes before making his announcement that he was leaving them to go on home. "I'm tired. I've had a long day."

Albert and Lucien exchanged glances, knowing exactly why Paul sought to depart and they bid him goodnight as he rose up from his chair to leave the noisy cabaret. As soon as Paul had left them, Albert and Lucien huddled together as Albert laid out his plans for Tiffany Renaud.

Chad Morrow was convinced that the rumors he'd heard ever since he'd arrived in Paris were true, now that he'd had a chance to see both of the lovely Renaud ladies—Tiffany and her mother. It was not by chance that he happened to be in the park where he'd been told that they would be attending a concert this afternoon.

An innocent remark made by the charming elderly lady he was visiting in Paris had prompted him to go to the park. Madame Evelyn St. Clair had spoken of the Renauds as they'd dined the night before, after his arrival in Paris to carry out his mother's request that her jewels be given to Evelyn. Chad had not carried out that mission as soon as he should have and he felt guilty about it.

He did not try to excuse it for he saw no reason for doing so. There were priorities in life, Chad considered.

He allowed nothing to distract him from a goal he'd set for himself. When he'd finally found time to make this little jaunt to Paris, he'd come as he'd promised his mother he would do.

He recalled the day she had summoned him to her bedside and urged him to promise to see that all her jewels were given to her dear, devoted friend, Evelyn who lived in Paris. "Now, don't you fail to do this, Chadwick," she'd whimpered with a pathetic look on her face.

God, how he detested that name—Chadwick! By the time he was eighteen he'd shortened it to just Chad. No one but his mother had ever called him Chadwick and as far as he was concerned no one else ever would.

He'd not planned on lingering long in Paris once his long overdue mission was completed. But now, he was having second thoughts. He had to admit that his hostess was a very likable earthy lady, who enjoyed smoking her little clay pipe after she dined. He wondered what common bond she had shared with his mother, who had seemed so restrained and aloof.

He always resented the fact that she had returned to England before he was born so he never got to know the father she'd left behind in the United States, far across the Atlantic Ocean.

To know his father became an obsession with Chad and he knew he must seek him out, which was exactly what he did when he was seventeen.

But by the time Chad found his father, their time together was brief, for the old riverboat captain was fatally ill. Chad was with him when he died. He, too, had drawn a promise from his young son. "Go back to England, my boy, and take care of your mother. She—she is such a fragile lady. That was why she couldn't make it here with me. I—I never held that against her. It was a strange circumstance that brought me and Elizabeth together in the first place. Me, a rowdy old riverboat captain with no schoolin', and her a fine English lady."

He never got the chance to tell Chad his side of the story, for he died that very night. Once his father was buried, Chad had obeyed his father's last wishes and returned to England and his mother. But there was no contentment to be found for Chad on the country estate on the outskirts of London.

He knew he'd inherited a lot of the traits of that old, rugged riverboat man he'd met back in the New World. He thought about him fondly and often in the months that followed his return to England.

Some would say that Chad's father had left him no legacy, but he treasured the old, yellowed journals he'd discovered in his father's quarters on his riverboat. Hours had been spent perusing them after he'd returned to England.

Perhaps his mother had considered him a crude, unrefined gent she'd impulsively married while she was there in the New World across the ocean from her native country, but Chad had a different opinion of his father after he read all the journals. He had been a man capable of great depth of feeling and an insatiable desire to live his life to the fullest.

He sought to impress no one as long as he pleased himself. Yet, he was a most generous man, always ready to lend a helping hand to the settlers along the riverbank as his boat made its runs up and down the winding Mississippi River.

Chad never told his mother about the journals he'd brought back to England after his father's death. He realized that his mother, Elizabeth Chadwick, was not the love of his father's life. There was another lady who'd stolen his heart completely the first moment he set eyes on her, but her heart belonged to another. The very brief interlude they'd shared was never enough for her to forget the man she'd first loved.

According to the journals, fate placed Elizabeth and Chad's father together and it happened at a vulnerable time in both their lives. Foolishly, they married, but after a few weeks of living together as man and wife they were both miserable. Chad's father was in love with the other woman.

Eagerly, Elizabeth welcomed the opportunity to return to England. Chad's father felt no loneliness when she left. In fact, he enjoyed returning to his former lifestyle. He'd lived his vagabond life too long.

Elizabeth's prosperous family gathered her back into the Chadwick family circle, pampering her generously when she discovered she was pregnant by the crude American who'd enticed her to marry him.

The Chadwick ideals and mold were not for Chad, he discovered by the time he was fourteen and started rebelling. The disapproving looks from his mother or his uncles mattered not a whit to him. They were all to learn that he was very stubborn, headstrong like his father. Each time he was admonished with these particular remarks, he smiled. It only tended to whet his curiosity to seek out this stranger who was his father.

As a stowaway, he left the shores of England to find the father he'd never known or seen. Being a daring, adventuresome lad, he never doubted for a minute that he would succeed.

Those four weeks Chad had spent with his ill father aboard his riverboat were a special time to the young man. The fiesty old riverboat captain was no longer able to pilot his boat, so he'd been forced to tie up by the docks weeks before Chad had appeared unexpectedly. This had galled Captain Morrow.

But Captain Morrow put forth the bravest front he could for his fine son who'd traveled all the way from England just to see him. It was the grandest gift he could have received. It made this cantankerous old man more willing to accept the fact that he was dying.

Chad knew he would be changed forever by this interlude in his life. When he arrived back in England a few weeks later, he was convinced of it.

Elizabeth had seen the change immediately and knew that she would never be able to influence him again. So she never tried from that time until she, too, died.

For the last few years, Chad had sought to exclude himself from the Chadwick family circle and had gone his own way. He did not need them or their money, he'd quickly realized. He certainly never accepted the guilt they tried to lay at his feet that he'd caused his mother's death. He never swallowed their lies that he'd broken her heart when he'd gone to search for his father. His mother had been an unhappy woman for as long as he could remember.

However, he had respected her last request that he see that all her jewels be given to her old, dear friend in France. This mission had brought Chad Morrow to Paris and the elderly Evelyn St. Clair.

Now, though his mission had been carried out and he was free to leave, he found that he wanted to linger in this exciting city just a little longer.

He could not admit to himself that it might just be the beautiful, black-haired mademoiselle he'd spied in the park. Carving himself a future had been his obsession, for he had to prove to the Chadwicks that he could make it on his own and without their wealth or influence. He was pridefully happy to say that he had done it.

According to his original plans, this should have been his last night in Paris and the last evening he would share with Evelyn St. Clair. But as they dined, he confessed to her that he would like to stay one more night. She was absolutely delighted.

"Oh, Chad, my dear—I've enjoyed your visit. Stay as

long as you like."

"I thank you, Madame St. Clair, for your graciousness," he told her. But Chad had this urgent need to go to the park one more time before he left in hopes of seeing that breathtakingly beautiful girl. Something told him he would, too.

Before the meal was over, Chad found himself talking to Evelyn St. Clair about the little beauty with the black hair. As he described her and the older lady riding in the carriage with her, a sly smile came to Evelyn's face.

"My goodness, young man, what a way you have with words. You've given me such a vivid description of these two ladies that there is no doubt in my mind about whom you saw there in the park. That lady and her daughter are considered two of the most beautiful women in Paris. You saw Madame Charmaine Renaud and her daughter, Tiffany. The Renauds are wealthy industrialists with holdings all over the world."

"This is all very interesting, Madame St. Clair."

A gleam was in her piercing blue eyes as she remarked, "I've no doubt it is. You and many young men in Paris find the lovely Tiffany a fetching young lady. But let me warn you, she has a doting old grandfather who can be difficult to deal with. There is an adoring father, as well as three older brothers. So just remember that I warned you."

He laughed, "I am warned, madame. But I am a very stubborn man when I set my mind to something. I've never had anything come easy for me and I don't expect it to. It's much more gratifying if you have to work for it."

"I like that attitude, young man. I like that very much."

"Well, that is why I struck out on my own after my mother died. I wanted to be independent."

She gave a soft chuckle. "Now, somehow I thought you just might. Chad Morrow, I have to think that you are a great deal like your father. It's too bad dear Elizabeth could not have been a little more daring. I often wondered how we got along so well because we were completely opposite in personality."

"Ah, Madame—I was well aware of that as soon as we met. You and my mother were two different types of woman. Someday, that is a story you must tell me."

"Oh, I shall, Chad—I shall."

The young man rose up from the overstuffed chair where he'd been sitting. His silver-gray eyes danced over the elderly lady and glowed with warm affection as he told her, "I will enjoy hearing it, Madame St. Clair. Now, I shall bid you goodnight and may you rest well."

"You too, my dear." Silently, she was thinking to herself what a magnificent son Elizabeth had been blessed with. He was worth any price her friend might have paid during that sojourn in the New World across the ocean.

She watched his tall, powerful figure move out of her parlor to go to the hallway and mount the stairs. There was nothing about this young man that reminded her of the Chadwicks. No, he must surely be like his father. Now that she'd met the son, Madame St. Clair found her interest whetted about this husband that Elizabeth had spoken about with such disgust and utter distaste.

She'd be interested in hearing Chad's impression of the father he'd visited in America. Perhaps before young Morrow left France, they should exchange stories of the two people they knew. Already, she knew that Chad's story was going to be different from the one Elizabeth had told her years ago when she'd returned to England.

Elizabeth could have been a happy woman if only she'd given Chad's father a chance, Madame St. Clair decided, now that she'd met the child of their union.

Elizabeth had no one to blame but herself and that austere, grim Chadwick upbringing for all her unhappiness!

Chapter 3

The gown she wore was the same shade of bright blue as the wildflowers that bloomed so profusely in the countryside of France. Tiffany's hat was ecru straw with a wide brim surrounded by a band of bright blue velvet ribbon and streamers hanging down. The dainty parasol she carried to shelter her satiny complexion from the midafternoon sun was bright blue with a ruffled edging.

The lunch she'd enjoyed with Denise on the terrace of her friend's home had been pleasant and she'd excitedly told her about the enchanting stranger she'd encountered at the concert. "Mon Dieu, I wish you could have been with me, Denise!"

"Oh, so do I, Tiffany, but I've had this miserable cold I can't get rid of," Denise told her.

"Well, I was hoping you were better today so you could accompany me. I must go back in hopes that I will see him again."

"You are going there alone?"

"Oh, I must! I have the feeling that he will be there."

"But there is no concert today. You might not want to encounter some of the scoundrels that gather there, Tiffany. I—I wish you'd not do this while you're all alone. You know the stories we've heard about the things

30

Lucien glanced back to observe the problem his friend was having with the little beauty. "She is a real little hellion, Albert!" He threw back his head, giving out a lusty laugh.

That stupid fool! Why had he spoken his name, Albert thought as he still struggled with the little firebrand. Conquering her was not going to be as easy as he thought.

"Pull in here," Albert shouted to his friend. The trees and the shrubs were thick and concealing. By now, he was desperate to have his way with this luscious lady. In her struggle with him, he viewed the tempting mounds of the silken flesh of her breasts from the low-scooped neckline of her silk gown. God, she was a tantalizing little bitch and he was determined to possess all the sweet, sweet nectar tempting him.

When Lucien brought the carriage to an abrupt halt, Albert lifted Tiffany roughly from the carriage seat down to the thick carpeted grass. A lusty grin broke on his face as he looked up at Lucien still sitting there on the driver's seat. "I'll take my pleasure and then you can have yours, my friend," he told him. This miss was no fragile little flower, he'd decided.

Tiffany realized then and there what the two intended to do and she fought more vigorously until weakness overcame her and she found herself being flung to the ground, Albert's strong body pressing against her.

His mouth assaulted her soft lips and his tongue was prodding for entry which she would not allow. "Bitch!" he hissed in his frenzy. She was going to fight him all the way, Albert realized.

She felt his fumbling fingers trying to invade the front of her bodice and it sickened her. But as she tried to fight him and arch against his male body, it only frenzied his determination to subdue her.

The chuckles of the man observing this little scenerio up in her father's carriage only heightened the suffering she was enduring. But suddenly she heard a deep groan of pain and she could not know what was taking place a short distance away.

It was only when she felt the pressing weight of the male body being lifted off that she realized that some good Samaritan had happened her way.

It mattered not who this wonderful person was as she slowly raised herself off the ground to sit up, looking wide-eyed at the powerful figure of her rescuer.

Her heart started pounding erratically when she suddenly realized that it was the same man she'd observed and admired yesterday in the park. He was the reason she'd come to the park today and now he'd been the one to save her from these two ruffians and this horrible, embarrassing situation.

Obviously he had taken care of the two of them. The one in the carriage had received a fierce blow, for he was slumped in the carriage seat. The one who had been determined to have his way with her was now lying limp and motionless on the thick carpet of grass.

Tiffany felt herself being lifted up from the ground. The silver-gray eyes of the man who'd just saved her were now scrutinizing her. "I trust you are not hurt, mademoiselle?"

To be this close to the handsome man she'd admired from afar yesterday and now to find herself enclosed in his arms left Tiffany breathless. It was not exactly how she'd imagined their first encounter in her dreams last night. For a moment, she found it hard to utter a word as she stared wide-eyed up at his face.

"My thanks to you and that I am not hurt, monsieur. I am most grateful to you." Her blue eyes locked with his. Chad's hand reached out to smooth away her beautiful black hair away from her face and he realized the fright she had experienced in those brief moments, for her lovely face was tear-stained. He saw the damage to her frock and the crushed brim of the beautiful straw bonnet where that lust-crazed bastard had flung her to the ground. A fury mounted in him to kill the son-of-a-bitch.

Instead, his deep voice softly assured her, "I am glad I just happened to be coming this way, mademoiselle. Now, if you will allow me to help you into your carriage and see that you are safely away from the scum lying over there, it will be my great pleasure. By the way, may I introduce myself. I am Chad Morrow."

By now Tiffany was standing by his side with his strong arm encircling her waist. "I am Tiffany Renaud, monsieur." Her black head tilted back to gaze up into his eyes. Chad Morrow couldn't deny that he would have loved to bend down and kiss those tempting, sensuous lips. But there would be the right time, and this was certainly not that time.

"Well, Mademoiselle Renaud, it is an honor to meet you," he said, allowing his eyes to appraise her loveliness. She was far more beautiful than he'd remembered. It took a strong will not to take a kiss from those luscious lips.

"My driver—poor Noah—he must be frantic by now. We must find him. He is an elderly man, Monsieur Morrow."

"Never you worry about that. We shall find him," he assured her. He lifted her up into the carriage and moved swiftly around to leap up in the driver's seat.

Chad had turned the carriage around and guided the bay back toward the main trail of the park when Tiffany called out, "There he is, monsieur—see over there." Her dainty finger pointed to the grove of trees where a couple of park benches stood. Noah sat on one of them, his head bowed dejectedly.

As Chad guided the carriage in the direction she had pointed Tiffany yelled out to the elderly black man, "Noah—Noah!"

His white-haired head raised up to see the reassuring sight of her in the carriage. A broad grin broke on his face and he gave a deep sigh of relief. "Oh, thank God—thank God! Our Miss Tiffany—she has not come to harm," he moaned softly. By the time the carriage was pulling up to where he was standing, Noah was there to lift Tiffany down.

Chad watched the touching scene of the elderly servant clasping the young girl in his arms and he knew the genuine feeling of devotion the two of them shared.

Tears flowed down the old man's face as he confessed, "Lordy, Miss Tiffany—I was scared to death!"

"So was I, Noah. So was I! Thanks to this wonderful Monsieur Morrow, I was spared a most terrible fate," she told Noah, turning to look back at Chad. "Monsieur, this is my dear Noah—Noah Mathews. Noah, this is Monsieur Chad Morrow."

The two men greeted one another. Now that she was with the devoted black man she would be safe, Chad realized. Besides, he was not through with the two fellows back there.

"A pleasure to know you, Noah, and now that I've placed Mademoiselle Renaud in your capable hands I suppose I should take my leave." Chad leaped out of the carriage so that Noah could take up his post.

As old Noah took charge of the reins, he declared, "Can't tell you how grateful I am for what you did for my Miss Tiffany, sir."

The young man's eyes darted over in Tiffany's direction. His deep voice addressed her," Until we meet again, mademoiselle."

"And we shall meet again, monsieur?" she asked with a bright gleam in her dark blue eyes.

"Oh, we shall!"

"I'm sure my parents would welcome you so that they might personally thank you. Please call on us monsieur.

Once again, my thanks."

"My pleasure, mademoiselle. Take care of her, Noah," he grinned, as he turned to stroll back across the grounds of the park.

Tiffany watched his towering, muscled figure walk away. She could still feel the heat of his strong arms when she was enclosed in them.

It was a very thoughtful Miss Tiffany that Noah took home in the carriage and he, too, was having his own private musings. He always figured that it would take some unusual man to win and tame Miss Tiffany. The old man figured that she might have met that man today.

The only thing Tiffany knew was that she had found the man she'd gone to the park to see. Now she knew his name and he'd held her for one brief moment in his arms. That was enough to make her yearn to know more about him.

No other man had ever affected her as Chad Morrow had!

Chapter 4

Tiffany and Noah had not been home two hours before the servants were talking about the latest episode of the young mademoiselle. It only took one servant hearing a brief moment of conversation for the word to be passed throughout the huge mansion.

Madame Renaud felt that something was wrong when her daughter and their devoted driver returned so late. She was utterly shocked by Tiffany's tale about what had happened in the park. She felt almost as sorry for poor Noah as she did for Tiffany.

She gave the black man a gentle pat on his shoulder and urged him to go to his quarters. "You'll not be needed the rest of the evening, Noah. I think you've had enough excitement for one day."

He shook his graying head. "Hope to never live through another time like this afternoon, Madame Renaud. I surely don't. If anything had happened to our Miss Tiffany I could have not forgiven myself."

"It would not have been your fault, Noah, but I am just grateful that nothing did happen. You go and get some rest. Lou will bring you some dinner." Madame Renaud was genuinely concerned about the old man. Perhaps he was getting too old to be Tiffany's driver.

Now that this had happened today, she was going to have a talk with Pierre. They could find something Noah could do that might not be so trying on him.

Noah looked at Tiffany; she was giving him one of her sweet, loving smiles. "Goodnight, Miss Tiffany and goodnight to you, madame," Noah said as he slowly began to walk away.

Tiffany turned to look at her mother. "Poor dear . . . he was scared to death, Mother. I . . . I love that dear old man."

Charmaine Renaud put her arm around her daughter. "As you should, since he's so devoted to you. Your father and I consider him a part of this family. It began long ago when your father and I met up with Noah on the Mississippi. Why, he's shared all our joys, as well as our sorrows for over twenty years, Tiffany. You can see why he is so dear to us."

Madame Renaud began to mount the winding stairway with her daughter following behind her.

As they reached the second landing, Madame Renaud kissed her daughter's cheek. "Shall we both refresh ourselves, ma petite? Your father will be home soon and he will want to know all about what happened to you, so I will question you no more right now. I'm—I'm just so happy to see that you were not harmed."

"Thank you, mother. I—I would like to relax and catch my breath before Father gets home." Tiffany turned to go into her room.

She thought how fortunate she was to have a mother who was so understanding. Thank goodness, she didn't have a demanding, overbearing mother like her friend Denise did. She could have imagined the severe grilling Denise would have gotten if this had happened to her.

She ordered a bath as soon as she got inside her bedroom. It was sheer luxury to enjoy the sweet perfumed scent of the bath oils washing over her body.

Reluctantly, she finally motioned for her maid to bring the huge towel to her. At the same time, she told her that she would be wearing the pale pink gown this evening. Her maid, Magdelaine, wanted to know if she wished her pink satin slippers or her white leather ones.

"The pink ones, Magdelaine." Tiffany found that she had an ugly bruise on her thigh from the rough treatment her soft body had received some hours ago as she was tossed to the ground by that horrible man in the park. She quickly draped the towel around her naked body.

Magdelaine had not yet heard the gossip about her young mistress. It was only after she'd helped the young mademoiselle get dressed and done her hair in one of her own favorite hairstyles that she was dismissed to go down to the kitchen to have her dinner.

She had just taken a seat at the little oak table in the corner of the kitchen where she and the madame's maid usually had their meals, when Roxanna sat down to join her. Leaning close to whisper in Magdelaine's ear, she asked, "Is the young mistress all right?"

"You mean Mademoiselle Tiffany?"

"Of course!"

"She is fine. Why shouldn't she be?" A frown creased her brow.

"She mentioned nothing to you about what happened to her this afternoon—about being attacked in the park?"

"Mademoiselle? She was attacked?"

Roxanna was quick to inform her about the brief conversation she'd overheard when she was in the master suite, as the monsieur and madame talked in the adjoining sitting room off their bedroom.

"Mon Dieu—she said not a word to me!" Magdelaine admitted to Roxanna. "She is as cool and calm as she usually is. I—I had no idea. She had no marks on her, Roxanna—not any I saw when she was taking her bath."

As she was finishing her meal, she saw the cook at the back door. A youth stood there, holding a basket filled with pale pink rosebuds and greenery. He handed the basket to the cook and hastily left.

The robust servant called out to Magdelaine, "Here's something for you to take up to Mademoiselle Tiffany, so that young lad told me."

Magdelaine went to get the basket. It must be nice to have an admirer who sent such beautiful flowers as these. But then Mademoiselle Tiffany was always getting lovely gifts from her many suitors. She could not help thinking as she carried the basket up the stairway how perfect a match these flowers were for the gown she would be wearing tonight.

As she entered the room, Tiffany was preparing to go downstairs. She wore a sly smile as she read the card enclosed and plucked one of the perfect rosebuds from the basket. Then she bounced out of the room without saying a word.

Magdelaine was left there alone to wonder just who this new admirer was.

To have Chad Morrow rescue her had almost been worth the ordeal she experienced this afternoon, Tiffany thought as she moved down the long winding stairway. Why had he chosen rosebuds to send her? she pondered. How could he have possibly known that he'd picked her favorite color?

When she entered the elegant parlor, so lavishingly furnished in her mother's favorite colors, her mother and father were already there, enjoying a glass of their favorite wine before the three of them went in to dinner.

When she made her entrance, her father immediately rose up from his chair to come to her and take her in a warm, fatherly embrace. "Oh, ma petite—I am one grate-

41

ful father this evening. Oh, Tiffany—my little Tiffany!"

When he released Tiffany from his loving arms, he led her over to sit down beside him. His warm, dark eyes darted over to his wife as she sat watching the two of them together.

"We shall enjoy our dinner and then you must tell your father about this afternoon, dear," Charmaine Renaud told her daughter.

As she had been preparing to dress after she'd had her refreshing bath, Tiffany had had time to reflect on the events as they'd occurred. She knew one thing: she'd never forget the faces of those two rascals, should she ever see them again. She'd heard a name—Albert—as she frantically wrestled with the dreadful man!

When dinner was announced, the three of them went into the spacious dining room to sit at the candlelit table and enjoy the good food and fine wine. There was even a shared lighthearted laughter as the three enjoyed their meal. But this was always the rule that Madame Renaud insisted upon when her family gathered in the evening. Problems of any kind must wait until after dinner. It had always been that way when her older brothers were at home to gather around the long mahogany dining table, Tiffany recalled.

After dinner, they retired to the parlor where Tiffany told her father what had happened to her. Pierre listened intensely to every word. "Now, this young man who came to your rescue, Tiffany—what is his name?"

"Chad Morrow, Father." Her dark blue eyes gleamed excitedly when she exclaimed, "Oh, you should have seen how quickly he took care of those two! His fist must have a powerful blow."

Pierre smiled. "Sounds like a young man I've got to meet and thank for what he did for my daughter."

"You will, Father. I'm sure of that."

"I'd bet you are right, Tiffany," Pierre declared,

glancing over to see the smile on his wife's face. There were no need for words to be spoken between the two of them. Each seemed to sense what the other was thinking.

Each of them knew that Tiffany was already in love with this paragon who'd rushed in to save her from the clutches of two ruffians.

But the smile on Pierre's face quickly changed to a frown when his daughter told him that she'd heard one of the men call the other one Albert. "The one who sat there ogling while his friend was trying to have his way with me called him that name, Papa."

Pierre could hardly contain his rage. His black eyes flashed with fury and fire. But he cleverly concealed all this from his daughter. His calm, cool voice reflected nothing of this to Tiffany.

"This could be a great help, ma petite, in finding these men. They will be punished for what they did to you today."

His wife understood why Pierre sought to excuse himself shortly after that to go upstairs. She followed him, leaving Tiffany alone. Tiffany had told her mother she planned to take a leisurely stroll out on the terrace.

As soon as they had left the room, Tiffany went out the double door leading out on the railed terrace. She stood there in the moonlight, gently playing with the stem of the pink rosebud Chad Morrow had sent her. As she took a seat on the iron bench she tucked the stem in the low-scooped neckline of her gown. She found the soothing sound of the spraying mist of the fountain so pleasant that she closed her eyes and leaned back against the back of the grilled iron bench.

She did not hear the soft footsteps of the towering figure moving closer and closer to the steps of the terrace because of the thick carpet of grass. To Chad, she looked like something out of this world sitting there in the shimmering pale pink silk gown with that black head of hers tossed back. The beauty of that face could compare to that of a goddess.

He immediately noticed where she had placed one of the pink rosebuds, and he smiled with delight. A more ravishing beauty his eyes had never beheld.

Something made her sit up with a startled look. Her thick black lashes fluttered nervously as she stared at him, wide-eyed and surprised. "Is—is that you, Chad?"

"It is I, Tiffany. Do you mind that I came in hopes that I might see you?"

This was not the conventional way her suitors came to call on her, but she found it a pleasant surprise. And after all, Chad Morrow was no ordinary man.

"You could have come to our front door, Chad."

"Ah, but I would have missed the beautiful sight of you sitting here in the moonlight, wouldn't I?" His eyes were now devouring her as he stood there, towering over her. "I like where you are wearing my rose—close to your heart."

She was slightly embarrassed, remembering where she'd tucked the rosebud, but before she could make any kind of reply, Chad's nimble finger was removing it. She felt the warmth of his finger brushing against her soft flesh.

Without saying a word, he reached out to extend his hand to her and she took it. He led her down the steps of the terrace and she followed as he guided her into the darkness of the garden beyond.

She was like someone in a trance as she walked with him through the garden and looked up to see his silver-gray eyes appraising her.

When they reached the far side of the gardens, he urged her to sit down on the bench by the fountain. Suddenly, she found herself enclosed in his powerful arms and his lips were capturing hers in a kiss. Never had a man kissed her as Chad Morrow was kissing her, with his tongue prodding her lips for entry. She surrendered helplessly.

She was breathless when he finally released her to whisper huskily in her ear, "God, Tiffany—your lips are sweeter than honey."

Such overwhelming love-making had left Tiffany shaken as she stared up at the face of the rugged Morrow. Never had she felt so stirred by any of her suitors' kisses. With this man, she was rendered helpless.

Now suddenly, she felt the caress of his hand cupping her breast and a flame seemed to travel all through her body. Everything within her urged her to surrender to the glorious feeling, but that fierce Renaud pride and indignation came alive and she forcefully pushed away from him. Her dainty hand swung back and slapped his face with a fierce blow.

It was Chad who was taken by surprise as she leaped up, her hands firmly placed on her hips as she angrily spit at him, "How dare you take such liberties, Chad Morrow! Just because you rescue me doesn't give you the right to think you have special privileges. I—I never want to see you again!"

She dashed across the ground with her flowing skirt swaying to and fro. She held it high so she could run as fast as she could to get away from him.

But she could hear his words echoing as she fled, "Ah, but you will see me again and next time you'll come to my arms willingly."

Never will I come to your arms, Chad Morrow, Tiffany swore to herself as she rushed toward the terrace.

Chapter 5

Long after Tiffany was safely inside her bedroom and the door was closed, she was still trembling from the effects of her late night encounter with Chad Morrow. He challenged her as no other man ever had. She might know how to sweet-talk her Grand-père Etienne or her father. There was no doubt that her brothers were easy for her to win her way with. All the young Frenchmen who came to call on her were helpless against her beguiling wiles. But this man, Chad Morrow, had his own kind of magic he worked on her.

She didn't trust herself when she was around him. She became a different person, it seemed to Tiffany. This was a feeling she'd never known before. She was not in charge as she usually was. This was what intrigued her about Morrow!

As she undressed and slipped into her nightgown, the lingering heat of his touch was still there with her. The caress of his finger was recalled when he removed the rose from her bodice and she could never forget the sensation he stirred within her when she felt his strong hand move slowly to cup her breast. That rogue probably sensed how crazily her heart started beating. Damn him!

Well, Chad Morrow would not be given that opportunity again, she promised herself as she crawled into bed. She wouldn't allow herself to be humiliated like that a second time. It appalled her that he should have had the audacious gall to do such a thing to her.

She comforted herself as she dimmed the light by her bed on the nightstand by telling herself in a few short weeks she would be going to London to enjoy the theatre and all the grand parties. There would be time spent with her friend, Sabrina. All those handsome, gallant young English lords would be fawning over her as they had for the last two years when she'd come to England with her parents.

Of all the places she enjoyed visiting, London was one of her favorite cities. She thought about all the things she would be telling Sabrina when the two of them got together again. There was no doubt that she and Sabrina had more in common than she and Denise did. But naturally, she and Denise were together more, since she lived in Paris.

She lay down on her soft pillows and went to sleep thinking about all the beautiful gowns the dressmaker was now making for her to take to London. All thoughts about that despicable Chad Morrow were pushed aside.

When Chad Morrow left the grounds of the Renaud mansion, he decided that it was time he left Paris and got back to his own world. He'd had his brief moment of folly and enjoyed every moment of it. The beautiful Tiffany was a mere child. Oh, she possessed a most sensuously curved body and the provocative look in her eyes could lead a man to believe almost anything, but the truth was she was innocent to the ways of a real man. Right now, he did not have the time or patience to teach her.

Oh, she might allow him to gently kiss her and she'd enjoy teasing him to the limits, but Morrow was not able

47

to indulge her that way.

Besides, his job at Penbrook Lines was demanding his attention. He would board the ship the first thing in the morning to assume those duties again. His mission here was over. A fond farewell to the delightful Evelyn St. Clair in the morning and he would take up his residence in his cabin aboard the ship, *Majestic Queen*, preparing to cross the Atlantic Ocean for the eastern coastline of the United States. Chad had thought many times about how it had been a Penbrook ship on which he'd been a stowaway to get to his father when he was just a youth. Now, he was their agent and a most successful one.

But Chad knew that there must come a day when he would return to Paris to pay another visit on this fine lady who'd been so cordial to him during the few days' visit he shared with her. Besides, she had a story to tell him and he wanted to hear it.

He bid her farewell the next morning and she smiled, placing a small case in his hand. "Young man, I will accept all the exquisite jewelry your dear mother wished me to have but there is one rare piece that I feel has to go to a very special person. A special young lady in your life, when that time comes to you. It is a magnificent black opal, a very rare stone. It is superb—like none I've ever seen before and I'm curious where Elizabeth got it."

Chad had not scrutinized the jewelry he'd brought to Madame St. Clair, but when he looked down at the ring she handed him, he saw what she was talking about.

It was like no other opal he'd ever seen before. He saw the blue-green flaring fire with the jet-black veins winding its way through the stone.

"If this is what you wish, Madame St. Clair," he told her, as she placed the ring in the palm of his hand.

"This is what I wish, Chad. Give this ring to the woman you love when you ask her to be your wife."

A slow grin came to his face as he placed the ring in his

pocket and bent down to give the tiny lady a farewell kiss before he left for the harbor. But he made her a promise before he left, "I shall return to Paris and to you, Madame St. Clair."

She gave a chuckle, "I'm going to hold you to that promise, young man."

He took his leave then but he turned back to wave to her before he jauntily went on down the street. She had no doubt as she walked back inside her house that he would come to see her again.

Pierre Renaud rarely arrived home from his office early, but tonight was the exception. Today, he'd been a busy man, attending to business details and talking to the officials about what had happened to his daughter. He'd pointed the finger of suspicion at Albert Charboneau and his constant companion, Lucien, to the authorities for what they'd attempted to do to his daughter. If the authorities could not catch the rascals, then Pierre would handle the situation himself, he decided.

But there was another reason that he wanted to get home early this evening. He'd received a letter—a plea for help from Etienne Bernay. The letter had come across the vast Atlantic Ocean from a small hamlet called New Madrid. Etienne was the son of his and Charmaine's dear friend, Tasha Bernay. The young man had written that his father, Jacques, had died and his mother was seriously ill. He was writing to Pierre as his father had told him to do if he should ever need help, for it seemed that Jacques knew he was a dying man.

"We must go, Charmaine. I owe them," he said, his black eyes searching her face for her reaction to his news. But then he should have known what she would have felt, loving Tasha as she did.

"Of course, we must go, mon cher. Tasha needs us.

49

Oh, I find it hard to accept that Jacques is dead. He was such a healthy, husky fellow," she sighed sadly.

"But that was some twenty-odd years ago, my dear," he reminded her as he held her in a warm embrace. The two of them were both thinking about those young days when they shared so much time with Jacques and Tasha Bernay.

"It means so much to me that you agree to make this long journey, and I feel that we should take Tiffany with us. I have no intention of leaving her behind. Grand-père can't assume the responsibility of such a lively miss as Tiffany. Would you not agree with me?"

"I agree, mon cher," his wife hastily agreed. "It is settled. She will go with us, Pierre."

He reached over to give her hand an affectionate pat. "I'm glad we feel the same way about this, Charmaine."

There was no doubt in Madame Renaud's mind that they were going to witness a fiery outburst of temper when they made their announcement. Tiffany was going to be crushed that she would not be seeing her best friend, Sabrina, and the excitement of London. But she guessed that this was a good time for Tiffany to learn that the whole world didn't revolve around her. Lately, she had began to wonder if this wasn't her feeling.

When their daughter did join them for the evening meal, her mother noticed a very quiet, withdrawn Tiffany. Now that she thought about it, the young woman had been in her room most of the day.

"Are you not feeling well, Tiffany?" Charmaine inquired as she noticed how she picked at the delectable dessert.

"I feel just fine, Maman. I guess yesterday drained me more than I'd realized. I enjoyed the comfort of being in my room and feeling lazy today." She had a most convincing way about her and her mother didn't doubt what she'd just told her.

Once the three of them left the dining room to go into the parlor, Pierre saw no reason to delay informing Tiffany about the future plans.

In that cool, authoritative air of his, he told her about the need for them to leave immediately to go to the aid of their dear friends in America.

"Then you must go, Papa. I have plenty of people here to look after me, along with a household of servants. I shall be fine," she quickly assured her father.

A slow smile came to Pierre's face as he responded, "Oh, we shall be sure of that, Tiffany. You shall accompany us on the voyage. Besides, it could be a grand experience for you since you've never crossed the ocean. You'd be seeing a whole different world you've never seen before."

Madame Renaud watched her daughter's blue eyes flash as they always did when she was overexcited or angry. "But I don't wish to go on a voyage and miss my trip to London and my visit with Sabrina. I always look forward to that, Papa, and you know it!"

"Yes, I know that Tiffany, but if I can change my plans, then so can you." His tone was so strong and firm Tiffany knew he was not going to change his mind or relent to her wishes to remain behind when they left.

She clenched her fist tightly. What could she possibly do to change his mind? she wondered.

"It would mean so much to Grand-père for me to spend some special time with him, Papa. Poor Sabrina will be brokenhearted that I'm not coming. The two of us had made such plans," she appealed to him.

Pierre applauded her efforts privately and he glanced over at his wife with an amused grin on his face. "You will have to give your grandfather some special time when we return, ma petite. While Sabrina's heart may be broken, I think I might be saving a few young Englishmen a case of broken hearts when I recall our trip to

London last year."

She took a deep breath, knowing she was defeated, for there was no way he was going to change his mind. She gave him a weak little smile and said no more. After a brief moment, she slowly rose from her chair and asked to be excused so that she might go upstairs to write a letter to Sabrina. Hoping to make her father feel guilty, she remarked, "I should let her know as soon as possible so she won't be counting on me."

"That's very thoughtful of you, Tiffany," her father told her as she was making her hasty exit from the room. When she was gone, the older Renauds exchanged smiles and Pierre rose from his chair to go over to his wife and plant a kiss on her lips. "We have a very unhappy daughter tonight but I'm sure she'll get over it."

How swiftly the plans were being made for them to depart from France! Already, her mother had instructed her to start packing her belongings and advised her about the type of clothing she should select for such a voyage. "Nothing fancy, dear. Things like your riding ensembles, Tiffany, for there will be no grand balls or soirees where we are going. Take a couple of woolen shawls and the simple little berry-colored wool cape."

"When are we leaving, Maman? It sounds like it must be in a few days," Tiffany inquired of her.

"We are leaving the day after tomorrow, Tiffany. Your father booked passage for us the afternoon he got the letter from Tasha's son and came home to tell us of his plans." She quickly took her leave from the room, telling Tiffany she had many things to see to and go over with Sadie, her housekeeper, since they could be away for many weeks.

Tiffany stood there for several minutes in a state of utter confusion.

If there were to be no fancy gowns packed, then she certainly had no reason to take any of her fine pieces of jewelry, but she would put a few pieces in her reticule to take along. Her pearls and the little miniature cameo on the pink velvet ribbon would not take up that much room. Her mother need not know about that.

The simple black twill riding outfit and her bottle-green cloak should be right for the kind of traveling they were going to be doing, and the two plain jacket and skirt outfits that she always took when they went to their country estate just outside Cherbourg. When she flung these across her bed, she was urged to add a simple silk frock and one pastel floral voile which she considered would not take up too much space. What if the occasion did come up for her to wear them? she reasoned.

When Magdelaine came into the room and saw the mammoth pile of clothes on the bed, Tiffany informed her that those were to be packed, for she would be leaving with her parents for several weeks.

"I shall be lonely with you gone, mademoiselle," the young maid told her.

"I fear I shall be the lonely one, Magdelaine," Tiffany replied. Her maid knew that she did not wish to make this trip with her parents.

Perhaps she was sad about leaving the handsome young man Magdelaine had seen in the darkened gardens a few nights ago.

As if to confirm this, her mistress turned away, and gave a sigh that made her lips tremble slightly with an unspoken emotion.

Chapter 6

Pierre Renaud always swelled with pride when he escorted his lovely wife and his beautiful daughter anywhere. Today was no exception as they boarded the ship that would take them to America. No lady was ever more elegant than his fair-haired, blue-eyed Charmaine in her simple blue frock and the matching bonnet framing her lovely face.

Fatherly pride consumed him as he looked at his lovely daughter, so fetching in her gold-colored gown with a jacket of the same color. Her gold bonnet with its black feathers swaying with the breeze provided a most flattering frame for her lovely face.

He could understand why every seaman on the deck of the ship stopped to stare at her as she walked aboard. She was a magnificent sight to behold!

He was convinced that he had made the right decision by insisting that she come with them. Before this journey was over, he knew, she was going to learn many lessons about life.

Madame Renaud had decided by the time they were ushered to their quarters that she was certainly going to keep an eagle-eye on Tiffany throughout this voyage, for she'd noticed the lusty gleam in the deck hands' eyes as they'd passed. To have a daughter as beautiful as Tiffany could prove taxing at times, she concluded. Her sons had not been such a problem.

She feared that she was not going to be too relaxed during the crossing and she wished that Pierre could have gotten adjoining quarters instead of Tiffany's quarters being across the passageway from theirs. True, it was not that far away, but it was enough to disturb her.

Pierre would not like what she was going to suggest to him but she was going to suggest it anyway. She and Tiffany could share their quarters at night and Pierre could go across the passageway to sleep in Tiffany's quarters. Once they were alone, she made her proposal to him and she saw a frown come to his handsome face. She was flattered that her husband didn't want to be separated from her during the night.

With the look of a coquette on her face, she teased, "The rest of the day will be ours to enjoy, mon cher. Tiffany is worth that small sacrifice. Did you see how those men were leering at her when we went across the deck? Oh, Pierre, what if Tiffany did not secure her cabin door at night?"

As usual she was right, Pierre knew. Everything she said made good sense. A slow grin came on his face as he grumbled, "Well, how can I refuse when you put it that way? But I shall pray that this crossing goes a lot faster than the last time we came across the Atlantic."

They both enjoyed a good laugh and a warm embrace.

Across the passageway, Tiffany found nothing pleasant about her cramped quarters—not even half the size of her bedroom back home! The idea of having to be a prisoner in this small cubicle left her in a depth of despair.

She flung off her bonnet and removed her jacket. It suddenly dawned on her that she'd not have the devoted services of Magdelaine. She'd be tending to her own clothing and fixing her own hair. Right now, she didn't feel too fondly toward her father for dragging her away from her friends and her comfortable home to go on this crusade. After all, these people meant nothing to her and they were not her concern. Why should months of her life be disturbed for them?

It was the first time in her whole life that she had felt that her father was being unfair to her. Usually, her slightest wish had been granted, but this one time he was adamant, unwilling to yield to her wishes.

She pouted and fumed for the next two hours as she flung the articles from her valise. She had decided that she was not going to be a pleasant traveling companion. She'd have her own little revenge on her father by showing him a sulky, sullen daughter. Before this trip was over he'd wish he had left her back with Grand-père or her brother, Charles.

Madame Renaud did not leave her cabin to go across the passageway to see Tiffany until she had all her own things in proper order. Pierre had left to go up on deck to seek out the captain of the ship and enjoy one of his cheroots.

Tiffany's mother had only to look at her face to know how unhappy she was. Charmaine felt sorry for her because she knew her bitter disappointment about not going to London. Perhaps Pierre had been asking too much of her to expect her to come willingly on this long journey. It was a mission they felt urged to make, but Tiffany had no feelings for these people. How could they expect her to feel differently?

"I've ordered our tubs brought to the room along with water for a bath, Tiffany. I—I think we will both feel better." She sauntered over to the bed to sit down by her and give her a warm, motherly smile. "We'll have dinner served in our cabin tonight, so when you are dressed and ready, just come on over."

56

Her dark blue eyes turned toward her mother as she sighed, "Oh, Maman—I'm so miserable! I hate this ship and I'm going to hate every minute of this horrible trip. I can't believe Papa could have been this mean to me."

Charmaine realized the intense resentment seething within her daughter, and she did not know how to soothe her. Pierre might not have the solution, either. This was not the time to try to justify his reasons, so she didn't try to do it. She rose up from the bed and patted Tiffany's hand.

"Maybe by the time the journey is over something will change the way you feel, my dear Tiffany." Without saying another word, she left the cabin to return to her own quarters.

It was a strange, unsettling evening the three Renauds shared as the ship plowed farther out into the ocean. As his wife had suspected, Pierre was surprised by Tiffany's air. There was no lighthearted laughter and gaiety such as the three of them usually shared.

Tiffany ate her dinner in silence and only spoke when her father or mother asked her a question, which she answered politely before withdrawing into her shell.

When two more days had passed and nothing had changed, Pierre announced to his wife, "If she is to act this way during the entire crossing, then I shall have you to comfort me at night, Charmaine. She will sleep in her cabin and I shall sleep in mine. As of tonight, Charmaine, I stay in my own cabin. Is that understood?"

"Whatever you wish, mon cher," she soothed him, for she had seen how distraught he had been with his obstinate daughter.

When Charmaine informed her daughter of this, Tiffany gave her a sassy tongue.

"Well, that suits me fine. I felt like I was being treated like a baby, having to sleep with you. I know how to lock a door, Maman."

Tiffany couldn't know how her sharp words hurt, for Madame Renaud's expression did not change, but the hurt was there.

But Madame Renaud did welcome the warmth of her husband by her side. It was comforting to have him there to kiss her goodnight and talk to her when sleep would not come.

He comforted her by making her recall all the many obstacles they'd overcome in their past. "Tiffany shall not conquer us, ma petite. We will show her that we are just a little smarter than she thinks we are. I've got an idea that she thinks she's punishing both of us. Well, that young mademoiselle has a rude awakening to face!"

Both of them enjoyed the best sleep they'd had for three nights.

Chad Morrow had shared the evening meal with the captain of the ship the last three nights. He and the affable Captain Shelby enjoyed one another's company. He'd sailed many a journey on Shelby's ship since he'd worked for the Penbrook Lines. As far as Shelby was concerned, this *Majestic Queen* wasn't owned by Penbrook Lines, it was his ship!

After they ate a hearty meal and when Shelby's duties allowed it, they enjoyed playing cards until the late night hour when Chad bid him goodnight to go to his own cabin.

During the daytime hours, Chad was sequestered in his cabin, going over his records and working on his reports to turn in once they made port. According to Shelby, they were making grand time on this voyage and the weather was ideal for a fast crossing.

It was not until that third night out that Chad was startled to see that the Renaud family were passengers aboard the *Majestic Queen*. The log listed Monsieur and

Madame Renaud and daughter, Tiffany.

A sly smile came to his face. He recalled that night in the garden and how he'd taunted her that they would meet again. Damned if they weren't going to, and sooner than he'd planned on it!

When he had finished his work, he dimmed the lamp on his desk and left his cabin to roam around the ship. He moved slowly down the passageway that quartered the passengers until he had satisfied himself that he knew which cabins Tiffany and her parents were staying in.

For one brief moment he lingered outside the door. To think she was just inside that door! He recalled the soft feel of her body when he'd held her in his arms.

Chad recalled their encounter in the moonlit gardens. God, how magnificent she was with her temper riled and her blue eyes flashing! He was stirred as intensely as he'd been when she was smiling sweetly at him. As angry as she was at him, he suspected she was a little provoked at herself, too. She wasn't repulsed by his caresses and he damned well knew it. The truth was, Tiffany Renaud was afraid of herself.

That sophisticated air of hers did not mean that she was experienced where men were concerned. Her flight from him had proven that. He'd wager he haunted her sleep that night!

Next time they met he was curious how she would react toward him. Now that he knew she was aboard the ship he was certainly going to be seeing her, unless she spent the whole time inside her cabin.

Outside the small window of her cabin, Tiffany could see the silvery beams of the moonlight shining through to play against the walls of her cabin. Such a quiet surrounded her that she swore she suddenly heard a slight noise outside her door. She sat up to listen but she heard no other sounds.

Nevertheless, a sudden chill rushed over her and for

several moments, she sat there on the bed before lying back to rest her head on the pillows.

But when her glossy black head did come to rest on the pillows, she found herself thinking about that devilish Chad Morrow. She chided herself harshly for allowing such thoughts to occupy her mind. Of all the young men who could have been there in her mind, why did it have to be that rogue?

But Tiffany knew the answer to that: he was the most exciting man she'd ever met!

Chapter 7

The privacy of her own cabin for the night seemed to have put Tiffany in a more pleasant mood, Madame Renaud noticed the next afternoon when Pierre escorted them for a stroll along the deck.

A stiff breeze blew across the deck and the women's skirts were billowing around their legs. Madame Renaud's silvery blonde hair was secured by two large coils at the back of her neck but Tiffany's hair was loose and she'd not thought about securing it with a ribbon or comb. It swept across her face and she could hardly see where she was walking.

Pierre held each of their arms. His hair was also blowing, as he wore no hat, which was a good thing, for it would have been swept off his head and into the sea.

Captain Shelby walked up to join the strolling trio. After the introductions were made, the captain remarked, "You have a very fine-looking family, Monsieur Renaud."

"Thank you, Captain. I have to agree with you about that. We were enjoying a walk around your fine ship. This is my daughter's first crossing."

"Well, mademoiselle—I hope that it will be an experience you'll remember for a long time. We'll try to make it that way for you." He gave Tiffany a broad grin.

She told the husky sea captain that she was sure it would be. What she didn't say was that it was an experience she would look back on as the most unpleasant time of her whole life.

In a well-concealed spot, Chad stood watching the scene below. Ah, the view of the luscious Tiffany was a sight for his eyes to behold! Now, he was getting his first glimpse of the father of the girl who had made him linger longer in Paris than he'd planned. There was no doubt that Madame Renaud deserved the reputation she had for being one of the most beautiful ladies in Paris, as Evelyn St. Clair had told him. She was striking in her deep green gown beside her daughter attired in a gown topped by a bobbed jacket of a deep purple color.

Before the captain parted company with them, he invited the family to have dinner with him in his cabin that evening and Pierre graciously accepted his invitation.

As they strolled the length of the deck, Charmaine remarked to her husband that that was very fine of the captain.

He gave a lighthearted laugh as he declared, "I wanted the best for my two ladies. He carries my most precious cargo."

Charmaine squeezed her husband's hand. "Now isn't that nice to know, Tiffany? Pierre, you are sweet!"

Tiffany agreed, giving them both the first warm smile since they'd boarded the ship. Her mother was delighted to see that smile instead of the sullen pout. She knew that it made Pierre happy, too.

That evening when they were to depart from their cabins to make their way to the captain's quarters, it was like old times as they walked down the passageway in a gay, lighthearted mood. Pierre complimented them on how beautiful they both looked and declared that Captain

Shelby would never find more exquisite ladies to grace his table or his cabin.

"Pierre Renaud, you are the most prejudiced man I know and I love it!" Charmaine laughed.

When Shelby opened the door to greet his guests, he would have certainly agreed with Pierre Renaud that two lovelier ladies never passed through the portals of his cabin.

"Come in," he greeted them. "I am truly honored." Shelby had made an effort to dress in his best attire for the occasion. His usual thick mane of gray hair had been neatly brushed, and he'd had the young cabin boy clean up his quarters. A candle was burning in a pewter holder in the center of the table.

Tiffany was amazed at the spacious area of his quarters, comparing it to hers and her parents'. When she remarked about it, the captain gave a deep chuckle, "I guess you might say that this is my home all year long. Passengers are only aboard for a few weeks. All my worldly goods are right here in this cabin, mademoiselle."

He watched her surveying the entire cabin, especially his shelves which held his collection of books. Those big blue eyes took in everything. She was a most curious little minx, the captain figured. He liked that!

"Well, mademoiselle—what do you think? You like my cabin?" he sought to tease her.

"Oh, yes, Capitaine—there's a quaint, interesting charm about it. Perhaps, it is because I've never seen the capitaine's quarters on a ship before."

"Well, young lady, I'm flattered that mine was the first, but then I'm sure it won't be the last."

Monsieur and Madame Renaud stood listening, glad to see that something about this sea voyage was finally drawing Tiffany's interest. Maybe, before it was all over, many things would intrigue Tiffany that she'd not expected.

She had surely not expected that when another guest arrived it would be the towering figure of Chad Morrow sauntering through the door. His silver-gray eyes seemed to be devouring her as they turned in her direction.

"Monsieur and Madame Renaud, I'd like you to meet my good friend, Chad Morrow. Chad, this is Mademoiselle Tiffany Renaud," Captain Shelby introduced his guest.

Tiffany was embarrassed that she could not hide her surprise. Her mother glanced over to see her fluttering long lashes and the reflection in her dark blue eyes as her hand raised to cover her mouth. Madame Renaud's curious eyes darted back to the young man standing there with an amused look on his rugged face. Then she knew instantly who he was and why Tiffany was so stunned.

This was the young gentleman in the park who had drawn Tiffany's interest the day of the concert and who had also come to her rescue the next day. Charmaine suspected that the voyage would become much more exciting for Tiffany now.

When Tiffany introduced Chad as the man who'd rescued her, she did it begrudgingly, remembering the encounter in the garden. Pierre was quick to thank the young man for what he'd done for his daughter.

Chad assured him that he was happy that he was there to come to his daughter's side.

A smirk came to Tiffany's pretty face as she listened to the two men talking. What would her father say if he knew the liberties this young man tried to take there in the garden? she wondered.

All during the meal she found herself ill-at-ease for she felt the heat of Chad's eyes on her. The intensity of his gaze was too much to ignore. What was it about this man that affected her as no other man ever had?

Tiffany was utterly taken by surprise when Chad

turned to her father to ask his permission to take her for a stroll along the deck.

A romantic at heart, and remembering himself when he was Chad's age, he willingly gave his permission to the young man.

"Should I escort her back to her cabin, sir, or back here?" Chad asked Monsieur Renaud.

"Oh, no, we shall be going to our quarters shortly. To her cabin, Chad. The captain has to get up early and we must not make him lose his sleep."

Reluctantly, Tiffany got up to take Chad's arm after she graciously thanked the captain for the delicious meal.

She wondered if her father realized what kind of scoundrel he'd entrusted her to. Obviously, he didn't. But she wasted no time once they were alone in the passageway telling Chad just this. "You have a silken tongue, Chad Morrow, and my father feels beholden to you. But I remember the rake you were, there in the garden." All the time she was telling him this, she was aware of the force of his hand holding her arm.

His deep voice murmured softly in her ear, "Tiffany, let's say that we got started on the wrong foot. I was out of order and I blame it on only one thing. I'll never force my attentions on you again. I promise! Believe me."

For a moment she said nothing. They walked for a moment in silence before she sought to ask him what he was doing aboard this ship.

"I'm an agent for the Penbrook Lines. I'm going back to our next port, on the east coast of the United States. Then I have some time off. Now, tell me, where are you bound for?"

"Some miserable place, I can't remember the name. We're going to help my parents' dear friends."

"And you are most unhappy about it?"

"I'm very unhappy," she confessed. She did not see the amused grin on his face, for she looked like an adorable child pouting.

Chad could not have known that a group of the deckhands had been sitting at the far end of the ship indulging themselves with some whiskey after they'd gone off duty. They'd been watching the couple stroll leisurely around the deck. As Chad was about to suggest that they head back to her cabin, he sensed that a couple of the seamen were stalking them.

He bent his head close to hers to whisper, "Don't be surprised if I make a sudden move, Tiffany. We've got a couple of drunk deck hands coming up behind us. I'll take care of them, never you fear! Just stay close to me."

As they moved down the steps to the landing below, Tiffany heard the shuffling footsteps of the two following them. It seemed that the sounds became louder but she dared not look back.

She leaned closer to Chad to whisper, "I think they're closer."

"I know they are. My quarters are the last at the end of this passageway. Here's my key. Take it and get inside as fast as you can. Lock the door until you hear my voice." He added that he was about to make his move and leave her side.

She felt the release of her arm from his strong hand and she was prepared to make the dash into his room as he'd told her to do. Everything happened so fast that her pretty head was whirling. She felt his agile body come alive as it turned away from her and his hand gave her an urgent push to get into his room. She went through the motions of unlocking the door and rushing inside, quickly bolting it securely. She heard the scuffling outside, not knowing if it was Chad or the seamen winning the battle.

It was a most welcome sound when she heard his deep voice calling to her to open the door. When she did, it was so good to see that he had fared well that she rushed into his arms, flinging her arms around his neck. "Oh, Chad!

I'm—I'm so happy you didn't get hurt!"

His lips met hers in a kiss that told both of them that one kiss would never be enough.

Feeling her soft body clinging to him, Chad could not resist the desires surging in his virile male body.

Tonight, she did not want him to stop kissing her as she had in the gardens. Tonight, she wanted to know the power that this man possessed, the power that affected her so completely. Her mood was a wild and reckless one and she wanted to give way to this feeling. Never had she expected to see him again, but he had appeared, and that had changed everything for her.

She found it easy to surrender to his sensuous lips and his prodding hands. She did not protest when she felt herself being led to his bed or when he bent her down as he hovered over her. But her dark eyes locked into his gray ones.

"Oh, Tiffany, I pray you won't hate me tomorrow, but tonight you're going to love me as you've never loved any other man," he moaned in her ear as he lowered the bodice of her gown.

She felt his hot, searing lips making a trail down her throat until they came to rest on the rosy tip of her breast. There was a magic he played that she'd never known before and her body arched with the new sensations. She knew nothing of this world of ecstasy he was drawing her into. "Chad! Oh, Chad!" she sighed.

"I know, ma petite! Now you know that we were pulled to each other as bees are lured to honey, ever since that day our eyes met in the park at the concert."

Caught up in such a whirlwind of passion, nothing mattered to Tiffany except that Chad keep making his wild, wonderful love. She was not even aware that she was no longer wearing her gown and that he was also bare of his clothes. She only became very conscious of that when his firm, muscled thighs were pressing against

67

her flesh.

She gasped suddenly when she felt the powerful force of him penetrate her but he immediately captured her lips as she felt the piercing stab. As quickly as it had happened, it was over and she felt herself being carried to a new, more thrilling height of rapture.

She had no idea how long the two of them soared to the heights of the heavens but she felt herself finally calming as she lay enclosed in Chad's arms and heard his sweet words of love whispered in her ear.

"My darling, I tried to be the tender lover since I knew it was your first time with a man. Tell me, was I?"

"You were, Chad," she stammered, feeling suddenly embarrassed now that she'd so recklessly and wantonly given herself to this man she hardly knew. Yet, she had given him no protest nor did she find it unpleasant lying there now with his naked body resting against her own.

But she was glad it was dark and she didn't have to face him. It became very urgent for her to leave his cabin; she should have been in her own cabin a long while ago. "My parents will be getting concerned about me." She pushed away from him and hastily started scrambling to find her clothes.

"Please don't light the lamp, Chad," she requested when she heard him move out of the bed.

"As you wish, love," he slowly drawled, noticing a sudden distant air about her.

"I—I don't . . . I've never dressed before a man before in my life."

"I understand, Tiffany—really I do. I just want you to know that this night meant a great deal to me. I've not taken it lightly. You've done nothing to feel ashamed about—not with me." He hoped to soothe any misgiving she might be having.

Indignantly, she retorted, "I feel no shame!" She began to dress even faster.

Chad would love to have seen that lovely face, but darkness denied him that. By now he was through dressing and was pulling on his boots. "Could I assist you in some way, Tiffany?"

"No, thank you—I'm almost ready," she curtly informed him.

When the two of them emerged from his quarters, the passageway was dimly lit, but the expression on her face told him nothing as she walked quietly by his side.

When they stood in front of her door, he whispered goodnight. She nodded her head without saying anything.

But before he turned on his heels to leave, he whispered, "I love you, Tiffany Renaud." His gray eyes warmed with passion as he watched her slip cautiously through the door.

She lay in her bed, feeling the flaming flush of his caress against her silken, supple body.

It seemed Chad Morrow had the capacity to make her take all leave of her sanity. She must be aware of that in the future.

Chapter 8

Her husband was fast asleep, but Madame Renaud heard the footsteps moving down the passageway to come to an abrupt halt in front of Tiffany's door. The hour was late and she was curious: was Tiffany already in her room, or still out with Chad Morrow?

She couldn't exactly put her finger on why young Morrow caused her a bit of concern. She supposed it was because he was not like the other young men who had courted her daughter. There was a devil-may-care air about him that she figured Tiffany would find very new and exciting. She could see why.

In his young days, her Pierre had been that same type of reckless rogue and he had captured her heart so completely that no other man had ever excited her. So how could she fault Tiffany?

Now that Tiffany had met Chad Morrow, Charmaine could only ponder what would happen before they reached port. There were many days and nights to be spent aboard this ship.

Ah, she swore, sons had been much easier to rear than this beautiful daughter! But nothing had given her more joy than her lovely Tiffany.

*　　　*　　　*

As the days passed and the *Majestic Queen* plowed through the choppy waters of the Atlantic, the Renauds found their daugher to be more congenial and easier to get along with, but one thing kept plaguing Madame Renaud. This young man reminded her of somebody from the past. Everytime she looked at him, she was reminded of another man. There was a certain swagger to his walk that she knew she'd seen in another man's gait. It was no lover, for Pierre was the only man she'd ever loved. But other men had been infatuated with her and she was well aware of that, too. Who could it have been, she wondered.

Chad's company was making the trip more bearable for Tiffany. She accepted his invitation to go for strolls along the deck in the afternoons but she did not make another trip to his cabin, nor did he try to lure her there.

She could not have asked that a man be more gallant and polite. He didn't even try to kiss her when they were in some obscure place. After several days, Tiffany began to question this unusual behavior.

Was he just being polite, now that he'd had his way with her? Was that all he'd ever wanted? He certainly was eager to kiss her before that night when they'd made passionate love in his cabin. Now, he could have been one of her older brothers taking her for walks. This was enough to perplex her as time went on.

Chad had his reasons. Back in the Renauds' gardens, he'd vowed to her that he'd never force his attentions on her again. The next time she would come willingly into his arms—and she had, that night in his cabin. But then she'd become very aloof and cool when they'd parted company, so he was content and patient to wait for her to give him some hint about her desires. Oh, he desired her desperately and more than ever he ached for the sweetness of her lips and the feel of her sensuous body next to

71

his. But he was not going to force himself on her. Once again, he was going to wait for her to come to him. He had no intentions of being one of her little French "lap dogs," as he imagined most of her ardent French suitors were. The impressive name of Renaud meant nothing to Morrow as it did to the young Frenchmen.

He had no doubt that she found him different from her friends; but Chad knew one thing, and that was she had surrendered to him as she had never done before. That was enough to make him feel a little smug. Right now, he figured that fierce Renaud pride was rearing its ugly head, making her act as she'd been acting lately. But that was all right with Chad.

He watched her displaying that nonchalant, saucy air when they were together but he sensed the last day or two that she was getting a little puzzled because he didn't try to kiss her or take her into his arms. Today, when he'd left her at the door of her cabin to return to his own quarters, he saw it in her dark blue eyes.

He wanted to take her into his arms and assure her of how much he adored her. He wanted to kiss those sweet lips, but he didn't. Instead, he bid her farewell and gave way to a devious impulse to remark as he turned to leave her, "I've a lot of work to get done, Tiffany, so I may not allow myself the pleasure of your company tomorrow."

Her head tilted to the side as she glared at him. He suspected her smile was forced as she remarked, "Oh, don't fret about that, Chad. A man's work must come first. I understand . . . really!"

Her full skirts swished as she hastily turned away from him to dash into her cabin. Oh, she detested that conceited way of his! Did he think that she would be devastated by the fact that they couldn't take that routine afternoon stroll around the deck of the ship? More than ever she yearned to be back in Paris or in London as she should have been but for the whim of her stubborn father. Somehow, Tiffany believed that her mother would not have been so firm as her father had been about her coming on this trip with them.

She thought about how she could have stayed at her Grand-père's palatial mansion and enjoyed all the luxuries she was used to indulging herself in. She would even have been happier staying with her brother and his wife at their country estate outside Cherbourg than being on this miserable ship where time was hanging so heavily on her hands. The only excitement seemed to be Chad Morrow, and that diversion was beginning to perplex and confuse her. Morrow was a strange man.

The endless ocean she observed every day as she walked along the deck was enough to depress Tiffany. The sea did not entrance her. That ugly gray-green water lapping against the hull of the ship had no soothing effect on her and she detested the constant gales of wind that were always blowing when she went on deck. Her lovely tresses were constantly tangled by their assault.

She was displeased by the effects of the wind and the salt spray when she examined her delicate, satiny skin. Like her mother, she had a fair gardenia complexion and the golden glow appearing left her devastated. She was going to look horrible by the time she returned to Paris. Her satinlike complexion was always admired by her friends and she could imagine what they'd think when they saw her after this long voyage.

It amazed her that the sea breezes and salt spray did not seem to disturb her lovely mother, for she possessed the same flawless complexion. She was beginning to think this voyage would be one vexation after another. From what Morrow had told her the other day, he would be leaving the ship in New Orleans too and taking a riverboat up the river as she and her parents would be doing.

She might have been happy if she had known what the captain had told her father this afternoon. They would be making their first port any day now.

"Can't say that the trip always runs as smoothly as it has this time, but the truth is we are a couple of days ahead of schedule. We aren't very far from New Orleans, Monsieur Renaud."

"Wonderful!" Pierre exclaimed. Maybe getting back on land would brighten Tiffany's mood, which had become sullen and withdrawn again, he'd noticed.

Both the Renauds expressed their delight. They recalled how long it had taken them to make a similar crossing years ago when they were returning to France from New Orleans, where they'd chanced to meet up with Noah as they waited to board a ship to take them back to their homeland.

Dear Lord, that seemed like such a lifetime ago, they were both thinking. For the two of them, this was a sentimental journey. They were returning to a place where they'd discovered their great love for one another.

This, Tiffany could not know.

Chad Morrow was looking forward to docking in New Orleans and seeing some acquaintances of his. There was no city more exciting and alive than New Orleans and that included Paris and London. There was something about this flamboyant city that other places found hard to match.

New Orleans embodied the cultures of the French and Spanish, along with that of the West Indies. That was what made it so interesting to Chad. He swore that there were no more beautiful women anywhere than the Creole ladies he'd seen in New Orleans. At least, there were no more beautiful ladies until he'd chanced to see Tiffany Renaud. She could have been a Creole except for her fair skin. Her black hair was a distinct feature of the Creole lady.

74

Tiffany would like the city of New Orleans, for she would be reminded of France. He planned to take her on a grand tour once they arrived, if she'd agree to accompany him.

He figured that there would be a few days to lay over there before they'd all be catching a boat to take them up the river. He smiled with the thought that she was going to find the old riverboat most primitive if she thought the *Majestic Queen* provided her with small, dull quarters. She was a delightful but spoiled brat! But still he adored her, and with time he figured that she would become one hell of a woman. Just a little maturing was all that was needed.

He and Monsieur Renaud had enjoyed a nice talk a few days ago and he had informed him that he was going to have a few surprises in store for him when he arrived in New Orleans. It had been more than twenty-five years since he'd traveled through the city on his way back to France with his young bride, Charmaine.

"Guess I certainly will, Chad," he'd said. "It hadn't really dawned on me just how many years had gone by. I should not have allowed so much time to pass without returning to see my old friends." Chad noted a look of remorse on Renaud's face—the look that had haunted Pierre ever since he'd received the letter from Tasha's son. He regretted that he'd allowed his life to become so involved with running his father's business and raising his family that he'd forgotten about his old friend, Jacques Bernay. But Jacques had been more than just a friend—and this was what pained Pierre even more.

Just before he'd left the Missouri region in 1811, he had found out that Jacques Bernay was his half-brother. Old Etienne had fathered Jacques as well as him but he'd never acknowledged it. Etienne's affair with Jacques's mother had gone on while he was married to Pierre's mother, so he would not acknowledge or accept a bastard

75

son, so Jacques Bernay had told Pierre.

Now, Pierre felt the need to accept the responsibility that Etienne had neglected over the years. He would give the help to Jacques's wife and son and see that they would live comfortably.

Lately, he'd realized that it was time his sons and his daughter be told this secret about Jacques Bernay. His wife agreed with him.

Yes, the secret was long overdue to be told!

Chapter 9

Defying her father's firm orders that she never leave her cabin without him, Tiffany did exactly that. It was early morning and she couldn't sleep. She could see no danger threatening her since it was daylight. The deck hands ogled her when she paraded past them in the company of Chad Morrow or her parents, but she decided there was no harm in them.

A refreshing breeze was blowing through her porthole as she hastily dressed in one of her simple muslin gowns. There was no need to wrap a shawl around her shoulders. She cared not that her hair blew wild and free, so she did not restrain it with a ribbon or comb.

She slipped cautiously out of her stateroom so that she would not wake her parents. She mounted the steps to go up on the deck. It was divine to inhale the early morning air as she stepped out on the deck of the ship and jauntily walked to the railing to look out over the churning waters of the ocean.

So bright and blue the sky was, without one single cloud floating up above! She stood there with her full skirt billowing out as the breeze flowed across the deck. Her long black hair blew back from her face and she tilted back to enjoy the full thrust of the sea spray gently pelting her face.

This was the enchanting sight to greet Chad Morrow's eyes as he ambled along the deck in his faded blue pants and an open-necked shirt. He'd not put on his cap, so his hair blew around his face.

What was that little minx doing over there by the railing so early and all alone? he wondered. He sauntered slowly in her direction for he wanted to savor the glorious sight of her. The Renauds were still sleeping, he'd wager.

She was so engrossed in her own private thoughts that she had no inkling of his approach, even when he was standing directly behind her. For a moment, he said not a word. Instead, he stood, inhaling the sweet fragrance of her. Her long hair swished across his face as he stood there.

Tiffany turned when she sensed the nearness of him behind her. She did not greet him as he might have expected but she gave him a most beguiling smile which made him hope that some of that coldness had melted.

He moved closer so that their bodies touched. She did not seem offended by his nearness nor by the fact that his arm had snaked around the back of her waist.

For a long moment neither of them spoke. Then suddenly something caught Tiffany's attention, up high in the sky, soaring the heights of the horizon. "Look, Chad—up there! It's a gull!"

"Sure is, love. We're not too far from land," he told her.

"Oh, Chad—really? Mon Dieu, that is the best news I've heard in a long, long time. I'm so tired of this damned ship I could scream."

"Well, that will soon be over, Tiffany, and I can't wait to show you New Orleans. You're going to think you've been transported back to Paris. You'll love New Orleans!"

"Really, Chad?" Her dark blue eyes flashed with

excitement and anticipation.

"Really, Tiffany. Most of the people there speak French and you will feel right at home."

He could tell that he had brightened her day; she was like the vivacious young lady he'd first spied in the park.

"Oh, Chad, you have really whetted my curiosity about New Orleans. I—I can't wait to get there."

Chad laughed. Never had he seen her look more enchanting or more alluring than she did this early morning in her simple muslin frock. She needed no frills and fluffs to make her beautiful.

The wharves of New Orleans were a beehive of activity. Chad secured a carriage to take the Renauds to a hotel and help them with their luggage. Pierre invited the young man to join them for dinner that night in the hotel's dining room.

Tiffany felt ill-at-ease around her parents and Chad Morrow. She heard her father invite Chad to join them for dinner, and she wished he hadn't. What irritated her was that Chad seemed to be perfectly comfortable with her father or mother.

It was unnerving to Tiffany that he allowed his gray eyes to dance over her with that certain glint in them, just as he did when they were alone. Dear Lord, she felt herself blushing!

The shameless rascal seemed not to care that her parents would see him ogling her so lustily! She wondered just how long she could deny herself the exciting pleasure she knew she would find if only she'd allow his arms to hold her . . .

She'd found it puzzling that he had not tried to force his attentions on her. Not once had he bent over to kiss her lips. Morrow was a most complex man. What *was* this little game he was playing with her?

79

Sooner or later, she was going to find out. Maybe tonight would be the night that she'd taunt and tease him without mercy until he could not resist kissing her when they were alone. Perhaps, though, if he leaned over or bent down to kiss her, she should turn her head and refuse him.

But she forgot about Chad as they traveled down the quaint streets of the city and admired the buildings with their iron-railed balconies. She enjoyed the many street vendors going up and down the avenues selling their wares. There were the aromas of flowers and the smells of foods. Flat-bedded wagons were filled with fresh fruits and vegetables on their way to the farmers' marketplace.

Instead of one of the hotels in the center of the city, Chad directed them to a place on the outskirts called Plantation House. He'd told her father it used to be a fine home of one of the wealthy sugar cane landowners who'd lost it in a card game. The new owner had turned it into an elegant inn.

"You'll find it much nicer, I think, sir, much quieter than the hotels with the noisy streets below. Being a port city, you know how that can be," Chad had told Pierre.

When the carriage rolled past the busy streets of the city, the driver guided the horses off the main road to a side road. For a short distance they moved through a wooded area that was pleasantly cool since tall trees shaded them from the midafternoon sun.

It was Madame Renaud who spied the lovely two-story white framed house with its massive columns. A huge porch extended around the second landing of the house. Two young black boys dressed in deep green livery stood at the front steps as though they were expecting their arrival.

"How beautiful this is, Chad. I'm so glad you directed us here," she exclaimed. Everything she saw appealed to her. Huge, massive urns flourished with colorful blooming flowers and the old mansion was surrounded with a thick carpet of lush green grass.

Pierre laughed, "Seems you've made my wife very happy, Chad. One would surmise she's delighted."

"Then I am happy, too, Madame Renaud." He got no response from Tiffany when he glanced her way.

"Will you be staying here too?" Madame Renaud inquired.

"Oh, of course. I don't care for the city's hotels." He added that wherever he traveled he always picked the wayside inns or lodging houses when he could find them.

By the time the four of them were settled into the inn, Tiffany was as pleased as her mother by the elegant surroundings. Maybe the worst of this trip was behind her, she thought as she followed her parents toward their suite of rooms on the second landing.

Charmaine took her arms and smiled, "This is nice—oui?"

"Oui, Maman!" Her dark blue eyes gleamed as she returned her mother's bright smile.

What sheer pleasure it was to see the spacious rooms once they were inside the suite. Nothing could have pleased Tiffany more than to find that her bedroom was decorated in shades of delicate pink. Her mother laughed and told her it was as if they had known her favorite color. Tiffany roamed all around her room to inspect each and every corner. How grand it was to have a room large enough to stroll around in after that tiny cabin on the ship!

Behind a lovely painted screen she found a roomy bronzed tub in which she planned to have a luxurious bath very shortly. Neatly piled on a small gilt bench was a supply of snowy white towels and on top were two bars of perfumed soap. She picked them up to smell the sweet fragrance of lilac and knew they surely had to be imported from France.

Oh, how she wished she had Magdelaine here to help her wash and style her hair! If she dared to hope that it would be dry before evening she decided she'd have to do that for herself and immediately. Without wasting any more time, she started to remove her clothing.

By the time the sun was setting over the Plantation House's grounds, Tiffany felt like a new person. Her long black hair was washed and now drying, looking like glossy black satin. The bath had refreshed her and the sweet scent of lilac permeated the room as she sat propped up in her bed to rest before dressing.

So light and gay was her mood that she hummed a happy tune and patted her foot to the tempo of the melody. It had been a long time since she'd been in such high spirits.

In the next room, her mother was also enjoying the luxury of washing her hair and taking a bath. Pierre sat at the desk, going over some papers. He hoped in a way that their trip up the Mississippi River would be delayed for a few days so his wife and daughter could enjoy their grand accommodations after the sea voyage.

For his own personal reasons, Chad had made arrangements so that the Renauds would not have to leave the next day, as they could have done. Selfishly he wanted some time in this romantic city of New Orleans before they started up the river. He knew that once they left New Orleans he might not have another chance to be alone with Tiffany before they parted their separate ways.

The thought of saying farewell to her made him sad, but if he had the sweet memory of her kisses it might ease the pain of leaving her.

One more time, he had to hold her in his arms!

Chapter 10

It was obvious to Morrow that the Plantation House was enjoying a prosperous business from the number of people dining in its elegant dining room. Mirrored walls gave it the air of being far more spacious than it was. Cut crystal chandeliers added to the grandeur of the room.

Waiters serving the tables wore scarlet coats that matched the rich, scarlet velvet-cushioned chairs around the tables. Frosty white tablecloths draped each of the tables and small vases of crystal held red rosebuds.

Chad noticed the people as the four of them strolled into the dining room and most of them turned to stare at the Renaud party. Chad was proud to be accompanying the impressive French couple and their beautiful daughter.

Perhaps she was meant for this kind of setting and for wearing her beautiful fancy gowns. He'd never seen her more bewitching and breathtakingly beautiful than she was tonight in her floral silk gown with white lace lining the sweetheart neckline. She wore pearl earrings to match the pearl choker around her neck. Her lovely black hair was pulled away from her face to fall in a cluster of soft curls down her back. Pastel velvet flowers were pinned at the sides of the cluster of curls.

Madame Renaud was a striking-looking lady in her rich brilliant blue gown and the sparkling deep blue sapphires dangling from her ears. There was an exquisite ring to match them on her long, slender hand.

They all enjoyed the fine choice beef sautéed with fresh mushrooms and tomatoes in a wine sauce. Pierre Renaud chose a bottle of red wine for them to enjoy with the meal. Chad noted that the two very petite ladies certainly had a hearty appetite, but it obviously had not done any harm to their fine figures.

Seeing that everyone was in such a gala mood, Pierre ordered a bottle of champagne after the meal.

They sat there sipping the champagne and listening to the strolling musicians serenading the diners.

Tiffany had not enjoyed herself so much for a long time. Her face glowed radiantly. Chad watched her dainty foot patting out a beat to the music and he wished that the room had a dance floor so that he could take her in his arms and whirl her around.

Madame Renaud leaned over toward him to remark, "I want to thank you once again, Chad, for finding this marvelous place. I've not seen Tiffany so happy since she had to leave Paris to come with us on this trip."

"I can't tell you when I've enjoyed such a wonderful evening," he replied. "It's been my pleasure to share it with you, your husband and Tiffany."

Tiffany overheard their conversation and saw that the Morrow charm was having its effect on her own mother, whom she'd always credited with being so worldly-wise and sophisticated.

When Chad asked her parents for permission to take her for a walk in the gardens as they departed from the dining room, they readily consented.

Her silk gown swished to and fro as she walked beside him toward the front door. With a perky tilt of her head, she turned to him to say, "What about me, Chad? What about my consent to go for a stroll with you?"

"Now, Tiffany, you're going to go and hurt my feelings if you talk that way, love."

She placed her hands at her waistline and frowned, "Now, why do you always call me 'love,' Chad. Thank goodness you didn't let that slip out around my parents!"

His hand snaked around the back of her waist as he pulled her closer. "Now, Tiffany . . . I would be merely stating the truth. You are my love. My one and only love!"

"Oh, Chad Morrow, I bet you've told that to a dozen girls."

Before she realized what he was about, he'd bent down to give her cheek a featherlike kiss. "That's just the trouble, my beautiful Tiffany, because you don't know me at all. But you will, my pet. There's going to come a day when I might just be your one and only love."

"I swear, Chad Morrow, you have to be the most conceited man I've ever met!"

"And what's wrong with a little conceit, Tiffany? It is true I am a man who knows what he wants out of life and what he's ready to do to get it. I feel the same way about a lady I find myself very attracted to—you, Tiffany."

She suddenly found herself without a retort so she said nothing as they slowly strolled into the darkness of the grounds around the Plantation House.

Chad Morrow was not a man to be taken lightly, she realized. He was not like most of her suitors with their gallant ways and lighthearted chatter or gracious compliments about her beauty. There was a force in this man who took no time or effort for the frivolous games of courtship that she'd been used to up to now. They had not prepared her for such an encounter as she'd experienced in meeting Chad.

Boldly, he'd dared her and challenged her every time they'd been together. He had succeeded in bending her to his will and she resented it, for she had always been the one bending the men to *her* will.

Never would it be with Chad Morrow and she knew it. Her brothers would be astounded to know that there was such a man as Morrow. Why, they'd probably applaud and join forces with him.

She had become so quiet that Chad wondered what was going on in her pretty head. He began telling her about the interesting places of the city and how he'd like to show them to her.

"Yes, I'd love to go with you, Chad. Shall we go on this grand tour tomorrow?" she glanced up at him.

"If you'd like."

"Then we will do it, but now I must be getting back to my room or my parents will be concerned."

"Well, we don't want that, do we?" he replied. He turned on the pathway to direct them back toward the inn. As they walked back down the path, the darkness concealed Chad's solemn face, for he was now the one who'd turned quiet and thoughtful.

It was only when he had escorted her to the door of her parents' suite that he announced that he would pick her up at 11:30. "There's a little tearoom where I thought it would be nice for us to have lunch. They serve a very good fish chowder."

"I'll be ready. Goodnight, Chad."

"I'll be here. Goodnight, Tiffany." He turned to leave when he saw the door opening and Tiffany going inside. As he slowly walked on toward his own room, he seriously pondered whether there was any hope that he could ever win Tiffany's love, for their worlds were so far apart. About the time he thought she was willing to give her love and affections to him willingly, she'd drawn back with a chilling aloofness that shattered him. Tonight there was warmth in those sapphire blue eyes—but what would tomorrow bring? he wondered. The only time he was sure of her love was after he'd tamed her by holding and kissing her. But that was not what Chad wanted. He wanted that impassioned look of love on her pretty face all the time.

They spent the next day taking in the sights of the fabulous city. He had the carriage take them around Lake Pontchartrain and they went down Royal Street toward the little tearoom where he swore she would eat the best fish chowder.

He pointed out to her that all the wrought-iron grill-work she saw on the balconies of the two-story buildings was imported from the south of Spain during the time that country had ruled the city before the French took over. She was thoroughly enjoying herself by the time he finally took her back to the Plantation House.

He craved to share one more glorious day with her while she was in this lighthearted, gay mood, so he asked if she would enjoy seeing more of the city tomorrow.

"I—I suppose so, Chad." She gave a soft laugh.

"Same time then?" he inquired.

"I guess so," she said hesitantly.

"I'll be here. Goodbye Tiffany." He turned to leave without any attempt at a kiss. As she wandered through the sitting room occupied by her parents, she pondered what his plans were for the evening. Obviously, he was not planning on sharing the evening with the Renauds again.

In a way she was glad that her parents were not in the suite. By the time they did return, she had enjoyed a refreshing bath and lay across her bed, relaxing in her robe.

Madame Renaud gently rapped on her door and Tiffany bid her to enter.

"Well, ma petite, you look pretty and relaxed. Did you and Chad have a nice day?"

"Oh, yes, Maman. I had the grand tour," she laughed.

87

"That is good," she smiled. Tiffany was going to find the trip up the river as dull and boring as she'd found the sea voyage, her mother figured, so it was nice that she could have a brief spell of lighthearted gaiety as young girls her age enjoyed. She had decided not to tell Tiffany that this was the last night they would be in New Orleans.

Her pampered daughter was hardly going to be prepared for the crude, primitive traveling on the riverboat they would be taking to go to New Madrid. Madame Renaud had to be the first to confess that she, too had been pampered and spoiled by her devoted husband, but she had an advantage over Tiffany: when she was her daughter's age, she was not used to such luxuries and she'd known what it was like to live and work on her uncle's farm on the Isle of Jersey.

When fate had cast her and Pierre in the backwoods of the faraway country across the ocean called the Missouri region, there had many hardships to bear. She was no older than Tiffany was now. Charmaine knew that this trip would not have the impact on her and Pierre that it would on Tiffany. She and Pierre would have to be aware of this in the days to come. They should be patient with her.

Charmaine bent down to kiss her daughter before departing to indulge herself in a refreshing bath. "I'll let you know when we are ready to go down to the dining room, Tiffany. We shall be dining without the company of Monsieur Morrow. He told your father that he had some personal business to attend to tonight."

Tiffany made no reply and gave her mother an accepting nod of her head. "I'll look forward to another fine meal like the one we had last night, Maman. It was delicious!" Charmaine had no inkling of the clever little miss she'd raised and that she could conceal her feelings when she chose to, as she was doing now.

Once her mother had left the room, Tiffany leaped up

from the bed. Angrily, she paced the room. She just bet it was *very* personal business Chad was attending to, now that he was in this fabulously lively city of New Orleans.

Later, while she dined with her parents, she pretended to be having as gay a time as she had when Chad was sitting across the table from her with his flashing gray eyes dancing over her face. But the excitement was not there tonight for Tiffany.

As they dined, Charmaine Renaud's keen eyes had chanced to spot Chad Morrow dining with two people. One was a very charming lady who appeared to be in her twenties.

As they were leaving the dining room after the meal, Pierre turned to his wife to say, "You and Tiffany will excuse me. I'll be back in just a minute, ma cherie."

She and Tiffany sat down on the velvet-covered long benches while Pierre disappeared through the archway leading into the spacious dining room. Shortly, he returned to join his wife and daughter, and as they were climbing the stairs to the second landing, he casually mentioned that he'd happened to see Morrow in the dining room and thought he should inform him that they would be leaving the first thing in the morning.

Charmaine saw the stunned look on Tiffany's face as she heard her father's announcement. "We're—we're leaving in the morning, Papa?" she stammered.

"Yes, Tiffany—we are," he replied, not noticing the effect his news had had on her.

Charmaine sighed as she observed the wave of sadness sweep over Tiffany's face. She could have told her daughter that the joy and ecstasy of falling in love with a man can also bring pain and heartache. She wished she could spare Tiffany that pain, but she knew she couldn't!

Chapter 11

Chad Morrow learned something about Pierre Renaud, and that was that no man took charge of his affairs. It was obvious that he had checked with the riverboat captain whose boat they would board and found out that they could leave a day or two earlier than Morrow had intended. Chad gained a new degree of respect for Renaud.

It was no wonder that he was one of the most successful businessmen in France! Chad would remember that in the future. This new turn of events changed his plans for the next day, and there was nothing he could do about it. He could not take Tiffany to the places he'd planned to take her before they left. He wanted to show her the old French Market that dated all the way back to 1791 and the Ursuline Convent that went all the way back to 1734 and the story about this convent's part in New Orleans' history. But the biggest disappointment to Chad was strictly a personal matter and now that would have to wait, he realized. Nothing was going as he'd planned.

It made Chad wonder if the old riverboat captain, Don Boxley, had said anything to Renaud about his requesting him to hold up the departure for one extra day. It put him in an embarrassing position, for he had told Boxley that he needed the extra day to gather supplies, which was a lie. He'd only wanted some extra time in New Orleans with Renaud's beautiful daughter.

Renaud had taken the initiative to make his own arrangements so that settled that, it would seem.

It was no shock to Morrow the next morning, when they all boarded the *River Queen*, to receive a cordial welcome from Monsier and Madame Renaud but a very cool reception from Tiffany. In fact, she practically ignored him, merely giving him a slight nod of her pretty head.

With a shrug of his broad shoulders, he left the Renauds on their own to wander around the old riverboat. For Chad it brought back a wave of nostalgia, memories of times spent with his father. This was his reason for returning to this part of the country after some seven or eight years had gone by. When he'd talked to Boxley a day or two ago, he'd told him who he was and the old riverboat captain had remembered that lanky young son of Cat Morrow. He'd given a chuckle and remarked, "You've grown a bit since then, I gotta say, son."

Chad had an overwhelming desire to do something for that old man he had gotten to know in the brief time he'd been with him. He could think of nothing that would have made Captain Cat Morrow happier than to have his old boat restored. He figured this was the tribute he wished to pay to a man he had come to respect even though he'd been denied the privilege of getting to know him as he was growing up. Chad regretted all those wasted years he'd been forced to spend around the Chadwick family. None of the Chadwick men had inspired him, nor had he admired them.

He realized that it was going to cost him a handsome price to put his father's old boat in running order, but he had the funds. While he'd not be here to see it in operation once it was able to make its runs up and down the river, he knew a man who could do that for him. From time to time, he would return. There was still the need of the old riverboats along this vast Mississippi River, he figured.

When he finally picked up his luggage and went to his assigned cabin, he chuckled thinking about Tiffany. If the ship's quarters had not met with her approval then she would surely find these not to her taste.

Madame Renaud had already witnessed this reaction as the three of them had been shown to their quarters. The minute Tiffany had stepped into her cabin, she'd turned around to voice her disgust, "Mon Dieu, Is . . . is *this* what we have to put up with? For how many days must we live like this? It's horrible!"

Her father turned on his booted heels, a disapproving frown etching his dignified face. His dark eyes glared at his pouting daughter. Rarely did he admonish her as he was about to do, but Pierre thought it was time he prepared her for the conditions they might find when they arrived in New Madrid. He would not have her insulting Tasha and Etienne when they arrived there.

The time had arrived for her to learn that few people enjoyed the lavish lifestyle that she'd known all her life. "Tiffany, you will survive, I assure you! Your mother and I did when our own lives were not so grand as they are now. I think your mother will agree that it made us stronger individuals. Now, I will hear no more complaining from you, ma petite!"

His angry tone was enough to make Tiffany go on into the cabin without saying another word and close her door. She was a little dazed by the harsh tone of her father's voice, for he never spoke angrily to her or her brothers. Usually, he was the most calm, gentle person she'd ever known. She'd seen her grand-père give way to a fit of temper, and even her mother, but not her father!

She had no desire to unpack her valise and she certainly had no interest in surveying this terrible cabin. She wondered if she'd find spiders in her bed, for she spied their cobwebs up in the corner. She sat down on her bunkbed and gave way to a flood of tears. How long would she have to endure this horrible odyssey?

If she ever got back to Paris, she knew her grand-père would be shocked to hear what misery this had caused her. She was convinced that even Charles, Phillipe and Jacques would not have enjoyed such a journey as this if they had been in her shoes.

Oh, if she ever got back there she'd never wish for anything else as long as she lived, she swore it!

As she sat there on her bunk she felt the slow, easy motion of the boat. She assumed they were departing from New Orleans to start that trek up the river to this place, wherever it might be, that her father was taking her and her mother. At this rate, she figured, the trip would last forever, for the boat seemed hardly to be moving.

She sat on the bunk for the longest time, then finally she began to go through the motions of unpacking her valise. She had no wish to join her parents for lunch and she suspected that the food on this boat would be terrible anyway.

Stripping out of her gown and jacket, she decided that if she was expected to live like the roaming gypsies she'd seen at the country fairs in England, she'd dress the part. She chose the berry-colored skirt she wore for riding and the pale pink voile blouse. She sat on the bed with her silver hand mirror to work her thick black hair into two long braids and tied the ends of the braids with pink ribbons.

What she could not know was that this simple outfit and her hair in braids made her look most fetching. She was to find this out the minute she left her cabin to roam around the riverboat without informing her parents.

She figured that there was no danger to threaten her on this small boat. Right now, Tiffany was feeling a little reckless and she cared not if her parents were riled. Her father was displeased with her anyway.

The first person she encountered was a short, paunchy fellow with an abundant amount of black hair on his face as well as his head. He sat on the deck of the riverboat barechested with his tremendous potbelly hanging over the waistline of his faded blue pants. But he gave her a warm friendly smile and greeted her, "Bonjour, mademoiselle."

"Bonjour, monsieur," she returned her friendly greeting.

"I must say you are a most beautiful sight for the likes of this old boat to have aboard. They call me Dom and I will hope to please you with my cooking. I'm the cook."

Tiffany took an instant liking to this grizzly-looking creature with his broad, friendly grin. "Well, it's nice to meet you, Dom. I am Tiffany Renaud."

He tilted his huge head to the side as he echoed her name. "Tiffany, eh? Tiffany—it is a name just right for you, I think!"

Tiffany giggled, "I guess my maman thought so or she would not have named me that."

"Ah, your maman must be a very smart lady and pretty like you, I bet. Well, old Dom will try to do his best for you and keep you happy with the food. You ever tasted our Louisiana crawfish, eh?"

"No, I haven't, Dom."

"Well, mademoiselle—you are in for a rare treat and I'll assure you that you will love them the way old Dom fixes them."

"I'll look forward to that, Dom," she smiled at him. Something about him made her warm toward him and she suddenly realized that it was her brother's foreman at their country estate that Dom reminded her of. He and Michael could have been brothers.

Tiffany turned to go in another direction. She had no way of knowing that her entire encounter with Dom had been observed by Chad Morrow.

From afar he watched where she sought to roam, for he didn't like a couple of unsavory characters he'd chanced to come upon since boarding the boat a few hours ago. He considered that the two of them were asking too many questions about the trio that had boarded the riverboat back in New Orleans. Chad had immediately decided to keep an eagle eye on them, as well as on the beautiful Tiffany, as long as they stayed on the riverboat.

This was what he had been doing since the moment he'd seen her walking along the deck. His gray eyes followed her wherever she strolled.

He watched the sensuous sway of her hips causing the flounce of her full skirt to flow back and forth. The longer he watched her, the madder he got. Didn't she know what she was doing to any of the boatmen who happened to be around? The little fool should not taunt a man like she did. She'd find herself in the same kind of trouble she had back in the park in Paris.

Suddenly, Tiffany turned slightly around to find Chad Morrow there behind her. "Well, hello!" she greeted him but there was no smile on her face as there had been when she was talking to the boat's cook.

"Hello. Enjoying yourself, Tiffany? I saw that you met old Dominic." His eyes danced over her face as he walked by her side.

"As a matter of fact I was enjoying myself talking to the cook. He's made me anxious to try those crawfish he talked about."

He gave a light laugh, "Oh, he didn't lie about that. Dom makes the best. I know, 'cause I've tried them."

"So you've been to this place before?"

"Came this way a few years ago and stayed around here awhile. Dom happened to be a friend of my father's."

"Your father lived around here?"

"That's right."

"But I thought you told me you were from England," Tiffany remarked. She had no doubt that she'd caught him in a lie.

"I am, but my father lived here. My mother left my father and went back to her native England before I was born. So it was in England that I grew up. Now, is that all cleared away?" he grinned down at her.

She found it hard to resist his charm. There were no two ways about it, Chad Morrow did have a winning way about him. Perhaps that was why she didn't trust herself around him sometimes.

When he was walking close to her side, as he was now, and his hand brushed against hers, she felt the heat of his nearness. Her heart beat faster and her face felt flushed.

"I'm sorry I didn't get to show you all the places I'd planned to, Tiffany. I didn't know that your father was going to make the arrangements for us to leave this soon," he told her.

"Well, it seems Papa is very anxious to reach his destination," she declared solemnly.

"I'm sorry this whole journey is so dull for you. I got the impression that a part of it had been rather—shall we say exciting and pleasant?"

She looked up to see a smile on his face. She knew he was thinking about the time they'd made love in his cabin aboard the *Majestic Queen*.

With a disgruntled look on her face, she snapped at him, "Oh, I should know that you couldn't be nice too long, Chad Morrow. I might just add that it goes to show how wrong an impression you got about that night. It was neither pleasant nor exciting!"

Hastily, she turned from him and Chad was left with a puzzled look on his face. Damned if he could figure that young woman out! He'd been talking about the day he'd shown her the sights of New Orleans!

After a moment, he began to laugh. Oh, what a charming little liar she was! He knew she'd enjoyed that night in his cabin. She just didn't want to admit it!

96

Chapter 12

For two days, Charmaine watched her daughter's mercurial moods. She thought she had the answer to what was troubling her. Tiffany had had a spat with Chad Morrow. By now, her experienced eyes had observed Morrow enough to know that he was more than fond of her daughter.

Perhaps, she should say something to Pierre, but he had so many things on his mind right now. He had details to attend to about his business back in France and he was constantly writing letters to be mailed from various places they stopped. He was also concerned about the situation once they arrived in New Madrid and how long it was going to take to put things in order there.

This evening they'd docked in Natchez and taken on new passengers. Their next stop would be Vicksburg. Soon Chad would be going his way and they would be going theirs.

There seemed to be one person aboard who could always bring a smile to Tiffany's face, Charmaine had noticed, and that was the hefty cook with his bushy black beard. He was a jovial character. There was no denying that they weren't being deprived of delicious food, even though there were no luxurious accommodations.

When they arrived in Vicksburg, the boat stayed at the wharf for over an hour. No new passengers boarded the boat but they took on a load of cargo destined for Memphis.

The captain told Pierre that if he and his wife would like to walk around the wharf or visit the nearby shops, they'd have plenty of time. Madame Renaud eagerly accepted the opportunity to do so, but she could not find Tiffany. She was not in her stateroom and the Renauds went around the deck to search for her. Neither of them was prepared for the sight they saw when they finally spied her.

Sitting on a rickety old bench beside Dom was Tiffany with a fishing pole in her dainty hand. They certainly didn't recognize the garb she had on or where she'd acquired it. She wore an old faded shirt that swallowed her and old, full-flowing trousers. Atop her pretty head was a very unfashionable old straw hat.

When Tiffany turned to see them, a most radiant smile was on her face as she excitedly exclaimed, "Maman, I— I caught my first fish! A catfish, oui, Dom?"

"A catfish it was, mademoiselle," he chuckled as his warm black eyes glanced toward Tiffany's parents.

Pierre and Charmaine exchanged glances and began to laugh. What a charming sight she was! In that strange garb, enjoying fishing with the old cook, they knew that she was going to be just fine when they arrived in New Madrid. Pierre suddenly realized that she was excited because she'd never enjoyed simple pastimes before. The humble surroundings of New Madrid might be very rewarding for Tiffany, he decided as he stood there looking down at her happy face.

"Well, we'll be on our way, Tiffany. Your mother and I are going to walk around the wharf since we'll have about an hour before the *River Queen* leaves. You and Dom catch a lot of fish so we can enjoy them tonight, eh?"

"We'll try, won't we Dom?" she said and smiled, looking over at Dominic.

"We'll do better than that! We'll do it," he assured her. As he watched Tiffany's parents walk away, he turned to Tiffany and remarked, "You've got fine parents, Tiffany. They're good people."

"Yes, they're wonderful," she replied, but her eyes were on the fishing pole to see if the cork was going under the water and if she might have another fish on the line. An amused look lit up on Dom's face. He was happy he'd made the suggestion that she try fishing with him while the boat lingered in Vicksburg.

The garb he'd furnished for her to wear were rags compared to her beautiful clothing, but that old faded shirt and trousers were clean, for Dom had scrubbed them himself. She looked adorable in them. Even that old straw hat took on a fashionable flair atop her pretty head.

Tiffany did catch another fish, and Dom matched her catch, so before they left the bench they had four fine fish. Dom promised he would prepare them tonight in golden corn meal crust, and he assured her that they would do this again as they went on up the river.

"This old river is full of these critters and we will catch us a few. Bet no other lady from Paris can brag that she done caught herself some fish in the Mississippi River, mademoiselle," he laughed. Tiffany laughed with him. She felt in the highest spirits when she returned to her cabin to take a bath and get dressed.

For Tiffany it had been a wonderful afternoon in the company of Dom, doing something she'd never done before in her life. She'd loved it!

As Dom puttered around his galley, Chad kept him company. "So this is why you come back this time, eh Chad? You are going to do this thing for old Cat? Ah, he would be most happy—that old rascal! We had us some fun and good times. I've missed him, Chad. I've missed him these last eight years. Going up and down the river hasn't been the same without meeting him coming or going."

"He was one of a kind. They didn't make two Cat Morrows, I don't think," Chad told Dom, adding that he just wished he'd had more time with him.

"At least, you had some time, and I know that meant a lot to him, son."

"It did. My mother had no right to deny me that time for all those years."

Dom looked at the pained expression on Chad's rugged face. "You got to know, Chad, those were crazy times around these parts when the quakes kept shaking the countryside for weeks. Wives got separated from husbands. Kids were lost from their parents. Your parents met under those strained times and they would never have married in the first place under normal circumstances."

Chad agreed that he knew this after reading his father's journals.

"No, Cat only loved one woman as far as I know, and she loved another. As old Cat told me, she never deceived him but he just kept hoping. When that quake hit she got separated from her man and for a few days, Cat had her all to himself, but she strayed away from him in that dazed state that so many people wandered in during those days. God, Chad it was an awful time!"

"It must have been."

"It was. As Cat told me, the man she loved came looking for her and Cat told him what had happened, so he went hunting for her. Cat often wondered about that special woman. Figured that she had to be a pretty nice lady for Cat to think so highly of her."

"I think you are probably right, Dom. And I think I know who the lady is."

Dom confessed that he never knew her but he recalled

the name of the lady Cat was always lamenting about when he got drunk. "Was no one who could get drunker than your dad when he decided to do it. When your mom left him, he was celebrating her departure. Please forgive me, Chad, for I mean no disrespect to your mother, but this is just the truth. Cat was glad to see her go. Said he couldn't stand her snobbish ways that didn't mix good with his ways."

"Oh, Dom—I understand completely."

"Well, he got drunk as a skunk—said he was celebrating. He told me that if he could not have the woman he really loved, he should never have married at all. Said he'd never worshipped any woman but one, and that was Charmaine. That's what he told me."

Chad's silver-gray eyes flashed brightly. Dom had just confirmed what he'd suspected for several weeks: the woman his father had truly loved was Charmaine Renaud, Tiffany's mother.

Now that old Dom had confirmed this, he had to wonder if perhaps Madame Renaud was questioning many things about him. Had she made the connection between him and old Cat? Did something about him remind her of her old friend? More than once he had found her deep blue eyes scrutinizing him carefully.

Maybe, someday they might find a moment to talk about his father. He'd love to hear her tales about the Cat Morrow she had known. Somehow, he felt that she would speak about him more kindly than his own mother had.

Before he went back aboard the *River Queen*, Chad paused by the flower vendor's cart to purchase two bunches of asters so he might give one to Tiffany and the other to her mother. The pink ones were for Tiffany and the lavender ones were for Madame Renaud.

But when he walked across the deck to see Tiffany saying goodbye to his old friend, Dom, and then walking down the deck in that old straw hat and faded breeches, he broke into a gale of laughter. She looked like one of the

101

street urchins he'd seen in the gutters of London. He could not decide which one she looked most like.

He made no effort to catch up with her now. He'd give her and Madame the flowers later. She looked too happy and gay as she hastily walked toward the steps, and he would have hated to see that happy face change at the sight of him. When they last parted, he well remembered that she was quite angry with him.

Tiffany's moods were very unpredictable, Chad was learning. She was a delightful distraction that had already caused him a few sleepless nights, he had to admit, but damned if he could dismiss her from his life. He'd heard other men talk about the women in their life and how they could become a fever that seemed to have no cure. He'd never allowed himself to become so involved with any woman before—until Tiffany came along!

By the time Chad got to his cabin and placed the two clusters of flowers into a glass of water to keep them fresh, he felt the slow motion of the boat pulling away from the wharf. They were leaving Vicksburg and heading for their next stop, which would be Memphis.

Once they reached Memphis, Chad realized that he would soon be parting with the Renauds and Tiffany. The time was growing short. God knew when he'd see her again.

He had to make the most of the next few days, he decided. Some way, somehow, he had to make that head-strong little vixen understand that she did love him and to hell with that stubborn Renaud pride that was holding her back.

Her sweet surrender to him had told him she cared and cared very deeply.

But how could he convince that headstrong, stubborn little imp of this?

Chapter 13

Monsieur and Madame Renaud strolled along the wharf, sharing a conversation about their daughter. "I'll never forget the excited look on her face when she told us about catching her first fish," Pierre said.

"I think we should insist that Dom share the evening meal with us, Pierre. We'll dine late so he can. He has been so good for Tiffany."

"I think you've just had a marvelous idea, ma chèrie!" Pierre agreed with his wife.

Before they returned to the *River Queen*, they bought two bottles of the best vintage white wine Pierre could find.

In a festive mood, Charmaine suggested to Pierre that he seek out young Morrow. "We shall have a gala affair in our little riverboat cabin this evening—oui, Pierre?"

"We shall!" He saw her to their cabin and went to do as she suggested.

Chad was pleasantly surprised by the visit of Pierre Renaud to his cabin and the invitation to join them for dinner. From there, Pierre sought out Dom. If Chad was surprised, Dom was overwhelmed by the gracious Frenchman's invitation.

"Are you sure, Monsieur Renaud?" Dom questioned.

"Your wife wishes this?"

"My wife was the one who suggested it, Dom. Besides, Tiffany would be delighted."

"Then this man will be honored and pleased and this will be the best fried fish you've ever eaten, I assure you!"

Pierre went back to his cabin happy to announce to his wife that young Morrow and Dom had accepted his invitation.

Their daughter knew nothing about this as she took her bath and dressed to join them in their cabin, but she was in such a good mood that she decided to wear one of her prettier gowns.

It was a paisley pastel voile frock. The low scoop neckline of the gown and the full puffed sleeves were edged with delicate white lace. Around her neck she wore a miniature cameo that Grand-père Renaud had given her on her sixteenth birthday. It was an exquisite piece of jewelry and she prized it because it had belonged to her grandmother.

After sitting on the deck fishing with old Dom during the warm, humid afternoon, her hair was unruly, so she'd pulled it high atop her head, tied a pink ribbon around it, and coiled it high.

She left her cabin to cross the passageway and join her parents. Old Dom had told her that their next stop was a place called Memphis, and he had promised her that they would be stopping over long enough for them to enjoy another afternoon of fishing. Tiffany was looking forward to this. It was fun to see the fish dangling on the line. Crazy as it might have seemed to her friends back in Paris, she had thoroughly enjoyed her afternoon with Dom.

When she entered her parents' cabin, she found her mother dressed in a lovely lavender gown. As she entered, her father was pouring a glass of wine for his wife. "Ah, Tiffany, how very beautiful you look tonight. As usual, I have two of the most beautiful ladies in the world to grace my table. What a very lucky man I am!"

"Ah, Papa—you have a smooth tongue," she giggled. "It's no wonder you won my beautiful mother. Did he sweep you off your feet the moment you met him, Maman?"

"Oui, Tiffany—he did just that!" She gave a soft little laugh and winked at Pierre.

It was this gay, jovial trio that greeted Dom and Chad as they met at the Renauds' cabin door and were greeted by Monsieur Renaud. Tiffany was wide-eyed with surprise as she saw Chad accompanying the hefty Dom inside the cabin. His attire was as finely tailored as her father's. No one had to tell her the elegant white shirt was expensive. He most likely had his shirts made for him in London, as her father did. What was really astonishing to her was that he brought two lovely little bouquets; one lavender, which he gave to her mother, and a pink one for her.

It was obvious that her mother was impressed by Morrow's thoughtfulness. Tiffany could hardly suppress a smile when she watched her mother pluck one of the blossoms from the bouquet and tuck it inside the neckline of her gown, as she herself had done when she'd received Chad's first flowers.

Her dark blue eyes seemed to have a will of their own; she glanced in Chad's direction and saw that he was smiling.

Quickly, she turned her attention in the direction of Dom. "Did you cook our fish, Dom?"

"Oh, mademoiselle—you just wait until you taste them. Why, this is what this occasion is all about, is it not so, Monsieur Renaud?"

"Ah, oui, Dom, and we even purchased some special white wine for the occasion," he declared as he moved over to the small table to pour each of them a glass of the wine. Then he hoisted his glass and declared, "To Tiffany and Dom! We celebrate Tiffany's first catch!" Everyone laughed and took a sip of the wine.

It was perfect timing that Dom's young helper in his galley rapped on the door to announce that their dinner was ready to be served.

A dinner guest he might have been, but Dom could not resist moving from his seat to go to his young helper's side to assist with the dishes he'd prepared for their repast. The aroma was delightful. Chad's appetite was already whetted by the smells of the delicious fried catfish and Dom's special way of making his corn bread.

Dom had sent his young helper out when they were docked in Vicksburg to buy some fresh garden vegetables. There were fresh garden peas and green onions. Small roasted potatoes surrounded the golden crusted fillets of the fish.

Old Dom watched with great joy as the diners enjoyed his cuisine. He felt himself swelling with pride, for they did not have to tell him how good it tasted; their faces reflected that.

Tiffany looked across the table to see Dom's smiling face and gave him a wink. He winked back at her. He knew that he'd never forget this trip up the river.

The first comment was made by Chad as he looked over at Tiffany. "Tiffany, you can catch fish for me any time you wish, as long as Dom will cook them." That brought forth a roar of laughter there in the cabin.

Pierre was glad that he had purchased two bottles of the wine, for this jovial crowd had finished the first one and he had already opened the second before the meal was finished. It was a very happy evening they were sharing and no one was enjoying it more than he was.

It was Dom's idea that they all stroll around the deck of the riverboat before they retired.

"I think that would be a splendid idea, Dom. Chad, would you like to join us? It would be our pleasure."

Chad eagerly accepted the invitation for he felt the need after such a hearty meal. So all the occupants of the cabin left at the same time, leaving Dom and his helper to clean up. Pierre and his wife were followed by Chad escorting Tiffany.

Before she left, Tiffany quickly reminded Dom that they must try their luck at fishing again, once they arrived in Memphis.

Chad tried to walk slowly so he and Tiffany would be far enough behind her parents so they could not hear everything he yearned to say to her.

"I never figured a girl like you would like fishing," he began as he took her arm.

"And why not, Chad? I thought it was great fun."

"And so do I, but I just didn't expect you to like it."

"Well, that just goes to show you that you don't know me very well, Chad," she declared with a saucy tone in her voice.

"Guess you are right about that, love. But I'll try to get to know you better," he answered her.

"Oh, Chad Morrow, you are insufferable! Maybe I don't want you to know me any better than you do already."

He sought to taunt her. "Now, Tiffany—don't try to deceive me or yourself. I recall how you welcomed my embrace in the park and in my cabin on the *Majestic Queen*. Lie to yourself if you will, but don't lie to me."

His gray eyes were staring down at her as though he was demanding she confess the truth to him. But this she could not do, for her pride would not allow it.

"I don't wish to discuss this any more, Chad," she announced stubbornly. She noticed how his pace suddenly picked up; before she realized it they were walking beside her parents. Chad's next words took her by utter surprise. "Monsieur and Madame, I want to thank you for a marvelous dinner and your pleasant company, but I must say goodnight so I can speak to the captain before he retires. Tiffany, I must say again that I enjoyed your catch and I shall hope that you and Dom are as successful in Memphis. Goodnight."

"Goodnight, Chad, I'm glad you could join us," Madame Renaud replied. Her husband echoed her sentiments. Tiffany mumbled a goodnight as well, but she was befuddled by his sudden departure.

He had to be the most unpredictable and the strangest man she'd ever known.

Chad turned sharply to go in a different direction. He had no intention of talking to the captain about anything, but he was damned well not going to be her little lap dog. If that was what Tiffany wanted out of him, she'd best look in a different direction. This child-woman he found himself in love with had a lot to learn about him. He was more than willing to teach her how to be a woman if she was willing to let him love her as he yearned to do, but he would not waste his time in silly, childish games.

Her haughty little remark about not wanting him to know her better struck Chad the wrong way.

He had hoped to steal a kiss from those tempting lips in the darkness as they'd walked behind her parents, but he was damned if he was going to linger any longer to be tormented by her cool aloofness. Only one woman had put him through hell in his life and that was his mother. He vowed that it would never happen again.

As beguiling as Tiffany Renaud was, he'd not allow her to drive him crazy!

Chapter 14

Madame Renaud linked her arm with her daughter's as they finished their promenade. "Monsieur Morrow, he is a very nice man, Tiffany."

Tiffany would not have dared to debate that with her beloved maman. "Oui, Maman. He is nice." But she was unsure about so many things where Chad Morrow was concerned. A part of her said that she should be forever grateful to him for rescuing her from those horrible men in the park and that he had shown her that he cared for her. But he overwhelmed her so completely! She felt helpless that she had allowed herself to give way to the natural impulses as she had that night in his cabin.

There was no denying it any longer; Chad Morrow frightened as well as thrilled her. This unnerved her, for she felt herself out of control when she was around him. His rugged face haunted her dreams and he'd made her question many things about herself that she'd never questioned before. The force and power of this most unusual man challenged her as no other man ever had! This, the proud Tiffany Renaud could not dismiss. She felt that he had to be the same type of man as her father, whom she'd always admired so much. This type of man did not come along often in life, she was sure.

When she was finally inside her own cabin after she'd told her parents goodnight, she paced the floor. She muttered to the empty room and to herself, "Chad Morrow, surely you must be the most confusing man I've ever met. But, damn you, I think I love you anyway!"

Distractedly, she went about the routine of undressing and getting into her nightgown. She did not bother to brush her hair as she usually did. Instead, she dimmed the lamp and crawled into her bunk.

Tomorrow, she would show Chad Morrow that she was not his to treat as he wished or be with when he wished. She resented how he'd so swiftly taken his leave tonight as though he was suddenly bored and found her company dull.

Well, tomorrow she would have no time for him. There'd be no stroll around the deck. She might just spend the entire day in her cabin.

The next day no one saw Tiffany except her mother, when she went across the passageway to check in on her after she didn't join them for breakfast.

"I may just spend the day attending to a few things I've not done for a while. I am going to wash my hair and write a long letter to Denise and one to Grand-père. Then I shall read that book he gave me before I left Paris."

Charmaine Renaud smiled at her daughter. "It hurts no one to enjoy a nice day of solitude sometimes."

"Guess that is what my mood is today," Tiffany told her.

"Then, ma petite—I shall leave you to your solitude. We'll see you this evening, won't we?"

"Oh, of course, Maman. I shall be hungry by then," she laughed.

Charmaine went out the door and back to her own cabin and made no effort to disturb her daughter the rest of the day.

Chad waited over an hour on the deck for her to join him for an afternoon stroll, but after an hour, he finally moved from the spot where he'd been standing and ambled toward the galley.

Dom was busily washing up all the dishes and pans from the noon meal so he could start preparing for dinner.

"Chad, my good lad—what kind of a day is it? I've not had a chance to notice," he chuckled.

"Grand day, Dom. Got to tell you again that that was one fine meal last night," Chad remarked as he strolled on into the galley and sat down on one of the old oak chairs.

Dom finished drying the last of the pans. "Ah, did you ever see anything more beautiful than Mademoiselle Tiffany was last night?" Dom was baiting the young man, for he'd watched the two of them last night and his dark eyes didn't miss the looks passing between them.

"She was surely that, Dom," Chad said.

Dom took a seat on the other chair and tucked up his apron. "You in love with that pretty little lady, Chad?"

Morrow hesitated for a moment before replying. "Can't figure that out myself right now, Dom. I never wasted much time on ladies, if you know what I mean. I've been on the move a lot so I never lingered long with any one woman."

"And with Mademoiselle Tiffany you find that you want to, oui?"

"She drives me crazy," he confessed to a grinning Dom.

Dom had a quick response for the young man. "When a woman drives you crazy, mon ami, it means a fever in the blood. I've known that fever a time or two."

"So suppose you tell me the cure, Dom. I could use your advice."

"Well, I can only speak for myself. I took two different cures, Chad. One woman that affected me so, I turned and walked away. I never looked back. The other lady that gave me such a fever I married and loved until she died. I was living in New Orleans at the time and working on a shrimp boat. No one could have been happier than me and my Angelique, but all my love couldn't save her when yellow fever hit there."

Chad saw a mist of tear gather in the old cook's eyes. He knew not what to say so he just sat there in silence.

Deep emotion filled Dom's bearded face as he added, "I never felt that so-called fever again, Chad, so I never remarried. Some men might think I lie but I tell you, Chad, that I never took another woman to my bed. I had no wish to." He gave out a weak laugh. "I ate instead."

"Obviously, you enjoyed much pleasure, my friend," Chad declared.

"That is obvious, isn't it? I have probably not given you much help, Chad, but it is the best I can do. Each of us is so different, I don't guess there is an exact answer to your question. You'll have to find yours as I found mine. She's worth all your time and patience. She's like that rare treasure a man would hunt for all his life and hope to find. She reminded me of my black-eyed, black-haired Angelique the first time I saw her."

Dom was like a man bearing his soul to young Chad Morrow. "I know it sounds crazy but the other day when we sat together fishing, I allowed myself to pretend that it was my beautiful Angelique that was sitting there with me as we talked and laughed together. It was the happiest afternoon I've spent in years. Mademoiselle Tiffany will never know how much joy she gave to me that day but I tell it to you, mon ami."

"I'm—I'm glad you have, Dom." He reached over to pat the cook's shoulder. "I feel very honored that you've talked with me and shared your thoughts with me this

112

afternoon. You've helped me more than you will ever know. As you felt when you pretended that Tiffany was your beloved Angelique, I feel that I've shared a time with my father just sitting here talking with you as I would have liked to have done with him. I thank you, Dom."

The hefty cook rose up from his chair and embraced Chad's shoulders. "Wherever old Cat is, I can tell you he is smiling down on us right now. I know it!"

Chad would agree with him about that. By the time he took his leave of Dom, he realized that he'd forgotten to ask him if he'd seen Tiffany today.

But Dom had told him to have patience and so he would.

Patience was not one of Chad's virtues, he realized by the time another day had gone by and he'd not seen the lovely face of Tiffany. It was like a day without sunshine and a night without the glowing rays of moonlight.

When he finally encountered the Renauds on deck, he inquired about her, but he was told that she was not ill. Madame Renaud tried to explain. "Tiffany is in one of her reading moods, which I must say are rare, but her grandfather gave her this book before we left Paris."

"It must be a very interesting book," Chad remarked.

"I was just thinking the same thing, Chad," Pierre Renaud said. "I guess I should have examined that book before I let her read it."

"Well, give her my best regards and tell her I have missed our strolls around the deck," Chad gallantly professed.

"We certainly shall, Chad," Charmaine told him as he turned to go. To her husband, she said, "I like that young man, Pierre."

"I rather suspect that Tiffany does, too . . . and far more than she wants us or him to know right now."

Pierre pressed his wife closer with an arm that was still strong. His dark eyes looked down at her as he declared, "Oh, Charmaine, I'm finding a daughter is a much more worrisome offspring than a son. I've already decided that Charles, Phillipe or Jacques are never going to cause me the sleepless nights I will have over our Tiffany."

"Ah, mon cher—she will be all right. She will have us to help her, which I didn't have as a young girl and I did all right, n'est-ce pas?"

"Ah, but you were lucky that you met and fell in love with me," he teased her.

"But there was a time when I thought you had taken advantage of my innocence, Pierre Renaud."

"Time proved that wrong. I proved that I loved you with all my heart and I might add that I still do." He suddenly found himself fired with a passion as great and fierce as those he'd felt over twenty years ago. He turned his beautiful wife around to guide her back toward their cabin.

She was aware of that special gleam in his black eyes. Pierre might not realize it, but she was as eager as he was to make love. The many years they'd shared had not dimmed the all-consuming passions they'd discovered back when they were young and fell so helplessly in love.

Behind the closed doors of their cabin, they became those two young lovers once again!

Part II

The Fury Of
A Summer Storm

Chapter 15

When the *River Queen* pulled into the wharves of Memphis, the vast Mississippi river was high due to the daily rains they'd been having in the region. The waters were near the edge of the banks. It was an ugly, muddy water that Tiffany looked down on as she stood by the side of Dom. He declared that there was a lot of muddy water due to the torrents of rain just before their arrival there.

In anticipation that they would be fishing again this afternoon, she'd worn the old faded shirt and full legged pants when she went to meet Dom. Atop her head, she'd placed the wide-brimmed straw hat but she removed it to wipe the sweat from her forehead.

"This Memphis is a miserably hot place, Dom," she sighed, wishing that she'd piled her hair on her head for it was damp and clinging to her neck.

"It is usually not this uncomfortable, but two days of rain and now this bright sun can do this to any place situated along the river."

"And this place my parents are going is beside the river—yes?"

"This is true, mademoiselle."

"Oh, Dom, I wish they'd left me back in Paris with Grand-père."

"Maybe they did not wish to be away from you that long. Your parents are very fond of you." He smiled at her.

"I know that, Dom, and I'm fond of them, but these people they want to help are not known to me."

"You may come to like them as much as your parents do. Then you will be happy that you came here."

"I suppose you are right, Dom," she mumbled as she sat down on the old wooden bench by the rail of the riverboat.

"Of course I am right," he chuckled.

Dom turned to notice the new passengers arriving on the *River Queen*. He realized that he was going to have to prepare an extra pot of food for the evening meal. As much as he hated to do it, he had to excuse himself to get to his galley so he could start preparing dinner.

In a way Tiffany was glad to get out of the oppressive heat and back to her cabin, where she stripped out of the pants and blouse to sit there in her undergarments. Once the old riverboat began to move she could feel the hint of a breeze coming through the small cabin window. She welcomed the movement of the boat for she figured that the sooner they arrived at New Madrid, the sooner her father could get that business taken care of and they could return to Paris.

Tiffany wondered why her parents had never spoken of Tasha or her son. If they were such devoted friends, why had she never heard them mentioned? It seemed strange that suddenly, out of the blue, there came an urgent letter from this Etienne Bernay and everyone's life had to be disrupted. Her father dropped everything, her mother had to cancel all her social engagements that had been made weeks in advance, and her own visit with her dear friend Sabrina had to be cancelled, too.

It seemed to Tiffany that this was a tremendous sacrifice to make for a family that she'd never heard mentioned in her whole life.

She aimed to ask her mother tomorrow just why this family demanded so much attention and consideration from the Renauds. Her brother, Charles, had had no answers to give her when she'd asked him, and Charles never lied to her.

The Mississippi River had a lot of winding bends and its waters flowed with a swift current from the torrents of rain that had fallen over the area. The flat delta lands and the cotton fields were flooded, as well as the pasturelands where cattle grazed.

Chad watched from the riverboat as his own father had done in the past when he pulled in to take on the farmers stranded on a dock and wharves. He watched the men and their wives eagerly board the riverboat with their small bundles of belongings, happy for the rescue provided by the passing vessel. He could see it in the faces of women with babes clutched in their arms and the eyes of the men, grateful that their family was not going to be swept away and swallowed up in the muddy waters of the overflowing river. They were gratified to see the riverboat coming their way.

Chad knew there and then that his idea to have his father's old riverboat restored and operating, as Cat Morrow would have done, was the right one. He must do it, no matter what it cost him. It was a mission he must carry out as surely as he'd seen that his mother's jewelry was delivered to her dear friend, Evelyn St. Clair.

Today convinced him of that. The pursuit of Tiffany Renaud would have to wait until he accomplished this, he reminded himself. But his esteem for the Renaud family grew as this day went on and never would he question the warmth and compassion of Charmaine Renaud when he watched her distribute her expensive light wool shawls to

119

some of the ladies to wrap around their babies or make a soft bed for them there on the open deck.

If Tiffany was half the woman her mother was, then she would be one hell of a woman, Chad was convinced.

With all this unexpected confusion, Tiffany did not manage to have the talk with her mother that she'd planned. She did not know about all the additional passengers until midafternoon when her mother told her about the poor people who were flooded out of their houses and had had to board the boat to get to higher ground.

"This happens around this part of the country quite often in the spring and summer when the rains come," her mother told her. Tiffany realized that she must remember those times when she had lived here, even though it was over twenty years ago.

"What will they do, Maman?"

"They'll get by however they can until the waters go back down. Then they'll go home and clean up the mess the floods have made, Tiffany."

Charmaine saw the look on her daughter's face and she wondered how Tiffany would have faced what she was forced to face when she was her age. "Tiffany, ma petite—it is not your fault, but you have never known what it's like to be desperate and I hope you never have to, but let me tell you that it is a very frightening thing."

"I gather you have lived through such a time?"

"Oui, ma petite—I have."

"I would like to hear about it, Maman," Tiffany told her mother as her dark blue eyes searched her mother's face.

"I think you have that right, Tiffany. Oui, I think it is time I told you."

As they sat there together, Charmaine asked her daughter how she would feel if she was faced with leaving everything she owned behind to flee, when the only thing

120

occupying her thoughts was to save her life.

"I would be petrified, Maman," Tiffany confessed.

"And so was I once in my life, Tiffany. You never forget it. These poor people that boarded this riverboat were confronted with that this afternoon. It is the most helpless, hopeless situation anyone can face."

Tiffany looked at the lovely face of her mother and realized why a magnificent man like her father was so ardently in love with her. She was a most remarkable lady!

"I'll look forward to the time when we can talk and you can tell me about all these things that happened in your life, Maman. I feel the need to know."

Charmaine moved to embrace her daughter as she told her, "You know they say there is a time and a season for all things and I think this is the time and the season that you know more about your maman and your papa."

Tiffany's curiosity was stimulated about this revelation that her mother was going to make. Was there some deep, dark mystery in her family that she'd never been aware of? Her mother had a strange air about her as she spoke. Never had Tiffany questioned her mother or father about anything in her whole life.

Now, she did!

It was midnight, but Tiffany could not sleep. She'd shared the evening meal with her mother and father and excused herself to go to her own cabin. But sleep evaded her, so she quietly slipped out to go for a walk on the deck. She saw the poor homeless people that her mother had spoken about. She saw a husband and wife sitting by the railing, with the woman cradling a sleeping baby in her arms. She thought about that empty bunk over the one she slept in and she knew what she must do. She could sleep in the upper one and give the lower one to the poor lady and her tiny baby, with the thick coverlet so that they could have a good night's sleep. They would be cozy and warm.

Tiffany walked over and bent down to speak to the young woman. "Hello, I—I was sorry to hear about your farm being flooded. I just wanted to offer you and your baby a place to sleep in my cabin, if you'd like." Tiffany spoke softly so she would not wake the baby.

The woman looked up and managed a weak smile as she told Tiffany, "Well I appreciate your kindness, miss, but I couldn't do that."

"I have an extra bunk that no one is going to sleep in. You and your baby could enjoy a good night's sleep," Tiffany pointed out to her. "Guess I should introduce myself. My name's Tiffany—Tiffany Renaud."

"Our name's Phillips. I'm Nell and this is my husband, Tom."

By now Nell Phillips' husband had roused up and heard the young lady's generous offer. "Nell, honey— this young lady is mighty nice and I thank you, ma'am, on behalf of my wife. Now, you and Betsy go get yourself a good night's rest and I'll be right here in the morning."

At her husband's and Tiffany's urging, Nell rose and followed Tiffany to her cabin. But the baby roused from its sleep and began to cry.

"She's fretting so 'cause I seemed to have such a fright when I saw those waters coming so close to our house that I can't seem to have the milk to nurse her. Seems like I just dried up," Nell told Tiffany.

Tiffany had a remedy for that. She knew that old Dom would not be in his galley, but she didn't figure he'd mind if she helped herself to a small jug of milk.

"I'll be right back and we'll see if we can't get little Betsy content so she will sleep," Tiffany said as she dashed back through the door. Nell had barely time to lay the baby back on the bunk and change her wet diaper

122

before Tiffany had returned to the cabin with the milk.

There was no bottle to put the milk in, so Nell took small amounts in a spoon to allow the baby to sip slowly. It took an endless amount of time to quench the baby's hunger but finally she was sated. Nell and Tiffany exchanged smiles when they noticed the baby's eyes getting heavy with sleep once she'd had her fill of the milk.

Carefully, Nell placed the baby to the side of the bunk that adjoined the wall of the cabin. Whispering her thanks to Tiffany, she told Tiffany that the two of them might be able to get to sleep now.

Tiffany got one of the soft white batiste gowns she'd brought along with her on the trip and handed it to Nell. "I think you'll rest more comfortable in this and it will give your dress a chance to dry overnight. I noticed that it is still damp around the hem."

Nell Phillips was amazed by this young lady. Not only was she the most beautiful girl she'd ever seen, but she was also the kindest and most generous. Maybe she was an angel from heaven, Nell Phillips secretly mused. One thing was for certain; she'd never forget Tiffany Renaud as long as she lived.

She took the gown and felt the softness of the thin cotton material and wasted no time stripping off her own damp clothing to drape it across a chair. When she had pulled the gown over her head and slipped under the sheet beside her sleeping baby, she thanked Tiffany again. "Hope you sleep well, Miss Tiffany."

"Oh, I will and you do the same, Nell," Tiffany said and she crawled up into the top bunk. Once she knew that Tiffany was up in the bunk, Nell dimmed the lamp on the nightstand. She immediately gave way to the weariness consuming her body.

Only for a fleeting second did she feel guilty about the leisure she was enjoying while poor Tom slept up on the deck.

Chapter 16

Tom Phillips had been as lucky as his wife, for he had not had to sleep on the deck of the riverboat either. Chad Morrow had ambled along the deck to find him sleeping there and offered him the extra bunk in his cabin as Tiffany had for his wife.

As the two men talked, Chad learned that Phillips and his wife were heading for New Madrid. They would spend a couple of weeks with his older brother until the waters subsided and they could return to their farm to survey the damage the flood had done to their home and crops.

"Didn't know what else to do with a small baby like Betsy so it was the only choice we had," the tall, lanky farmer told Morrow.

"Well, the captain tells me that we should be getting to New Madrid tomorrow afternoon."

"That sounds like good news to me. My brother's got a nice little place there and they don't seem to have the threat of flood waters where he lives." Tom Phillips sat on one of the oak chairs in Chad's cabin, removing his high-top shoes to rid himself of his damp socks.

He looked up to inquire of Chad, "You heading up New Madrid way too, eh? You got kin livin' there?"

"No, not now. My father used to spend a part of his

124

time there. He was a riverboat captain, so his boat was his home up and down the river."

The two men talked for a while longer before Chad dimmed the lamp after Phillips crawled up to the top bunk. But by the time Chad woke up the next morning, the upper bunk was empty. Tom dared not sleep too long and allow his wife, Nell to go to the deck and not find him where she'd left him the night before. The poor woman had had enough frights in the last few days, so he had no intention of giving her another one. Besides, he'd enjoyed six good hours of sleep and that was enough for Tom.

Tiffany also found the lower bunk of her cabin vacant when she roused up from her sound sleep. The gown she'd given Nell was neatly folded on the lower bunk.

The couple greeted one another on the deck, happy to be back together after being separated for the night. But each had a tale to tell the other about two complete strangers who'd opened their generous hearts to them.

Tom gave his wife a hug. "There's a lot of good people around, right, honey?"

"More than I realized, Tom. Why she even let me sleep in one of her pretty nightgowns! Prettiest thing—so soft and sheer."

"Now, Lordy—that I would have liked to have seen, Nell!" he teased her. This brought a rosy flush to his wife's face and it made Tom realize that even though they'd been married for almost two years and she'd had a baby, she was still modest and shy.

"We'll be arrivin' in New Madrid sometime today, honey. How about that, Nell?"

"Oh, that will be nice, Tom," she said.

As he sat there with his arm around her, Tom hoped that someday he could get her a pretty nightgown like the one she slept in last night.

As they sat there on the deck looking out at the river as

125

the riverboat surged its way up the stream, Tiffany Renaud came scampering across the deck with a small bundle in her arms. Her long black curls bounced over her shoulders as she walked directly toward them.

"Oh, Nell—there you are! Glad I found you. I—I wanted you to have this," Tiffany gave her a warm smile that made Nell dare not refuse the small bundle which she knew contained the soft batiste gown.

"Oh, now, Miss Tiffany—you don't have to do this."

"But I want to. Please, Nell." The young mother obliged her by accepting her gift.

Tiffany did not wish to intrude on them any longer so she said goodbye and turned to leave. But she slammed into the firm, muscled body of Chad Morrow who was standing behind her.

"Oh, Chad! I—I didn't know . . ." she stammered as she stared up into his face. "I was saying goodbye to the Phillipses."

"Well, I was about to do the same thing," Chad told her. Looking beyond her to address Tom, he bid the farmer goodbye and good luck.

"Same to you, Chad. Hope we meet again," Phillips replied.

"Oh, we probably will, Tom" he said, as he took hold of Tiffany's arm. In his masterful way, his strong hand guided her down the deck. She allowed him to do so.

"You—you know the Phillipses?" Tiffany asked him as she tried to match his pace.

"I only met Tom last night. I asked him to share my cabin."

Tiffany gave a soft little giggle, "And his wife shared mine."

Their eyes met and Chad laughed. He was tempted to say how much nicer it would have been if they'd allowed the Phillipses to share one of the cabins and the two of them had taken the other one. But he bit his tongue just

126

in time.

He led her over to the railing, for it suddenly dawned on Chad that this might just be the last private moment he'd have with her before they docked. That didn't exactly make him happy.

His hand had now snaked around her tiny waist. His deep voice commented about swift currents of the river due to the torrents of rain that had hit the area a few days earlier. Tiffany noted a serious tone to his voice and his manner. She saw a different side of Morrow.

She listened as he began to speak about his father and his days as a riverboat captain on this muddy Mississippi River.

"Is this why you are coming back here, Chad? I thought you called England your home."

"England was my home, but my father lived here. You might say I'm coming back here because of my father, Tiffany." His rugged face wore a serious expression as his eyes gazed down at her. "I've something I must do for him."

Her dark blue eyes locked with his but she said nothing as she looked at him. Perhaps she had judged him wrong, for at this moment she saw a side of this man she'd not seen before. He was not always the devil-may-care, reckless individual she had thought him to be.

"How long will you be here?" she asked him.

"That I can not tell you, Tiffany. As long as it takes me to do what I want to do. And you?" he asked her.

She felt his powerful hand clasping her waist tighter and she felt herself sway closer to him. "I have no way of knowing, how long Chad. That is up to my parents."

His gray eyes danced over her face and the heat of passion Tiffany saw reflected there was enough to stir a flame of desire in her. She suddenly yearned desperately for his sensuous kiss.

"I shall miss you, love, when we have to say goodbye. I

127

want you to know that. I want to kiss you, Tiffany—I want to so bad it hurts, for I know not when I'll see your beautiful face again."

Her half-parted lips invited him to do just that as she murmured softly, "Then for God's sake, do it, Chad! If you don't I think I shall die!"

He needed no more urging as he turned her around to face him and his head bent down to take those tempting lips in a long, lingering kiss. Neither of them cared who might be watching. The only thing consuming them was the need and hunger for the ecstasy they'd known before. But a kiss was all they could share now.

When Chad finally released her, she stood looking up at him as though she could not believe the sensations he'd stirred within her.

"God, Tiffany—I love you!" he murmured. His silver-gray eyes were piercing her and there was sincerity etched on his tanned face. She wasn't sure what would have happened next if a couple of the boatmen had not come sauntering down the deck.

Tiffany realized that there in broad daylight anyone could have seen them kissing. She felt ill-at-ease as Chad's strong arms were still encircling her waist. While it didn't bother him who might be watching them, he saw that Tiffany was feeling uncomfortable.

"I'll not try to kiss you again, love, even though I'd damned well like to. You know this might be the last time we see one another for a while, don't you, love?"

He wondered what she was truly thinking as she stared up at him. She looked like a sweet innocent angel but he also knew how easily all of this could change and she could cut him to the quick with that sharp little tongue of hers.

But he prodded her anyway, "Will you miss me just a little, Tiffany?"

"Oh, Chad—what am I to say? I'll certainly miss the

devilment you've cast my way." She was fighting to keep from confessing to him that she would miss him very much and it had not dawned on her that they would soon be going their separate ways. Trying to sound more casual than she was feeling, she smiled up at him to declare, "You must know I'll miss you, Chad Morrow, you conceited devil! There, is that what you wanted to hear?"

He laughed. "Well, at least that is something, to hear you say that." He noticed the sudden scurrying of the deck hands and he informed Tiffany that she was about to get her first glimpses of New Madrid; the docks were straight ahead.

"I see nothing but woods lining either side of the river. I see no houses or a town."

"The small town is beyond the woods, as I recall. You see, it's been sometime since I was back here." His arm was still encircling her waist and she seemed to enjoy it being there, he was convinced.

Neither of them was aware that Monsieur and Madame Renaud had spied them at the far side of the boat and were coming over to join them. They had wondered where their daughter was when her mother had found her absent from her cabin. Both of them immediately noticed the cozy manner the two were enjoying in this last moment of the long riverboat trip since they'd left New Orleans. Pierre and his wife exchanged glances and smiled.

They both considered that they had to credit Morrow for bringing Tiffany out of her sullen, pouting mood when they'd first left France. For that, they were truly grateful. What a miserable time that would have been if she'd remained in that mood all these many weeks!

When they were within a few feet of the young couple, Pierre announced their presence. Tiffany turned to see her parents standing behind them and she felt a flush coming to her face, for Chad's arm was still around her. It certainly didn't seem to trouble him. He had to be the coolest, calmest man she'd ever met. Most of her suitors would have become flustered and nervous that her father had come upon them in an embrace. But she could have sworn that not one muscle flinched in Chad Morrow's body.

Chad felt her move from his side. "I must go see Dom and tell him goodbye," she said. Before anyone could say a word or stop her, she was dashing across the deck.

The three left standing there laughed as they watched her rush away. All were secretly admiring the lovely sight of her with her long black curls bobbing down her back.

"I think I can say that Dom made himself a friend during this trip," Pierre Renaud observed.

"That lucky Dom!" Chad muttered without even thinking about what he'd said. Right now, he wasn't exactly sure what she considered him.

Chapter 17

When the *Majestic Queen* had docked at New Orleans, the wharves had been alive with activity and people milling around. The streets were lined with wagons and carriages, reminding Tiffany of the streets of Paris.

The first sights of New Madrid were completely different. No lady wore a fancy chapeau. All Tiffany saw were simply dressed women wearing cotton bonnets or straw hats.

Chad had left the riverboat before the Renauds. He had traveled light, so there was no luggage to wait for. Besides, he had spied his father's old friend standing on the wharf the minute the riverboat came to a halt.

He called out to old Bickford and waved his hand to get his attention. Chad had not expected him to be there.

Tiffany happened to be standing by the railing as Chad walked down the wharf with the weathered, hump-shouldered gent and the two of them laughed and talked as they swiftly faded from sight. A sudden sadness filled her as she watched him walk away and she wondered if she'd ever see him again. Perhaps he would disappear from her life as suddenly as he'd entered it that lovely spring day back in Paris.

Pierre hired a man with a one-horse buggy to take them

to the Bernay house. The driver seemed to be curious as to who they were and asked a dozen questions. Pierre answered some of them and others he chose to dismiss. Tiffany saw him smile at her mother.

It did not disturb Pierre, for he recalled how it was in a small town like this one. When he saw the smile on Charmaine's face, he knew she did, too.

He knew that his beautiful daughter was going to be startled by many things she was going to encounter here in New Madrid. He vowed to himself to be more patient with her than he had been when they first started out on this journey.

The house that the Bernay family lived in was like no home Tiffany had ever seen. The grounds were overgrown with high grass and weeds. Only the narrow stone path was free for one to walk to the front steps. Across the front of the house there was a porch with a wooden railing edging it. Numerous pots and urns filled with rich black soil sat along the walls, but it seemed no one had taken the time to plant anything in them.

When her father rapped on the door, no one came to greet them. Unceremoniously, Pierre Renaud checked the door to find it unlocked so he did not hesitate in entering. His wife followed him as she called out, "Tasha, dear—are you here?"

She thought she heard a soft moan and rushed ahead of her husband toward the pathetic sound. It did not take her long to discover her dear friend, Tasha in the back bedroom, trying to struggle to sit up in bed. Charmaine rushed to embrace her. They clung together as tears streamed down their cheeks.

For an endless moment the two women held one another as Pierre stood looking on. Tasha's dark, hollow eyes glanced up to see Pierre and she gave him a weak smile.

"I—I never hoped to see you again, Pierre. You and Charmaine being here is like a prayer being answered," she stammered. Pierre moved to sink down on the bed beside his wife and take Tasha's hand as he kissed her gently on the cheek.

"Tasha, I'm sorry we didn't get here sooner. But we are here now and everything will be taken care of. We will get you well."

Tiffany stood there feeling like a stranger in these new surroundings as she listened to her parents talking to this woman. It was hard to believe that there had been a gap of some twenty-odd years since they'd last been together.

Charmaine's hand finally reached out to her daughter and urged her to join their circle. "Tasha, my daughter—this is Tiffany. Tiffany, ma petite, this is our dear friend, Tasha Bernay."

"I am pleased to meet you, Madame Bernay," Tiffany responded.

Tasha gave a sigh. "Your mother was about your age the first time we met. Is that not so, Charmaine? My, but you are beautiful, as she was and still is!"

Tasha's black eyes stared at her as though she could not take her eyes off her. Tiffany felt awkward, for she knew not what to say to this lady.

Before the next couple of hours had passed, Tiffany found herself feeling very much the stranger as her father and mother took charge like a team. Tiffany roamed aimlessly around as the two of them moved with resolute vigor to put some order in this house which seemed to have been so sadly neglected.

She heard her mother tell her father that it was obvious that poor Tasha had been unable to do a normal day's chores for a long time.

Pierre carried all their luggage into one of the extra bedrooms and inquired of his wife, "What about

Tiffany? Where shall she sleep?"

"I have to ask Tasha about her son and if he lives here with her," she told her husband as she busily moved around the room to open up some of the windows to allow some fresh air in. She flung aside her blue twill jacket and began to roll up the sleeves of her white silk blouse. "The first thing I'm going to do to rid this house of this horrible sick smell."

Tiffany had taken a cue from her mother and rolled up her sleeves and piled her long hair atop her head after removing her bonnet. With the fresh air flowing through the windows, the oppressive, stuffy feeling of the house disappeared.

By the time the sun was setting and Pierre was going around to fill all the lamps, her mother had a cast-iron pot of stew simmering on the cookstove. While their supper cooked, Charmaine took that time to refresh her ailing friend with a bath and dress her in a clean nightgown.

"You'll feel much better now, dear, and a bowl of stew will give you some strength, Tasha."

"Oh, Charmaine, you—you are so sweet and kind, but then you always were. Poor Etienne, he's done the best he could, but he is only a young man and trying to work for the lumber mill all day long to pay off his father's debts. He just hasn't known how to deal with it all. We depended on Jacques to take care of us," she confessed to her old friend as Charmaine washed her arms and dried them with a towel.

"And you've been here all day by yourself, Tasha?"

"Had to be, except for a neighbor occasionally coming by with a bowl of food and a few hours' visit. Etienne had to work to have food on the table and buy my medicine."

Charmaine assured her that she'd not lack for medicine or food. "Now all you've got to worry about is getting well," she said in her comforting tone.

Tasha indeed felt stronger after the bowl of delicious

134

stew. Poor Etienne wasn't a very good cook and she'd not had the vigor to go into her kitchen for many weeks.

Darkness was already covering the small village when Etienne arrived from the lumber mill. He was dirty and tired as he trudged up the path to the steps. It was only when he walked across the front porch that he realized that lights were blazing all over the house. Why, it looked like it used to before his mother became ill! It was always a cheerful, welcoming sight when he'd come home in the evening, always exhausted but hungry for the good meal he knew would be waiting for him.

As he moved slowly through the front door, his nose inhaled the delicious aroma of the stew and he wondered if a miracle had happened since he'd left early this morning. His mother was hardly able to get out of bed to prepare a pot of stew that smelled this good.

He moved slowly, almost afraid to venture into the house that seemed to have taken on a completely different air since he'd last been there.

He knew he must surely be dreaming when his eyes beheld a vision that had to surely be an angel. She moved down the darkened hallway. Her black hair fell all around her dainty shoulders. She wore a white blouse with a wide ruffle edging the scooped neckline displaying her bare arms. He swore he'd never seen a smaller waist than hers as she swayed down the hall in the full gathered skirt of scarlet. But what really took his attention was the fact that she was without shoes and padded barefooted. Oh, there was no doubt in Etienne's mind that she was surely a vision. This lady could not be real!

However, when she kept coming toward him, Etienne had to accept that she was no ghost—she *was* real! When her soft, accented voice greeted him, he returned her greeting. "I am Tiffany Renaud. Are you Tasha's son? Are you Etienne?" she asked of him.

"I am." He felt very conscious of the fact that he must

have looked terrible to her with the dirt and grime on his face and clothes. In an uneasy voice, he asked, "You and your family did come?"

"We came. We arrived this afternoon."

Etienne felt very ill at ease and embarrassed to be greeting the Renauds in the condition he was in, but he could hardly be clean after his ten-hour day at the mill. They had come as his father had told him they would do if he asked them.

"Come—I'll introduce you to my parents, Etienne." She had such a warm, friendly smile that he relaxed a little as he followed her into the parlor.

After Etienne met the Renauds, he was no longer apprehensive about how he looked. But he did excuse himself so that he might change out of his dirty cothes. No one had to tell him what a miracle they'd performed in a few hours.

His mother was in much better spirits and the house looked and smelled much better. Once he'd bathed and changed into clean clothes, Madame Renaud immediately went into the kitchen to serve him a steaming bowl of the stew which she'd kept warm on the stove. "We were famished, Etienne. I apologize for not waiting for you. Besides, I wanted to give some to your dear mother."

"Oh, Madame Renaud, you don't have to apologize to me. I'm—I'm just grateful for all you've already done for my mother. She—she seems so much better than when I left her this morning." He did not tell her all he was thinking as the two of them were in the kitchen alone. He found it hard to believe this woman who had servants waiting on her back in Paris had come to this backwoods place and done what she'd done this afternoon.

"Oh, I hope so, Etienne. I love Tasha as she loves me. We shared so much and went through so much together. I am happy to do anything I can to get her well and we shall, Etienne."

She sounded so positive that Etienne had to believe her. Now he knew why his mother and father always raved about the beauty Pierre Renaud had married. Ah, yes, he saw that for himself now!

Tiffany and her father kept one another company in the parlor while Charmaine served Etienne his supper. But shortly he joined her and her father and Tiffany saw a different man from the one she'd greeted in the dark hallway.

He was clean-shaven and his jet-black hair was neatly brushed back from his face, but the long sideburns were still curling wisps of hair. There was no way to control the curling hair that teased the collar of his shirt.

Pierre looked at him and saw the very distinct resemblance to his father, Jacques Bernay. He even had the man's stout, husky body.

So many memories rushed back through Pierre's mind when he thought of the times he and Jacques had shared. God, he would love to relive those times! There was an exception and that was the devastating earthquakes that hit this area in 1811. Never would he want to relive that horrible time! But he and Jacques had both survived that.

Tiffany saw a young man she considered to be very handsome. He had a magnificent physique and his features were enough to hold any young lady's interest.

As the evening went on and Tiffany found her piercing black eyes turned in her direction, she found herself entranced by the intensity there. They almost had a hypnotic effect on her. He was not the rugged, sensuous man that Chad Morrow was, but something about Etienne Bernay whetted her curiosity and interest.

Suddenly, she found herself thinking that this backwoods place might not be so dull and boring after all!

Chapter 18

Etienne Bernay insisted that Tiffany have the use of his bedroom.

"I haven't used my room in so long, I'm used to that cot in Mother's room," he assured her. "It's made it simpler, because I'm there if she needs something during the night."

So it was settled, and they all retired to their separate rooms. Tasha had not felt so contented and secure since Jacques had died. It was such a comfort to have Charmaine and Pierre here with her.

By the time Tiffany woke up the next morning and got dressed, Etienne had left for his job at the lumber mill a few miles out of town. Her father had gone to town to look into the affairs of Jacques Bernay to try to set everything straight once and for all. He was going to pay off all the debts and look into the possibility of selling the property so that they could take Tasha and her son back to France with them when Tasha was able to travel.

He intended to speak to the doctor and see just how serious her illness was. He knew that she had not been getting adequate care, but all that would be remedied now.

His business took him most of the day, but the Bernay

family was free of debt when he walked away from the bank. It took him much longer to get an audience with the doctor, but by the time he left his office he was feeling in much better spirits about Tasha.

The doctor had told Pierre, "In case you don't know, Mister Renaud, Jacques was the rock, the strength of the family, and Tasha was simply overcome with grief when he died. Etienne is a fine young man but he was brought up taking orders from Jacques and Tasha. Tasha completely collapsed. She didn't eat or sleep. She just fell into a deep mourning period and there was no one to insist that she pull herself out of it."

"So you are saying that she just got weakened from her mourning?" Pierre asked him.

"Exactly! Then she got a bad cold, had chills and a high fever this last winter that weakened her even more. But there is no reason that Tasha Bernay can't get well. All she needs is some hearty meals and I'll give you a tonic to help her along. She could be as vibrant a woman as she once was."

Pierre assured him that he and his wife would see that this happened. "I'll let you know how things are going, Doctor Christy. When she is well enough we plan to take her back to France. We'll see that she and Etienne have a good life where they will be close to us."

"Well, Mister Renaud . . . all I can say is that Tasha and Etienne are lucky to have such a good friend as you. I'll be very anxious to hear about the progress she makes now that you and your wife are taking charge."

Pierre promised that he would be speaking with him again in a week or so.

He was encouraged as he once again walked out to the street. He felt like he'd put in a very productive day. As he passed a peddler on the dirt road selling his vegetables off his old rickety cart, Pierre bought a variety of the fresh wares. He was so generous with the peddler and spent so much that the farmer offered him one of his baskets to carry the cabbage, carrots, shell peas and ears of corn.

It seemed to be market day in New Madrid. As he was walking down the dirt road toward the Bernay house, he met another fellow with his wagon loaded with wired coops filled with fine young pullets.

"I'll buy those young hens if you'll deliver them just a short distance away. As a matter of fact I'll make it well worth your while. I'll take the whole coop of six."

The fellow could hardly refuse that offer, and nodded eagerly.

Pierre figured that some good chicken broth and roasted chicken with fresh vegetables should do wonders for Tasha.

Amusement played on his dignified face as he fancied what some of his colleagues would think if they could see him walking down this country lane, his arms laden with vegetables, following a man in a cart delivering chickens. But it would probably be a more shocking surprise to Charmaine's friends back in Paris if they saw her slaving away in Tasha's kitchen and being the housekeeper there in the Bernay's humble home.

When his wife saw what he'd been doing during the morning and early afternoon, she found herself falling in love all over again with this fascinating man. It was a special time in both of their lives and she realized that they were being allowed to recapture a glorious interlude of their past.

She did not mind the cooking or the cleaning. In a way she realized that she'd missed it by having servants do practically everything for her. Back in Paris, this would not have been possible, nor could she have done it in London. There it was the role of Pierre Renaud's charming wife that she played, and she enjoyed that life she'd shared with him throughout the years, too.

140

She was happy to tell Pierre that Tiffany had spent some time at Tasha's bedside and she'd heard the two of them laughing.

"Ah, Pierre—Tiffany does have a good heart. She is not completely selfish even though I'll be the first to admit that she's spoiled and pampered. That was very sweet of her to spend so much time with Tasha."

"So maybe we did the right thing after all by insisting that she come with us—oui? Maybe, she will go back to France realizing that other people don't live as extravagantly as we do. Should she lose her heart to some young man that can't spoil her as we have, she won't become disenchanted and disillusioned with life. This, I hope, ma cherie."

Charmaine smiled her agreement.

A week in New Madrid had gone by so swiftly that Tiffany could not believe it. She found herself charmed by the handsome Etienne and he had opened doors to the simple world he lived in in that backwoods village, a world so different from the one she lived in. They roamed through the woods and he told her about the beautiful wildflowers she picked as they walked along the verdant grounds. One lovely delicate flower she found by the riverbank was a swamp lily, he told her.

All of Tasha's vases were filled as a result of these strolls through the woods. Tiffany and Etienne dug up clusters of the wild verbena, ferns and buttercups so that they could take them back to the house. She endeared herself to Tasha for the bouquets she took to her after these walks in the woods.

Etienne was so different from any of the men she'd known. As they spent time together, Tiffany was attracted to him. He helped her forget that dominating force of the rugged Chad Morrow. Etienne's nature was kind and gentle. Never did she feel nervous or uneasy around him as she had with Chad.

Etienne was as predictable and trustworthy as one of her brothers, so their times together were wonderful. He made fishing poles out of tree branches and they sat by the riverbank and fished as she'd done with old Dom on the riverboat. Some days, their catch was enough to provide a fine supper for the five of them.

But Tiffany did not sense the torment she was stirring in Etienne. She didn't know that his hands were now aching to touch her and he yearned to kiss her sweet, rosy lips. Never had he gazed on a more beautiful face than Tiffany's and her slender, graceful body reminded him of the young does he spied moving through the woods. She was like a bewitching nymph that roamed in the woods.

He had to draw upon all his willpower so that he did not bend over and kiss her when she stumbled on a rock and fell against him. Etienne knew that he was going to be tested sorely the more they were together.

How long would he be able to restrain himself from doing what any red-blooded man would want to do with a girl as beautiful and tempting as Tiffany?

He knew he had no right to feel this way and he knew not how to fight it. He could not resist the urge to grasp every private moment he could share with her, for she was the most exciting thing to come into his life.

He marveled at the changes that had come about in his mother since the Renauds had arrived. Each day he could see her improving and he had the Renauds to thank for that. Now, he knew why his father had told him to get in touch with Pierre Renaud if something happened to him.

Each day he saw the Frenchman go away from the house and come back with baskets of edibles. His wife spent her time in the small kitchen cooking up delicious pots of good food. How close and dear the friendship must have been between his mother and Madame

Renaud! he thought as he heard their girlish laughter in the evening.

Never could he do something dishonorable by allowing his passions and desires to overcome his good sense, Etienne reminded himself. After all, he was older than Tiffany. But today, he sensed that she would have allowed him to kiss her if he'd tried.

Tomorrow, he would not spend so much time around the house. He'd take the cart and go into the woods to cut some firewood; that would take him away from her tantalizing presence. With these plans in mind, Etienne slept easier and sounder. Tonight, he did not dream about Tiffany as he'd been doing lately.

But Tiffany dreamed about Etienne. At least, it made the haunting image of Chad Morrow fade from her dreams.

But the searing heat of his kisses could not be forgotten nor the wild desires they stirred!

Chapter 19

The day had been long and time had hung heavily on
Tiffany, with Etienne away all day. Her mood wasn't the
best when her father returned to the Bernay cottage to
announce that he had chanced to meet Chad Morrow in
town. Just the mention of his name was enough to make
Tiffany flinch.

"He asked about you, ma petite. I told him that you
were becoming a little backwoods girl, roaming the woods
and going fishing. He got a chuckle out of that." Her
father laughed lightheartedly.

So this is what he thought, Tiffany mused to herself as
she swelled with resentment. She was hardly ready to
become a backwoods girl and she quickly informed him of
that.

"I fear you are wrong, Papa. I can't wait to get back to
Paris." Her tone of voice startled her father and her
haughty air did not please him at all.

"Guess I was wrong, Tiffany. I assumed you had been
enjoying yourself with Etienne. New Madrid is not Paris
but both places have a lot to offer." He glared at her
before he turned to walk out of the room. He was a little
vexed with his pretty daughter. He'd bought her a little
trinket box from a woodcarver on the street but he did

144

not take it out of his coat pocket to give it to her. Perhaps, another time would be better, he decided.

As he moved on through the house, he saw that Charmaine was not in the kitchen and Tasha was not in her bed. He moved hastily on through the back of the house.

It was a pleasant sight for him to see that his dear wife had coaxed Tasha to sit out on the back porch and enjoy the sunshine and the fresh air. Standing in the doorway watching the two women, he could have sworn that Tasha had put on a few pounds since they'd arrived. She certainly wasn't so pale and drawn. Charmaine had done this by her tender loving care. Tremendous admiration swelled in him as he gazed at his wife.

As he watched the two of them sitting there, he noticed a new sparkle in Tasha's black eyes. He was reminded of those times when all of them were so young—he, Charmaine, Jacques and Tasha.

He did not hesitate to come out on the back porch and give the two ladies the little trinket boxes he'd purchased for them. Both of them generously thanked him and he sat on the railing that surrounded the plank porch to enjoy the pleasant summer afternoon.

Tiffany saw the three of them out there but sought not to join them. Instead, she went out on the front porch and sat in the wooden swing. She saw how all the various ferns and plants she and Etienne had brought back from the woods seemed to be thriving and growing in the urns and pots on the porch. She realized that she'd lied to her father, for she'd had some glorious times with Etienne. She had deliberately set out to startle him but she did not know why.

But she had no time to ponder her reasons, for she spied Etienne driving the wagon down the lane. How handsome he looked, with his black curly hair falling over his forehead and his faded shirt opened to give himself comfort from the afternoon heat.

She watched him coming closer. A broad grin broke on his face at the sight of her. She leaped up from the swing and rushed down the path to greet him. He had certainly put in a full day's work; the bed of the wagon was filled with the sawed wood.

The minute Etienne saw her he realized how helpless he was to fight the bewitching magic she created whenever she was near him. She was like a fever in his blood and the heat of desire consumed him.

He guided the wagon to the back of the house to unload the wood close to the back door so that it would be handy to gather for use in the cookstove. He was delighted to see his mother sitting there. How good it was to see her looking happy and content and her hair neatly combed. He did not recognize the lovely pale blue wrapper she wore and suspected that it might be one of Madame Renaud's.

He called out to her and she waved to him. Things were looking up around the Bernay household, thanks to the Renauds!

He took the time to bend down and kiss his mother before excusing himself so he might have a bath and a change of clothes before dinner.

Tiffany decided to join her parents and Tasha as Etienne left them. Charmaine suggested that they start their evening meal. "Will you help me, Tiffany? You might set the table while I add some vegetables to the roast I'm cooking."

Tiffany followed her mother into the kitchen.

Tiffany's mother sensed that her daughter's mood wasn't as lighthearted and gay as it had been lately. She had blamed it on the absence of Etienne's company, until Pierre mentioned that he'd run into Chad Morrow. Charmaine wondered if that might be what was causing Tiffany's subdued air.

146

Curious to see what Tiffany's reaction would be, she remarked as she busily sought to prepare the vegetables, "So obviously Chad Morrow is still here in New Madrid."

Tiffany took the plates from the cupboard, along with the glasses and silverware, and aimlessly moved toward the table. "Obviously, he is."

"I would have expected him to look us up."

"Well, he hasn't," Tiffany replied stiffly, wishing that her mother would stop talking about Chad. She did not wish to talk about him. He certainly had no urgent need to see her or he could have sought her out. He knew where they were staying but he'd made no effort to pay a call.

"Is there anything else I can do to help you, Maman? I have the table set," she asked, hoping that she could be dismissed so she would not have to listen to any more talk about Morrow.

"I think everything is done. I can leave it now to cook on its own. But Tiffany, may I say something to you that I think you will be delighted to hear?"

"Oh, course, Maman," she answered, turning back around toward her mother.

Charmaine smiled as she told her that they would not be here much longer. "Your father has found a man in New Madrid who is interested in this property. Now that Tasha grows stronger every day, we can take her and Etienne back to France with us."

"They are going home with us?" Her dark eyes flashed with surprise at her mother's revelation.

"I'm sorry, my dear. I guess your father or I had not mentioned this to you. Yes, your father wants to take them back to France with us so he can see to their having a good life and security. He thinks the two of them would enjoy living at our country place."

For a moment, Tiffany stared at her mother with a quizzical look on her young face. This relationship her parents shared with the Bernay family was a loyal, binding one that she could not completely understand.

"And they have accepted Papa's most generous offer?" she finally asked her mother.

"Tasha has and I'm sure Etienne will, too," Charmaine told her daughter.

"I see." Privately, she pondered how her brother and his wife would accept strangers moving into the country estate which they considered their home. It seemed to her that her mother and father were asking a lot of the family. She had to question what Grand-père would think of this, too.

She went to her room to brush out her hair and tie it back in a ribbon. She decided to put on a fresh blouse before she joined the others for dinner. The soft voile dress she'd worn all day did not look fresh and the warm summer day urged her to wash her face in cool water.

But as she passed by the window she saw a sight in the lane that made her halt in attending to her toilette. Who was the pretty, tiny blonde-haired girl talking with Etienne? she wondered. The look on her face seemed to reflect anger as she talked up to Etienne.

That assumption on Tiffany's part was absolutely correct. It was an angry Sandra Michaels making jealous accusations at Etienne for neglecting her.

"I'll not be made the laugh of New Madrid, Etienne Bernay. Now I know why you've not been coming over in the evening. It's your uppity friends from France and I heard today about that very attractive daughter of theirs. Well, I just may not be interested in you coming around the next time and they'll be going back to France. Just maybe then I won't have any time for you." She turned to dash away but Etienne caught her by the arm and tried to soothe her. "What you say is not true, Sandra. The Renauds are family friends and they're here to help my mother. But it is true that their daughter came with

148

them." He realized that the day would soon come that Tiffany and her parents would go out of his life. He would possibly never see her again and it would be the pretty blonde-haired girl he'd court, as he had for the last year and a half.

If he had to be honest he would have probably asked her to marry him had his mother not taken so ill and his father had not died, leaving all the responsibility on his back.

Tiffany stood in the window watching as Etienne's two hands clasped the girl's arms in a most possessive way. Her dark eyes flashed with resentment when she saw him bend down to give her a quick kiss on the cheek. She noticed a sudden change on the girl's face as a pleased expression brightened her mood.

For a moment they lingered there to talk some more before the girl finally broke away to go on down the lane and Etienne walked back through the gate and up the path to the house.

He looked especially handsome, Tiffany thought, in a vivid plaid shirt and a pair of dark pants. His hair was as black and shining as a raven's wing and she could envision how dashing he could have looked if he wore fine-tailored clothing like Chad Morrow had worn in Paris.

Oh, why was she always thinking of Chad? Why couldn't she forget him as she yearned to do? He was nothing but trouble and torment and she knew it. He was out of her life now that he'd parted to go his own way and that's the way she should leave it if she had any sense at all, she told herself.

But thoughts of him hit her at the most unsuspecting times, as they had just now, and she knew not how to stop that from happening. God, if only she could!

She tucked her blouse neatly inside her full gathered skirt and checked her image in the mirror before leaving the room. She dabbed some of the lilac toilet water at her throat for the pleasant cooling fragrance it gave forth.

She made a divine sight in her berry-colored skirt and soft batiste pink blouse when she entered the parlor. Etienne and her father paused to observe her entrance.

Before Pierre glanced up to see that his lovely daughter had entered the room, he was very cognizant that something had captured Etienne's attention and the look in the young man's eyes was enough to alert Pierre of problems that could arise. Such problems of this nature he'd not thought to consider until now.

He'd come this long way to solve the tragedy of the Bernay family, but he'd not allow his daughter to be innocently caught up in a dilemma because of it. Pierre made a hasty decision as he sat there observing young Etienne as his daughter entered the room to greet them. They were going to be leaving here sooner than he'd planned. Maybe he'd not been so wise after all to bring Tiffany here to New Madrid. Maybe he should have left her back in Paris with Grand-père!

One thing he did know and that was that his darling Tiffany meant more to him than all the Bernays!

Chapter 20

All of Etienne's plans to go calling on Sandra Michaels the next morning fell by the wayside when Tiffany came down the pathway behind him with her straw bonnet in her hand and her muslin skirt swishing to and fro.

"Isn't it a wonderful day, Etienne?" she greeted him, a radiant smile on her face. Ever since her mother had told her that they'd soon be leaving, she had felt her spirits lift. Once she got back to Paris she could get back to her own life and that's what she wanted more than anything, she decided.

The sight of her was enough to mesmerize any man, Etienne thought as he surveyed her lovely black hair flowing over her shoulders. Her dainty feet were shod in sandals and he noticed that she wore no stockings.

The soft fabric of the bodice of her frock displayed the tempting mounds of her breasts. His two huge hands could have spanned her wasplike waist. That feisty way she walked was enough to drive any man crazy with desire and Etienne considered himself to be a red-blooded man with a healthy sexual appetite.

Suddenly, he found himself trailing aimlessly at her side. All thoughts of Sandra had faded now that the sensuous Tiffany was near him.

"By the way, where are we going, Etienne?" she asked with a giggle.

"Darned if I know." They walked down a slight grassy incline to get to a clearer pathway and he took her hand in his. She followed as he led her for it mattered not where they roamed; it was far nicer being in Etienne's company than idly wandering around the house all day long.

He'd become accustomed to her suddenly stopping to pick wildflowers. Playfully, he took one of the yellow blossoms from her hand to tuck it behind her ear.

"There—how pretty that looks against that black hair of yours," he remarked.

Time went by swiftly when he was with Tiffany. Neither of them realized that the sun was not so bright now. The thick branches blotted out a lot of the sunshine anyway now that they were in the thick of the forest, so neither of them were aware that the bright blue sky now had clouds quickly moving in. High fluffy white thunderheads had built over the last half-hour. Their tops seemed to reach into the heavens.

It was Tiffany's idea that they sit down for a moment to rest. "We've surely walked a good mile from the way my feet feel, Etienne."

"Oh, Tiffany—I never thought about that! You're wearing your sandals instead of your boots. How completely thoughtless of me. I apologize!"

As he took a seat beside her, he felt the bulk of the two apples he'd stuck in the pockets of his sleeveless cotton vest. "May I offer you some refreshment while we rest, Tiffany?" He offered her one of the shiny red apples.

"Thank you, Etienne. They look delicious and I ate no breakfast this morning."

"Shame on you, Tiffany. That's not good for you," he gently chided her.

"But I've never eaten breakfast."

"You sound like my mother. Neither does she. It's no

wonder both of you are such tiny ladies," he laughed.

Tiffany's attention was pulled elsewhere and she listened intensely to something she'd heard over in the distance. Etienne asked her what was the matter.

"Did you hear that, Etienne?" she asked, tilting her head to listen to see if she might hear the same sound again.

"No, I heard nothing. Guess I was too busy eating my apple."

"You saw no flash of light through the trees over there? And I thought I heard the rumble of thunder."

"Oh, Tiffany—on a beautiful day like this? I can't see how," he scoffed at such an idea. But he changed his mind a second later when a loud reverberation resounded through the thick forest and he, too, saw the sharp flashes of lightning.

"Tiffany—you were right." He knew that they were too far into the forest to try to beat this storm. For her safety, he had better get them to a cave he knew about, a short distance away, and wait for the storm to pass before they tried to make it back to the house. Lightning like that could be a deadly force.

His hand grabbed hers to urge her to get up and follow him. Together they started running back.

As close as the cave was, Etienne didn't manage to get them to its sheltering cover before the skies erupted with torrents of rain. Both of them were drenched to the skin by the time they rushed through the wide opening of the cave.

Tiffany could not help flinching as the fierce bolts of lightning struck, lighting up the cave as she and Etienne hovered together against the rocky wall. The dampness had molded her sheer bodice to her bosom and her black hair dripped with water.

She sought the comfort of Etienne's strong arms holding her securely as she jumped nervously from the roar of the thunder and cracking lightning. Tenderly he placed his hands on her face and soothed her. "We are safe here, Tiffany. It will all be over soon and we can go home."

She gazed up at him and her long lashes fluttered. Her half-opened lips tempted him beyond all reason, especially with her supple body pressing against him. A wild fury exploded within him and his head bent down to take that long-awaited kiss he'd yearned for since the minute she'd arrived at his house.

The kiss took Tiffany by surprise, but she didn't try to stop him as his lips lingered. Maybe Etienne had the power to blot out the memory of those compelling, amorous kisses of Chad Morrow. Maybe Etienne could bring her to that same passionate frenzy that Morrow had, and then she would know that he wasn't the only one who had such a hold on her.

Etienne felt her surrendering to his ardent lovemaking; he felt as if a giant flame were consuming his body. Oh, how sweet were her lips, and the feel of her curvy body was sheer ecstasy!

Giving a husky gasp, he abruptly released her and stared down at her as she stood breathlessly next to him. "I've—I've no right to do that, Tiffany! I just got carried away. Dear God!"

He had such a strange look on his face! Tiffany stood there silently. It seemed to her that the handsome Etienne was as moody as the rugged Chad Morrow. She was beginning to wonder if all men were so hard to understand.

"You've nothing to apologize about, Etienne. Don't look as if it's the end of the world. It . . . it was just a kiss."

A frown came to Etienne's face. Was that all it really meant to her? Had she realized that in another second it would have been much more than a mere kiss? Maybe he had figured Tiffany wrong. Was she a sweet innocent or a promiscuous coquette? Maybe back in Paris, she gave her kisses and her love freely. He'd heard about the ways of the wealthy Frenchmen from his father who had told him about the worldly, exciting city of Paris. Etienne had allowed himself to forget that Tiffany was no Sandra Michaels who lived in the backwoods as he did. No, hers was a far more sophisticated world. For a brief moment, he'd forgotten that.

He welcomed the calm he heard outside the cave, for he could get started for home. He was grateful that he'd not reached the point of no return and had come to his senses in time.

"It's stopped storming, Tiffany. The rains seem to have let up. Stay in here and I'll take a look outside."

He came back to give her a nod of his damp head and to tell her that there were just a few sprinkles falling. "Shall we go?"

"If you like," she stammered, finding herself very confused about Etienne Bernay and his sudden change of mood.

They walked through the woods without much conversation. The branches of the tall trees were still dripping from the heavy showers but the creatures of the woods were emerging from their nests and burrows to explore the woods again.

They spotted a squirrel enjoying the apple that Tiffany never finished when the storm suddenly caught them.

They both laughed, so the silence was finally broken between them. The rest of the way they resumed the warmth they'd shared, but Tiffany was still feeling puzzled about the handsome young man walking by her side.

It was not exactly the afternoon Chad Morrow had

155

planned for himself when he borrowed a horse from Bickford to ride into New Madrid to see Tiffany. He'd thought about her constantly since the last day he'd seen her, but he could not allow the tempting distraction to interrupt his plans for his father's old riverboat.

But running into Pierre Renaud the last time he was in town had brought the vivid image of that raven-haired beauty to his thoughts and he had an overwhelming desire to see her beautiful face again. He cared not what his reception was when they met; he felt sure he could change her mood if she was displeased with him for not appearing sooner.

Now that he had all the repairs on the boat priced and had contracted a man to do them, he had some time to call his own. In fact, he had everything so settled that he could soon leave the rest in Bickford's hands and he would be free to leave New Madrid. Penbrook Lines had been very generous to give him this much time away from his job.

The closer he got to the Bernay home the higher his anticipation soared about seeing Tiffany again after all this time. But that anticipation was sorely wounded when he galloped down the dirt lane only to give the horse a hasty yank on the reins when he spied the saucy-looking Tiffany sashaying along, holding hands with Etienne.

He sat astride the horse and observed those blue flashing eyes gazing up at the young man and he'd once known the impact of that look of Tiffany's. Oh, yes, he'd known how those blue eyes could blaze with passion and desire and he'd also known the fire of her volatile fury.

He watched the two of them until the dense woods seemed to swallow them up and he could no longer see them. All the time he sat there, his jealousy mounted to such a height that his fist clenched the reins tighter and tighter.

It was obvious that she had certainly not been pining

away because he had not come around. He was convinced that he'd been smart doing just what he'd done the last few weeks.

That frivolous little minx would not take up any more of his time, he swore. It was best he found out just where he stood with her as he had this afternoon. To hell with that kind of foolish fancy!

He knew a pretty young lady who'd welcome his company. At least, he figured she just might. The truth was he'd only met her the other day but something about the way she looked at him led him to believe that she'd welcome a visit from him.

So he reined the horse around to pay a visit on the young lady he'd escorted home after he'd bumped into her coming out of one of the local stores with his arms full of packages.

Tiffany Renaud was not the only pretty girl in New Madrid. That blonde Sandy was a good-looking miss!

Chapter 21

It didn't seem to be Chad's lucky day where the ladies were concerned. When he went to the Michaels household to call upon their daughter, he was met at the door by her mother and told that Sandra wasn't home. Something about her manner told Chad that she disapproved of him since he was a stranger in this small hamlet.

A crooked smile broke on his face as he turned to go back down the path. Perhaps his best bet for a little company and companionship was the local tavern for a few drinks and some lighthearted chatter with the always-friendly barmaids there.

In a place as small as New Madrid there was no other choice to be made. The Bee Hive served as a meeting place for the fellows to gather in the afternoon and evening to do their drinking and their talking. There was always a poker game or two going on.

When he arrived, there were several horses tied at the hitching post so he figured to find a crowd when he entered the door. The aroma of liquor and tobacco filled the room.

As he had in the past when he'd come here, he walked to one of the empty tables in the corner of the room. It took a moment or two for his eyes to get accustomed to the dim lighting.

He'd paid no attention to the other occupants at the surrounding tables but one of the men had recognized him the minute he'd walked through the door. Dom knew that it was Morrow as he watched the tall man amble toward a table.

Old Dom sat for a moment just observing the young man as he ordered a drink. Dom figured that this fellow could hold his own with just about anyone. Over the last few weeks, he'd thought about Chad and Tiffany and wondered what had been happening to them. Since he'd last told them goodbye, he'd gone back up the muddy Mississippi and now he'd traveled back down it again.

The only reason he had this lazy afternoon to enjoy was that the riverboat needed minor repairs so they'd remain in dock at New Madrid overnight.

When Dom was satisfied that Morrow was not expecting anyone else, he moved from his table to join him. He got the impression that Chad was not in too jolly a mood this afternoon. While he never had the ability to bring himself out of a melancholy mood, he did have the knack to pull others out of their doldrums by the funny tales he was always telling. Besides, he found himself curious about any news he might find out from Morrow about the little mademoiselle.

"Mon ami, it is you, isn't it?" Dom asked as he moved up by Chad's chair.

"It bloody well is, Dom, and how are you?" Chad grinned as he saw the black-bearded cook standing there. "Sit down, Dom! It's good to see you!"

"Good to see you, too, Chad. Thought about you often since we parted company. Hope all your plans are coming along."

"Slowly but surely, and I'm not too far away from getting back down that river to catch a ship back to England."

159

Dom told Chad that he admired him for this special deed he was going to do for his father. "You're a good man, Chad, and old Cat was a lucky man to have had you for his son. I got myself a hell of an idea, Chad. Your riverboat is going to be needing a fine cook, isn't it?"

"Of course, Dom."

"Well what would you say to me applying for the job when that boat is ready to get going?"

Chad laughed, "I think it would be a great idea. I'll tell Bickford tonight. The job's yours if you want it."

"I want it, Chad!" Dom gave a boisterous laugh as he told him, "Got a feeling old Cat's ghost will be stalking around that boat, and it would be nice to be there if he did."

"Never thought about that, Dom but I bet you're right. Yes, sir, I'll bet you're right!"

The two of them shared a grand afternoon and time went by so fast that neither of them realized that the sun was sinking lower and lower. It was Dom who happened to notice this when another group of men came through the door of the tavern.

"Guess I got to leave good company, Chad. My services will be needed shortly. But before I go, I must ask you about the mademoiselle. How is she?"

Chad grimaced as he muttered, "That's a good question, Dom. I wish I knew. I've not had a chance to find out since the last day I saw you. That is the last time I've talked to her."

Dom was surprised to hear this. "Guess I had the two of you figured wrong then. I'd have sworn that the two of you were . . . well, how do I say it . . . I thought the two of you cared for one another."

"I saw her today from afar, Dom. I'd been on my way to call on her, but I happened to see her in the company of another man walking toward the woods and her mood led me to believe she would not like being disturbed."

The sarcasm lacing his words as he spoke was enough to tell Dom that Chad was riled.

"Was it a man you knew?"

"I suspect it was Etienne Bernay. I don't know him but I know about him and he's not for Tiffany, Dom," he firmly declared. Dom saw the fury in his gray eyes. A storm had passed over the area while they'd been in the tavern but Chad's mood was still stormy.

"Don't jump to conclusions, son. Things aren't always as they appear. Take an old fool's advice." Dom gave him a pat on the shoulder as they prepared to go their separate ways.

Chad was quick to remind him that he had a job on his boat if he wanted it, for he wanted no more discussion about Tiffany Renaud. Dom nodded his head as he went in one direction and Chad mounted his horse to travel in the opposite one.

As he traveled back toward Bickford's houseboat, where he'd been staying, he thought about what old Dom had said. Maybe he should have ridden on up to Tiffany and the young man she was with. Maybe his pride had gotten in the way. He'd not deny that.

No woman had ever had the impact on him that Tiffany Renaud had. No woman had ever occupied his thoughts as she had. This was a new, strange situation Chad Morrow found himself in. Sometimes he wished he had not happened to be in that park in Paris. Until then, he'd been the happy-go-lucky, elusive bachelor and enjoying his life.

He'd had his life expertly planned out, and it did not include any woman. Oh, he could have a woman any time he wished it but there was no particular woman that would change the course of his life.

From the moment he'd rescued her from those scoundrels hellbent on having their way with her, Chad felt she was his to protect. Not only that, but he had lost his heart to her.

But he found it impossible to tame her. That night in his cabin aboard the *Majestic Queen* he thought he had, for she surrendered so willingly to him. But how soon he had found out that this was not the case at all!

Today when he saw her with another man, and this man was holding her dainty hand, he seethed with a jealousy he'd never felt before.

By the time he reached the banks of the river where Bickford's houseboat was secured near the small dock built out over the river's edge, the sun was down and twilight had settled over the area. He could see the lamps were already lit inside the houseboat and he figured that a good supper was already being prepared by Bickford. It was a funny thing about these people in this part of the country; none of them seem to have any wealth to speak of, but everyone seemed to set a bountiful table.

Chad figured that he was going to be eating some savory chicken tonight that Bickford had been given yesterday for the nice string of fish he'd taken to the widow Dixon. While he'd been there he'd repaired her back steps and she'd included some tender ears of corn with the chicken.

By the time he'd stepped on the deck of the houseboat, he knew he was right about what they'd be dining on tonight. Bill Bickford's frying chicken gave forth a delicious aroma as it cooked in the old cast-iron skillet.

"Everything sure smells mighty fine, Bill," Chad greeted the old man as he was putting the lid back on the skillet.

"Bet your boots, boy! Widow Dixon's roasting ears and fried chicken are going to make us a fine supper. Think that with a little corn bread will fill your belly?" he chuckled, turning around toward Chad. Chad was reminded of the gypsy men who roamed the English countryside as he observed old Bill, who stood there in his baggy pants without a shirt on. His gray hair grew long and curled around his shoulders and he had a full thick set of eyebrows. His weathered skin was as tanned as any sea captain's Chad had ever seen.

"That will fill my belly fine," Chad laughed, but added that he'd need some of that strong coffee Bill brewed.

"Oh, we'll have some of that, too."

They did have that, and a cup or two after the hearty meal, laced with some of Bill's prized brandy. He rationed that out very sparingly. Chad decided that he'd have to see that the old boatman got a supply of his favorite brand after he left New Madrid. He'd have it sent to him.

After dinner as they sat with Chad puffing on his cheroot and Bill smoking his favorite pipe, Chad asked him, "I'm going to have to pull out of here in a week, Bill. Think you can oversee the work I've hired Herb Webster to do for me? You know the route I want the boat to take and I know you can hire the crew you need. The funds are available for you at the bank in town. I've seen to that."

The best news of all was when Chad told him that he'd already hired a cook for the riverboat. Bickford gave a yell of delight. "That fat Frenchie is the best damned cook around these parts. You are going to have one old riverboat captain mad at you, Chad, for taking his cook away from him."

"It was Dom's idea and he asked me for the job."

"Dang—it's going to be like old times. Damned if it isn't! You ought to stick around here, young fellow. Might just get to enjoying yourself," Bickford challenged Chad.

"Perhaps, Bill, but I've a job to do. There's my place in London to check into from time to time."

Bill gave him an understanding nod of his head. "Oh, I know how it's like with a young man like you. You got a lot of irons in the fire, as they say."

"Guess that's it, Bill."

163

Morrow figured that he'd righted a wrong done to his father years ago by restoring his old riverboat. It was his way of saying that he was proud that Cat Morrow was his father.

When he returned to London to report to the office of Penbrook Lines, he hoped to hear from his solicitor that the land he'd wished to acquire had been purchased during the last few months he'd been away.

It was important to Chad that this land became his, for it was Chadwick land that he felt he'd been cheated out of when his mother died. One of his mother's brothers had gained control of it but he'd made the stupid mistake of turning it over to his oldest son. The son was a wastrel and to pay his debtors the land had been put up for sale, parcel by parcel. Chad had acquired the first lot which had a small, but very attractive stone cottage. Chad had made this his home when he was in England until he'd bought a townhouse in the city.

Last year the second lot had been put up for sale and he'd instructed his solicitor to purchase it for him because the lot adjoined the property he already owned and was a beautiful wooded area, with a crystal-clear creek and spring running through it.

The third lot was a picturesque rolling English countryside which joined the lands next to the lavish country estate which the Chadwick family called their home. Chad's restless soul would not be content until he had that land, too. Only then would he be satisfied, for he could flaunt the fact that he had more Chadwick land than he was due to inherit. He had bought it all with money that he had earned without any help from the Chadwick family.

Only then would he be able to say that this riverboat captain's son had managed to outfox those snobbish, haughty relatives of his who'd dared to look down their aristocratic noses at his father.

Only then would he be content!

Chapter 22

Since the afternoon they'd taken refuge from the storm, Tiffany had seen very little of Etienne. She could not understand a young man who'd kissed her so passionately and now was treating her as if she were a leper. If that was the way he wanted it, then she could play that little game too, she decided. So she made no effort to rush out to greet him when he returned to the house in the evening.

She went her own way and made no move to single him out. Etienne Bernay was not going to give her sleepless nights as Chad Morrow had after she allowed her heart to take control.

Tiffany knew she'd never been so homesick as she was now. Dear Lord, she would have loved to have Denise to talk to or a nice visit with Sabrina. A pleasant afternoon visit with her Grand-père or a trip out to her brother's place would have been something to look forward to. She was growing to hate this place more and more every day.

Perhaps, it was this stinging resentment that made her leave the house without telling her mother that she was going for a walk. Maybe there in the shade of the woods she would find it cooler than it had been back at the house. She'd worn a lightweight muslin frock with short puffed sleeves because of the warm late summer day.

She'd piled her thick hair atop her head and tied a ribbon around it. With pins, she'd secured the long curling wisps. Little curling ringlets framed her face due to the moisture in the air that had lingered in the area after the stormy afternoon.

When she came to a spot in the woods that pleased her, she sat down on a log and made herself comfortable. She yanked her skirt to her knees for she had no reason to fret that anyone was around to see her exposed legs. Besides, it was so cool to have the long skirt swept aside.

There she sat for a long time and enjoyed watching the squirrels and the birds. Except for the singing of the birds and the chattering of the squirrels, the woods were perfectly quiet.

Her lovely face took on various expressions as her thoughts strayed to and fro. She just had to be back in Paris before her eighteenth birthday, she mused. That was a most special birthday to her and she prayed that it did not have to be spent in a place like this or in the middle of the ocean. That celebration had to be in Paris.

She finally got off the old log to stroll on into the woods. She and Etienne had taken so many trails in this woods she was beginning to think she knew them as well as he did. She wanted to go to a spot where she could gather some wildflowers before she started back to the house. The sun was still high in the sky and there was certainly no threat of rain in these cloudless skies.

But when she walked a certain distance she did not come to the spot she sought and she knew somehow she'd gone in a wrong direction. So once again she took a seat on a fallen tree trunk to look around and get her bearings.

"That's all I need is to get myself lost," she muttered to herself. Her blue eyes roamed over the area to try to figure out when she'd strayed in a wrong direction. She came up with no answers to her dilemma.

The heat of the summer afternoon seemed to be as

intense in the woods as it had been back at the house, and she yanked up her flowing skirt to cool her shapely legs and held out the scoop of the neckline of her muslin gown for air to cool her.

She had no inkling that a pair of eyes was devouring her. He could not believe the vision he was seeing, after staggering through the woods.

He'd never seen her around New Madrid and that he knew. He'd lived in New Madrid all his life. Such a beautiful thing as this he would not have missed, Cleve Marshall told himself as he leaned against the tall pine tree.

Now no one had to tell him that he was good and drunk because he knew that when he left the local tavern to start for home, but he was damned if he was dreaming this sight up. There was a black-haired beauty sitting over there with her skirts hoisted up to her knees showing off the prettiest legs his eyes had ever seen.

Marshall could have sworn that she was the kind of gal that could ever be conjured up by any man's wildest fantasies.

He ogled the full mounds of her breasts jutting out temptingly and his eyes trailed down to her tiny waist. God, she was something!

But who in the hell was she? No respectable gal would stroll the woods all alone. He knew the families of New Madrid and they just didn't allow their daughters to do this. But she sure didn't look like any tavern maid he'd ever seen. Maybe she'd just arrived in town.

Right then it really didn't matter to Cleve because she was sitting over there all alone, and he was fired with the wildest desire to have his way with her.

He moved out of the thicket and away from the pine where he'd been standing. He'd covered some fifty feet that separated them before Tiffany realized that she was not the only person in the woods when she heard the

167

breaking branches underneath his boots as he approached her.

When she saw the approaching figure and noticed his swaying body as he walked, she knew he was drunk. The stupid grin on his face and the lecherous glint in his eyes alerted her to the danger she faced.

She swiftly leaped up from the log and surveyed the ground around her feet in the hope of finding something she might use as a club to defend herself.

But there was nothing and she felt herself panicking. A voice urged her to run and that was what she did. Swiftly, she turned and bolted through the woods as she held her skirt high so she would not get it tangled in the underbrush. Behind her she heard the man's lusty laugh and the sound of his heavy boots beating a path toward her.

His deep voice gave forth a gusto of cusses and she turned to see that he had fallen down. Maybe she had the advantage, for she was not drunk and more agile. She dashed on and on into the woods. By now, she had no idea where she was running because the only thing important to her was to get away from him.

While she held her skirts high, she'd not thought about her long flowing hair getting caught on a low-hanging branch. She found herself a prisoner as she struggled to release it. She gasped with frustration as she yanked and pulled at her hair in her frenzy to be free, for she saw that the man was gaining on her.

The more he laughed, the more she yanked at her long hair even though she seemed to be held there helplessly. In anguish, she moaned. "Oh, God! No!" His awesome figure was only a few feet away from her now.

Frantically, she gave a mighty jerk, enduring the agony and pain, but her freedom came too late. The man lunged to grab her around her leg, which brought her tumbling to the earth. Her small body slammed to the ground.

She sensed the man's scrambling to cover her body

with his and his hands rushing to cover her screams. But she gathered her forces and began to struggle and fight him and Cleve found it impossible to shut up her screams.

She arched her leg to fling it at his groin with all the force she could muster, but it did not hit with the force and power that she had hoped it would. Nevertheless, it had told Cleve that he was dealing with one little hellcat who would not be easily subdued.

He flung the full force of his male body against her petite figure. She had to endure his slobbering mouth touching her cheek and it sickened her. She was forced to recall the incident in the park back in Paris. Oh, God, if only Chad Morrow would come along again!

"You're something else, little lady, but I'll have you before it's over with and you might as well resign yourself to that," Cleve told her.

"You'll not have me unless you kill me first," she challenged him. Her blue eyes blazed with determination.

"He'll not kill you, Tiffany, but I fear I may have to kill him." A deep, familiar voice resounded in Tiffany's ear. She looked up to see the formidable figure of Chad Morrow standing there looking down at her. "Get away from her, you bastard," he ordered.

Slowly, the man moved away from Tiffany, for he figured he was looking at the devil himself. Those cold steel-gray eyes were piercing him and he saw the danger lurking there. He figured himself to be a dead man! His afternoon folly was going to prove to be the death of him.

Chad ordered the man to get up and walk in a certain direction and Cleve dared not disobey him. Tiffany lay there on the ground allowing Chad to take charge. She knew not how long Chad was away but she heard the anguished moans of the man who'd attacked her and she supposed that Chad was giving him the beating of his life.

She truly didn't care if he did kill the man and the way

169

he looked, he could have done just that. Never had she seen such fury on a man's face.

This was the second time he'd kept her from being harmed by someone hellbent on hurting her.

She could tell herself that she didn't care for him and he meant nothing to her when that stubborn pride took over, but now she accepted Morrow was more than just a passing fancy. Everything had been different with him from the minute his arms had held her. She trembled as she thought about what could have happened to her if he hadn't come along.

It was as if some mighty force pulled them toward one another. As it was in the park when she'd needed some dashing knight to come to save her, he came to her. Now after all these weeks that she had not seen him, he suddenly appeared to be her avenger. She could not take this incident lightly. No, there was something so compelling that she could no longer try to deny that it existed.

As she sat there quietly, giving way to these private musings, Chad emerged through the thicket. She was not aware that her face had been scratched by branches when she fell to the ground after Cleve had seized her from behind.

But it was the first thing Chad noticed when he came to stand there and look down at her. She noticed the strange look on his face and he quickly sank to the ground and took the kerchief from his face. "Damn sonofabitch!" he muttered as he gently wiped the blood from the three-inch scratch.

As she started to give him a mild protest, he told her, "Only wiping away a little blood from your pretty face, love. You got a little scratch."

Her hand went up to the spot where Chad had dabbed the kerchief. "I—I didn't know."

"You had more urgent worries at the time than this,"

Chad remarked, letting his gray eyes carefully survey her. How enchantingly lovely she was, sitting there with those blue eyes gazing up at him. There was a childlike air about the way she looked right then—nothing resembling that haughty arrogance he'd last witnessed.

In a stammering voice, she asked him, "How did you happen to be around here, Chad?"

A devious twinkle sparked in his eyes and he grinned, "Why, love . . . don't you know that I appointed myself to be your protector?"

"Oh, Chad!" She could not resist allowing a slow smile. She found it hard not to give way to the exciting charms he possessed, especially when he was looking at her the way he was just now. He was utterly irresistible!

Before she knew what he was about, he had snaked his hands under her legs to swoop her up in his arms. His long legs were taking giant strides as he marched through the woods with Tiffany in his arms.

"Where are you taking me, Chad?" she asked. "Home?"

"Not just yet. I'm going to show you what I'm doing here, since you asked," he said.

"We're near the river, aren't we Chad?"

"That we are, love." It was not much farther until she would be seeing the dock where his father's riverboat was secured. A short distance away from it was Bickford's houseboat.

He wanted to tell Tiffany about his plans and why he'd made this trip in the first place. At least this was his intention when he started toward the riverbank as he carried her in his arms. But by the time he'd felt her soft, sensuous body resting against his chest as he moved through the woods and arrived at the wooden dock built out over the river, something else was occupying his thoughts.

He knew that the houseboat was deserted this afternoon. Bickford had left this morning to be gone all day to visit his brother who lived in a nearby town.

When he finally released her from his arms so that her feet came to rest on the plank floor of the dock, he announced that this was where he was staying while he was here in New Madrid. "Would you like to see what a houseboat looks like, Tiffany?"

"Yes, I would." She'd never seen a houseboat before. It looked like a small cottage set atop a flat boat. There were small clay pots of flowers sitting around the floor that gave her the feeling she was entering a small house instead of a boat. Against the wall of the cabin she spotted fishing poles propped, and she was reminded of old Dom and wondered how he was doing. He had been a bright spot of her long journey.

Inside, she saw immediately the little things that had been done to give the quarters a homey look. Bright floral curtains were hung at the small windows. Wooden bunks were built in one corner of the room and a worn old settee sat against the opposite wall. In the center of the room was a rough-hewn table and two straight-back chairs. There was no dividing wall from this area to what appeared to be the kitchen of the houseboat.

What she did marvel about was how every inch of space seemed to be used. The entire back wall was shelves except one small area where an old cookstove was situated.

Chad watched her surveying the one room that old Bickford had called his home for many years.

"Isn't exactly like anything you've ever seen before, is it Tiffany?"

"I think I like it better than those cramped quarters of the *Majestic Queen*," she quickly responded. "I was miserable during that crossing."

He walked over to where she was standing in the center of the room. His hands clasped her tiny waist and he turned her around to face him. There was something about the look on his face that was demanding that she be honest with him when he asked, "Love, you weren't miserable the night we were in my cabin. I won't believe that for one minute, Tiffany. Tell me—tell me the truth!"

His gray eyes locked into her and there was something so forceful that she dared not lie to him. "No, Chad—no, I was not miserable. For that brief moment I was deliriously happy."

A broad grin came on his tanned face as he lifted her high from the floor. Tiffany felt his strong hands holding her so effortlessly and the passionate look in his silvery eyes told her he was going to kiss her.

And she wanted him to do just that!

Chapter 23

Slowly, he brought her down until their lips touched in a searing kiss that both of them were yearning eagerly for, and from that moment, neither of them had any control of their willpower. The force and power was too overwhelming for Tiffany, for she wanted only one thing and that was for Chad to make love to her.

Chad ached to do just that. His arms clutched her close so that he could feel the throbbing of her heart against his strong, broad chest. His lips hungrily let Tiffany know how much he'd missed her kisses.

When he finally was forced to release her so they could both catch their breaths, he huskily admitted, "God, love. I've—I've missed those sweet, sweet kisses. Your lips were meant for kissing, Tiffany. My kisses!"

She did not try to argue with that. He spoke the truth.

Neither did she argue with him when he swept her up in his arms and carried her over to the lower bunk. Her arms encircled his neck as she laid her head against his chest. His hand gently caressed her face where the ugly scratch was etched on her cheek and it suddenly riled him about what had happened or could have happened if he had not been close by.

She was so damned beautiful that no man could look at

her without wanting her just as he wanted her right now. She was his, he told himself, and no other man was going to have her.

Tiffany was hardly aware of how his long, slender fingers had lifted her frock over her head so quickly and now he stood there towering over her barechested. For the first time she noticed the curling ringlets of brown hair on his broad chest. For such a broad chest he had such a trim waist! Her dark blue eyes watched as he removed his pants and he watched her ogling him as her eyes traveled down the length of his body.

It was obvious that she was admiring the fine male body he possessed and this pleased him. He'd known from the first minute that he'd met her that she was a young woman full of passion and fire. He also knew he was the first to spark that fire and curiosity.

As he removed each and every undergarment of her clothing he savored the lovely sight of her soft, satiny skin. "You are so beautiful, Tiffany, from the top of your head down to those tiny toes." He gave her a devious smile.

"Well, if anyone should know, you would, Chad," she grinned. "No one else has seen me as you have."

"And no one ever shall, love, if I can help it! I'm a selfish man, Tiffany. I'd never share you."

By now he was lying by her side, his nude body pressed against hers, and his lips were giving featherlike touches down her neck and down to her pulsing breasts.

She gave a soft moan of pleasure, "Chad! Oh, Chad! You might as well know I'm selfish too!"

With a sudden move, Chad had moved her to rest atop of him and she felt the pulsing force of him as his lips played a tantalizing magic with the rosy tips of each of her breasts. Such sensual pleasure Tiffany had not realized until now. She gasped as he continued to tease and taunt her with his overwhelming love-making.

175

This time he carried her to a new height of lofty ecstasy as their two bodies fused. She felt herself being swept by such a surging wave of passion she clasped her arms around his neck for fear that she would lose him in the swift ascension they seemed to be whirling in.

She felt his mighty shudder and she gasped breathlessly with her fingernails digging into his neck from the sensation he'd stirred within her.

For a glorious moment time stood still.

As they finally lay quietly enclosed in one another's arms, Chad gently caressed her face and once again he gazed on the ugly scratch. He was content to lie there and just look at her, but he knew that soon he was going to have to escort her back to the Bernays' house. Just a glance out the small houseboat window told him that the afternoon was growing late. Old Bickford could be returning about sunset.

"Love, I guess I'd better think about getting you home safely."

She roused only slightly to smile up at him. It rather pleased him that she seemed in no hurry to leave his side.

His deep voice murmured in her ear, "You know we're going to have to explain that angry-looking scratch on your face. God knows, I don't intend that they think I caused it."

"Oh, Chad, they wouldn't think that!" she laughed as she sat up in the bed to look down at him.

Sitting there like that, with her lovely bosom exposed, he found himself instantly stirred again. "For God's sake, Tiffany—have you no mercy! I'll never get you back home if you don't get yourself covered or dressed." He leaped out of the bed before he dared to pull her back in his arms and hastily began to get dressed as he heard her soft laughter echoing in his ear.

"Why, Chad Morrow—you mean to tell me I have such power over a big, strong-willed man as you?" She leisurely moved to get out of the bunk and began to slip into her undergarments.

"Don't taunt me too much, love. I swear I might just throw caution to the wind!" By now, he had on his pants and shirt and sat down on the bunk to pull on his boots.

Tiffany had had a chance to glance out the window to see that the sun was sinking fast in the western sky and she realized that her parents would be worried about her. It suddenly dawned on her that she had not told them that she was even leaving the house. Looking at the clock on the wall, she was astonished that it had been over four hours since she'd started out for her walk.

But then she'd not expected this to have happened when she innocently ambled out of the yard of the Bernay property to take a simple stroll in the woods.

Now, it was she who was hastily getting her frock on and brushing back her tousled hair from her face. She slipped into the sandals, standing up to declare to Chad that she was ready.

Together, they left the houseboat and Chad left her on the bank of the river to go get his horse quartered in a small lean-to shelter a short distance away.

A short time later, they were riding into the woods along a small, narrow trail. Feeling still flushed by Chad's love-making, she enjoyed the feel of his warm body close to hers as his arms encircled her to hold the reins guiding the horse.

As they rode along, more than once Chad whispered sweet words of endearment in her ear and when she'd turn around to look at him and smile he planted a kiss on her cheek. Playfully he admonished her that once he got her back to the house, he expected her to behave herself. "No more foolish roaming in these woods alone, love. I might not be so handy the next time."

"I promise! Once was enough for me, I can assure you," she vowed and smiled back at him.

177

It was obvious that Chad knew the exact direction to go, for it seemed all too soon that they were emerging out of the woods into the small clearing where the Bernay house was situated.

Now that Chad had entered her life again, she was reluctant to part company with him so soon. It seemed that Chad must have been reading her thoughts, for he told her, "I've no intentions, Tiffany, for us to be apart again for so long when I tell you goodbye. Never that long do I want to be without the sight of your beautiful face."

Saucily, she teased him, "Then I expect to see you before I leave to go back to France, which could be soon."

"You are leaving shortly?"

"That is what my mother told me just the other day."

A somber look was on his face as he assured her that they would see one another before she left. "My business is almost finished and I shall be going back to England myself."

By now, the horse was approaching the hitching post by the gate. Chad glanced toward the front porch to see Pierre and Charmaine Renaud rushing down the steps. He knew their last precious moment to be alone had passed.

After Morrow bid the Renaud family farewell and rode away, he turned his thoughts to the young man he'd met just as he was taking his leave. He didn't particularly like Etienne Bernay nor the possessive way he went to Tiffany's side to declare how concerned he was about her. Tiffany's blue eyes had looked at him as she apologized for causing him to worry. Damned, if it didn't rub Chad the wrong way! He didn't consider that she had to explain her whereabouts to Bernay. Her parents were a different matter and that was why Chad didn't linger any longer, for he had only to look at the fierce dark eyes of

Pierre Renaud to know that Tiffany was going to receive a harsh reprimand for going into the woods alone.

This Chad approved of, for he shuddered to think about what could have happened this afternoon. On his way back to the houseboat he veered off the trail to the spot where he'd left the unconscious Cleve lying on the ground. He'd given him a vicious beating combined with a firm order never to come within spitting distance of Tiffany or he'd find himself dead the next time.

When he arrived at the place where he'd left the man, there was nothing left but some blood-spattered leaves. Drops of blood indicated the man crawled along the ground until he'd found the strength to stand up and walk.

The fact that the overwhelming smell of liquor had been on the man's breath had not lessened Chad's fury. Nothing excused that low-life Cleve from trying to harm Tiffany!

By the time Chad arrived back at the houseboat he had decided that he wasn't going to let too much time go by before he was going back over to the Bernay's to see Tiffany.

After he had shared the evening meal with Bickford, he curled up in his bunk and carefully perused the yellowed journals of his father's. Something gnawed at him, something he'd read in them a few years ago when he'd returned from here and arrived back in England at his mother's home.

With the lit lantern hanging there on the upper bunk where he slept, he read through two of them but what he was searching for was not in those. It was not an easy task, reading old Cat's crude writing. The third journal was started but his eyes got too heavy with sleep to finish it so he had to give up for tonight. But he would read every one of them, for he was certain there was something he must find.

Tomorrow, he would find it. It was just a matter of reading all of the journals if he must. He had come to the part where his father had entered the data about bringing one Jacques Bernay, Pierre Renaud, Charmaine Lamoureaux and her friend, Tasha to the town of New Madrid and Renaud's uncle's home there. This was many months before the first of the devastating earthquakes struck on December 11, 1811.

These journals fascinated Chad once again when he read them, for it was like reading history and his father had lived it.

If ever he'd needed a reason to restore that old keelboat of his father's, he had it now. It mattered not that few keelboats were still around now that the steamboat was dominating the wide river. A few of them were still afloat to carry freight from one place to another. Maybe, just maybe, there were people who'd like to experience the run up the river on a keelboat.

If nothing more, Chad knew that his plans had excited and pleased two of his father's old friends—Bickford and Dom. That's why he was sure those plans would have delighted Captain Cat Morrow.

For tonight, his curiosity would have to wait.

Chapter 24

Bickford had seen the young couple leave his houseboat late that afternoon and he'd wondered who the pretty young thing was that Chad had lifted up on his horse, then hoisted himself up behind her. He didn't recognize her as one of the local young lovelies of the small town. Chad had not mentioned anything about it after he'd returned to the houseboat later so Bickford figured that he intended to keep that his little secret.

The old riverboat man didn't fault him for that. He'd had his fling with a lot of pretty maidens up and down this river in days gone by, so if he was a virile, handsome rooster like Chad he'd have been doing the same thing.

He didn't try to pry any talk out of him that evening, for the young man seemed very occupied with his own thoughts and was concentrating on something. Bickford respected his wishes to do as he wanted.

Nevertheless, the old riverboat captain was curious about young Morrow's interest in his father's old journals he was so carefully reading.

Bickford had become very fond of the young man staying with him. Cat had had himself one hell of a son, he'd have to say that. A couple of times he'd been tempted to advise young Morrow not to pour so much money into that old keelboat, for it was a poor investment the way things were changing on this old river. But Bickford knew this didn't bother Chad. It was sentiment urging him to do what he was doing about the boat, so Bickford said nothing to try to persuade him any differently.

The only thing Bickford did plan to tell him before he left New Madrid was that he'd not see any profit from the runs of the keelboat. He wanted no hard feelings about their business relationship after Chad departed to go back to London.

It was the steamboats dominating the river because they could plow through those muddy waters of the Mississippi River at a much faster speed. The hours spent to get from one stop to another along the river were drastically reduced.

But Bickford didn't have to tell Chad this because since he'd tallied all the figures up for repairs, he knew he'd yield no harvest of profit. But the project was so important to him he didn't care.

The cost didn't matter to him since he had the funds to do it. Now that he thought about it, if he'd not come here to accomplish this for his father he would not have gotten to share this time with Tiffany aboard the *Majestic Queen* and the long trip up the Mississippi River. Now he had this afternoon to remember, but memories were not going to be enough to satisfy Chad—not after today.

Tiffany could not be just a passing fancy for she meant too much to him. Only today when he'd had to ride away and leave her behind he suddenly realized that he wanted her with him all the time. Damned if he didn't want her sleeping in his bed every night and sharing all his days as well!

A voice prodded at him, quizzing him about his well-laid plans to remain a bachelor until he'd accomplished all the different projects he'd so carefully plotted a few years ago.

He turned a deaf ear to that annoying voice and he justified his change of mind by arguing that he lacked so little now. He felt sure that when he returned to England the land would have been acquired by his solicitor. That left one more plot he aimed to buy to satisfy his insatiable desire to right the wrong the Chadwick family had done to him. Only then would he feel at peace.

The dignified Pierre Renaud rarely lost control of his temper, whether he was dealing with business matters or the members of his family. But this late afternoon, he was furious with his beautiful daughter who stood there acting as if nothing had happened when she'd caused both him and her mother several long hours of worry and fretting.

He was not going to dismiss the irresponsible episode just because she'd returned without any harm coming to her, because, God knew, it could have been different.

"Please excuse us, Charmaine, and you too, Etienne. My daughter and I are going to take a little walk," he said.

Tiffany was not the only one taken by surprise. It startled Charmaine as well as Etienne as he took Madame Renaud's arm to lead her back up the path toward the house, leaving Tiffany and Pierre back at the gate.

But Madame Renaud did not have to be told that her dear husband was upset and he had a right to be. They had been terribly worried to find Tiffany absent from the house without so much as a word from her that she was going to leave. This just wasn't like Tiffany, even though her mother knew she was quite an independent, spirited miss with a will of her own.

But she'd been unable to tell Pierre just how long Tiffany had been gone because she didn't know when she'd left the house, for she'd been busy helping Tasha take a bath and wash her hair. This was a tedious task which had taken a great deal of time so it was only after this that Charmaine had searched the house to find no sign of her daughter.

When Pierre had returned to the house and inquired about Tiffany, she was forced to tell him the truth and he flew into a rage. It was at this moment that Etienne returned from the mill and suggested that he knew all the places in the woods where Tiffany liked to stop to pick her favorite wildflowers, so he left immediately to seek her out.

But Charmaine found that there were no soothing words that stopped Pierre from pacing the floor after Etienne left. Not even the glass of wine she served him did anything to calm him.

She knew that this was one time Tiffany was going to receive a thorough tongue-lashing from her father as they took their walk together. There was nothing she could do after she entered the house but go about the chores of preparing the table. Etienne graciously set the table as Tiffany usually did. He, too, was concerned about what was going on between father and daughter.

Pierre wasted no time or words once he and his daughter were alone and he took her arm to stroll around the grounds of the Bernay property. "Tiffany, I've never taken you to be an addle-brained idiot. In fact, like your grand-père, I've considered you to be very smart—maybe the smartest of my children."

While she had always respected and honored her father and never had talked back to him, she indignantly declared, "I'm no addle-brained idiot, Papa! I was bored to death! Blame it on that if you must, for that would be the truth! I did not want to come on this trip but I was forced to do so."

Black eyes flashed with blue eyes. Pierre saw that her

fury matched his own and he had to admire her spunk. He knew that she was speaking honestly, and what more could he ask of his daughter than that? So he had to be as honest as she was being with him. Perhaps, he could not know the depth of her loneliness because he'd taken her away from all her friends and her surroundings she was accustomed to all her life.

But before he could say anything, Tiffany confessed, "Yes, it was foolish and obviously it was dangerous, Papa. I could have been lying out there ravaged or dead. I know this."

The very thought of that made all of Pierre's anger mellow. The very thought of something like that happening to his daughter was more than he could have endured.

He patted her hand and told her, "Tiffany, I—I can understand that this has been no pleasant time for you. But I've something to tell you that I've not even had a chance to tell your mother yet. I've negotiated a deal today for the sale of Tasha's property. There's nothing more to hold us here, ma petite. I think Tasha is able to travel now so would it make you happy if I told you that we will be leaving in just a few days?"

Her blue eyes sparkled brightly as she flung her arms around his neck and declared, "Oh, Papa—it would make me so very, very happy!"

"Then I am very happy, too!" he laughed.

He knew it would delight her to hear that he'd spoken to old Dom today as they'd docked for a brief moment before the *River Queen* went farther up the river to the next little hamlet. Then she would be returning back down the river, and that is when the Renauds would board the boat to go back toward New Orleans to catch their ship to cross the Atlantic Ocean before the winter months set in. The ocean was too turbulent and treacherous during that time of the year.

Renaud had given the whole summer to help the

185

Bernay family and being a very practical man, he knew that his own business was needing his services back in France. Come the autumn, he had to be back home in Paris!

"Come, Tiffany—let us go in the house and join your mother. I must ease her pretty head that I've not turned you over my lap and spanked you as I felt tempted to do a short time ago," he laughed.

"Now, Papa—you know I'm a little too old for you to do that!" she playfully taunted him.

"Oh, I don't know about that, little one. You are like your mother. You are a wee one, but oh, what a lot of spice in tiny ladies I've come to realize, having both a wife and a daughter. Between the two of you I can't afford to grow too old."

Tiffany giggled, "See, Papa—Maman and I shall keep you forever young!"

Pierre leaned over to kiss her cheek gently. "Is that the secret of this eternal youth I've been blessed with?"

"Why of course, it is! Oh, Papa, you'll never be old to me. I think you are the most handsome man I've ever seen in the whole world. I think I shall always feel this way."

His black eyes warmed with a swelling fatherly pride. All men yearn for a son, and he had three, but always and forever there would be something so very special about his one and only daughter, Tiffany.

He knew that his beautiful Charmaine understood the special spot Tiffany held in his heart. He, of all people, knew how she welcomed the birth of their daughter after she'd borne him three sons.

No precious, exquisite gem could he have purchased for his wife would she have prized more on their anniversary than the gift of their daughter.

There was no denying that Tiffany was that rare jewel!

* * *

It was a glorious sight to Charmaine to see the two of them laughingly walking up the pathway with their arms linked together. She watched her daughter's smiling face looking up at her father and she knew that her beloved Pierre had not been too harsh.

What pleased her more was to see the peaceful, serene look on her husband's face as he laughed while the two of them walked along. No longer was he furious with Tiffany.

It was going to be a pleasant evening after all and she was delighted. She called to Etienne to look out the window. "See them, Etienne. It would seem the angry storm has passed and a calm has set in." She gave a soft laugh.

Etienne strolled to the window and saw what she was talking about as he watched the two of them come up the steps.

Usually Etienne did not speak so impulsively but this moment he did and he could have bit his tongue as soon as the words were uttered. He heard himself saying to Madame Renaud, "Tiffany could bewitch the devil himself."

"Oh, how true it is, Etienne," Charmaine agreed with a casual air.

Etienne was just grateful that she had taken his comment so lightheartedly. For Etienne, it was much more serious and discerning!

Chapter 25

For twenty-three years New Madrid was the only place Etienne had ever lived. This was his home. The news that he was to accompany his mother to France was not entirely welcome, but he understood why she felt the way she did, for she had lived in France and England before coming to this country and marrying his father.

He also knew that since his father's death she had nothing to hold her here and, since the Renauds were such close friends, she would feel a peace and security being near them. He knew he could not refuse her. He must go whether he wanted to or not.

How could he not be grateful to the Renauds for all the things they'd done in the last weeks? Charmaine Renaud had nursed his mother back to health and she was like her old self again. That itself was a miracle.

Monsieur Renaud had paid all his father's debts and made the deal today to sell the property. Etienne had to confess that it would have taken him much longer to have accomplished what the clever Frenchman had done in a very short time. He felt an overwhelming admiration for Pierre Renaud.

Etienne decided that should he go to France and find it not to his liking, after he'd gotten his mother comfortably settled, he was not doomed to live there forever. He could seek out his future somewhere else.

However, he had to admit that Pierre had painted a most magnificent picture of the country estate where he was taking them to live just outside the city of Cherbourg. That certainly appealed to Etienne more than the city of Paris. He'd hardly feel at ease in a flamboyant, sophisticated place like that. He was a backwoods fellow and he would feel awkward and ill at ease in the kind of world that Tiffany and her parents inhabited.

He found it interesting that the Renauds' three sons liked their individual lifestyles. Each seemed to take his separate path to pursue their futures. Already, he was of the opinion that he would find the most in common with the son who was the farmer and the vintner in the French countryside.

Many things were on Etienne's mind as he roamed around the grounds of his house after the family had dined. He certainly wasn't ready to retire.

As Chad Morrow had not liked him, Etienne did not care for Morrow. It did no good for him to admonish himself about the jealousy swelling in him when he thought about Morrow's arrogant air. He had no right to feel that way but damn it, he did!

He resented the look he saw in Tiffany's deep blue eyes when they gazed up at the rugged Englishman who presented himself as a tower of masterful power and strength. He towered over Etienne in height by four or five inches and Etienne had always considered himself a tall man. He had also considered himself to have a fair physique, but his chest and broad shoulders could not compare to Chad Morrow's. When Chad mounted his horse to ride away, Etienne noticed how his pants molded to the firm muscled thighs as he straddled the horse.

A man like Chad Morrow could make any young lady lose her heart and he feared that Tiffany had already lost hers to him. Yes, he resented it even though he had no right to feel that way!

When he did finally go to his bed that night he knew there was only one salvation for him: he must forget about Tiffany and this romantic fancy he'd indulged himself in for too many weeks now. Someone like Tiffany had never entered his life before.

So the next morning he left for the mill and on his way home that evening he stopped by the Michaels' house. Sandra was overjoyed that he had asked if he might come over after supper to visit her. She eagerly agreed.

Her mother heartily approved, for she liked Etienne Bernay as a suitor for her daughter. Now she didn't care for that stranger who'd come to call the other day. She had labeled him a scoundrel who was just stopping through their village, and she wanted her Sandra to have no part of him.

Tiffany had not been lonely or bored since she'd had the talk with her father and he'd assured her that they would be leaving soon. The other thing that had lifted her spirits was the afterglow of the afternoon she'd spent with Chad. All she had to do was think about that and she began to shiver, recalling the wonderful ecstasy he'd given her that she'd never known before.

So her day went by swiftly and the four of them gathered at the dinner table to share the evening meal. It did not matter to her that Etienne was not among them. It was only when her parents went for their evening stroll and she found herself alone with Tasha that she realized Etienne was absent.

They happened to meet when Tiffany came out on the front porch and found Tasha sitting there in the swing. "Autumn's coming soon, Tiffany. I've watched the squirrels all afternoon gathering the pecans and scurrying away with them. Oh, how bushy their tails are. They say that's the sign of a cold, harsh winter, but then I won't be here this winter," she told the girl as she light-heartedly laughed.

It was good to hear the sound. She had an infectious laugh, Tiffany realized. She was hardly like the pale-faced woman Tiffany had first seen when they'd arrived here. Now, her skin had a light olive hue and there was spark of life in her dark eyes. While her features were not delicate like Tiffany's mother's, Tasha was not the homely woman Tiffany had first considered her to be. There was a warmth to her smile and a love that glowed in her eyes when she looked at those around her.

"Will you be happy to get back home, Tiffany?"

"Oui, Tasha—I can't wait."

"Can I confess I am excited about crossing that ocean? The last time I crossed it was when your mother and I were young maidens and neither of us was too sure about what the future held. Oh, Tiffany, those were the most exciting, wonderful days of my life! Few have a friend-ship like the one Charmaine and I have shared. I'd not take anything for that."

"I've—I've two very good friends, Denise and Sabrina, but I can't say that our friendship is all that strong."

Tasha gave her a warm smile. "Well, ma petite—you are lucky. You have two loving parents. I had no parents by that time and neither did your mother."

"I—I guess I had not realized that. I'd never been told that Maman was an orphan."

"Well, Tiffany, it can be a very frightening thing to be all alone when you are as young as the two of us were and have no one to turn to. We clung together, I guess you might say, and the two of us gave one another strength to endure many, many things."

Tiffany listened as Tasha spoke with such feeling and

emotions and she found that she was liking this sharp-featured little lady more and more. By the time Pierre and Charmaine returned from their walk to join them, the seventeen-year-old daughter of Charmaine Renaud knew she had many questions to ask her mother. She found herself most curious to know about that time in her life that Tasha had lightly touched on.

Now that she'd been awakened to love by Chad Morrow, she wanted to know how her mother had met and fallen in love with her father. She was curious about Charmaine's life before she met Pierre Renaud. Her pretty head was whirling with a hundred questions. A woman like her mother, whose astonishing beauty was always being praised and admired, must have had many suitors before Pierre Renaud made her his bride.

Tiffany watched the two of them now as they approached and saw the intimate way they held hands and their eyes met when they looked at one another. After all these years, they had surely found the secret of keeping their romance glowing and exciting. This is what she wanted when she gave her heart to a man. She wanted that love to glow forever as her parents' affection for one another did. She would not settle for less, she decided.

None of her beaux back in Paris would fill this tall order. Only one man she knew could measure up to this, and it was Chad Morrow!

As handsome as Etienne was, and as intriguing as she had found him to be when they were together, he still didn't block out the impact of Chad Morrow. Right now, she rather doubted that any man could.

When she went to bed that night, it was Chad Morrow she dreamed about and how his sensuous mouth thrilled her and how his hands felt against her flesh when he so lovingly caressed her. She wished that he was there snuggling by her side.

A few miles away, where Chad lay on the top bunk of

the houseboat, he was occupied with the same thoughts as Tiffany. He ached for the soft touch of her body next to his and he knew that his soul would be in torment until that was the way it was.

His hand wanted to be able to reach out and feel that silken flesh and his arms wanted to be able to encircle her curvy body and draw it close so that it fit to his as it was surely meant to do. His hungry mouth wanted to be sated by the sweet nectar of her lips.

He was bloody well not going to be in this state too much longer, he vowed to himself. He'd have Tiffany Renaud for his own. Nothing was going to stop that from happening. She was meant to be his!

To get his mind off Tiffany he turned his attentions to the old journals to read on into the third one. There was still an answer to uncover before his curiosity could be satisfied. He knew it was in there.

When he'd first read all of them, it had not held any importance but now he knew that it did. He knew that it had to do with Tiffany, as crazy as that might seem, because those journals were written long before she was even born.

But he turned one page after another that told of numerous little incidents that old Cat experienced as he moved that old keelboat up and down the river, taking his cargo and passengers to various towns. Those he had mentioned earlier in the journal caught Chad's interest, especially his father's very descriptive words about one Charmaine Lamoureaux who he knew was now Madame Charmaine Renaud.

Chad had to conclude that several weeks must have passed without another encounter with any of them. This was not what he was seeking to find in the journals so he hastily went over these pages. But finally he came to a page where his father had written about a night when he had gotten drunk and was lamenting about the lady he loved. He wrote about the amulet he'd slipped in her reticule before she'd left his boat and he had wondered why he'd acted so impulsively. As he'd written that night in his journal, he just hoped the amulet would protect "that silver-haired angel" from any harm that might come her way now that they were parting and she was leaving his boat.

The next page of Captain Cat Morrow's journal was filled with his very personal feeling for the lovely lady he knew could never be his but nevertheless, could never be forgotten. He had written that she would always be the lady of his dreams.

As much as Chad wanted to read on and on, he could not do it for his eyes were too heavy with sleep. But it was obvious that the beguiling charms of Charmaine Renaud had been passed on to her ravishing daughter, Tiffany. He felt about her as his father had surely felt about her mother over twenty years ago.

Well, he was different from his father, for he would fight for Tiffany! Whatever it took to make her love him as he loved her, he would do.

No other man would have her!

Chapter 26

The hour was late when Etienne slipped back into the house and into the bedroom to the cot where he slept. For the first time since the Renauds had arrived, he wished that he had his own room, the one that Tiffany was now occupying.

As quietly as he could, he managed to get undressed and sink down on the cot. But as quiet as he was, Tasha knew when he entered the room but he had no inkling of that. She lay there without stirring. No one had to tell her that Etienne had been over to the Michaels' house to see the promiscuous Sandra.

She would not have made a good wife for her son but she did not have to worry about that now, for they would be leaving here. Tasha had no doubt that sooner or later Etienne would have been tricked into marrying the girl if they had remained here.

In a reflective mood, she thought about the time when she and Charmaine were crossing the Atlantic Ocean and the handsome, robust Jacques Bernay started paying attention to her one day on deck of the ship. How excited she'd been when she returned to the cabin to tell Charmaine about him.

Later when the two of them had been alone by the

railing of the ship and he'd kissed her, Tasha had never been so stirred by the touch of a man. Being a plain-looking young lady, she could not believe it when Jacques told her how attracted he was to her. It was a miracle, for Tasha had never expected to attract such a man as Jacques but she found that he was quite sincere about how he felt about her. When they arrived in New Orleans, she and Jacques were married before they boarded the riverboat with Pierre and Charmaine to travel on up to New Madrid. How could she have possibly been the one to be married before her friend, the beautiful Charmaine?

They'd only been in New Madrid a few weeks before she discovered she was expecting their first child and Jacques Bernay could not have been happier.

A soft flow of tears dampened her pillow as she thought of all those wonderful days. Never could there have been enough years to satisfy her to have spent with her beloved Jacques. All through the years she'd felt herself the luckiest lady in the world to have Jacques love her as he did. He had a way about him that made her believe herself to be beautiful at least in his eyes. So she ignored what her mirror told her.

She knew instinctively that Jacques would approve of what she was doing by leaving New Madrid. She felt this so firmly or else she could not have done it and agreed to Pierre's plans for them. Perhaps it was Etienne's destiny that they return to France, his father's native country.

Tasha knew she could be content there and it would be nice to be able to see Charmaine when she could manage to come to the countryside from Paris. It would be nice to get to know her dear friend's sons. They surely had to be fine young men if they were sons of Pierre and Charmaine. Perhaps Etienne would find himself a pretty little French girl to claim as his wife after they were there a while.

To look at Charmaine, Tasha had to think that the years had been very gentle and kind to her or maybe, it was the generous love she'd received from her devoted Pierre, for she was as exquisitely lovely as she had been when she was young. Her figure had not suffered at all from bearing four children.

When Tasha finally gave way to sleep, she was thinking about the first winter they'd spent in New Madrid when the terrible earthquake had struck the area. Somehow, she was looking forward to this winter that she would be enjoying in the countryside of France. It was going to be a good life they were going to—she firmly believed that!

There were few things that Pierre kept from his wife. That was part of the reason their marriage was so grand, but there were some things he felt might concern her pretty head that he wanted to spare her. This was one of those times and he had rushed to promote their departure even sooner than he'd told Charmaine originally.

He could already imagine the sparking of surprise in her blue eyes when he informed her tonight that they would be catching the boat to take them down to New Orleans the day after tomorrow. But he knew that most of Tasha's packing was done and he'd already made a deal with her neighbor to purchase all the household items she'd not be taking.

But it was Tiffany who was the jubilant one at the evening meal when he made his startling announcement. Charmaine and Tasha sat there tongue-tied for a few moments.

"Day after tomorrow, Pierre? Mon Dieu, can we get it all done, Tasha?" Charmaine stammered.

Tasha threw back her head and gave a jovial laugh. "I guess we'll have to."

Charmaine looked over at her husband sitting there with an amused look on his face. He had no doubt that they'd manage.

Pierre turned his attention to Tiffany. "And what about you, ma petite? Can you be ready?" He already knew what her answer would be.

"Oui, Papa—I shall be ready!"

It was only then that Pierre chanced to glance over at the sober face of Etienne, and he decided to ignore it. So he asked no opinion from him.

That first gusto of elation and joy for Tiffany subsided once she was alone in her room and her thoughts drifted across the way to that place where an old houseboat was moored. It suddenly dawned on her that she would be leaving Chad Morrow in New Madrid. This time he would not be accompanying them on the riverboat when they traveled back down the river toward New Orleans.

She also recalled those dull, long days as the riverboat plowed slowly up its course and she was sure that it would travel at the same pace going back down. Chad would not be there to enliven the time for her and neither would there be Dom. The chances were he'd not be on the riverboat they'd be taking this time.

The next day she hoped and prayed that Chad would come to see her as he'd promised, but he could not know that their departure date had been moved up and the time was growing shorter and shorter.

She was tempted to saddle one of the horses in the Bernays' barn and ride to the riverboat to see him. But she knew he was quite serious about her roaming and wandering through the woods alone, so she dismissed that impulse.

As adventuresome as she was, she didn't relish the idea of being in that woods again by herself after what had almost happened.

When there were only twenty-four hours left before

she and her parents were due to leave New Madrid, she was forced to face the fact that she might not see Chad before they left. Nothing about leaving New Madrid filled her with sadness except leaving Chad behind. That was obviously not the case with Etienne and she had only to look at his face to come to that conclusion.

Actually, since Chad had escorted her back to the house that late afternoon, Etienne hardly spoke to her. They might be making a long journey together, but if Etienne didn't wish to be friends it was not going to cause her to lose any sleep. It truly didn't matter to her.

After Chad's rapturous love-making, Etienne and any other man paled for Tiffany!

It never dawned on Tiffany as her father helped her, her mother and Tasha onto the deck of the boat while Etienne and one of the boatmen loaded on the baggage, that it was the very same riverboat they'd traveled up the river on in late spring. Summer had gone by and autumn was in the air.

But when a chummy little black-bearded fellow came waddling across the plank deck with a big, broad smile on his face, she recognized him immediately.

"Dom! Oh Dom," she shrieked as she scurried across the deck, her black curls bobbing up and down around her back and shoulders. Her parents, Tasha, and Etienne watched her rushing to meet the old cook she'd become so fond of during the days they'd plowed up the Mississippi. Her parents exchanged smiles but Tasha and Etienne had no idea who the man was until Charmaine turned to Tasha to tell her about Dom.

Tasha laughed when Charmaine told her about Dom and how he'd introduced Tiffany to fishing off the deck of the boat.

"I can't imagine Tiffany holding a fishing pole or

enjoying fishing. However, Tiffany has so very many sides about her, I'm discovering. She's an amazing young lady, Charmaine. I can see why you're so proud of her."

"She is just that, Tasha."

By now, Dom and Tiffany had joined her family and he greeted the Renauds, telling them what a pleasure it was for him to have them on the boat for their return to New Orleans.

"Well, Dom—it's going to be nice to eat some more of that good food of yours for a while," Pierre declared. "These are good friends, Dom. I'd like you to meet Madame Bernay and her son, Etienne. Now they'll get to see what I've been talking about when I praised your fine fried catfish."

"Ah, we'll look forward to that, Dom," Tasha told the cook.

"Well, now—you heard that, didn't you, Mademoiselle Tiffany? We got to get them catfish caught so we can give the nice little lady a treat," he teased Tiffany in that jovial manner of his.

Her blue eyes sparkled. "Any time you say, Dom."

By now, all their baggage was aboard. Dom excused himself so the boatman could show the newly arrived passengers to their quarters before the boat was pushed away from the banks of the river to begin the long trek southward toward the gulf.

Sluggishly, slowly, the boat began to move by the time the passengers were in their cabins. Tasha and Etienne occupied the same cabin Tiffany had been assigned when they'd come up the river. She now was put in the one next to her parents which had only one bunk instead of two. It was much smaller quarters, which met with her displeasure, and there was only one small window.

At least the weather was cooler, she consoled herself as she surveyed the small area before she attempted to start unpacking. When she saw just a few pegs on the wall, she decided to take out of her valise just what she would need for the next few days.

Another thing she consoled herself about was the fact that each day that went by now brought her just a day sooner to being back in France. That was enough to lighten her spirits. She was going home!

By now she could feel the motion of the boat moving at a steady pace and she realized that they were really leaving New Madrid behind. A strange thought struck her that made her stop taking the garments from her valise: somewhere back there in the distance was Chad Morrow. A wave of sadness washed over her just thinking about him. She sank down on the bunk and stared at the walls of her cabin.

Under her breath she cursed him for not coming to her as promised before she'd left.

When would she quit believing that smooth-tongued devil with all his empty words and promises? Never had she been so utterly helpless with any other man in her life except this one. God knows, he wasn't the handsomest gent she'd attracted but that reckless, rugged air of his had fascinated her far more than any of the others fawning over her. Perhaps that was the secret hold Morrow had on her. He didn't bend to her slightest wish as the others had. Maybe that was the overpowering charm which had captured her restless, fickle heart.

An overwhelming, driving force made Chad Morrow ride over to the Bernay place at midday. All morning Tiffany had been on his mind and he could not shake the feeling that he must see her before the day was over.

Chad saddled his horse and rode the few miles to the Bernays. But when he arrived, a ghostly quiet seemed to have settled around the grounds and the house. All the drapes were drawn and all the wooden doors were closed and secured. There was no life or movement around the house or the grounds.

A young lad walked along the path in front of the fenced-in front yard and near the hitching post where Chad had secured his horse.

The youth bounced his ball against the ground as he slowly moved in front of the Bernay property. As Chad came down the path from the house to go back to the hitching post, the young boy was quick to inform him that the Bernays were gone.

"They left this morning and they ain't comin' back, my momma says. They're going a long way from here," he told Chad.

"Thanks, fellow," Chad said as he untied the reins of his horse and mounted the animal. He knew where they were going and all that mattered to him right now was that he might be lucky enough to get to the river before the boat left New Madrid. As if the demons of hell were after him, he rode toward the river.

But luck was not with him this time. By the time he reached the long wharf, the boat was going around the first bend of the river that was constantly winding its way toward New Orleans.

Seeing the boat carrying Tiffany away from him was a devastating blow Chad had not been prepared for. What was it about that tantalizing little sorceress that drove him crazy? Damned if he knew!

All he knew was that he was going to make some hasty plans to get back to England just as soon as he could!

Chapter 27

A dispirited, dark mood settled in Chad as he rode back toward the houseboat. His gray eyes gazed aimlessly ahead on the narrow lane he traveled now that he was on the outskirts of the town. It agitated him to think that Etienne Bernay would be on that riverboat with her instead of him. There were those many days and nights he would be sharing the crossing of the ocean long after the boat trip was over.

A deep frown etched his face as he spurred the horse into a faster pace as a release to this sudden spark of anger. He wasn't exactly in the best of spirits when he arrived back at the houseboat. It was just as well that Bickford wasn't there when he arrived nor was he going to be there all night. Chad found his crudely scribbled note saying that he might be gone for a couple of days.

So Chad was left with preparing his own supper and his talent didn't lie in that direction. He searched Bickford's cupboards to see what was available and finally decided that the slab bacon and eggs were his best bet. However, he almost burned the bacon and the eggs had a miserable look to them when he scooped them out of the cast iron skillet. He had a disgruntled look on his face as he surveyed his plate before sitting down at the table.

At least, the bread and jam was tasty and the milk tasted good.

After the meal was over he found himself impatient with the chore of trying to clean the skillet. Saying to hell with it, he walked away to go out on the small deck built around the living quarters of the houseboat and sat down on the wooden bench to enjoy one of his cheroots. A big full moon, so golden, was shining down on the gentle, rippling waters of the river and the night air was fresh and good-smelling. Across the river he could hear the calling of the nightbirds and flitting over the dark deck he could see five or six fireflies. He heard a rather large splash out in the middle of the river and he figured that to be a fair size fish. It made him think of his beautiful, blue-eyed Tiffany and the night they'd shared that fantastic dinner in the Renauds' cabin when Dom prepared the catfish he and Tiffany had caught that afternoon.

He strolled back into the houseboat and poured himself a generous glass of whiskey from his flask. With the glass in his hand he ambled back on deck. It was pleasant and peaceful out there. He allowed himself to enjoy the night's quiet and sip on the whiskey, while he let his thoughts roam down the river where he knew Tiffany to be tonight.

But after a while, he knew that too much thinking was only tormenting him so he took his half-empty glass to go inside. Turning up the lamp, he took out the journals to start reading through them again. Tonight, maybe he would find the answer he was searching for in those old yellowed pages.

Chad found the place where sleep had overtaken him the other night when he had to put the third journal aside. Getting himself cozy in the chair after he'd refilled his glass of whiskey, he began to read the pages once again. Cat wrote about seeing Renaud and Charmaine, along with the Bernays when his riverboat would make

204

the stop in New Madrid. He wrote about Tasha Bernay being pregnant with their first child.

Chad found himself completely engrossed as he read about the disaster in December of 1811 that they were all swept up in, and the panic that followed. A huge crack so vast and deep had separated Charmaine from Pierre and the Bernays. Cat had been the one to find her in a dazed state.

For days, he took care of her and held her in his arms as the aftershocks hit the area. Never did he make love to her but it was a precious time to Cat that he could just hold her this way. Never did he try to fool himself that Charmaine could love him but he dared to hope so when days went by and Pierre did not come to get her.

But one day when she strayed away to search for her little pup, White Wolf, she roamed too far away and when Cat got concerned, he went out to hunt for her. But fate handed him a cruel blow, and he slipped on one of the steep cliffs, injuring his leg so badly that he had to crawl back to the small cabin where they'd taken refuge.

That was where Pierre Renaud had finally come in search of Charmaine, and Cat could only tell him the truth: he didn't know where she'd wandered off to.

Cat had not known the sequence that had followed that day until many weeks later when he finally managed to get back to New Madrid and seek out Jacques Bernay.

Jacques had been the one, Cat had written in his journal, who had informed him that Charmaine had been found by Pierre a few nights later as she sat on a cliff overlooking the river, clutching the little white pup. Cat wrote that he was happy that Pierre had found her safe and sound.

Pierre and Charmaine were mentioned no more in Cat's journal. His last entry about them was that Bernay had told him that a short time later they left New Madrid and returned to France. The two of them were happily married, Cat was informed.

The last yellowed page of the journal contained the first mention of Chad's mother, Elizabeth Chadwick, and how Cat thought her to be an awfully pretty English miss. Cat wrote about presenting her with a large black opal ring he had won in a card game—at least now Chad knew the origin of the stone Madame St. Clair had given back to him. Chad read this last page and gave up on finding the answer he sought.

But the next night, he began to peruse the fourth and final journal, and it was a strange one. Months went by with no entries being made and Chad flipped to the back of the journal to find it was the same way. It mentioned briefly that in April of 1812 Cat was married to Elizabeth Chadwick, but then there were long gaps of days and months when he wrote nothing. There was an entry where Cat wrote about receiving a cool, polite letter from Elizabeth that she'd had a son but she'd not be returning to New Madrid. She planned to stay in England and raise their child. But Cat had noted the birthdate: January 16, 1813.

After many hours of reading, Chad Morrow finally found the passages he sought. It was an entry his father had made after he'd chanced to meet Jacques Bernay in the local tavern. Both of them were in a depressed mood and making certain confessions to the other. Cat was bemoaning the fact that he had a son he'd never get to see and Jacques was decrying the fact that he'd never got to know his father either because he was the illegitimate son of a wealthy man back in France.

Each of them was giving sympathy to the other one. In a weak moment, Jacques confessed that he never held any animosity toward Pierre. When Cat questioned him about that, Jacques told him that Pierre was his half-brother. It was the old, respected Etienne Renaud who'd sired him as well as Pierre.

Cat had let out a flow of cuss words of astonishment and written it exactly that way in his journal.

He'd also written that after that night he and Jacques Bernay never spent time together again. When they met on streets of New Madrid, Bernay had been very cool and unfriendly, so Cat figured that he recalled what he'd revealed to him and regretted it.

Chad read no more for he'd found the information he sought. He was satisfied that this was what had kept prodding at him to seek the answer.

Etienne had no right to claims for Tiffany, especially romantic ones. They were half-cousins. Something told Chad that Tiffany was not aware of this. For whatever reasons her parents might have to conceal this from her, that was what they'd obviously done. He recalled many of their conversations when they were crossing the ocean and she was so displeased about making this trip; she'd referred to the Bernays as her parents' old friends. Never had she said family.

But being a fair-minded man, Chad had to wonder if Etienne was as ignorant about the past as Tiffany was. That disturbed him all the more as he thought about it!

By the time Chad placed all the journals back in the leather case, he'd made a decision: he was catching the first boat he could for New Orleans. Maybe he would be a few days behind them, but he would be trailing them fairly closely.

When Bickford returned the next evening at sunset, Chad told him that he had urgent business calling him back, so he was leaving his unfinished project in Bickford's hands.

"The funds are there in the bank, Bill. There's more than enough to get that old lady rolling back down the river. There's enough to also keep you in business for six months, and if it doesn't work, then dock her here by your houseboat until I return," Chad told the old captain.

"Hey, sonny—you just never fear! Me and that old girl will make it fine. Why, we'll run up and down this old muddy just as spry as we did when we were both young and full of ginger."

Chad laughed, "You don't have to convince me, Bill. I believe you!"

"You just get your tail going to attend to that business you speak about and then get back here to see us in action. Everyone up and down this river is going to know the *Fancy Lady* is running this river again. Yes sir! Why I couldn't let old Cat down. If I did, he'd come back and haunt me . . . sure as hell he would!"

The two of them broke into a gale of laughter.

Two days later, Chad left New Madrid. His accommodations were not exactly to his liking, for it was a small boat, and he was not too happy about the gent who was sharing his quarters. Under normal conditions, he would never have accepted such an arrangement, but time was urgent to him right now so it was worth the inconvenience.

Everything about the man, from his slicked-back black hair to that thin mustache over his lip, labeled him some kind of unsavory drifter who most likely preyed on innocent victims for his livelihood.

Chad didn't intend to be one, so he played it very cautiously. He left nothing in his luggage of any value except his clothing. At night, he slept with a little deringer under his pillow. He wanted the little short-barreled pocket pistol handy in case he would need it.

Often this fellow returned to the cabin late at night and he figured he'd been in card games with some of the other passengers or some of the crew. Chad always listened to his movements around the dark room before he finally crawled into the bunk.

By the time they'd docked in Memphis, Chad's clever trickery had revealed to him that his suspicions about this Del Adams had been right. He'd placed things in his luggage a certain way to see if the man was nosing around when he wasn't in the room. It didn't surprise him when he asked the man where he was heading for and he told him New Orleans.

"That's a place that never sleeps. No place like New Orleans anywhere I've ever been and I been a lot of places," Del boasted. "Ever been there?"

"I've been there," Chad replied.

"You don't seem taken with it," Adams commented with his beady eyes giving Chad a skeptical glare.

"I was there on business, not pleasure, Del."

"Hey, New Orleans is a place for a man to pleasure himself to the fullest, Morrow. Prettiest ladies—and the most obliging, I might add." Del gave a lusty laugh.

Giving a shrug of his shoulders, Chad casually responded, "Maybe I'll have time to indulge myself this time."

"Hey, let me tell you if you want some good places to go while you're there, just let old Del here direct you. I know all of them."

"That right?" Chad baited him.

"That's exactly right. Listen, a good-looking gent like you could have himself a hell of a time. I know what I'm talking about."

"Well, you've given me something to anticipate when I arrive, Del." Chad laughed good-naturedly.

Del Adams was quite an expert about judging people. He'd been sizing people up for years because that was how he was able to take advantage of them as he did. Chad Morrow's clothing was not cheap and neither was that ring he wore on his finger. Those fine soft leather boots of his did not come cheap, either. He held himself aloof from the other passengers as though he felt himself a

209

little better than the rest, Del Adams decided.

Already, he'd gone through the luggage to see if he might fined any money concealed there, or jewelry in a pouch, but he'd found nothing—so he had to conclude Morrow carried his money on his person.

But tonight, he'd noticed a bulge in the pocket of his coat that he'd hung on the post at the head of his bunk. He planned to wait out until he knew Chad was asleep and then he would try to investigate that.

Del Adams was no fool. He wanted no trouble with the likes of Chad Morrow, for the man was twice his size and a few years younger, too. No, he'd wait to make his move until the last night they were sharing this cabin and due to arrive in New Orleans.

Once again, Chad threw out the bait for Del by pretending to be asleep when he wasn't. He lay there in the dark, quietly allowing him the liberty to prod his jacket pockets. There in the dark, he wore an amused smile on his face as he knew the moment that Del's hand found his pouch stuffed with money. All the time his hand firmly held the deringer as he waited to see if Del removed it. Chad found it interesting that he didn't. He listened as his feet padded back to get in his bunk. For a few moments Chad was puzzled and then he came up with the answer as to why he'd left the pouch there in the pocket.

Del would wait until the last night they were out on the river and then he would help himself to Chad's money. He'd make a hasty departure from the riverboat just before they arrived at the docks. A short swim in the river was worth it to a man like Del Adams if the purse was rich enough. Chad's was, and Del knew it.

Now Morrow knew what to expect out of this gent and he'd be ready for him!

Chapter 28

Old Dom made a point of inviting Tiffany to join him during their stops in Vicksburg and Natchez so that they might enjoy the brief hour or two together trying to catch themselves another nice line of fish. Both times they were lucky and Dom told her she was like a good luck charm.

"Wish I had you around all the time, Mademoiselle Tiffany! Why, I'd always have a fine mess of fish to fry."

She laughed gaily, "Oh, Dom—I adore you!"

"Now do you, mademoiselle?" he laughed. Dom had been tempted both times they'd been together to bring up the subject of Chad Morrow, but somehow, something had prevented it. He wondered about the young man and he was also curious about the two of them. Often during that trip up the Mississippi River he'd observed them together when they were not aware of it. He'd had the impression that there was a strong attraction between them. During the stop in Vicksburg as they'd started to part company, Dom was about to approach the subject, but the young man traveling with the Renaud party joined them so Dom didn't say anything.

Today's stopover for two hours in Natchez to take on new cargo and six more passengers would most likely be their last one before they arrived in New Orleans.

Today, he would inquire about Chad since both of them had been in New Madrid at the same time for many weeks now. Obviously, Morrow was still back there since he wasn't returning on the boat with them. But the plans he had for going to New Madrid were a tremendous undertaking and Dom could imagine the many obstacles he had faced.

They had four fine fish on their line after the first hour. Dom laughed, "Well, we did it again, didn't we? I will never forget that night and our grand dinner in your parents' cabin when we were going up the river, mademoiselle. I got the impression that your papa was surprised at your exuberance about fishing."

"I think he was."

"I think Chad was, too. He told me that you never cease to amaze him," Dom remarked.

"Oh, he told you that, did he? Well, he never ceases to amaze me either," Tiffany replied with an expression on her face that told Dom she was not too pleased with Chad Morrow at the moment. Dom wondered what had her so out of sorts with him.

"Is he still in New Madrid?" the old cook wanted to know.

"As far as I know, Dom." Her lovely face reflected that the mention of Morrow seemed to depress her and Dom almost wished that he'd not brought up the subject at all. He wanted to tell her he was sorry about that, but before he could say anything, Etienne Bernay sauntered up to the bench. Dom suddenly felt a resentment that he was always interfering with this special time they shared. He wondered if he stood back in the shadows watching them, taking on the role of Tiffany's protector.

For the second time, Etienne took Tiffany's arm to lead her away after her goodbyes were said to Dom. There was something about the possessive air he had with

Tiffany that the old cook found to his distaste. He had not felt that way when he'd seen Chad holding her arm as the two of them had strolled around the deck of the riverboat. Something about that had seemed right and proper to Dom. That was the only way he could explain it to himself as he went to his galley to start preparing his evening meal for the passengers.

As the two of them walked toward their cabins, Tiffany asked Etienne if he was enjoying his trip down the river. "Is this not your first time to be out of New Madrid? I think this is what your mother told me when we were talking the other day," Tiffany asked him. Lately, she'd found herself feeling very restrained around Etienne and this was not like it had been all the time she'd been there in the Bernay home. But it was Etienne who had changed, not she. It had happened that stormy day they'd sought refuge in the cave and he'd ardently kissed her. She found this all very strange and confusing.

She was beginning to wonder if all men were complicated, complex creatures. It seemed to be the case with both Etienne and Chad Morrow. She had soothed herself since they'd left New Madrid that it would be nice to get back to Paris and those easygoing young Frenchmen who squired her around the city. They were far easier to understand, Tiffany was convinced.

She recalled that Natchez was not too far from New Orleans and she eagerly anticipated arriving there, for she had found that was the most exciting city she'd visited since she'd last seen her wonderful Paris.

This time she intended to see the places Chad had told her about—places that they never got to visit because of her father's sudden decision that they catch the riverboat two days sooner than they'd planned.

Suddenly, it struck her that Chad would not be with her to share the fun and excitement of the jaunts around the city, visiting the quaint little shops she'd like to go to so she might purchase gifts for Magdelaine and her brothers before they boarded the ship for home.

Somehow, she could not see Etienne enjoying this. The bustling, busy streets of New Orleans and the hodge-podge of mingling people would not appeal to Etienne at all. He liked the peaceful quiet of his woods and the river-banks of his town and countryside where he'd lived all his life. She had to admit that her father's idea to situate him and his mother, Tasha, out on their country estate was a wise decision. Neither of them would be happy in Paris.

By the time Etienne escorted her to her cabin and she'd politely said goodbye, she closed the door, feeling glad to be alone with her thoughts. Why had that dear Dom innocently brought up the subject of Chad Morrow and that dinner all of them had shared? Oh, that was a wonderful night and all of them were so gay and light-hearted! She could see his face now and those gray eyes with the devious glint in them, and she ached so much to feel his sensuous mouth capturing hers. Those strong arms held her like no others ever could, she was certain of that.

All she had to do was remember the intimacy they'd shared to give out a soft sigh. Maybe, it was a moan of the sweet anguish that love had caused her. Oh, Chad, she silently moaned, why did you do this to me? Was this her punishment for so recklessly and loosely playing with the affections of so many young men back in Paris? Perhaps it was!

She comforted herself as she sat there in her cabin that once she was back in Paris there would be her friends and all the social affairs that she and her family were con-stantly invited to attend. Once they were home, she would not have to pay the price she'd paid for these friends, the Bernays. Surely her parents would expect no more from her as far as they were concerned. They could live their own lives and she would live hers. Since she'd been denied her annual trip to London for the autumn season and visit with her friend, Sabrina, they would surely allow her to spend a part of the holiday season with her.

Thinking about all these happy possibilities helped lighten the disturbing thoughts about Chad Morrow. She finally moved off the bunk to remove the old faded pants and shirt she'd worn to sit on the deck and fish during the afternoon. She looked in the mirror and saw what a miserable state her hair was in from the afternoon heat with the humidity so thick from the river. She decided to brush the long, thick strands in the same style her mother wore. Letting the naturally curly wisps linger around her ears, she pulled all her hair up to make one huge coil at the crown of her head.

A refreshing bath in the perfumed bath oil had a relaxing, calming effect on her. She put on a light, soft, blue sprigged muslin frock with short, puffed sleeves and a low-scooped neckline. She wore no jewelry.

As she dabbed toilet water behind her ears and at her throat, she looked in the mirror at her reflection and smiled. Mon Dieu, it would be fun to get back to Paris just to enjoy dressing up! There was little incentive to do that on this old riverboat.

The wall dividing her cabin from that of her parents' was thick enough that she could not overhear their very serious discussion this early evening before the group joined for the evening meal.

Pierre's beautiful wife was very adamant and determined when she sought to be. This was one of those times as she expressed her views to her husband as she sipped the wine he'd just poured.

"We are being unfair to Tiffany, Pierre. Now that I look back over all these months, I think we should have told her before we ever left Paris. She could have understood why this was so important to us that we go so far

215

away to help Tasha. Tiffany is clever and I'm sure she's been perplexed and wondered why we would disrupt our lives and hers for a friend way across the ocean. There is another thing I've worried about lately, mon cher."

Pierre voiced her fear before she could, for he, too, had spent a moment or two with that concern. "I know it is Étienne you are speaking about. I have also had some moments of worry, but lately they have been together alone very few times. Oh, believe me—I've had my eye on both of them. Like you, it was such a concern that I spurred all the deals I had to make so we would be able to leave much sooner than I'd planned. What I'd like to know is if Étienne knows, but my hands are tied, for I cannot mention it to him in case Jacques and Tasha never told him."

"I have also wondered and I've been tempted to ask Tasha, but she's been so sick I hated to bring up the subject," Charmaine told her husband.

Pierre took his wife's hand in his and vowed to her that as soon as they got back to Paris they would have the long overdue talk with Tiffany as well as with their sons. "I'm afraid Father's feelings have been spared for too many years. Just because of his age now, he can't expect us to live a lie the rest of our lives. I shouldn't have waited this long. I should have gone to him, Charmaine, the minute you and I returned to France and told him about meeting Jacques Bernay and what the two of us discovered about one another quite by accident. Poor Jacques—he got cheated all his life. He could have deeply resented me but he didn't."

"He might have only been your half-brother but he loved you as a brother, Pierre. You felt the same way about him," Charmaine declared.

"I feel I might have failed him and his family by not telling my father what I found out and demanding that he claim Jacques as his son, too."

216

"No, Pierre! No, you ask the impossible of yourself and you must know that. Jacques did not wish you to tell him and he told you as much. Besides, you'd never force Etienne Renaud to do anything if he did not want to and this you must surely know, too."

Pierre made no reply, for he could not. She was right as she usually was.

She sat there beside him as he remained quiet and thoughtful. In that soft, soothing voice of hers, she comforted him, "It will all work out just fine, Pierre. You will see. Jacques would bless you for what you've done for Tasha. When Grand-père sees his grandson who bears his name and looks so very much like him, his heart will surely mellow. He will not be able to resist or fight the truth."

His black eyes glanced to look at her lovely, confident face and he had to believe what she said would prove to be true. His arms went around her and he pulled her close to him. He gave her a passionate kiss that left her breathless when he finally released her.

"Well, I can tell you, ma petite, that I was surely blessed the night I happened upon you on those cliffs on the Isle of Jersey. Still half-drunk as I was, I swore you were some kind of goddess there in the moonlight. Damned if I don't still believe it to this day!"

Charmaine still found him the most charming, handsome man she'd ever known and she was not that naive little farm girl that she'd been then, having come from France to live with her aunt and uncle in the Channel Islands off the coast of England.

The years had not dimmed that wild desire and passion he could always arouse in her and she always found herself eagerly surrendering when his arms held her close to him.

"Oh, Pierre—I find myself falling in love with you over and over again," she softly sighed as she snuggled there in his arms.

"I told you long ago that this would be the way it would always be with us, did I not, Charmaine?" His lips placed featherlike kisses on her face.

"And it has been," she murmured as his lips came to meet hers.

Monsieur and Madame Renaud did not join the others for the evening meal. They dined much later in the privacy of their cabin.

Chapter 29

Perhaps it was only because he and his mother and Tiffany had shared the evening meal that Etienne impulsively invited Tiffany to stroll around the deck with him.

It was a glorious autumn evening with a full harvest moon.

"I trust your parents were feeling all right tonight," Etienne remarked as he took her arm to guide her along the dark deck.

"Oh, I'm sure they were fine, Etienne," she said. "They often enjoy their time alone together. My parents are still in love after all these years. Were your parents this way?"

For a moment her bold question startled him and he hesitated for a moment before trying to reply. When he did, it was in a halting voice. "I—I guess they were, in their own way. Our ways are different from yours, Tiffany. You must understand that my father sat in no fancy office and my mother didn't live in a mansion with servants to pamper her."

Something about his tone vexed her. Her voice reflected that when she retorted, "My father works just as hard as your father did and my mother is no pampered little darling as you surely know, with what she's done in

219

your house, Etienne."

She felt herself swung around as his hands gripped her. "Tiffany—Tiffany, I do know! I meant no disrespect to either of them. Why, I think they're the finest people I've ever known." He reached over to kiss her on the cheek gently. "That is not what I meant at all. I was trying to say in my foolish way that there's never been much time for romance in the backwoods, when a man and a woman work from sunup to sunset. You understand now, Tiffany?"

"I guess so," she stammered, as Etienne's strong hands held her. Her nearness was affecting Etienne in that overwhelming way it had the day in the cave. For a while he'd been able to keep it under control, but now as they were here alone in the moonlight with its rays gleaming down on her beautiful face and those deep blue eyes looking at him, he was helpless to resist her charms.

"Good, I'm glad that is settled," he said with a laugh as he urged her to walk along with him on down the deck.

She liked the renewed warmth she was feeling as she walked beside him. It was as it had been those first weeks when they'd shared so much time together. There was no denying that they'd shared many pleasant hours. Etienne did not challenge her as Chad Morrow always seemed to do when she was around him. She relaxed around Etienne.

"Do you think you could love someone that long, Etienne—like my mother and father have, I mean?"

He bent down to look at her. "I suppose I could if it was the right woman for me." He tried to sound casual, for her question had taken him by surprise. He knew he could be forever in love if that woman could be Tiffany. Forever, she could have kept him intrigued and interested in exploring how that pretty head of hers worked. But Etienne knew that he could never have her as his wife.

220

"And who would be the right woman for you, Etienne? Have you met such a woman yet?"

He broke into a laugh, "You are not going to get the answers to those questions, mademoiselle. That is for me to know and not you. If I tell you yes then your next question will be who is the lady."

She giggled, "You are right. I would have done just that!"

"You see, Tiffany I've learned a lot about you in the last months." He was glad to see that her mood was light and gay. Maybe she'd ask him no more questions that could get both of them in trouble if he answered her honestly. That was the way he wanted to keep it for the sake of both of them. He could fall from grace so easily when she was there bewitching him.

Seeking to change the subject, he asked her how long it would be before they would be getting into New Orleans and she told him most likely another twenty-four hours.

"That soon?"

"That is what Father said today." She added that she was anxious to get there because it was such an exciting place. "We shall have fun there, Etienne, if we get to stay over a day or two, which I'm sure we will. I'll take you to some—some places I went to before." She had to bite her tongue to keep from saying that she'd take him to some of the places that Chad Morrow had taken her.

"I'll be glad to get off this boat and get my feet back on the ground. I'll confess to you that I'm not looking forward to that ocean crossing at all," Etienne told her.

"Neither am I! It is a bore!"

She was such a delightful little creature when she was in this carefree mood. No one had to ponder the way Tiffany thought nor did she mince words about any of her feelings. He admired this in her. He could not resist comparing her to Sandra. Even though he'd courted her and allowed himself to become enamored with her blonde loveliness, he knew she was a conniving little liar. He knew that she was also a flirt who enjoyed the attentions of other gentlemen around town when she was professing to be in love with him.

When he finally took Tiffany to her cabin, he kissed her goodnight at the door, but his kiss was not the kind he yearned to give. "Thanks for a lovely evening, Tiffany. It was nice to walk with you."

"It was nice for me too, Etienne. I'll see you in the morning," she said as she turned to go into her cabin.

But once inside, she found herself puzzled as to why Etienne was fighting the truth. Why did men play such mysterious games with a lady's heart? Chad Morrow had done it and Etienne Bernay did the same thing. She knew he was attracted to her.

She knew he desired to make love to her. His reaction to her touch told her that. Chad had taught her how to sense that in a man. Maybe she hadn't known that the first time he made love to her but she certainly did when they made love in that old rickety houseboat. It was not conceit that made her know that she affected Etienne just as forcefully.

But she also realized that he was fighting his emotions and she wondered why. They were two young people whose right it was to feel romantic if they chose to. Chad Morrow might have made love to her but she was not going to deny herself the joys and pleasures of another man if Chad didn't care enough to pursue her as a man in love should. Perhaps he didn't love her!

She'd become no man's slave just because she was helpless to resist his irresistible charms. They weren't together now and she had no idea when they'd ever see one another again. Maybe she'd never again know the sweet rapture of Chad Morrow's loving. But she'd have the memories of it for the rest of her life. To know that ecstasy once and forever spoiled her to settle for less with

222

any other man.

As she slipped into her soft batiste gown and crawled into the bunk, she lay there looking out the narrow little window at the full moon, all glowing and golden. Wherever Chad was tonight, he had to be viewing the same moon. She wondered if he was thinking about her.

Nothing about this man resembled the aristocratic ways of her grandfather or her father with their fine-chiseled features. His unruly hair seemed always to be falling over his forehead and his devilish eyes seemed always to penetrate her, making her feel that there was no secret she could conceal from him even if she tried. The features of his tanned face weren't perfect but he possessed the most sensuous mouth, which seemed to always have a smirk on it even when he was being his most gracious self. Perhaps this was what gave him such an arrogant air.

Yet there was no denying that he was a many-faceted man who could be any person he chose to be. In Paris, he had been the fine-attired gent in his elegant frock coat and expensive tailored pants. On the riverboat, she'd seen him in his faded shirt and tight fitting twill pants. The sight of his magnificent male body had excited her, she could not deny. Few men possessed such broad shoulders, trim waist and hips.

Something about the way he walked with a lazy swagger reminded her of the fierce tigers she'd seen when her father had taken her to the circus in Paris a few years ago.

There wasn't any denying it; the likes of Chad Morrow did not come along too often in a young lady's life. He was a rare breed of man.

She tossed back and forth on the bed, fluffing her pillow harshly to give vent to the frustration the thoughts of Morrow stirred within her.

Why did she do this to herself? Why punish herself by

even thinking about him? she wondered. The answer was simple. She couldn't help thinking about him. It mattered not how much she vowed that she was going to forget him. She couldn't do it!

Sleep did finally come, but only due to sheer tossing and turning. The dawn was breaking before her eyes finally closed.

Tiffany was not the only one having a restless night. Etienne found sleep evading him as he tried desperately to close his eyes and get some rest. He hoped his mother was not aware of his restlessness as she seemed to be sleeping soundly. He'd tried to be very quiet as he'd entered the darkened room. The bright moon helped as its rays glowed through the small window.

A cool breeze permeated the cabin and he was glad that his mother had opened the window before she'd retired. He would have sworn that he would sleep the minute his head hit the pillow, but such was not the case. Tiffany's beautiful face haunted his thoughts and her sensuous figure in that pretty gown tantalized his senses, tormenting him unmercifully.

Etienne realized that he had not cured himself of the spellbinding curse that Tiffany had put on him. She innocently did not even know it, so how could he fault her. He questioned why her parents had never told her the truth, as his father had told him. It wasn't fair to her. Did they feel shame about the fact that her grandfather had sired an illegitimate son? They didn't seem like that sort. After all, they'd come all the way from France just to help him and his mother. So why? he asked himself. There had to be some explanation for their motives in not telling her.

Suddenly, he was struck with the idea that they might be thinking that he, too, didn't know the truth. Lying there in the dark, Etienne wondered if he should not have a talk with Pierre Renaud and tell him that he knew that

Pierre was his half-uncle and that his father was his half-brother.

Tomorrow, he was going to do just that. Making this decision seemed to relax him so that sleep would finally come.

Tasha was aware of her son's tossing in his bunk and she wondered what was worrying him so much. She feared that she knew the answer.

Tiffany was a breathtakingly beautiful young lady!

Chapter 30

Chad Morrow found Del Adams a despicable character as he was forced to spend more nights in the same small quarters with him. He reminded Chad of a snake, with those beady little black eyes and that reedlike body. He had no idea with what concoction he greased down his black hair, but the smell of it was totally obnoxious.

Having traveled with many different breeds of men from various parts of the world, Chad had found few that were as abhorrent as Del. He was glad that this was going to be the last night aboard this boat.

He also figured that tonight Del would try to rob him and abscond with his money before they arrived in New Orleans.

Chad was going to be ready for him. The captain had informed him this evening that they should be making the wharves at New Orleans by late morning.

After the evening meal he'd enjoy the privacy of the cabin alone, for Del was not there. Chad had the opportunity to bait his trap by filling his coat pocket with an enticing roll of bills that was bound to whet Del's greedy appetite.

He prepared his luggage to leave the boat and laid out his clothes on the chair. By midnight, he crawled into his

226

bunk with the little pocket pistol neatly tucked under his pillow. Dimming the lamp, he lay back on the bunk to wait for the action to begin.

He did not have long to wait before he heard the squeaky sound of the wooden cabin door opening. Chad's gray eyes watched the thin figure pause to survey the room and him. Chad conjured up a snore to convince Del that he was sound asleep. Instinctively, he sensed that Del was feeling very cocksure and confident as he sauntered across the room. He couldn't tell what he was doing as he lay there in his bunk.

If he could have seen Del he would have observed the man making a compact pouch of his belongings. He would take it with him when he jumped from the boat with Chad's money to swim to the bank of the river.

Morrow heard his soft footpads as he moved toward his bunk and tensed, as his hand gripped the deringer. He waited patiently until Del's hand had pilfered the coat pocket and pulled out the fat roll of bills.

"Found what you were looking for, Del?" Chad's powerful body raised up out of the bunk with the pistol firmly aimed directly at a point between Del's beady little eyes.

In a faltering voice, Del stammered. "Wait a minute, Chad! Listen, I—I can—"

"I've been waiting, Del—just waiting for you to make the move I knew you were going to make. I had you figured out days ago, fellow. You bloody well did just what I expected you to do. Now, hand over my money."

Del didn't hesitate. He was nervous as hell when that huge man started moving out of the bunk. He hardly expected what that deep voice ordered him to do next.

"What did you say, Morrow?" Del asked in a quaking voice.

"You heard me, Del! Take off your clothes!"

Nervously, Del started fumbling with his clothing, not

knowing what fate had in store for him. He knew one thing and that was he'd never been so damned scared in all his life.

He did as he was ordered until he stood stark naked. Chad ordered him to go out the door and Del did as he was told. They marched down the narrow passageway until they got to the deserted deck.

"Jump, Del! Jump as you intended to do after you had my money," Chad's gruff voice demanded.

"God, man—have a heart!" Del pleaded with him.

Chad gave a deep, throaty laugh, "I've as generous a heart as you have, Del. Jump before I put a bullet between those lying eyes of yours!"

Del knew Chad Morrow had been the wrong man to try to outfox. He should have known better but his greed had been his undoing. He'd played this little scam a dozen times or more but never had he left a boat without his clothes and a hefty pocketbook to sustain him for a while in the city of New Orleans.

He jumped into the muddy Mississippi River. As he swam desperately to the banks he prayed he would never meet up with Chad Morrow again. Once in a lifetime was enough!

By the time he reached the bank he was trembling. Del Adams was faced with the dilemma of how he was going to manage to get himself some clothes so he could go on into New Orleans.

He had only once choice and that was to go to a nearby farmhouse and tell a very convincing tale of how he'd been robbed along the road and his clothes had been taken from him. Once he had obtained some clothes, he'd plot his next maneuver. Morrow had only slowed him down for a few days, Del consoled himself as he raised himself up off the bank of the river to start walking down the road.

One thing was for sure, if the opportunity ever came

that he could even the score with Morrow, he would take great delight in doing it. No man had ever outsmarted Del Adams before, so he could hardly forget that Morrow had.

Chad was relieved that he had finally gotten that scoundrel out of his life. All he could think about was that he was alone. Chad sank into his bunk and his sleep was sweet and peaceful.

By the time he woke up, the port of New Orleans was just ahead. He hastily dressed and prepared to disembark as soon as the boat pulled up by the loading wharves. He felt that he would surely find the Renauds quartered at the Plantation House, since they were so impressed by the place when they'd landed in New Orleans months ago.

He wasted no time in hiring himself a carriage to take him there. The closer the carriage got to the spacious white-columned mansion, the more his enthusiasm mounted at the thought of seeing the beautiful Tiffany again. It had pleased him that he'd not arrived that many days after she had.

To his dismay the desk clerk informed him that the Renauds had indeed arrived, but stayed just two days before they'd checked out.

Flabbergasted, Chad inquired to the clerk, "You mean they've already sailed?"

"I couldn't tell you that, Monsieur Morrow. All I do know is they left here day before yesterday."

Chad thanked the man and slowly ambled through the black and white tiled lobby to his carriage. He was so disturbed that he turned to go back to the desk clerk. After all, he had to have lodgings while he was in the city, unless he wanted to sleep out on the street.

The clerk gave him an understanding smile as he assigned him a room. "I'm sorry I couldn't help you any-more than I did, sir. I suppose you might check with the shipping lines. They'd be able to tell you if your friends took one of their ships in the last day or two."

"You're right. I'll—I'll do just that."

He did not want to accept for one minute that he'd missed Tiffany before she'd sailed away from him. But an hour later, he was just as perplexed after he'd visited a couple of the shipping line offices to be told that no party by the name of Renaud had boarded their ships. He was informed by one clerk that they'd have no ship sailing out of New Orleans for another week.

A good part of the afternoon had gone by when he went through the door of the third shipping office. There he was given the same answer.

When he arrived back at the Plantation House, the desk clerk saw the dejected expression on his face as he moved through the lobby and he knew he had been unsuccessful in finding out anything about his friends.

He found himself wishing that he could help him in some way.

Chad entered his room and went to his luggage to pull out his flask, for he felt the need for a drink of whiskey. Flinging open the double doors, he walked onto the second floor veranda that extended along this side of the building. Taking a seat, he took a hearty gulp of the whiskey as he tried to figure out what he should do next. Looking down the length of the open portico, he was glad to see that no one else was outside the rooms running along this part of the old mansion.

His mood was not such that he wished to be congenial and visit with anyone. The clerk had said that the Renaud entourage checked out day before yesterday, and yet, they'd not sailed on any ship leaving the port. That left him with only one conclusion: they were still in the city.

But where?

*   *   *

There was a very simple answer to the mystery Chad was trying to solve. Pierre Renaud found out that they were going to be unable to leave New Orleans for almost a week, so he decided to pay a visit on an acquaintance he'd met in London the previous year when he and Charmaine were spending some time at their home there. They had struck up a friendship with the Ronald Carrolls, who were visiting in London and lived here in New Orleans.

Pierre had called on Ronald and invited him and his wife, Renee, to dine with them at the Plantation House that evening. The Carrolls had insisted that they accept the hospitality of their palatial country house just outside the city the next day. At first, Pierre had declined, since there were five of them, but by the time the meal was over, Renee insisted that they share a few days with them before they sailed back to France.

"The truth is, Ronald and I miss having those rooms filled as they used to be when the children were home. We would enjoy it. Besides, Ronald would love to show you our fine thoroughbred. It was to purchase this horse that we'd made that trip to London where we first met you."

As they parted company that night, Pierre and Charmaine had accepted their invitation. The next morning, the Carroll carriage came to the Plantation House to get Pierre's party, and he checked out of the inn.

They might call it a country house, but to Etienne Bernay it was a palace. He'd never seen or been in a house so elegant or spacious. He enjoyed the afternoon riding on one of the thoroughbreds from the Carrolls' stable. He'd never seen such a fine animal around New Madrid. It surprised him to find out that Tiffany could hold her own astride the fast-paced horses.

She gave him a lighthearted giggle. "You look surprised, Etienne! I like to ride when I get the chance. I always go horseback riding when I visit my brother,

Phillipe. Remember I told you that he lives in our house just outside Cherbourg?"

Etienne wondered if their country estate was as grand as this place. He remembered Pierre telling his mother that this was where they would settle once they arrived in France. His head whirled crazily with thoughts that it would be something like this.

The first two days went by swiftly for Etienne, for there was so much to occupy him. It seemed to him that the Carrolls had everything a person could possibly want right here on the vast grounds of their property. Not only were there fine horses to ride, there was a fishing pond surrounded by willow trees and lush green grass at the back of the house. He and Tiffany spent one afternoon there enjoying a picnic lunch and fishing. She gave a moment of thought to her old friend, Dom, and how he would enjoy this spot.

She also sensed that Etienne was awestruck by all this grandeur. "The Carrolls are nice, aren't they?" she remarked to him as they strolled around the magnificent gardens surrounding the house one late afternoon.

"I've never met finer people. Why, you'd think we were family the way they're treating us," he said.

Tiffany had found Etienne much more fun to be around since they'd arrived in New Orleans. Maybe he might change and not be such a serious, moody young man now that he was away from New Madrid. She wondered if it was because all he'd known was hard work and there's never been any time just to be lighthearted and frivolous.

"Etienne, would you drive me in to do some shopping tomorrow? If I hope to get some gifts to take back to France I must do it soon. A week is going to be gone before we know it."

"If your parents approve, I'll drive you, Tiffany," he told her.

"Oh, they will approve, Etienne. I could always have the Carrolls' driver take me, but I'd enjoy your company." She smiled up at him sweetly.

He looked into those beautiful blue eyes gazing up at him. He knew that as long as he lived he'd never feel about any woman as he did about Tiffany.

Why did they have to be so cruelly cursed?

Chapter 31

Chad Morrow was not about to admit defeat, so he made the rounds of the shipping offices again the next morning. None of them had anything new to tell him, but at the branch office of the Penbrook Lines, he found a letter that had been awaiting him for many days. News from his solicitor brightened his dismal day: He was now the proud owner of the property he'd sought to acquire. That left one more plot of ground to fight for before he'd be satisfied.

Sooner or later, he knew he'd get that, too. Now, as he thought about it, what he'd sought to do a few years ago had not taken all that long.

While he was in the office he lined up his own departure to return to London. After all, he could not linger too many days in New Orleans if there was a Penbrook ship leaving port.

There was a ship leaving in two days, so he had a short time to scout around the city in the rare hope that he might locate the Renauds.

When he left the Penbrook office, he was famished, so he decided to go to the quaint tearoom where he'd taken Tiffany back in the spring. That thick crawfish chowder was going to taste mighty fine along with a thick slice of fresh bread.

The narrow street was crowded with carriages and buggies and as he approached the tearoom he saw that they were enjoying a thriving business. He only hoped there was a small table left for him, for his appetite was so whetted for the chowder he could taste it.

He leaped out of the carriage and marched through the door of the Red Lantern, delighted to see an empty table at the rear. He darted past the other tables to take a seat and he was promptly served that spicy, steaming crock of chowder. One bowl did not satisfy his hunger, so he asked for another.

He felt like a new man, his vigor restored by the good chowder. As he walked toward his carriage, he pulled out his case to take a cheroot to puff on after that fine meal. But as he was about to light it a carriage rolled slowly up the street. The lovely vision sitting on the seat, with her jet-black hair falling over her shoulders, was smiling at the man by her side—Etienne Bernay. Chad choked on the puff he'd just taken on his cheroot. His temper flared to see Tiffany having such a gay time in the company of Bernay.

Chad threw away the cheroot to rush out into the street as he gave out a yell, but he had not noticed an old fellow pushing his vending cart filled with vegetables, moving slowly from the opposite direction. The old vendor was taken by surprise by the swift dashing figure suddenly appearing in front of his cart, and it was impossible for him to halt. The cart tilted just enough so that all the baskets of vegetables came tumbling down on Chad. Amid a burst of cuss words and flinging the vegetables away from him, Chad rose up to meet the concerned look of the old vendor.

Chad hastily placed a roll of bills in the fellow's wrinkled hand as his gray eyes searched up the street for the carriage, but it had already disappeared from sight.

Still he didn't linger to listen to the old man's thanks or pay any attention to his protest that he'd given him too much money. Chad was consumed with one thought, and that was getting to his carriage to search up the street for some sign of that carriage carrying the lady he loved.

But after an hour of traveling up and down many adjoining streets, he realized the search was futile. As quickly as she'd appeared, she had also disappeared. So once again, Chad could only return to the Plantation House and try to think about his own neglected business affairs. He had Tiffany Renaud to thank for that. She had been a tormenting distraction since that first day he'd seen her in the park in Paris. How different his life would have been had he not made that trip!

But he had to honestly admit that he'd never known such heights of joy and happiness as he had shared with Tiffany.

At least, he knew one thing for certain: she was still here in New Orleans. Perhaps destiny would lead him to her. Their paths had almost crossed this afternoon and had he not rammed into that blasted cart, his long legs would have enabled him to catch up with their carriage.

It had been a wonderful day that Etienne knew he would treasure forever, and he thanked God that Tiffany had not seen Morrow back there on the street. Just one glance backward, and she would have recognized the Englishman.

Etienne found it ironic that less than an hour ago they'd dined at the Red Lantern, enjoying a marvelous lunch. Tiffany had insisted that they make one more stop before they return to the Carrolls. There was a little tobacco shop where she wanted to get some fine blend of tobacco to give to Noah.

But for a few minutes of time, they could have come to

236

face to face with Morrow!

Morrow had rubbed him the wrong way the first time they'd met. Bernay did not like the intimate way he looked at Tiffany. It disturbed him to think that Tiffany might care for Morrow. There was a presumptuous air about him, as if he thought he could have any woman he wanted. Well, he wasn't going to have his way with Tiffany, if Etienne could stop him!

He didn't mention seeing Chad on the street as they traveled back to the Carrolls, but he'd glanced back a second time to see Chad collide with the vending cart and it was all he could do to stifle a roar of laughter.

By avoiding the likes of Chad Morrow, their entire afternoon went quite pleasantly. Etienne felt very at ease as he escorted her around the various shops while she purchased her gifts. Perhaps, it was the grand spirit she'd instilled in him when they'd left the mansion to go into the city and she'd declared, "You look handsome today, Etienne. I like your new coat."

"I've your father to thank for all my nice clothes," he remarked. Fine-tailored clothing could do much for a man's morale, he decided when he'd brushed his dark hair before leaving the room to join her. He'd never owned a pair of nice pants like the fawn-colored ones he had on nor anything as fine as this bottle-green coat. He'd say one thing about Pierre Renaud, and that was he did things in a grand style. It was not one linen shirt he'd purchased for him, but a half dozen.

They did make a striking-looking couple as they'd rolled out of the Carrolls' drive. Both Charmaine and Tasha agreed on that as they watched them leave.

But neither of them voiced a private fear that each had been harboring, knowing how much time the two young people had spent alone together all during the late spring and summer. As close as the two ladies were, they were still reluctant to bring up the unpleasant subject.

When they returned Tiffany showed her mother and Tasha the gifts she'd purchased for everyone back in France. She had a hefty canister tin of tobacco for Noah and a lace scarf and brooch for her little maid, Magdelaine.

There was a gold-etched case for Charles to carry his cheroots in, and a magnificent waistcoat in a crème-colored brocade for her brother, Jacques. For Phillipe, she'd purchased a bright plaid scarf and matching cap.

Charmaine laughed softly, "It would seem to me that your choices were perfect for everyone, ma petite. Now, tell me what you bought for yourself to take back to France, eh?"

"Ah, Maman—I bought nothing. I shall wait until I return to Paris to buy something for myself." She smiled with a look of mischief that reminded her mother of the Tiffany she knew as a child.

When she excused herself to go to her room to refresh herself before dinner, Tiffany bent down to give each of the ladies a kiss. Her eyes sparkled as she told them, "It had been a wonderful day, but I feel the need for a bath and a change of clothes."

Tasha gave an admiring sigh as she told her friend, "Oh, Charmaine—she reminds me so much of you."

"Oui, sometimes I see her that way, Tasha. Other times, I see her so much like Pierre, but then there are those instances I see her like neither of us. She is Tiffany—her own person."

"And that is what makes her so very special, Charmaine," Tasha said.

"Oui, my Tiffany is very special and I knew that from the day she was born."

Tasha recalled to her friend the days of their youth when she was so in love with Jacques and Charmaine was attracted to Pierre Renaud. "It will take a most unusual man to hold Tiffany's love," Tasha told Charmaine.

"Ah, it is going to take a most remarkable man to conquer that fickle heart," Charmaine remarked, adding that her daughter had numerous suitors vying for her attention back in Paris. What she did not mention to her friend was that Tiffany had already met a man who could conquer and win her heart. Right now, Tiffany was just refusing to accept the truth, Madame Renaud believed.

A worldly-wise lady like Madame Renaud knew the look of love on a woman's face when she saw it and she'd already seen that on her daughter's face. She knew the man who'd put it there.

Chad Morrow was the man her daughter loved!

The Publishers of Zebra Books Make This Special Offer to Zebra Romance Readers...

AFTER YOU HAVE READ THIS BOOK WE'D LIKE TO SEND YOU
4 MORE FOR *FREE*
AN $18.00 VALUE

No Obligation!

ONLY ZEBRA HISTORICAL ROMANCES
"BURN WITH THE FIRE OF HISTORY"
(SEE INSIDE FOR MONEY SAVING DETAILS.)

MORE PASSION AND ADVENTURE AWAIT... YOUR TRIP TO A BIG ADVENTUROUS WORLD BEGINS WHEN YOU ACCEPT YOUR FIRST 4 NOVELS ABSOLUTELY *FREE*
(AN $18.00 VALUE)

Accept your Free gift and start to experience more of the passion and adventure you like in a historical romance novel. Each Zebra novel is filled with proud men, spirited women and tempestuous love that you'll remember long after you turn the last page.

Zebra Historical Romances are the finest novels of their kind. They are written by authors who really know how to weave tales of romance and adventure in the historical settings you love. You'll feel like you've actually gone back in time with the thrilling stories that each Zebra novel offers.

GET YOUR FREE GIFT WITH THE START OF YOUR HOME SUBSCRIPTION

Our readers tell us that these books sell out very fast in book stores and often they miss the newest titles. So Zebra has made arrangements for you to receive the four newest novels published each month.

You'll be guaranteed that you'll never miss a title, and home delivery is so convenient. And to show you just how easy it is to get Zebra Historical Romances, we'll send you your first 4 books absolutely FREE! Our gift to you just for trying our home subscription service.

BIG SAVINGS AND FREE HOME DELIVERY

Each month, you'll receive the four newest titles as soon as they are published. You'll probably receive them even before the bookstores do. What's more, you may preview these exciting novels free for 10 days. If you like them as much as we think you will, just pay the low preferred subscriber's price of just $3.75 each. *You'll save $3.00 each month off the publisher's price.* AND, your savings are even greater because there are never any shipping, handling or other hidden charges—FREE Home Delivery. Of course you can return any shipment within 10 days for full credit, no questions asked. There is no minimum number of books you must buy.

4 FREE BOOKS

TO GET YOUR 4 FREE BOOKS WORTH $18.00 —MAIL IN THE FREE BOOK CERTIFICATE T O D A Y

Fill in the Free Book Certificate below, and we'll send your FREE BOOKS to you as soon as we receive it.

If the certificate is missing below, write to: Zebra Home Subscription Service, Inc., P.O. Box 5214, 120 Brighton Road, Clifton, New Jersey 07015-5214.

FREE BOOK CERTIFICATE

4 FREE BOOKS

ZEBRA HOME SUBSCRIPTION SERVICE, INC.

YES! Please start my subscription to Zebra Historical Romances and send me my first 4 books absolutely FREE. I understand that each month I may preview four new Zebra Historical Romances free for 10 days. If I'm not satisfied with them, I may return the four books within 10 days and owe nothing. Otherwise, I will pay the low preferred subscriber's price of just $3.75 each; a total of $15.00, *a savings off the publisher's price of $3.00.* I may return any shipment and I may cancel this subscription at any time. There is no obligation to buy any shipment and there are no shipping, handling or other hidden charges. Regardless of what I decide, the four free books are mine to keep.

NAME

ADDRESS _____ APT

CITY _____ STATE ___ ZIP
(   )

TELEPHONE

SIGNATURE _____ (if under 18, parent or guardian must sign)

Terms, offer and prices subject to change without notice. Subscription subject to acceptance by Zebra Books. Zebra Books reserves the right to reject any order or cancel any subscription.   ZBMS02

GET
FOUR
FREE
BOOKS
(AN $18.00 VALUE)

AFFIX
STAMP
HERE

ZEBRA HOME SUBSCRIPTION
SERVICE, INC.
P.O. Box 5214
120 BRIGHTON ROAD
CLIFTON, NEW JERSEY 07015-5214

Part III

Autumn's Golden Splendor

Chapter 32

Like a bolt of lightning out of a stormy sky, Chad Morrow realized his own stupidity. He'd checked all the shipping lines except the branch office of the very line he worked for. It just proved to him that he was not thinking straight. It didn't please him to have to admit to himself that any woman could play such havoc with his usually sharp thinking.

Had it not been the Penbrook Lines that Pierre had booked their passage on to come here from France? Why he had not thought about that in the very beginning he'd never be able to explain to himself.

Damned if he could do one thing about it until the office opened in the morning! One thing for sure, and that was he'd be there the minute it opened and ask to check the list of passengers sailing on the same ship he himself would be taking day after tomorrow.

It was going to be an unbearably long night for someone with Chad's impatient nature, but he knew he'd have to endure it.

Since he had regained some of his ability to think more clearly, he reasoned that he might as well have a bath and a good meal. He was ready to sink his teeth in to a nice thick slice of beefsteak with a lot of rich brown juice.

When he stood in front of the mirror to give his brown hair a firm brushing, he had to admit that his clean-shaven face and a fresh white linen shirt made him much more presentable. He walked over to the bed to slip into his trim-lined gray flannel pants. Taking one last glance to see if his unruly hair was in place, he put on the gray pinstriped coat.

A man with Chad's unusual good looks and fine physique was bound to draw attention, and especially so when he appeared in a place like the elegant dining room of the Plantation House. The ladies stole fleeting glances and wondered why such a man would be dining alone; the men who observed him swagger into the room figured him to be a scoundrel there to attract the eyes of their ladies.

The pretty young miss serving as Chad's waitress was quivering with excitement as she watched the tall man take his seat. By the time she had served him his first glass of wine and taken his order, he was well aware that her name was Lorna. Chad tried to keep a smile from his face as he devoured his beefsteak, taking no notice of the admiring glances he was getting from the various ladies at the nearby tables.

It pleased Lorna to see him linger at the table after the meal to finish sipping his wine.

When he left the dining room, she was elated to see the handsome reward he left on the table to express his thanks for her services. He'd never know what that amount of money could do for her and her small baby she was struggling to raise alone.

She thought about the handsome gentleman whose name she'd never know who had enabled her to buy the medicine her ailing child needed. She blessed him from the bottom of her heart. Suddenly, she wished that she had not cheapened herself so that she'd so boldly flirted with him. But such a man as he was rarely visited the

Plantation House and she never expected such a night to happen again for a long time.

When she left the inn Lorna clutched the little pouch that carried the precious funds she'd earned for her long night's work. Her spirits soared as she walked through the darkness to her small cottage almost a half mile away.

Chad Morrow left the dining room and went directly to his room, unaware of the happiness he had created for the young woman who had served his meal. Only one woman consumed his thoughts tonight.

As he'd expected, the night was a long, restless one. He tossed and turned until sometime just before dawn; then he drifted off. Even then, he slept briefly and before seven he was ready to leave the bed. Once dressed he went down to the dining room for breakfast. An hour later he made his way to the office, approaching the door about the same time the clerk was unlocking it.

"'Morning, Jason," Chad addressed the clerk.

"Why, good morning to you, Mister Morrow," the young man greeted him as he turned around. "Didn't expect to see you until day after tomorrow."

"I need to check your list of passengers, Jason," Chad told him as he followed him into the office.

"Sure thing, Mister Morrow. I'll get them for you in just a minute."

Chad took a seat by the desk, privately telling himself that what he hoped to find on that list might not be there and he could be in for a big disappointment.

"Here it is, Mister Morrow," the clerk said, handing him the long sheet of paper.

He started scrutinizing the long list. Midway down the page there was no Renaud listed. The farther down the list he went, the more he felt disheartened.

Ironically, there almost at the end the Renauds were listed and his own name was the last name on the passenger list.

Handing the list back to Jason, he inquired about the Renauds, "Where are they staying while they wait to sail?"

"Give me just a minute and I can tell you." The clerk picked up a large black ledger. It took him only a second to tell Chad that they were quartered at the R and R Stables.

"You know where that is?"

"Sure do. It's a big country estate just outside New Orleans, owned and run for years by the Carrolls—Ronald and Renee. They are a highly respected New Orleans family. Something isn't wrong, is it?"

Chad gave a chuckle, "Hardly, Jason. In fact, everything is completely right now. I need to locate this family. I thank you very much, Jason!"

After Jason gave the directions to get to the R and R Stables, he had no trouble finding the impressive country place. A huge stone column sat on either side of the long drive off the main road, and a high arch extended from one column to the other with the estate's name.

He guided his carriage up the long drive lined with tall, slender poplar trees. As his carriage approached the front steps of the circling drive, it seemed to Chad that a very tranquil quiet surrounded the house for midmorning. He saw no one on the long portico with its white wicker settee and chairs. But suddenly from around the corner of the spacious two-story house came a young black boy offering to take charge of his carriage.

Chad returned the young lad's broad smile and gave him the full charge of his carriage. He'd ambled around the side of the carriage to mount the two steps leading up to the portico when he was met by the displeased face of Etienne Bernay charging out the front door.

"Well, Bernay—how are you?" Chad had a crooked grin on his tanned face, for he knew that the sight of him did not meet with Etienne's approval.

"Fine. If you're looking for Tiffany, she's not here. She and her mother have gone into the city to do some shopping."

"As you and she did yesterday?" Chad asked him. By the expression on Etienne's face, Chad suspected that Etienne had seen him. To prod at him, Chad inquired, "You did not hear my yell? I'm surprised!"

"No, Morrow, I did not hear you," Etienne replied, finding it hard to lie with Chad's gray eyes piercing him. The more he was around Morrow, the more he disliked him.

"What the devil are you about, Morrow?" Etienne asked as he walked up the step to take a seat in one of the wicker rockers.

"I'm about sitting here to wait for Tiffany to return," Chad said, making himself comfortable. "Now, it really isn't any of your business, is it, Etienne? And since you're in no position to object, then I think that would settle that once and for all!" Chad glared at him even though there was a hint of a smile on his mouth.

Anger seethed in Etienne at this bold, brash man. The thought of him having anything to do with Tiffany was abhorrent to him. His black eyes locked with Chad's as he muttered, "You're not good enough for Mademoiselle Tiffany, Morrow, and you know it!"

Chad broke into a gale of laughter. "I suppose *you* think you're the right man for her, eh?"

Etienne wished that he could have said yes, but he couldn't. Instead, he replied, "I haven't said that, but I know you're not!"

"Funny you should think that, Bernay. You and I hardly know one another, so I find it puzzling how you put your values on a person." A devious streak in Chad urged him to goad Bernay a little. "Now, I hope that Miss Tiffany has not been telling tales of mischief about me."

Etienne had never been a man of violence, but he was

247

now pushed to that point by the arrogant Chad Morrow. He felt his fists clench and was more than eager to slam them both into Morrow's smirking face.

Chad saw that the man was riled. He hoped that Bernay would make the first move so that he would be justified to defend himself.

But a commotion a short distance away pulled their attention to the road beyond, as a carriage approached the wide driveway gate.

Etienne was crestfallen to see that Tiffany and her mother were returning, but Chad was absolutely delighted to see that crown of glossy black hair blowing as the light winds whipped the long flowing tresses.

"Well, my wait was not in vain. There she is! See there, Bernay—patience and fortitude pay off. Remember that!"

Chapter 33

As the carriage came closer, the vision of Tiffany became clearer and clearer. Chad moved across the porch and down the steps.

Tiffany gave a soft gasp as she realized that the figure she spied was Chad Morrow, standing by the steps with strong legs slightly apart and his arms folded. That rugged face was turned in her direction and those eyes was staring at her.

She had to admit she was anxious to feel those powerful hands as they helped her down from the carriage as she knew he would.

Madame Renaud had only to glance over in her daughter's direction to know that she was delighted to see Chad Morrow waiting for her. A smile broke on her face just before the carriage came to an abrupt halt and Chad came rushing around to Tiffany's side to help her down. The young black boy assisted her mother, assuring her that he'd see to all her packages.

"Well, thank you, young Elrod," Charmaine said and smiled down at him. She handed him a small sack and told him, "I bought you a handful of those lemon drops you like."

The boy thanked her and scampered into the carriage

to gather up the packages while Madame Renaud moved on up the steps. She realized that neither Tiffany or Chad was aware of her presence.

It would have been impossible for Tiffany to disguise her joy, so she didn't try to as those two strong arms reached up to her. "Ah, Tiffany!" he greeted her, "What a beautiful sight you are!"

"Chad Morrow, what a surprise," she purred sweetly, returning his smile with one of her own.

"I hope it's a nice surprise for you, Tiffany."

She let her body sway leisurely next to his as they walked around the front of the carriage. "Oh, and here I figured that you were still back in New Madrid. I had no inkling that you were here in New Orleans."

His gray eyes were looking down at her, dancing over each and every lovely feature of her face. "My business in New Madrid is finished, so it's time for me to leave, Tiffany. I'm returning to London."

Her bright blue eyes sparkled with the brightness of a lively child as she said, "And I am returning to France!"

"And I can tell you are happy, Tiffany," he declared with a smile.

Neither Chad nor Tiffany had been aware of Charmaine's clever maneuver to urge Etienne to accompany her into the house, so that the two young people could enjoy the quiet solitude of the portico.

Charmaine had noticed Etienne glaring at Tiffany and Chad as they'd met by the side of the carriage. There was no question that he resented Morrow's presence. With a warm smile, she'd motioned to him to help her with the small packages in her arms that Elrod had not taken inside the house for her.

The black mood consuming Etienne was not good, she knew, and she felt the tenseness of the young man as he walked beside her into the house and down the hallway.

"I thank you, Etienne dear. Here, these two packages

are for your mother. Just a couple of little things I think she might be able to use. Perhaps you would be good enough to take them to her for me."

Etienne managed a weak smile. "I'll take them to her, Madame Renaud." He turned to mount the winding stairway and Charmaine watched the unhappy young man go up the steps as she removed her bonnet. She felt sorry for him, for if it was love for Tiffany he was feeling, he'd only suffer a broken heart.

She must have a talk with Pierre and very soon, she reminded herself. This could not be allowed to happen. Fate had placed them all in a situation that none of them could have anticipated years ago.

She took the time to straighten up her wisps of hair after she'd removed her bonnet. Looking at her reflection in the mirror she recalled another time and place so long ago. She had been right, she told herself, that day back in the spring when the two young people first exchanged glances in the park in Paris. Madame Renaud was a most romantic soul and she was convinced that once true lovers meet, nothing can ever change that love. That was the way it had been with her and Pierre. She felt that the same was true with Chad Morrow and Tiffany.

The feeling had been with her that day, she well recalled, when Tiffany had met her knight in shining armor.

It was almost an hour later that Tiffany finally mounted the steps to go up to her room. Her spirits were soaring. Chad had told her how he'd come to see her in New Madrid and had found the house deserted, and how he'd watched the riverboat go down the river carrying her away from him.

"I was devastated, love. You must believe me!" he declared. His words rang with such sincerity that she had to believe them. His eyes had adored her so when they'd talked and held hands as they'd sat there on the wicker settee all alone. She was grateful for her mother taking Etienne in tow so they might be by themselves.

He searched her face as he spoke of his plans and the business he had to attend to once he arrived back in London. But he told her, "I don't intend to be away from you too long, Tiffany love, once I get back to London. I shall be coming to Paris to find you. You've got to know I adore you. I've never felt about any woman as I feel about you."

"Oh, Chad I do so want to believe you," she sighed. He urged her never to doubt him or his love for her.

Before he left, he'd kissed her with such fierce ardor that the burning heat of him seemed to be consuming her. Now as she mounted the steps, her whole body felt flushed. That English devil had the most devastating effect on her and she might as well just accept it. All the foul names she'd called him and all the grand vows she'd made that he'd not do it all over again were useless once he came near her.

Anyone seeing her bounce up the steps and down the carpeted hall would have seen a very happy Tiffany Renaud. Etienne had cracked his door just slightly to watch her pass by. He, too, had to admit that the charms of Chad Morrow must play a certain magic on women. He even sensed that Morrow met with Madame Renaud's approval, or she would not have asked him to accompany her into the house so that Tiffany would have been left alone with Morrow.

He supposed that Monsieur Renaud shared her feelings. He'd mentioned, when they checked into the Plantation House, that it had been Morrow who directed them to the fine lodging house when they first arrived in New Orleans.

When Tiffany disappeared behind her bedroom door,

Etienne closed his door and paced the floor as he asked himself how he was to ever rid himself of the fever in his blood that Tiffany stirred.

On the other side of the wall, his mother heard the sound of Etienne's boots as he marched back and forth. Why was he so restless this afternoon? she wondered.

He had seemed content this morning when he escorted her back to her room after a pleasant stay out on the sunny veranda. She had been ready to have a rest and he had told her that he was going to enjoy the marvelous library downstairs. Renee Carroll had insisted that he do so whenever he liked.

Tasha had told him, "Well, you better make the most of your time there, Son, for we'll soon be leaving this wonderful place. It has been heavenly, hasn't it, Etienne?" Her warm, dark eyes had gazed up at her son, for she knew he was a bit awestruck by all this opulence. It had been obvious to Tasha that Tiffany was accustomed to such grandeur, so she was curious as to what awaited her and Etienne when they got to France. Could it be possible that Charmaine and Pierre lived in even grander surroundings than this?

Oh, she could only hope she'd made the right decision for her and her son by coming with her friends. But then how could she possibly refuse when Pierre was offering her and Etienne a future and New Madrid offered nothing?

Why, Etienne might now have a chance to be a grand gentleman like Pierre. Back in New Madrid, he would have worked from sunup to sunset just like his father and ended up with nothing more than a day-to-day existence.

No, she had made the right choice for both of them and someday Etienne would thank her for it. Oh, there were going to be many awkward times for him, but he was a smart young man and he could adjust to the new life they'd live in France. He would certainly have the help and support of Pierre. On that, Tasha knew she could depend!

She sat in her chair by the window and thought about the country estate Charmaine had told her about, where she and Etienne would be living. What contentment she would find if it was anything like this divine place! What care had gone into making these grounds such perfection with the laid-out flower beds and shrubs with the beautiful blendings of colors as the flowers blossomed. From this second story window she could see beyond the grounds surrounding the house. The fenced-in green pasture was there for her to see where the Carrolls' fine horses roamed around. When she looked in the opposite direction she could see the pond surrounded by graceful willows.

She could understand why Ronald and Renee felt such pride in their place. She would be sorry to have to leave all this to board a ship. The ocean was so desolate and lonely looking with its gray-green churning waters and endless horizon. She could never forget the horrible fury it could unleash without warning, as it had when she and Charmaine had been making their crossing when they were young women. The ship they were aboard was caught up in that turbulence. They never made their destination in Virginia but the strong, fierce winds tossed the *Sea Witch* miles south to the coast of Georgia.

Tasha wondered if Charmaine ever recalled the time when the two of them were in that strange place called Savannah, Georgia. She had not thought about that time until now that she was about to make another sea voyage. All of those times came back so vividly to her.

What a lifetime she had experienced since those days!

Now, Tasha mused, her son and Charmaine's daughter had reached the ages they had been back then when all this was happening. They would know those same heights of happiness and those same heartaches as they traveled the road of life.

A sudden shudder flooded Tasha, and she reached for the soft shawl Tiffany had purchased for her and draped it around her shoulders. As if a foreboding had come to her, Tasha felt a chill consume her small, frail body. Her fear was for her son and for Tiffany.

The vivacious Tiffany could be the most provocative coquette without even trying and her dear Etienne was a very unsophisticated person. Yet, she knew he was a very virile young man with the normal healthy sexual appetite. After all, he was Jacques's son. She'd figured long ago that he'd had his way with Sandra Michaels but this could not happen with Tiffany Renaud.

This was Tasha's great fear!

Chapter 34

As he traveled back to the Plantation House from the Carrolls' estate, Chad thought happily about meeting Tiffany for lunch tomorrow. The day after that would find them all aboard the ship carrying them back across the ocean. The last few months had been a bittersweet adventure for Chad in a lot of ways. To go back into the past as he had done to find it emerging with the present had been a little startling to Morrow.

When Chad got back to his room, he found himself in no hurry to go downstairs for an evening meal. He thought about all the things that had happened to him over the last six months. It had all started when he'd decided to go to Paris and see Madame St. Clair as his mother had requested. Now he could understand the same overwhelming impact his own father had experienced when he'd happened to meet Tiffany's mother for the first time on his riverboat almost three decades ago.

But a Frenchman by the name of Pierre Renaud had denied Cat the chance to claim his love for the beautiful Charmaine. Now, another man of French descent, Bernay, was hellbent that he, Chad, would not have Tiffany. But Etienne Bernay was not the man that Pierre Renaud had been back then. Etienne wouldn't interfere

256

with his plans to win the beautiful Tiffany. Chad would not allow it!

Chad figured that his sleep would be a peaceful one tonight; he was eager to have an early dinner so he could go to bed and get an early start in the morning. He had a couple of things to do before he met Tiffany for lunch.

Chad had always been a meticulous, calculating man about his business and his finances. He could show a magnificent degree of patience to attain what he wanted for himself. The same had been true in his personal life until Tiffany came on the scene. At that moment, a primitive instinct and wild impulse had arisen over which he seemed to have no control. He could not snap his fingers and instantly bring himself in line.

Tonight as his head hit the pillow, he'd decided that he was not going to wait until his business in London was finished and he traveled to France to ask Tiffany to be his wife. No, he'd not chance fate that long. He was going to ask her tomorrow at lunch and he was going to buy her the most magnificent ring the jeweler, Lazier, could offer him.

He smiled as he thought about the gem he would choose for her. It must be as rare and unique as Tiffany herself. No ordinary diamond would do, nor would a sapphire, even though that was what her lovely eyes reminded him of.

Tonight, he did not know what the gem would be—but if any jeweler in New Orleans could provide it for him, he knew that Paul Lazier was the man.

Chad Morrow and Pierre Renaud were two men sharing mutual thoughts this night about the women they loved. Pierre wanted to find something to present to his lovely wife for the sacrifices she'd made to help and support him as he went about his mission to help his half-brother's family. Not once had she complained about the hardships that she'd not been used to for many years. It was as if time had stood still for his beautiful Charmaine and she was that same hard working girl as she'd been when they'd first met.

Today, he'd spent a couple of hours looking for something worthy to express the depth of his gratitude. Ronald Carroll had suggested that he pay a visit to Paul Lazier's shop because the most exquisite gems coming into New Orleans could be seen there.

Pierre had taken Carroll's suggestion and stopped by the shop. He saw immediately that what Ronald had told him was true. The gems were magnificent, and many were flawless beauties. One ring took Pierre's eye and he was tempted to buy it immediately, but he told Lazier he would think about it. "I'll probably see you tomorrow, Monsieur Lazier. I shall sleep on this tonight. It is a most beautiful ring."

Pierre did think about that rare blue diamond all night, and he made his decision to return to the jeweler's shop and purchase it for Charmaine.

He had it all planned out about how he would present it to her the night they'd sail out of New Orleans to go homeward to France. It seemed the ideal time.

He was in grand spirits as he sat with the Carrolls that evening. They dined in the lavish dining room twinkling with all the cut crystal and reflecting candlelight. He applauded Renee Carroll that she always managed to run their palatial home with such perfection. Pierre appreciated the expertise of ladies like Charmaine and Renee. Without their ability to see that the numerous servants carried out their duties properly, all this would not be possible.

Pierre was too absorbed about the blue diamond and his plans for tomorrow to notice the withdrawn, sullen mood of Etienne during the dinner hour, but Tiffany noticed it. She decided that it had to be jealousy. He would surely be vexed at her when he found out that she was going to meet Chad for lunch tomorrow, but she could not be troubled by that. After all, Etienne had no claims on her!

Every time she glanced in his direction, he looked at her with a hurt look on his face as though she'd betrayed him. His petty, childish attitude quickly vexed Tiffany, so she ignored him the rest of the evening.

When the meal was over and the group left the dining room, Tiffany rushed to her mother to whisper in her ear that she'd like to be excused. "Chad is taking me out to lunch tomorrow, Maman, so I've some things I'd like to attend to. May I?"

"Of course, ma petite," Charmaine said and smiled.

Tiffany had graciously bid the others goodnight and scurried up the stairway as swiftly as she could so that Etienne could not catch up with her. She'd rushed so hastily up the steps and down the long hall that she was breathless by the time she went inside her room and closed the door.

The minute Chad's eyes opened to greet the new day, he knew it was going to be a grand and glorious one. The sun was bright and when he'd ambled over to look at the window, there was nothing but blue sky to greet him.

When he was dressed, he left his room to go downstairs for a couple of cups of coffee before departing from the Plantation House. By the time he had traveled into the city and made his way down the narrow street to Lazier's jewelry shop, the owner had just unlocked his door and was raising the shades at the windows.

Paul Lazier had only to look on the impressive figure of the man entering his shop to know that he had some gem he wished to purchase. Over the years that he'd dealt with people Paul knew the ones truly interested in buying his gems and those who just enjoyed wasting his time talking about the possible purchase of one. This one wanted to buy!

"Good morning, monsieur," Lazier greeted Chad eagerly as he ambled into the shop. "May I help you?"

Chad told him he hoped so, for he was looking for something unusual in a gem. Lazier surveyed the young man carefully and something about him intrigued the jeweler. He smiled as he inquired, "For a most unusual lady of exquisite beauty, n'est-ce pas?"

A sly smile creased Chad's face. He wondered if he was that obvious. "It is true, monsieur. She is a rare jewel."

"Then I have the gem for her. Please have a seat and I will bring out this gem for you to see." He could not wait in the hope that the other gentleman would return, even though he sensed that he was a man of means. Maybe he would return this afternoon eager to purchase the ring, but then maybe he wouldn't, so Lazier was not about to pass up this chance to show his exquisite ring to this young man.

From the safe, he lifted out the crimson velvet case holding the magnificent blue diamond encased in the gold mounting.

Moving back through the doorway into the front of his shop, Paul Lazier smiled. "Ah, monsieur, feast your eyes on this and tell me you've not seen anything to equal it."

In a dramatic slow gesture, Lazier opened the case to allow Chad's gray eyes to gaze appraisingly at the ring. The jeweler was not exaggerating about the ring. It was the most outstanding, gorgeous ring Chad had ever laid his eyes on.

"How much, Monsieur Lazier?" Chad asked him without blinking an eyelash.

Lazier quoted the price, expecting the young man to have grave second thoughts and sit there silently.

Chad pulled out a pouch from his coat pocket and laid a sizable sum there by the case. "My earnest money to assure you I want it. I shall return in a hour with the balance, monsieur. Do we have a deal?"

Paul nodded his head and chuckled excitedly, "We have a deal. I'll sign a bill of sale right now. Your name, monsieur?"

"Chad Morrow."

"Monsieur Chad Morrow. Monsieur, you are a man of exquisite taste and whoever the lovely lady is, she should be very happy, I would think," Lazier chuckled as he wrote out the bill of sale.

Chad laughed. "I shall hope so. One hour, monsieur."

Lazier was dazed at his good fortune this morning. Never had he expected to make such a quick sale on this particular piece of jewelry. It had not really troubled him that he might keep it in his possession for awhile, for he appreciated the magnificent beauty of the ring so much that he would have enjoyed just gazing upon it from time to time.

He went to the back of his shop to help himself to another cup of coffee while he awaited the return of Chad Morrow. He'd not finished the cup of coffee before the tall young man came striding back through the door with a big grin on his face.

Chad handed him the money and Lazier handed Chad the crimson case. "It's been a pleasure to do business with you, Monsieur Morrow. May my ring bring great happiness to you and to the one who wears it."

"I thank you, monsieur, and I shall hope so, too. Perhaps someday I shall be in your city again and I will have the need to see you to purchase another fine piece of jewelry," Chad declared as he tucked the case inside the pocket of his coat.

"Ah, monsieur, I shall hope so. You are leaving New Orleans?"

"Yes, I sail for London tomorrow, but I will be returning to this country one of these days. I—I have interests here."

"Good luck to you, young man," Lazier called to him as he strolled out the door. He watched the young man mount his carriage and a grand feeling washed over him as he thought about the gleam of happiness in some young lady's eyes when she first looked upon his magnificent ring.

He was glad this Monsieur Chad Morrow bought the ring instead of the older gentleman who'd come into his shop yesterday.

He guessed he was just a sentimental old fool, but he was not so old that he didn't recall that glorious state of young romantic love.

He knew this young man was going to give the ring to the young lady who'd stolen his heart. Surely he must worship her to buy such an expensive gift!

Chapter 35

Tiffany took special care with her toilette and the gown she'd picked to wear for her luncheon date with Chad. She knew the color was becoming to her, for the dressmaker had told her she should wear this particular shade of blue to flatter her blue eyes.

The gown enhanced the sensuous curves of Tiffany's young body without being too risqué. The scooped neckline was just low enough to flatter Tiffany's satiny soft flawless flesh without exposing the fullness of her rounded breasts.

The soft silk sleeves fastened at the wrists with pearl buttons. The same dainty pearl buttons lined the front of the bodice that molded to her figure so perfectly. The soft silk flowed gently as she walked.

To get the effect she wanted when she put on the matching bonnet, she'd pulled the back of her hair back with a comb so the long cluster of curls would fall down her back instead of around her shoulders. Only tiny wisps of curls teased her ears. She carried white lace gloves and a blue reticule.

If she had not been satisfied with the way she looked, her mother and Renee Carroll assured her of her exquisite appearance when she entered the parlor.

"Tiffany, it is almost sinful for anyone to be as beautiful as you," Renee declared, giving a soft, light-hearted laugh. "Is it not true, Charmaine?"

Charmaine had to agree with her friend. "You do look stunning, cherie! Madame Moreau was right. That color is very flattering on you. We shall have to get you another gown in that shade when we get back to Paris, I think."

Tiffany thanked them for their generous compliments as she took a seat to wait for Chad to arrive.

Soon the house servant ushered him into the parlor. He looked quite handsome in his fine-tailored deep gray coat and pants with a pearl gray waistcoat. Tiffany stared up at him, admiring how elegant he looked. Why, he was as debonair as any of the Frenchmen who'd been her suitors back in Paris!

Maybe there were many sides of Chad Morrow, she was beginning to think as she appraised him there in the Carrolls' parlor.

After a brief moment of conversation, Chad and Tiffany took their leave. Renee Carroll was the first to speak as the young pair left the room and strolled toward Chad's carriage. "My, they make a very striking couple, Charmaine!"

Another pair of eyes was observing the young couple walk down the path edged with boxwoods. His black eyes did not like what he saw. He did not like the sight of Morrow's arm braced around Tiffany's waist as the two of them walked side by side. He seethed at the sight of Tiffany's lovely face smiling so warmly as she looked up at Morrow. That smug, self-assured grin on Morrow's face ignited hate in Etienne for the man by Tiffany's side. He had no right to be there!

He clenched his fists, wishing he could slam them into Chad's face. Instead, he slammed them into the facing of the window. In a frenzy, he turned away from the window to pace angrily across the room.

He would be glad to see tomorrow come so that they would be sailing away from this place and leaving Morrow behind. Etienne had no way of knowing that they would not be leaving him behind, for Morrow would be sailing with them all the way—at least as far as London.

Tasha was perplexed by her son's snapping tone when he'd visited her room, but she didn't allow it to disturb her, because lately these moods seemed to come upon him quite often. Being a practical woman, she'd decided that Etienne was a man now and he'd have to learn to deal with life on his own terms. She was not going to coddle him.

The Renauds were enjoying the company of their host and hostess on this last day before they sailed, so neither of them concerned themselves with the sulking Etienne who roamed around the estate like a lost soul. This did not exactly lighten the black mood he lingered in during the morning and the afternoon.

He did not join the group as they all enjoyed a delightful lunch out on the roofed veranda. Tasha made some feeble excuse for her son's absence.

Every hour that went by and Tiffany had not returned to the house found Etienne more and more irritated. He was angry with the Renauds for allowing their daughter to be with that man alone for such a long time when the clock struck three in the afternoon and she had still not returned.

From the moment Chad woke up this morning and went to Lazier's shop to find the perfect gift for Tiffany, he knew it was going to be the most glorious day. When he'd arrived at the Carrolls' to pick her up and found her in the parlor waiting for him, looking so breathtakingly beautiful, he was sure of it.

265

They'd both seemed bewitched by the golden splendor of the early autumn day as they'd traveled toward the city. Chad had suddenly decided to change his plans as to where they were to have lunch. It was the perfect day to dine out on the terrace of the Plantation House instead of the little tearoom where he'd originally planned to take her.

It seemed that other people had the same idea, for the terrace area was crowded when they'd arrived—but they were ushered to a secluded table where a giant bougainvillaea bush filled with purple blossoms gave them a certain degree of privacy which Chad liked.

"Oh, Chad—this is a beautiful place. We didn't come here when we stopped here before," Tiffany declared as they were comfortably seated by the waiter.

"I know. There was not enough time, Tiffany. Remember?"

"My father was so eager to leave to get to New Madrid."

Chad wondered just how much Tiffany knew about her father's plans for the Bernay family once they got to Paris. "I am to assume his plans were completed and that is why you are now returning to France?"

"I guess you could say that. My parents do not exactly inform me of all their business," she replied with a smile. "We are taking Tasha and Etienne back to France with us so my father can see to them and help them. Is that what you mean?"

"I guess so, love. I guess that's it," Chad said, letting his eyes dance over her lovely face. He loved seeing her in the kind of mood she was in today. This was the Tiffany he'd first spied in Paris who had won his heart instantly, the minute he saw her in the park.

But he could not resist asking, "Will they live with you and your family?"

"Oh, no! They will live at my father's country place

just outside Cherbourg. That is where my brother lives."

This eased Chad's mind. A big, broad grin came to his face. "Your father is a most generous, kindhearted man."

"Yes, he surely is that!"

All the time they enjoyed the delectable light lunch there on the terrace, Chad was thinking about the ring nestled in the inside pocket of his frock coat. Somehow, this did not seem like the right place to give it to her. Yet, he dared not rile her by suggesting the privacy of his suite. Everything had been too perfect up to now.

When the waiter came by their table carrying an array of delicately decorated petits fours, he suggested that they have a glass of wine to complete the meal and Tiffany agreed.

As Tiffany nibbled on one of the petits fours and reached to her glass of wine for a sip, a butterfly swooped down out of the bougeinvillaea blossom to land on the rim of her glass. Taking a flick at the butterfly, she brushed her glass and it fell to the table.

"Oh, no!" she gasped as the whole glass of wine flowed on her lap.

Chad offered her his napkin, but suggested that they go to his suite so she could get some water on the large, damp stain. "It's such a beautiful gown! We'll take care of that, love."

It seemed to Chad that fate had stepped in to help him by tipping that glass of wine at just the right moment.

Hastily, they went to his suite. Tiffany was holding the folds of her skirt so no one could see the huge spot of dampness in the center. Once they were inside the room, Chad ordered her to remove the gown.

"Do *what?*" she shrieked.

"If you don't want a circle there on that lovely silk gown, you'd better do as I say!" He turned to look at her indignant face. A grin slowly creased his face. "It isn't as

267

if I've not seen you in your undergarments before—and a lot less. It isn't going to shock me and I don't think it's going to shock you, love."

As she fumbled and fumed with the gown, Chad walked over to assist her. "Quit wiggling, honey. Let me help you." In short order he had the gown unfastened and was slipping it down to her waist. He casually walked away to allow her to step out of it so he could wet a towel.

"Give it to me," he told her. Rubbing the stained gown vigorously, he glanced up at her as she sat on the bed watching him. He took the gown out on the small balcony to hang it over a chair so the air could dry it.

"Oh, I hope it doesn't set," Tiffany sighed dejectedly as he reentered the room. "I love that gown!"

He walked over to her with a warm smile on his face and bent low to kiss her lips. "If it's ruined, we'll get you another just like it, love."

No man's lips had such a devastating effect on Tiffany as Chad's did. She felt herself already flushed by the soft, gentle touch of them as he'd kissed her. He raised up to gaze down on her face and what he saw there pleased him. He saw passion in those sapphire blue eyes. He saw those half-parted lips asking for more of his kisses. He could hardly refuse her.

"Oh, Tiffany, love! Do you know how much I adore you?" He flung aside his coat, forgetting all about the precious ring he had in the pocket. His hand caressed her face as his other hand busily unbuttoned his fine white linen shirt.

She purred like a little kitten, "Do you truly adore me, Chad?"

"God—what do I have to do to convince you? I half broke my neck to get on the next boat to get down that Mississippi to catch up with you and then I went all over New Orleans to try to find you and your family."

She'd watched him hastily removing all his clothing as

he'd talked with a sly, devious smile on his face. "Well, you found me, Chad Morrow." Her jet-black hair was fanned out on the pillow and her eyes were boldly challenging him.

He met her eyes with the same bold challenge as he slowly bent down to meet her waiting lips. Now his hands moved with expertise to remove her undergarments.

His searing lips gently trailed down her throat to the tip of her jutting breast. His tongue teased and taunted as he listened to her sweet moans of pleasure. He felt the surge of her satiny flesh pressing against him and his passion soared. He wanted no part of her to not know the touch of him before this day was over. Today, he was determined to forever make her his woman. No other man could ever claim her once he loved her as he intended to do this day.

Tiffany found herself swept by the force and the power of Chad's fierce love-making and now she knew why Etienne paled in comparison when he'd kissed her that day. Suddenly, she felt herself leaning over his firm muscled body and looking down into his gray eyes. "Love me, Tiffany. Love me as I love you," he boldly dared her.

She bent down to meet his lips and his strong hands guided her hips so he could enter the velvety softness of her. She gasped from the strange sensation she'd never known before. He felt the quaking of her body against his.

"Oh, God, Chad! Oh God!"

He gave a husky laugh, "Ah, Tiffany, it is good with us—yes? I could have told you that a long time ago."

He felt the mounting passion of his body and Tiffany's seemed to be matching him. How could he make time stand still for just a few moments longer?

He gasped, "Tiffany—I love you! I love you like I've never loved before!"

She felt the full force and fury of his blazing passion penetrating her and she surrendered herself to it, letting it consume her.

Her fingernails dug into his neck as she held on to him and her body clung to him as she gasped breathlessly.

He heard her whisper softly, "Oh, Chad—Chad, I love you." That was all he needed to hear to make him the most happy man in the world.

As he held her close to him as they both descended slowly back to the world of reality, he planted featherlike kisses on her damp forehead and face and he knew that nothing could ever take her away from him. He would not allow it. Tiffany was his. She was meant to be his.

He lay there now, holding her soft body in his arms and the craziest thought paraded through his mind. A vision of old Cat Morrow came to him and he seemed to be telling Chad not to let her go.

Privately, Chad lay there vowing that he'd never let her go. She was his!

Chapter 36

Chad Morrow had always figured himself to be a clever fellow but after this afternoon he was not too sure. He'd gone to the jeweler this morning and laid out a small fortune to impress his ladylove of his affection and devotion. It wasn't until he was traveling back toward the Plantation House, after seeing Tiffany back to the Carrolls', that it dawned on him that he'd never given her the exquisite ring.

He shook his head in dismay about his stupidity. He'd been so bewitched by her love-making that the ring was forgotten.

When she'd finally roused from the cozy circle of his arms, she declared that she had to get back home, for the clock was striking five.

"Mon Dieu, Maman and Papa will be furious at me, Chad. You must bring me back quickly. I don't want to put them in a foul mood their last night at the Carrolls'."

He'd never seen her look so devilishly cute as she did scurrying out of the bed with her nude body moving so hastily to get her clothes on. Chad leaped out of bed, dressed, and assured her that he'd get her back to the Carrolls' and take the blame for her late arrival.

He watched as she stroked her hair into place with her

long slender fingers and placed the perky bonnet just so on her head.

"As beautiful as ever," he teased her. "I adore you, Tiffany Renaud. I hope you'll never forget that or ever doubt it."

She whirled around from the mirror to smile at him. "And I adore you too, Chad Morrow, but then I suppose that you may have guessed that by now."

A crooked grin came to his face as he teased, "Well, I'd certainly hoped so."

She turned back to the mirror to finish tying the bow of her bonnet. "You know so!"

He liked the way she snuggled close to him when they rode in the carriage all the way to the Carrolls', and he wondered if she was feeling as he was about the fact that they'd shortly have to say goodbye and part company. After the intimate closeness they'd shared this afternoon, he did not want to part from her even for one long evening.

When he had told her goodbye at the front door and mounted back up in his carriage to return to the Plantation House alone, he was already feeling the void of her not being by his side.

As he took a backward glance toward the house, he saw someone watching in one of the upstairs bedrooms. He'd wager it was Bernay spying on them. Angrily, he drove away. It was later that he realized the ring was still in his pocket. The effect of their passion always seemed to drive him a little bit crazy!

Chad Morrow was not the only man Tiffany drove a little crazy. Etienne had only to look at her from afar to be affected by her. Oh, how he yearned to hold her and kiss her as he'd done that stormy day in the cave.

He'd seen Tiffany when she'd finally returned. She'd been gone over five hours with Morrow.

He rushed out of his room the minute he saw Chad drive away. He stood there on the second landing to see Tiffany rushing down the hall to mount the stairway. The radiance there on her face was enough to tell Etienne that her mood was the very opposite of his.

She did not notice him until she reached the second floor. She stopped suddenly when she saw him standing there. "Oh, Etienne, I didn't see you," she casually exclaimed as she proceeded to go on by him. This stabbed Etienne that she had no time even to linger for a moment with him.

"Are you in a hurry, Tiffany?" he questioned her, but Tiffany did not detect the tenseness in his tone.

She said lightly, "I am. I'm getting in late and I must change for the evening meal. So if you'll excuse me, Etienne—I must go." She'd made a point of holding her reticule in front of her gown, for the stained spot was still there.

"You look very dressed up, Tiffany."

"But I wish to change, Etienne, so please excuse me."

"You didn't seem to be in such a rush to get home when you were with Morrow, Tiffany," he muttered to her.

His attitude and his tone of voice displeased her as she took a couple of steps backwards so she could stand before him and look at his face. He sounded like a sulking child. She stood there in front of him with fire sparking in her blue eyes as she spoke. "I was in no rush as long as I was with Chad, and how I spend my time with him is none of your business, is it Etienne?"

But before he could answer her, she'd lifted her skirt to rush on down the hallway.

He realized that he had been put in his place. He had to ask himself when he'd quit playing the fool.

When the group gathered for dinner that evening,

everyone seemed to be in a festive mood except her son, Tasha noticed. Why could he not enjoy this good fortune that had come their way? she wondered.

It bothered her to think that Charmaine and Pierre would consider him ungrateful when he acted as he did tonight. Tiffany had been thoughtful enough to gather her a lovely bouquet of white asters and bring them to her room this late afternoon. The girl charmingly confessed that she had kept one of the blossoms to wear in her hair tonight because her gown had white flowers on it.

Tasha thought she looked so attractive in her daisy-splashed gown with its black background trimmed with white lace ruffling. The white aster pinned in her jet-black hair was most flattering.

Tasha sat in the candlelit dining room and observed the people around her. Ronald and Renee Carroll and Charmaine and Pierre were such perfectly matched couples. It was no wonder that their marriages had been so happy and lasted through the years.

She had dared not confess to her dear friend Charmaine that she and Jacques had not retained that same glow of romance throughout their marriage. Having always considered herself ugly and unattractive as a young lady, Tasha was overwhelmed by the attentions of the dashing Jacques Bernay. When he'd asked her to marry him she could not believe her good fortune.

That romantic glow had lasted when they'd arrived in New Madrid and after their first child was born during that terrible disaster. Tasha had always considered the birth of her daughter a miracle, and she named her Charmaine Genevieve because she felt she owed Charmaine so much and Pierre's aunt had been so kind to her and Jacques. Never had she met a lady so generous of heart as Genevieve Renaud, Pierre's aunt. During that horrible time a bond had been fused and they comforted and supported one another during those next terrible months when the earth still shook and frightened them.

But when Pierre finally found Charmaine many miles away from New Madrid where she'd wandered aimlessly like many of the stunned, dazed people of the region, he was obsessed with only one thought and that was getting Charmaine out of the area.

A week later, they'd gone down river toward New Orleans. From there, they'd returned to France. Tasha and Jacques had received word that they had married and were living in Paris.

How fast time had gone by, Tasha thought as she sat there looking at her two dear friends. A vast ocean had separated them and ten years had passed them by suddenly. Then another ten years had come and gone.

Death took her beautiful daughter before she celebrated her sixteenth birthday, but she had a lively young son which softened the blow of losing her daughter.

But something happened to Jacques after the death of his daughter. She could never figure out what it was that turned him so politely cool toward her. Tasha's practical mind reasoned that it was nothing she had done, for she was the same loving wife she'd always been, so the problem was Jacques. Whatever that was he carried it to his grave.

She'd thought of many things, and now she was convinced that one of her ideas had been right. Why would he have finally told Etienne to seek out Pierre Renaud's help if things became too much for him to handle?

Tasha felt that at the end of Jacques's life he became a very embittered man, feeling that he had been cheated while Pierre, his half-brother, was enjoying the luxuries of life that he should have shared.

She could understand and sympathize with him, but then Jacques had never been bold enough or allowed his pride to demand anything. Often, she wondered what would have happened if Jacques had marched in to seek an audience with old Etienne Renaud and told him he was his son just as much as Pierre was.

Whatever troubled Jacques those last few years, he had shut her out. She had been lonely, helpless to do anything to comfort him.

But Tasha felt no guilt. She'd given all her love and devotion to Jacques all the years they spent together. Now that she'd been given a second chance at life—thanks to her two dear friends, Charmaine and Pierre—she was going to do a few things she wanted to do. Etienne was a grown man now, so he must make his own way.

Once she got to France she was going to pursue her first love—her sketching and drawing. She could not imagine a more delightful setting to do that than the beautiful countryside outside Cherbourg. Already, she could envision the endless rows of the vineyards and the lush, verdant valleys of the wine country. From the things Charmaine had told her, she already had a vision of the old stone two-story house she would be living in.

Maybe her son was not excited about their new life in France, but Tasha was elated. She was suddenly feeling very selfish. Maybe it was because she had been so close to death before Charmaine and Pierre arrived. They had given her a chance to live, along with the incentive. Tasha had not felt so alive in a long, long time and her son was not going to dampen her spirits about the new life she was anticipating.

Only one thing dampened Pierre Renaud's last evening with his friends, Ronald and Renee Carroll: once he and his family were back in France, Pierre knew many years could go by before he'd come this way again. Maybe he never would. But he'd extended an invitation to the Carrolls to come to Paris in the spring to visit him and Charmaine, and Ronald had accepted his invitation.

Pierre concealed his deep disappointment that some scoundrel had purchased the ring he'd gone back to buy for Charmaine. He was absolutely dumbfounded that such an exquisite, expensive ring had been sold in less than twenty-four hours since he was in the shop.

Renaud was used to getting what he wanted and he wanted that ring. If he could have found out the gentleman's name who'd purchased the ring that morning he would have made him an offer he'd have found hard to turn down. But of course, Lazier would never have told him the name of the man. The only information Lazier would tell him was that the gentleman did not live in New Orleans.

What really riled Renaud was that he could have had the ring if only he'd not hesitated and had purchased it the afternoon he'd first seen it. So the gift he'd hoped to give his wife would have to wait now until he returned to Paris for right now, nothing he would see could measure up to that magnificent ring.

A second choice would never do for his beautiful Charmaine. She deserved the very best and he would settle for no less.

Chapter 37

Chad arrived much earlier than the passengers who'd booked passage on the Penbrook ship, the *Bonnie Belle*. As the shipline's agent, Chad was always furnished with very comfortable quarters. When he was shown to his cabin and went about the chore of getting himself settled in, he thought about Tiffany. She should find her own quarters on this ship more pleasing than those on the *Majestic Queen*. The *Bonnie Belle* was a more luxurious ship sailing under the Penbrook flag.

Chad had seen the passenger list and a tremendous number of passengers were leaving the port of New Orleans to cross the Atlantic. Chad figured by the time they made two more port stops before the ship moved into its eastward route toward England, the ship would be filled to capacity.

The sun was not up when Chad had boarded the ship but now, an hour later, its first rays were gleaming over the waters of the bay and a brisk breeze gave a slight autumn chill. Chad looked out the small window of his cabin to see that passengers were now coming across the wharf to board the ship. But there were no signs of the Renaud party yet.

Chad was nervous about just where he wanted to keep

the expensive ring he'd purchased for Tiffany until he could find the right opportunity to present it to her. He did not want to carry it around with him nor did he feel safe to leave it in the cabin. In the end, Chad decided to keep the ring on his person.

He didn't have too long to wait before he saw the dignified Pierre Renaud appear with his lovely silvery-blonde wife on one arm and his beautiful black-haired daughter on the other. Behind them, Etienne Bernay accompanied his diminutive mother whose step seemed to be fairly lively for one who had been so sick. She seemed to be keeping up with her long-legged son's stride.

He watched Tiffany's pretty head turning from one direction to another, and he wondered if she might be seeking to spot him in the vast sea of faces milling around the deck. A smile broke on his face as he sat there watching her. Dear God, what a vision she was just to watch! He thought about those rapturous moments they'd shared yesterday. He found himself aching to hold her again as he'd held her yesterday.

Now that he'd seen her and knew that she was aboard, he returned to his cabin. He had a lot of business to catch up on and letters to write so he could place them aboard the faster clipper ship that would arrive in London sooner than the *Bonnie Belle*.

By the time the afternoon was over, Chad realized that his funds had taken a severe beating over the last few months. He was glad that he'd left the funds with his solicitor months ago to acquire the property he'd just recently managed to purchase.

Now that he'd taken the time to take stock of his extravagant ventures, he realized that he had overextended himself. Emotion and sentiment had prompted him to have his father's old riverboat restored, though he knew it would never repay him in funds Bickford would make when he started making the runs up the river.

He sat there with a grin on his face as he thought about how easily he'd given way to the impulse to buy Tiffany such an expensive ring. Dear Lord, he had really taken leave of his senses lately! Time you come back to reality, Morrow, he silently chided himself.

How far he'd strayed from his well-beaten path and the careful way he'd managed his affairs for well over five years! He grinned, thinking that it was a damned good thing that he had lived so frugally all those years so that he could afford this rash way he'd been spending his hard-earned money.

Chad came to the sudden realization that he must take leave of this spellbinding state he'd been in since he'd lost his heart to Tiffany Renaud. He was no Pierre Renaud with wealth and power. If Tiffany loved him, she'd have to accept him for what he was and what he could afford to give her.

Whether he wanted to or not, he had to turn his thoughts back to his job for Penbrook and Tiffany would have to accept that, too.

There in his cabin he decided that he'd been caught up in the fury of a summer storm and his emotions had been ruling his head as well as his heart. But summer was over now and he had to face his everyday responsibilities.

He closed the ledgers and placed them back in the desk drawer. Now it was time to shift his attentions to the reports the captain of the *Bonnie Belle* had turned over to him when he'd come aboard. He became so engrossed in the reading of the reports that he did not leave his cabin that evening and had his dinner sent in.

The absence of Chad all evening left Tiffany a little perplexed and puzzled, for she was so sure he would have made a call at her parents' cabin as soon as possible. When she did not see his towering figure emerge for the evening meal, she was devastated. Had he not sailed on this ship? she wondered.

She yanked the pins from her long hair impatiently. Her anger mounted when she thought about how she'd allowed that handsome devil to seduce her again yesterday, and now today he'd suddenly disappeared. What was it with Chad Morrow? She would have figured that he would be by the railing to meet her, especially after the intimate interlude they'd shared yesterday afternoon. But no—that seemed not to be the way it worked with Chad.

As she sat there, thoughtfully stroking her long hair with the brush, she recalled the times they'd made love. Each time, Chad had disappeared for several days or weeks before he had the urge to see her again.

Well, she thought to herself, maybe she should just make him wait a long, long time before he enjoyed the pleasure of her kisses. When they next met, she'd not be so eager to surrender to him. She'd not be his puppet she decided.

There was always Etienne, who would be more than willing to escort her around the ship's deck or keep her company in the evenings.

Tomorrow, she would forget about Chad Morrow and spend her time with Etienne. If Chad happened to come around, she'd treat him with coolness. Just maybe he'd learn to be a little more attentive in the future.

He was not the only man in the world. She knew that Etienne found her very attractive and desirable. There was something else she knew about Etienne, and that was that he wanted to make love to her. His kisses that day in the cave had told her that.

The next day she not only encouraged Etienne's attentions, but accepted them when he invited her for a walk during the afternoon when the sun was the brightest.

During the afternoon walk, Tiffany found she needed her light woolen cape to be comfortable and Etienne wore his coat. She remarked to him that it seemed strange that just a few days away from the mild New Orleans' climate, the weather should be so different.

Etienne did not know what had brought about the sudden change in Tiffany, but he did not care, for she was walking with him and smiling up at him as they strolled along the deck. The only thing that could possibly disturb their pleasant promenade would be the appearance of Chad Morrow.

Every now and then Etienne would glance over his shoulder to see if he saw the tall Englishman. He guided Tiffany toward a cozy little corner where they were not in sight of the deck hands and other people strolling along the deck.

When they were comfortably shielded from the strong wind, Etienne laughed, "Tell me, Tiffany, does France have harsh, cold winters?"

"Not as cold as your New Madrid winters from what Maman has told me. I could not know, Etienne," she smiled.

"No, I suppose you couldn't," he said, looking down at her with his dark eyes so warm with affection for her. He wished it could always be so nice when the two of them were together. She had the hood of her cape pulled up over her head and she looked like an adorable child. There was a lot of child in Tiffany, he realized. She was so guileless about so many things, even though she'd lived in a far more sophisticated world than he had. Maybe she'd had many young French suitors back in Paris, but Etienne believed that she had no inkling of the hellish torment she put a man through—just by a certain look in her eyes or the feisty wiggle of her hips when she walked.

Etienne knew that Sandra Michaels did those things just to drive a man crazy, but Tiffany was not like Sandra. Sandra's was an act but with Tiffany it was as natural as breathing.

He was tempted to snuggle her close to him and kiss

her, but he dared not give way to the urge pounding so crazily within him. Instead, he asked, "Are you cold? If you are, we'll go back to the cabin."

"I am just fine, Etienne," she said, taking his hand in hers. "You're sweet, Etienne, and so thoughtful."

Her gesture flustered him, for the mere touch of her hand flamed his desires that he was trying so desperately to keep under control. "You make it easy for someone to be that way with you, Tiffany."

She gave a soft little gale of laughter. But just as suddenly, Tiffany's mood changed. A strange feeling engulfed her like one of the waves there in the ocean, and she felt the heat of a pair of eyes watching them. A devious idea struck her.

Looking up at Etienne in the most seductive way, with her lips half-parted and inviting, she purred softly, "Kiss me, Etienne!"

So urgent was her plea that he could not refuse her and he bent down to let his lips meet hers. But he sensed that she did not wish him to linger there, so he pulled back.

"We should get back to the cabin, Etienne," she stammered, as she moved slightly away from him. He shook his head, agreeing with her, for he was in a state of utter confusion. He certainly didn't trust himself after what had just happened.

As they walked along the deck toward their quarters, Tiffany could not shake the feeling of those watchful eyes. She felt they were still watching every move she made.

Those cold gray eyes blazing with silver fire were Chad Morrow's. After being sequestered in his cabin for two days and nights, going over piles of paperwork, he had finally emerged for a breath of fresh air. Tonight, he had intended to seek out Tiffany.

283

But when his eyes caught the sight of her strolling arm in arm with young Bernay, he figured that she had not missed his company too much. But what galled him was the kiss he'd seen them share.

That damned little vixen! Lucky for her that he had not been closer, for he wasn't sure what he might have done! Lucky for both her and Bernay! He'd turned hastily to go back to his cabin. Calling the cabin boy into his quarters, he quickly scribbled a note to the captain of the ship who'd invited him to join him for dinner this evening. Chad suddenly decided to accept the invitation.

The ring that he'd carried so close to his heart all the time he'd boarded the ship was flung carelessly in his valise.

If he had not been on the high seas, he would have taken the ring back to Lazier in hopes of getting back the small fortune he'd spent on it.

Tiffany Renaud was a fickle-hearted filly and he'd played the fool!

Chapter 38

Tasha didn't figure she had to always have an escort to take a simple walk around the deck. Through her window of the cabin she could see a bright sun shining and she saw nothing wrong with taking a brief stroll by herself. Charmaine or Etienne could not always be expected to accompany her, she decided. The strength was back in her legs now and she desired to feel independent once again. She'd never relied on others as she had the last few months of her life, and she didn't like it!

With the warm woolen shawl draped around her small shoulders, she left the cabin. She saw no reason why she should disturb Charmaine to tell her where she was going.

When she had climbed the steps and moved out on the deck, she found that the bright sun was deceiving, for the wind had a bite to it that she had not expected. Her walk was probably going to be a short one, she decided. But as she looked around the deck it was obvious that a lot of the other passengers had the same idea, for the deck was alive with strolling couples. There were also single ladies like herself walking along, so Tasha did not feel ill at ease.

At the far end of the deck she saw the black head of her son with Tiffany by his side and she smiled, thinking that he would be shocked to know that she'd ventured out of her cabin alone.

She found the winds much stronger there by the railing so she moved back away from it. The structure of the ship acted as a buffer and she found this more to her liking.

A deep voice announced the presence of Captain Bergson coming up behind her. "Well, Madame Bernay—nice to see you out enjoying the fresh sea air. Nothing like it to invigorate a person," he declared.

"I'm hoping so, Captain Bergson."

The jovial, husky seaman assured her that by the time they arrived in England she'd see that what he was telling her was the truth. "Why, I'd swear your cheeks are already rosier."

She smiled, knowing he was trying to be nice. She appreciated his effort to make her feel better. "I'll take your word for that."

She found herself falling into the pace of his slow, unhurried stride as the two of them moved on down the deck. "This will be a pleasant crossing," he told her. "You will be arriving in England before the cold weather sets in."

"I'm happy to hear that, Captain, for I must confess my last crossing of the Atlantic ended in a frightful experience," Tasha told him.

"That right, Madame Tasha. Tell me—what happened?"

"Our ship was caught up in an awful storm off the east coast just before we were due to dock in Virginia and we were swept southward many miles away. I felt lucky to be alive, for many lost their lives."

"Oh, mercy ma'am—glad you made it. When was this?"

"Well, Captain Bergson, that was a number of years ago, back in 1810."

Captain Bergson assured her that ships were built much sturdier these days, but he also admitted to her that no one had more respect for the sea than he had. "She can be a treacherous lady. But we'll have a smooth sailing this trip, ma'am. I feel sure of it and I don't always feel that way."

By now they were turning a corner which provided a recessed area that was completely sheltered from the wind blowing across the deck. Captain Bergson figured it might be the spot to linger a moment before he took his leave from the nice lady. Duty called him to excuse himself.

But it seemed that the spot was already occupied by one of his passengers. He recognized the silver-haired artist immediately. "Well, good afternoon, Reuben. Finding an interesting scene to sketch this afternoon?"

"Ah, Capitaine, I usually find a picture I wish to get on my pad here," he said and laughed. Tasha stared at the face of the man standing before them with his silver-gray hair growing down to the collar of his faded shirt. A beard covered his face, along with a bushy mustache that matched his bushy eyebrows. But below those brows were the most alive, twinkling black eyes Tasha had ever seen.

"Madame Bernay, may I introduce you to Reuben Grodin. I think Reuben sails with me just to paint his magnificent pictures of the ocean."

"It is nice to meet you, Monsieur Grodin," Tasha replied.

"Ah, my pleasure, Madame Bernay. What Capitaine Bergson says is true. That and the fact that I must travel to New York once a year."

Grodin noticed how the winds seemed to be whipping the tiny lady's shawl and suggested that they move into his cozy corner. Tasha eagerly moved to the shelter, for the winds seemed to be cutting through the skirt of

287

her gown.

"More comfortable, isn't it?" Reuben asked her.

"Yes, it is." Standing so close to the man she could not resist asking him if she might see his sketching on the pad. When she did view them she saw the talent there. "Oh, Monsieur Grodin, these are magnificent!"

Captain Bergson smiled as he told her that Reuben's paintings hung in the galleries of London, Paris and New York. "I tell you this because Reuben here is such a modest fellow that he would have never told you."

"Ah, Capitaine—I need only to hear Madame praise my work to be happy. That is what inspires me."

"I apologize that I did not recognize the work of such a great artist, but it has been a long, long time since I've had the pleasure of visiting an art gallery. I used to go when I lived in England but that was long ago."

Grodin smiled warmly. "But you still appreciate the effort when you see it—yes?"

"Oh, yes, I do. In fact, when I was younger it was a great desire of mine to paint my own pictures like the ones I saw in the gallery in London," she confessed to him.

"Then, madame—what is stopping you, eh?" His eyes twinkled as they boldly challenged her.

She broke into a smile. "Absolutely nothing, I guess."

The two of them joined in laughter. The captain figured that Madame Bernay was enjoying the company of Reuben Grodin so much that she would not mind if he excused himself.

Tasha lingered in the company of Reuben Grodin and when she finally told him she must leave, he insisted that he escort her to her cabin. When they arrived at her cabin door, Reuben made a point of telling her, "If your party stays in London before traveling on to France, it would be my great pleasure to take you on a grand tour of London galleries, madame."

"And I can assure you I would enjoy that so much, Monsieur Grodin."

Reuben took her hand in his as he said to her, "Ah, let it be Tasha and Reuben. That is much nicer—yes?"

"Yes, Reuben—it is!"

They said their goodbyes and Tasha went into her cabin knowing that she had met a most unusual man. She had not felt so alive and excited in a long, long time. It reminded her of another time and place when she'd first met the handsome Jacques Bernay aboard another ship. With Jacques, it was a different kind of exhilaration than it was today with Reuben. But what had happened when she'd met Reuben Grodin just now had told her that life was not over for her. She had the promise of happiness for the future and that was enough to encourage Tasha to strive for whatever life had to offer her.

When Etienne returned to the cabin she made no mention of her afternoon or that she'd met a famous artist. She wanted to keep that her own little secret for the time being.

As close as she was to Charmaine, she sought not to tell her about meeting the interesting artist. For the time being, she just wanted to keep all this to herself.

For the moment, Tasha wanted time to question if she was just being a foolish old lady about what she saw in Reuben's eyes when he looked at her. She saw warmth and caring. It had been a long tme since she'd seen that in a man's eyes. But she knew how vulnerable a woman could be when she'd been wounded and hurt by love and she was too old to wallow in foolish folly.

She'd not give her heart and soul to Reuben Grodin as swiftly as she had to Jacques Bernay.

—

A little frivolous folly was exactly what had prompted Chad Morrow to accept Captain Bergson's invitation to dine with him and his guests in his cabin. He knew that Bergson considered him the ideal dinner companion for the young woman that he would be trying to impress in order to win her father's favor so that he would use the Penbrook Lines. Everett Roland and his wife Prudence had boarded the *Bonnie Belle* in Boston to sail to England. Accompanying them was their eighteen-year-old daughter, Priscilla, who'd spent the last year in Boston with her aunt.

Chad thoroughly understood that he was to be the entertaining guest for young Priscilla. This was a role he'd played numerous times in the past, all for the good of Penbrook Lines.

He'd not been plagued with any qualm of conscience about such a role before, but he would not have accepted this particular assignment tonight if he'd not seen Tiffany with Etienne in such an intimate embrace this afternoon.

That was enough for Chad to make a hasty decision after that. He'd gone to his cabin and pulled out the fine-tailored pants and coat from his valise, along with one of his white linen shirts.

At the appointed hour he arrived at Captain Bergson's cabin. He knew that he would at least enjoy a grand meal and a fine wine because Bergson would be striving to impress the Rolands.

When Captain Bergson opened the door to welcome Morrow, he saw that the Roland family had already arrived. As he might have expected, Everett and Prudence Roland were a fine-looking couple. He did not get a view of the daughter until he'd walked on into the cabin, and he had to admit that she was a very attractive-looking girl with her bright blue eyes and brilliant auburn hair. She had the same flawless, fair complexion as her mother.

After introductions were made, Bergson gave Chad a

glass of wine as they awaited the meal to be brought to the cabin from the ship's galley.

As Everett and Bergson talked, Chad was left to entertain the two ladies. Bergson was pleased to see that Morrow seemed to be doing it quite successfully, and he was glad that he'd invited Morrow to join his party this evening. It was a clever stroke on his part.

By the time the cook and his helper wheeled the cart to the cabin, bearing a most scrumptious meal, everyone seemed to be in a festive mood.

Gallantly, Chad assisted both of the ladies into their chairs while the captain and Roland continued to slowly amble to the table.

The meal was very tasty and quite a feast, which told Chad just how much Bergson was striving to impress the Rolands. A fine white wine was served to complement the crispy fish dish the cook had prepared with his special herbs and seasonings. Chad figured that the fresh vegetables were those bought just prior to leaving the last port before sailing out to sea.

A delectable custard was served for dessert. Its flaky crust was golden and delicious, topped with a thick cream. Chad was glad that he'd been invited to partake of such a fine dinner.

After dinner, Chad took the cue Bergson tossed at him to take Miss Priscilla for a stroll around the deck.

Chad offered Priscilla his arm as he invited her to join him, "Mademoiselle?"

She took Chad's arm as she gave him a warm, friendly smile.

As they emerged on the deck, the galelike breezes of the afternoon had seemed to calm as the sun had set. It was pleasant to be walking on the deck with a big, bright moon shining down to light their way. They stood by the railing, enjoying lighthearted casual conversation.

But something made Chad suddenly turn around to

look over his shoulder. He saw nothing when he did glance back in the darkness.

A pair of fiery blue eyes was piercing him. She stood back in the shadows to observe him standing close to a girl with flaming red hair. Who was she? Tiffany wondered. Now she knew why he'd not made any effort to see her. He'd been occupied with someone else. Oh, what a fool she'd been! That Morrow was a philanderer, taking his pleasure with her and then forgetting her until he wished to take his pleasure again. She, being the idiot that she was, had allowed it not once or twice but three times now. Well, no more would she be his plaything, she vowed.

All the time she was standing back there in the darkness, making all her promises to herself how she'd handle Morrow, he was having the strangest sensations and it was that tantalizing image of Tiffany that kept haunting him as he stood there beside Priscilla.

That wicked little witch! She was never going to allow him any peace of mind. Tiffany was disturbing and distracting him so that he was paying no attention to anything Priscilla was chattering about.

Priscilla gave a girlish giggle. "Chad, I don't think you've heard a thing I've said in the last ten minutes."

He gave her a weak smile as he looked down on her smiling face, for he could not lie to her. He hadn't. But he did apologize to her.

How could he tell her that there was a bewitching little goddess that cast her spells on him and drove him out of his mind to the point that he had no will of his own?

Even as he stood there by the railing with Priscilla and gazed up at the black skies above them with those many twinkling stars, he'd thought of her and how her deep blue-purple eyes sparkled just as brilliantly.

Tiffany Renaud was a sensuous little sorceress!

Chapter 39

The next day Captain Bergson was quick to tell Chad how pleased he was with him. "You did yourself proud, young man. Both the Rolands praised you—thought you were one charming fellow, so Everett Roland told me."

"That's nice to hear. I wasn't so sure that I was that successful in entertaining their daughter," Chad declared to the captain.

"Oh, quite the contrary, from the way Roland talked this morning when I ran into him and his wife as they were taking a walk. Just keep up the good work, Chad," Bergson chuckled.

Something about the captain's remarks rubbed Chad the wrong way and he wasn't in the best of moods this morning. "I have no intention, Captain, of entertaining Priscilla all the way to England. I just want you to know that right now."

Bergson sensed the sharp edge of Morrow's tone and he was not about to argue with him about anything. "Sure, Chad—if—if that's the way you feel."

"That is the way I feel. Penbrook does not pay me to be a gigolo. They pay me for my expertise as an agent."

"Oh, I understand, Chad. I figured you might just find

293

Priscilla Roland a very attractive lady," Bergson stammered.

"Attractive she is, Captain, but I'm not attracted—all right?"

"I understand, Chad. I'll say no more on the subject," the captain said.

"Thanks, sir, I'm glad we understand each other." Chad gave him a smile and turned to go on his way.

The captain watched the young man move down the deck. He couldn't help admiring the independent young man and he knew now why the Penbrook Lines held him in such high esteem as their agent. He was a man with a will and a way of his own, and nothing or no one swayed him if it did not meet with his approval.

What the captain did not know was that there was one petite miss with flashing blue eyes who could easily sway Chad Morrow!

The anticipation of getting home to Paris completely occupied Pierre's thoughts, for he'd been away from his home and his office for four months now. Charmaine was eagerly anticipating being reunited with her sons and preparing for the holidays. Neither of them realized the jealous torment their daughter was enduring. Etienne naively accepted her attentions without any questions.

The next week she made a point of suggesting to Etienne that they take endless strolls around the deck in hopes that Morrow would see her. Etienne was a very handsome escort and Tiffany noticed a number of the strolling ladies cast their eyes in his direction. But Etienne was too occupied with her to notice that.

During that long week she never saw Chad or the redheaded lady. What did she do during the long afternoons? Tiffany wondered. Where did Chad keep himself? Perhaps, they were spending time together.

Tiffany did often see Tasha and her new friend, Reuben Grodin. It did not seem to trouble Etienne that his mother had suddenly become so chummy with the artist.

She mentioned to Etienne that sea air and her new companion, Reuben, had certainly given Tasha a glowing radiance the last week.

"It's good to see that she's not fearful about the sea any more. She was when we were preparing to leave New Madrid, you know. All those fears of years ago when she and your mother were shipwrecked off the Virginia coast came back to haunt her."

"And Monsieur Grodin?" Tiffany prodded him for his opinion about the man who'd been spending so much time with his mother.

"Ah, Reuben Grodin is an interesting man, I must say, and I've not known my mother to be so gay and happy for a long time. He seems to have the capacity to make her laugh and enjoy life," Etienne told her.

"She certainly doesn't look or act like the same lady we first saw when we came to this country a few months ago," Tiffany remarked.

As she prodded him, Etienne now sought to do the same thing by quizzing her about the absent Chad Morrow, who he knew had not been coming around to see the Renauds or Tiffany. What were her feelings for him now? he was curious to know. Tiffany's moods and affections could change so swiftly, Etienne had come to realize.

All he knew was she seemed to be still desirous of his companionship and he willingly accepted the role.

But he knew that the next day she might treat him with a cool aloofness as she had in the past, so he didn't allow himself to think about the next day. He only enjoyed the present. Etienne had come to terms with the reality that this was the best attitude he could have where Tiffany was concerned. Somehow, it had calmed the fury of his passion for her when they were together as they'd been frequently. Besides, aboard a ship there was no refuge you could take, and this was why he found himself curious about Morrow.

"What has happened to Chad Morrow? I've not seen him on the ship or decks lately." Etienne felt her arm instantly stiffen as he held it.

"I've no idea where he's about," she snapped. She was not about to tell Etienne that she had seen him with another woman.

Etienne commented about his position as the ship's agent. "Guess that must be a pretty important job—traveling all over the world like he does," he said, glancing down at Tiffany's solemn face.

"Oh, I suppose so," she mumbled, shrugging her dainty shoulders.

"Must be nice to go to all those places and meet so many different people," he said.

Suddenly, she halted and looked up at him. "Dear God, Etienne—is that all you can talk about? If Chad Morrow is so interesting to you, then why don't you just take me back to my cabin and go seek him out. Maybe he could answer all your questions!"

Etienne could hardly suppress a smile, for her tone told him that she was at odds with Chad. That was enough to satisfy him.

"I apologize, Tiffany. I'm such a stupid dolt, I guess. Living all my life in a small place like New Madrid, I guess I can't help envying a fellow like Morrow who's been everywhere."

Something about the look on Etienne's face sent a wave of compassion rushing over Tiffany. There was no cause for her to take her venom out on him. It was Chad who deserved the sting of her tongue, not Etienne!

She turned to face him and her hand went up to touch

his cheek as she sweetly assured him, "You've no cause to envy Chad Morrow. You're a wonderful man, Etienne, and your life may take you many places." She gave a soft laugh. "My goodness, you're on your way to England now and from there we shall be going to France—and Paris. Oh, wait until you see Paris, Etienne. No city is as exciting!"

He found himself affected by her enthusiasm and he laughed. "Oh, Tiffany—you—you are good for me. You are exactly right. I'm going to faraway places that I never hoped to see. I've your father to thank for this opportunity."

"You see!" She turned those bright blue eyes up at him and he swore that no woman on this earth had a more beautiful face than Tiffany.

"Yes, I do see, Tiffany. And I thank you for making me see," Etienne said. Right now, he felt that there was no cause for him to envy the likes of Chad Morrow. As a man his ego had been given a tremendous boost.

Anyone seeing them would have taken them for young lovers. The sight of them was enough to convince Chad Morrow that Etienne Bernay had certainly taken advantage of the time alone with Tiffany since they'd boarded the ship.

He turned away from the sight of them to return to his cabin. As soon as he'd slammed the door with a mighty blow, he marched over to the nightstand by his bunk to pull out the flask from the drawer. He took no time to get a glass but hoisted the flask to his mouth to gulp a generous taste of the whiskey.

His long fingers nervously brushed aside the unruly hair from his forehead. Damn her! Damn her trifling little heart! Right now, he was wishing that he'd never met Tiffany Renaud in the park that spring day.

He sat there on his bunk and continued to drink from the flask as the tormenting thoughts of Tiffany looking so gay and happy as she strolled by Etienne's side made his anger heighten. When the flask was empty, he flung it across the room.

He staggered as he tried to get up off the bunk, so he sank back down. Suddenly the softness of the bunk beckoned to him and he gave way to the urge to lay his head on the pillow.

Quickly, he gave way to the drunken stupor he was in and fell asleep. For over six hours, he slept deeply. When he did wake up and looked at the clock, he realized that he had slept through the late afternoon and early evening. It was now ten at night and he was feeling the need of some food. There was a miserable, dry feeling in his mouth.

Slowly, he sauntered over to the washstand and poured some water into the bowl to wash his face. The cool cloth on his face did wonders. Taking the brush to his tousled hair, he gave it a few strokes.

Surely the ship's cook would still have something left in the galley to sate his ravenous apetite. He ambled down the passageway toward the stairway to take him up on the deck of the ship. But the first gust of the salt air did wonders to make him more alert. He inhaled deep and long, lingering there for a moment or two before he sought to move on.

He took no notice of the late evening strollers as they paraded down the deck nor the couples who were lingering by the railing. Instead, he made for the galley where the ship's cook, Timothy, was still there cleaning up his pots and pans.

"Well, Mister Morrow—good evening!"

"Evening, Timothy. Can a hungry bloke hope that you have something left over? I'm bloody well starved!"

The slender young Englishman laughed. "I've always something to eat in my galley. Suppose you just have a seat and I'll fix you a most tempting plate. I've some nice slices of a fine beef roast and there's a portion of buttered, herb dumplings. Now how does that sound to you, sir?"

"Sounds wonderful to me, Timothy!" Chad didn't hesitate in taking a seat as the cook began to dish up the dumplings. From a huge platter, he took two generous slices of the huge mountain of beef. Chad could not wait to devour the meal.

The aroma teased his nose before he ever put a knife and a fork to it. Never had a mouthful of food tasted so good.

Timothy turned back to his chores as Chad ate with relish. It always pleased the young English cook when someone obviously enjoyed his cuisine.

"Another cup of coffee, sir?"

Chad shook his head and declared, "I don't know where I'd put it, Timothy, and I thank you for the great meal."

"My pleasure, sir."

Morrow pushed himself away from the table. "I'll tell you goodnight, Timothy. I figure that you are more than ready to get to your own cabin as I intend to do now that I've had a hearty meal."

"Yes, sir, I think I'm ready to do just that," Timothy confessed.

Chad left the galley and it was his intention to go directly to his cabin. But as he walked down the deck toward the steps to go below, his gray eyes caught sight of a tiny figure by the railing, all alone.

There was no doubt who it was as Chad watched that thick long black hair hanging down her back and blowing away from her face by the gentle sea breeze.

Softly, he moved like a stalking mountain lion closing in on his prey. The pounding waters surging against the hull of the ship blocked out the sounds behind her so Tiffany did not hear Morrow approaching her.

What a bewitching little siren she was with the white

wool shawl draped around her shoulders. He could not resist letting his strong arms snake around her tiny waist to clasp together as he pressed himself against her back.

For one brief moment Tiffany stood frozen, saying nothing. She knew instantly whose arms encircled her waist, even without looking around.

Chapter 40

His face touched her cheek and his nose nuzzled the sweet fragrance of her glossy hair. "Hello, love," he murmured in her ear.

All the well-chosen words she'd planned to say to him the next time they met did not come out. Instead, she stood there swaying slightly against him. The heat of his male body flamed all over and her legs felt like jelly.

As she continued to stand there without turning around to face him, she mumbled, "Chad?"

"You know it is, Tiffany. Don't you know that we can't fight this thing between us? You know it and so do I." His arms pulled her around to face him. For a fleeting moment their eyes locked before his forceful lips were pressing against hers. With his lips kissing her as they were, she could not deny that he spoke the truth. Whatever this strange magic was between them, it would not be denied. Her arms instinctively rose to encircle his neck and she pressed herself against his broad chest.

The feel of her full breasts brushing his chest was enough to release a surging wave of passion in Morrow. His lips released hers long enough for him to give a deep moan of pleasure, "God, Tiffany—I want you! I want you so much I'm crazy!"

She clung to him closer as though she was afraid she would suddenly be freed from his arms and she did not want to be free. She wanted him to hold her and love her as he'd done that day at the Plantation House.

Her supple, sensuous body gave him the answer he wanted and he said nothing as he swept her up in his arms. All he prayed was that they didn't encounter Etienne or Monsieur Renaud as he carried her to his cabin.

But nothing stirred in the darkened passageway as he took his ladylove to his quarters. Even after he'd closed and locked his cabin door, he was reluctant to let her out of his arms.

"I—I missed you, Tiffany. Something is missing when you're away from me," he told her as he finally lowered her to his bunk. His gray eyes searched her lovely face for a moment before he declared, "It's too strong for us to fight it. Do you believe me, love?"

"I think I must, Chad."

Suddenly the two of them were moving toward each other. Once again her arms went around his neck and his arms circled her waist as their lips met in a long, lingering kiss. Slowly, he lowered her back on the bunk. She looked absolutely beautiful with her thick black hair fanned out on the pillow.

His nimble fingers trembled as he removed the top of her gown so that his eyes might savor the sight of her breasts overflowing the bodice of her undergarments. When his lips began to taunt her without mercy, she was the one impatient to wiggle out of the binding skirt of her gown.

He gave a deep chuckle. "Always knew you were a woman of fire and passion, Tiffany."

"You've yourself to blame for that, Chad Morrow!" she retorted.

He was hastily removing his clothing as he assured her

302

that he'd gladly take the blame. "I'll admit of being guilty of wanting to love you as I've never wanted to love any other woman, Tiffany Renaud. There, does that satisfy you?"

She smiled up at him and softly purred, "No, Chad— that doesn't satisfy me!"

He lowered his firm, muscled body and touched her satiny, flushed flesh. "Well, love—I want you to be completely satisfied." He sought to do just that as he burrowed himself in the velvet softness arching closer to him.

A blazing violence of passion burst forth in both of them like a wildfire out of control. Chad and Tiffany felt themselves both caught up in the torrid flames consuming them.

Moans of pleasure and delight came from Tiffany as she felt herself swept up in the fury of Chad's fierce love-making. Suddenly, she felt the violent explosion of his body and she gasped as she clung tighter to him.

Together, they lay enclosed in each other's arms as though they were waiting out the force of a devastating storm to pass by. Time seemed to stand still for both of them as they lay there. There was no world other than the lovers' paradise they sought to linger in.

When Chad finally roused from the pleasant lethargy that surrounded them, he knew that Tiffany must be convinced beyond any shadow of a doubt that they had a love so special that nothing could ever destroy it. It was as endless as that vast ocean out there.

He slipped from her warm side to get the ring that he'd so carelessly tossed in his valise when he'd first boarded the ship.

It was time that he should give it to her. After all, if he'd not been such a stupid idiot, he'd have remembered to give it to her back at the Plantation House.

When he found it, he slipped back into the bunk to lie

303

beside her. "Chad? Chad—where did you go?" she mumbled, rising up in the bunk to see that he was back there by her side.

He urged her to give him her hand. When she did, with a quizzical look on her face, he slipped the exquisite ring on her finger. It seemed to be a perfect fit. He confessed to her that he'd forgotten to give it to her the day they'd had lunch on the terrace at the Plantation House.

One look at the ring made her bend down to kiss him as she laughed. "You have to be the most perplexing man I've ever known. I never know what to expect from you, Chad Morrow. Oh, Chad—it is the most beautiful ring I've ever seen! What can I say?"

"Just say that you love me as I love you, darling."

"Oh, Chad, I must love you. How would tonight have happened if I didn't love you, mon cher?" Her blue-violet eyes were so warm with love when she looked at him that he had to believe her.

"I can't argue with that, Tiffany," he said, rising from the bunk to kiss her sweet lips.

"No other man has ever made love to me as you have and you know that," she boldly admitted.

"I do know that, Tiffany. I'm just a very possessive man and you might as well know that."

She gave him a challenging look and smile. "And I am a most demanding, possessive lady, too, and you might as well know that, Chad Morrow. I'll share you with no other woman!"

He laughed. "Well, I would say that we understand each other then."

"And I would say that you'd better get me back to my cabin because my parents would not be so understanding about this late night venture of mine."

So like two mischievous children, they cautiously and quietly moved down the passageway toward Tiffany's cabin. One hasty kiss was all Chad allowed himself to enjoy before he quickly turned to go back down the passageway after Tiffany was safely inside her cabin.

By the time he closed the door to his cabin and lit the lamp there by his bunk, he smelled the sweet fragrance of her still lingering on his pillow. But for that he could have wondered if he had dreamed all this had happened tonight.

In her own cabin, Tiffany lit her lamp but turned it down low. She had to look at the magnificent ring Chad had given her. For the longest time, she stared at the ring before she made any effort to get undressed. Chad had to care very much for her to give her such an expensive gift. Her own mother had a vast collection of jewels but no ring she possessed was more impressive than this one. She wondered what her mother and father would say when they saw this ring on her finger. Would they disapprove of her accepting it?

Maybe she should just keep this her little secret until they arrived back in Paris. Perhaps, that would be best for she would be shattered if they insisted that she return the ring to Chad.

She allowed it to remain on her finger as she undressed and she saw no reason why she should not leave it on her finger while she slept. So she did as she leaned over to turn off her lamp.

Gently, she let her cheek rest against the ring as she drifted off to sleep, her thoughts on Chad. She never dreamed that a man could make her feel as Chad did. Never had she imagined in all her romantic whimsy that love would be like this.

She knew one thing for certain after tonight and that was that she must quit using poor Etienne to seek her revenge against Chad every time she got riled. She wasn't being fair to him and he deserved better from her than that. There was no nice way to say it; she'd used Etienne sorely.

Her thick lashes fluttered lazily as sleep swiftly came upon her.

Etienne had found it impossible to go to sleep. He'd known the moment Tiffany had slipped quietly out of her cabin long after they'd all said goodnight after the evening meal.

As tempted as he was to rush to get dressed and slip into his boots, he feared that he would wake his mother, so he dismissed the thought. Nevertheless, he could hardly think about going to sleep, for he was curious about Tiffany's nocturnal wanderings at such a late hour.

For the next two hours, he fidgeted there on the bunk, staring out the small window and looking aimlessly around the darkened room.

The torment of Tiffany would not be so unbearable once he was off this damned ship and got himself occupied with work, he soothed himself. Besides, they would be in Cherbourg and she would be in Paris. For everyone's best interest that was a good thing.

When he was just about at the point of drifting off to sleep, a noise brought him wide-eyed and awake.

He knew it was soft footsteps he heard just outside his door. He sat up in the bunk and listened to see if he was right. Creeping quietly to the door, he strained to listen and what he thought he heard made him tense, for there were two out there.

When he was certain that he heard the clicking sound of Tiffany's door, he waited another moment before slowly cracking his own cabin door to peer out and the sight he saw was enough to make him angry.

There was no doubt in his mind who that tall, towering figure was sauntering slowly down the passageway. Tiffany had obviously met Chad Morrow. He'd escorted her back to her cabin.

What was it about that devil that Tiffany seemed unable to resist? Etienne wondered. He was no good and Tiffany would only be asking for heartbreak if she kept seeing this rogue. But he knew not how to stop her from seeing him.

Morrow was not worthy of such a beautiful girl as Tiffany, Etienne thought angrily. He'd love her and leave her as he'd probably done to many a fair maiden in ports all over the world.

Etienne made a vow to be there if she needed him to ease the pain she'd suffer when Morrow broke her heart, as he surely would.

307

Chapter 41

The glowing rays of the sun shining through her cabin window seemed to play off Tiffany's dainty hand as blue brilliance of the facets of the diamond sparkled as she opened her eyes. All she had to do as she stretched herself like a lazy cat was to remember Chad's marvelous caress and she, too, glowed with radiance.

As she sat up on the bunk she remembered that she was not ready to show the ring to her parents, so she walked over to the chest where her jewelry box was and opened one of the drawers to take out a gold chain. She put the ring on the chain and fastened the clasp of the chain around her neck.

When she had dressed, she tucked the chain inside the neckline of her frock so that the ring would not be displayed. There, it nestled at the cleavage of her firm breasts. Slyly, she smiled as she sat down to brush her hair, knowing that Chad would certainly approve of the secret place she'd placed his ring. It lay very close to her heart!

Looking at herself in the mirror, she pulled her long tresses back to secure them with a bright purple ribbon to match the deep purple frock she'd picked to wear. Maybe this was the look of love she was seeing in her reflection.

The long-sleeved, high-necked gown felt very comfortable, for the early morning breeze seemed to get cooler each morning as the ship came closer to the English coast. Tiffany had noticed this for the last few mornings and had closed her window.

With her high neckline no one would know that she had a chain around her neck.

It was not a morning that Chad Morrow and Etienne Bernay should have met. Chad was still feeling heady, intoxicated by the rapture of the love he'd shared. He was feeling quite cocky and self-assured as he swaggered jauntily down the deck and he was taken by surprise when the figure of Bernay surged forward, blocking his path. The sea breeze blew his jet-black hair across his forehead and side of his face, and his black eyes glared at Morrow as he stood in front of him.

"I've something to discuss with you, Morrow."

Chad raised a skeptical brow as his gray eyes pierced Etienne. "I can't imagine what we'd have to discuss, but I will hear you out."

"I just better warn you right now that I'll not stand by and see you play her wrong."

It took all his restraint and willpower not to grab Bernay by the shirt collar and sock his arrogant face. Instead, he spoke in a low, firm tone. "I hadn't heard anything about you becoming Tiffany's protector or taking over the authority of her father, Bernay! Has that happened? I think you're overstepping your bounds. Now, I just better warn you about something. You never lay your rules down for me. You never warn me about anything again. What I do with Tiffany is none of your business, Bernay. I have that right—you don't!"

Etienne suddenly flinched and his black eyes sparked. There was a cracking of his voice when he asked, "What

309

do you mean by that, Morrow?"

Chad began to turn and walk away. His deep voice taunted Etienne, "Oh, you know what I mean, Bernay. You know exactly what I mean!"

A pang of anxiety consumed Etienne as he watched the formidable figure of Chad Morrow stalk away from him.

What had Morrow meant by that last statement? Could he possibly mean what Etienne thought he was referring to? But how could he know about the strange, well-kept secret that existed between the Renaud and Bernay families for over twenty years?

No one but the two men themselves knew about this secret that linked Pierre and his father. It was obvious from what his mother, Tasha, had told him that Jacques had not told her the truth for several years. Etienne could not know when Pierre had told his wife.

There was one thing Etienne knew for certain: the Renauds had not told their daughter, Tiffany, about his father being a half-brother to her father. Perhaps, they wished to preserve the grand image of her grandfather, old Etienne Renaud. He recalled how she'd commented when they'd first met that her grandfather's name was Etienne. But that was the end of it.

There was no denying that Chad's words had made a tremendous impact on him, for what he'd said was absolutely true. He pondered now as he walked over to the ship's railing why he'd even approached the man. He should have known what Morrow's reaction would be.

Etienne walked to the far end of the ship and stood there to look out over the waters. He seemed to be completely alone; this part of the deck was deserted by the deck hands as well as any early morning strollers. He wanted this quiet time to be by himself, to think.

Suddenly, as if a bolt of lightning had struck him, he knew that Morrow *did* know the secret. His father was Cat Morrow and he knew everyone up and down the river. He also recalled his mother telling him that it had been Cat's riverboat that had brought them up from New Orleans to New Madrid. Cat must have known, too. Etienne also recalled a night when his father and old Cat had shared drinks at the local tavern, for he remembered Jacques stumbling into the house very drunk and he'd helped him to bed.

If Morrow sought to tell Tiffany, there was nothing he could do to stop him, Etienne reasoned. It was out of his hands. A devious rascal like Morrow would probably delight in doing just that.

Bernay finally left the spot of seclusion he'd lingered in for almost an hour to return to his cabin. There, he spent most of the day for he did not want to encounter the Renauds or Tiffany.

For the next few days Etienne isolated himself from the rest of his group. He found it more comforting and less disturbing to be by himself. His mother was so occupied during the afternoon in the company of Reuben Grodin that she accepted Etienne's explanation that he was interested in the book he was reading. It was obvious that Tiffany was not curious enough to come to the cabin to seek him out. He knew that it was Chad's company that was keeping her occupied.

Chad was trying to spend as much time with Tiffany as possible. The captain told him that the English coast was going to be coming in sight very soon. Morrow knew that he would have to be saying farewell to her for a few weeks. That wasn't too pleasant a thought.

He welcomed the fact that he'd had no more encounters with Etienne Bernay, for he was not so sure he would have been in control if Bernay had started lecturing him again.

It did not seem to disturb the Renauds that he was escorting their daughter around the ship daily. The same was true when he and Tiffany had chanced upon

Etienne's mother, Tasha, and her friend, Reuben. In fact, he found Tasha Bernay a very pleasant, friendly little lady. He also liked the very unconventional Grodin, who lived his life a particular way that pleased him.

Pierre and Charmaine Renaud shared the same feeling about the artist who'd attached himself to their friend, Tasha, as Chad Morrow did. They liked him!

But they felt poor Tasha was going to be terribly lonely once Grodin left the ship in England, since the couple had been inseparable lately.

"They are such an unlikely pair! It has amazed me that she and Reuben seem to enjoy each other's company so much," Charmaine remarked to her husband.

"It will be good to get home, mon cher," she added. "I am eager to see our sons." She smiled up at him as his arm rested around her shoulder.

He reached over to give her lovely cheek a gentle kiss and agreed with her. "I think this will be a very special holiday season for the Renaud family."

She wondered why he'd said that with such a smug look on his face. She knew Pierre well enough after all these many years to know that there was a hidden meaning behind that statement.

She pushed away from him to search his face. "Now, Pierre Renaud—just what are you keeping from me?"

"Why, not a thing, ma petite! Not a thing!" He had no intention of telling her just yet. That divine curiosity would just have to fret for a while. But it was part of his determination to get back to France well before November.

She gave him a playful slap on his shoulder, declaring that she knew he was keeping something from her. "Oh, Pierre—you can be a devil at times!"

Pierre had welcomed the sight of Tiffany spending her

afternoons in the company of Chad Morrow lately. It eased the concerns he'd secretly harbored when his daughter was in the company of Etienne. He had decided that Tasha's and Etienne's stay in Paris would be a brief one before he and Charmaine took them on to the country estate outside Cherbourg.

He liked Etienne very much, for he was Jacques and Tasha's son, but Etienne must never have any romantic ideas about his daughter. Pierre would never allow that to happen. He knew that there was only one of two ways that this could be ensured: Tiffany must become romantically involved with some other man, or he must tell her the truth. Whatever her reaction would be to the revelation, and regardless of how her grand-père would protest his plan, Pierre knew that sooner or later he must do it.

And so he was happy to see his daughter in the company of the attractive Englishman, Chad Morrow.

Chapter 42

Tiffany only wore her magnificent ring on her finger when she retired inside her cabin at night, or when she took a nightly stroll around the deck with Chad. Lately, they had been together every night on the ship's deck and several nights Chad had been invited by her father to share their table for the evening meal.

Last night as they'd roamed around the deck, holding hands and talking, Chad had remarked that they must surely be getting close now to the English coastline. "See this thick fog moving in?"

He took her hand to put it to his lips. "I could feel very sad at the sight of this fog because it means I will soon be saying goodbye to you, Tiffany. Tell me—tell me that I'm not fooling myself when I believe that you'll be as lonely when I leave you."

"Oh, you know I will, Chad. Tell me that you will not make me wait too long. I don't think I could stand it."

"I swear it won't be too long. Believe me!"

He pressed her close to him and held her tenderly in his arms. "Ah, Tiffany—you are so young and vulnerable, and I suppose that is what is bothering me. I feel so much older than you."

Playfully, she reached up to taunt him with her lips.

"Oh, you old man! I am not a child. Don't you remember that it was you who made me a woman—your woman, Chad!"

"For that, love, I shall always be glad. But I also know how different our backgrounds are. Believe me, I know that this can make a difference. My own parents were from two different backgrounds." This was the first time that Chad had ever mentioned anything to her about his life before he'd met her.

"You seem so serious, Chad. I've—I've never seen this side of you."

"No, I suppose you haven't."

She searched his rugged face and she saw something there that had escaped her before. She'd always seen him as a reckless, devil-may-care individual, who went his way doing as he pleased without a care in the world as long as it pleased him.

This was a different Chad Morrow that Tiffany had not known or seen before. This Chad Morrow fascinated and interested her just as intensely.

When she and Morrow parted company at her cabin door and he bent to give her one lingering kiss before he left, he had no inkling that his prediction was so correct that they were nearing the English coastline. The truth was that they were nearer than he knew. One long sweet kiss would have not satisfied him if he'd known that he wouldn't have the opportunity to hold her in his arms again before they would be forced to part.

During the late night hours and the early morning, a thicker fog gathered around the ship. Captain Bergson cut his sleep short to take full charge of his ship as he usually did in cases like this. None of the sleeping passengers aboard the ship were aware of the precautions being taken by the crew and their captain. Not even Chad knew about the tension on deck.

Pierre was the first of his party to be dressed and up on

the deck to see the thick, ghostly haze surrounding the ship and he also sensed the serious attitude of the scurrying deck hands as they moved around the vessel.

He didn't like the feeling in his gut. Another ship could so easily ram them in this dense fog. He marched along the deck in hopes of finding the captain. He had to search the deck and ship for several minutes before he spied him.

Bergson saw the look of concern on the Frenchman's face. "A bitch of a fog, sir. We are bloody well crawling in, I can tell you, but we are there. We're in England!"

It eased Renaud's mind a little to know that they were near the harbor. Bergson saw that he had calmed the fears of Monsieur Renaud.

"I'm a cautious captain. London is a busy port so I don't take any chances when I approach the harbor on a morning like this."

"You make me feel much better, Captain Bergson," Pierre said, feeling that he and his precious cargo were in capable hands.

He left the captain to do his work and he went below to wake up his wife and his daughter. Once he had his sleepy wife awake, he went down the passageway to Tiffany's door.

Tiffany was not accustomed to her father or mother disturbing her sleep in the early morning hours so when her sleep was interrupted by the rapping on her door, she was taken by surprise.

"Just a minute," she mumbled as she staggered to unlock her cabin door.

Her father marched into the cabin. "I thought you would be delighted to know we are ready to dock, ma petite. The crossing is over. We are so very close to home."

She stumbled back over to her bunk to sink back down on it and her father followed her to take a seat beside her.

It seemed the right time for Pierre to tell her that he knew how reluctant she had been to make this long journey and how proud of her he was that she'd accepted it and been so understanding.

He took her hand in his. "I know, ma petite, what we made you give up and I love you for being such a dear, devoted daughter. We shall make it up to you."

His hand holding hers felt the bulk of the ring on her finger and he glanced down to see it. He tensed instantly when he spied the exact ring he'd intended to purchase for his wife there on his daughter's finger.

For a moment, he found it impossible to speak. When he finally found his tongue, he still could not control the cracking of his voice. "Where—where did you get this ring, Tiffany?"

She was as tense and nervous as her father, for she had forgotten that she was wearing Chad's ring. She had certainly not expected this early morning visit from her father.

But she managed to look up at him with a lovely smile. "Isn't it absolutely breathtaking, Papa? I've never seen a more beautiful ring in my whole life!" She held her hand out to give it an admiring glance.

Pierre insisted on knowing where she had gotten it. Tiffany sensed her father's disgruntled manner, so she knew she must play him a certain way as she had in the past and as she always soothed her grand-père's vexed moods. Flippantly, she told him, "Chad got this for me in New Orleans. Now wasn't that sweet of him!"

Pierre once again lost his tongue as he looked at her in a state of shock. Did his daughter not realize what an expensive ring she wore on her finger? Obviously, she did not!

He mumbled, "You say Chad Morrow gave this to you?"

"Yes, papa—he did. Chad is a sweet, thoughtful man.

317

He must have known that I'd adore it."

Pierre sat there thinking to himself what woman would not adore it. His daughter seemed to take it so lightly that he was befuddled. He did not even have the desire to try to enlighten her that it was too expensive a gift for a young lady to accept from a gentleman unless this young man's attentions were serious enough for a commitment of marriage. Right now, he wasn't prepared to lecture her, for he was now in a daze himself.

All he could think about was that his daughter possessed the ring that he'd intended to purchase for his wife and Chad Morrow had been the man who'd denied him of that privilege.

"Best I leave so you can get yourself dressed," Pierre muttered as he opened the cabin door. Frustration was still consuming him as he left the cabin.

Tiffany did not know quite what to make of her father's strange reaction to the ring. As she moved around the cabin to prepare to dress, she thought her father acted a little awestruck when he picked up her hand to look at the ring. Even when he'd spoken to her, his eyes were not on her but staring at her ring.

Later as the Renauds and their daughter were standing on the deck watching the ship approach the harbor, Chad joined them. As they stood there talking, Chad noticed that Renaud glanced his way, giving him scrutinizing looks. Chad sensed that there might be something disturbing Pierre Renaud. But then maybe that was just his overactive imagination, for the Frenchman had greeted him as graciously as he usually did.

He also noticed that Tiffany was not wearing his ring this morning. Had her father seen it and forbidden her to wear it? He did not know that she always wore it around her neck on a chain except when they were alone together.

When she had dressed, she made a point of taking the ring from her finger to place it back on the chain. She wondered if her father had told her mother about the ring. If he had, she knew her mother would be most anxious to see it when she joined them there on the deck. But Charmaine had said nothing and this told Tiffany that her father had not mentioned her new ring.

While Chad could not say anything with the Renauds there, he made a point of surveying her fingers to see that he had been right about her not wearing his ring.

Suddenly he knew he must inquire about his ring. With a sly smile, she flipped the chain around her neck. "I wear it close to my heart when it is not on my finger. Does that meet with your approval, Chad?"

He looked into her deep blue eyes. He released the chain from her finger to nudge it back into the neckline of her frock. "Can't think of a nicer place for anything to be, love. I certainly approve of that."

As he finally moved reluctantly from her side, he gave her a fervent vow, "I'll be in Paris in three weeks—four at the most, love. I promise!"

Tiffany fought back the tears she felt welling up in her eyes as she stood watching him walk away from her. So intimately she knew that powerful physique now! She watched the swaggering gait of his muscled body move farther and farther away and a fierce wave of sadness washed over her. She watched those broad shoulders melt into the group of passengers. She stood in the spot where he had left her until she could not see that towering figure of his and his thick mane of hair any longer.

Then she made a dash to her room and closed the door and locked it so that she could give way to tears demanding to be released from her thick-lashed eyes.

All the time she cried, her heart called out to him to hurry to Paris!

Chapter 43

Tiffany was not the only one shedding tears after saying farewell to the man she loved. A loneliness instantly settled over Tasha Bernay as she'd left Reuben's side. She didn't dare return to her cabin to face Etienne, for he'd just think she was being a silly old woman if he saw her crying. But Tasha knew that it was possible to fall in love in a few short weeks. She had done exactly that with Jacques Bernay so it seemed that it had happened again.

When she had allowed all her tears to flow, she wiped her eyes and was ready to return to her cabin. After all, Reuben had sworn to her that before the holidays had come and gone he would come to Cherbourg to see her.

There was no sign of Etienne in her cabin and she figured that he was out on the deck watching the passengers leave the ship. So she took the time of privacy to place the gold chain Reuben had given her in a small leather pouch where she kept the few pieces of jewelry she owned.

At the last minute, he'd taken the chain off his neck and placed it in her hand, declaring, "Just a little of me will be with you while we're apart. I've nothing else to give you, Tasha. As I know you've guessed, I put little importance on material wealth, but this chain I treasure."

"You have more wealth than almost anyone I know, Reuben," she had told him. "You spend your days doing what you love doing. You are happy and content with your life. So few people are."

He'd smiled warmly at her. He'd known the minute he'd met and talked to her that first day that Tasha Bernay probably would understand him as few ladies could. Tasha was good for him and he could not say that for many ladies he'd known in his life. Most were too demanding of his time and jealous of his love to paint. There was never any question as to what was to be sacrificed as far as Reuben was concerned. The ladies were never as stimulating as his art. So he had never married. From time to time, he'd had a mistress who'd shared his loft studio in the outskirts of London. But the last two years, he'd tired of this arrangement, for the last lady he'd found was a handful to move out and rid himself of.

He knew when he left the ship that Tasha had made more of an impact on his life than any woman had for several years, because as he took a carriage to his studio he felt lonely. This was a new feeling for Reuben Grodin!

As Grodin's carriage pulled away from the wharves, Chad was just leaving the ship with his two heavy valises in each hand. He still wore his seafaring garb, for he'd not taken the time to change his clothes. He wasn't going to be the dapper young man when he entered his townhouse this morning but he didn't care about that.

He was just eager to get there and see what was awaiting his attention after so many months' absence. He could imagine the mountains of papers awaiting him and he expected that several messages would be on his desk.

321

He never worried about the running of his townhouse when he was away for long periods of time, for his manservant, Simon, and his good wife, Delphia, took excellent care of his home. Chad had always left Simon enough funds to take care of bills that might be due when he was away.

He was so eager to get home after so many months away that he didn't hesitate to accept a young man's offer of a carriage when he came up to him on the wharf. He figured the limping youth with a cap pulled down over his head needed the fees as much or more than the other drivers.

"Where's your carriage fellow?" Chad inquired.

"Right down at the end of the wharf, sir. Here—I'll take the baggage for you," the young man offered. Chad gave him one of the valises.

For the limp in his leg, Chad had to admit he walked at a pretty fast pace and he found himself admiring the fellow's spirit. They carried on a light conversation as the two of them moved on down to the end of the wharf where the crowd began to thin out.

When they reached the carriage, the young man carrying his valise tossed it up in the driver's perch. "Shall we go, sir?" The young man waited for Chad to open the door and climb inside.

In a split second, Chad felt two strong arms yank him inside. Out of the corner of his eye he caught sight of the limping young man running as if the demons of hell were after him. There was no hint of a limp as he sped away. But Chad had no time to defend himself as the sudden thrust of some blunt object slammed the side of his head with such a mighty blow that he felt the excruciating pain sending him into an abyss of blackness.

As he was sinking into that bottomless pit, he heard the echoes of laughter in his ears. What kind of hell had he entered? he wondered. It was his last conscious thought before he was rendered completely helpless.

"He was as easy as a baby—no problem at all," one of the men laughed, looking at the slumped figure of Morrow on the carriage seat. He urged the other man to get to the driver's perch and get the carriage away from here fast.

The man did as he was told, leaving his buddy in the carriage with the fellow they'd been hired to take care of the minute he stepped off the ship. If it all went as smoothly as it had so far, then the two of them had earned themselves some easy money, he figured.

As quickly as he could, the man pushed the carriage to the outskirts of the city—for he and his buddy were not through with this bloke yet.

He did not slow the carriage's pace until they'd reached the spot they'd decided upon to finish the task they'd been hired to do.

The driver of the carriage, Willie, was not a huge man but his buddy was a giant. It was Ural who would carry out the rest of their assignment to take care of Chad Morrow. Willie was glad that his own part of it was finished. He didn't have that particular sadistic streak in him that Ural possessed.

When Willie halted the carriage in the dense wooded area and Ural jumped out of the carriage, Willie walked away, knowing what was going to be done to the man.

The only thing that eased Willie's qualms was the vast sum of money they were getting for the few minutes of work. In an hour they were making more than they usually did in weeks.

Ural pulled the limp figure of Morrow out of the carriage and enjoyed every leap in the air he made to come down with a mighty impact on Chad's hand. When he was certain that he had broken the fingers of his right hand, he quit. Allowing his three-hundred-pound body to slam Morrow's hand had been what he'd been instructed to do, but Ural's overzealous nature could not rest with that; so he slammed Chad's leg with the same iron pipe he'd hit him with when he'd entered the carriage. Only then did he give one of his lionlike roars of laughter and beckon to Willie that they were ready to leave. When Willie came to the carriage and heard the animal sounds of the man lying there on the ground, he felt sick.

But he dared not offend his giantlike friend, so he said nothing as they drove away. He was glad to have it over and he just prayed that he wouldn't have nightmares about it.

By the time they'd traveled back to London and stopped by a pub on Fleet Street, Willie had calmed down a little. An hour or two later, with his fill of ale, he was much calmer and the sorry sight of Chad Morrow was fading fast.

Reuben enjoyed his first evening home with his artist friend, Jacob. They went to their favorite tavern to celebrate. He told Jacob about the excitement of his exhibits in the eastern coastal cities and he talked for hours about Tasha.

By the time they returned to the two-story house where they both lived, they had drunk so much wine that they were both ready to hit their beds and go to sleep.

But even though it was well past midnight when Reuben fell across his bed, he was wide-eyed and ready to get up to start the day by six in the morning. As he stirred around his small apartment, he noticed that Jacob had slept the night on his old settee and never made it to his own place.

He let him sleep while he brewed his coffee and drank it. From his high lofty window, he looked out over the beautiful countryside that he'd been away from for several months. God, it was a glorious sight!

As soon as he had another cup of strong, black coffee, he would take his pad and go roaming. He felt no need for food. If Jacob woke up, he would have plenty of coffee waiting for him.

He grabbed up his satchel, left the room, and went down the two flights of steps.

There was a crisp bite to the morning air and Reuben felt invigorated as he inhaled deeply. He was not bothered that his thick, bushy hair blew around his weathered face as he marched along. He gave a friendly greeting to one of the farmers traveling down the road in his wagon filled with farm products he was taking to the market in London.

But he soon took a trail off the main dirt road to go into the dense woods. He figured he was bound to find something interesting to watch and sketch—a playful squirrel or a mother bird feeding her young. Reuben always found something to catch his interest.

But he had barely entered the wooded area when his ear, which was as keen as his eye, heard a strange sound. He stopped to listen, for he'd often come upon an injured creature during his treks. Again, he heard the deep moan of agony and Reuben knew instantly that this was no small creature. He was no fool and he knew that a wounded animal could prove to be treacherous, so he moved cautiously through the bushes.

Another few moments went by and Reuben heard the sound again, but he saw nothing. He moved toward the direction he thought the sound was coming from.

Suddenly a sight came in view and he couldn't believe what he was seeing. Some poor bastard was slithering along on the ground and after three or four moves, he was forced to stop. Giving a deep moan of anguish, he tried to get himself moving again. Reuben just stood there a moment to convince himself that he was actually seeing what he was seeing.

The man lay on his left side and he was stretching out with his left hand and pushing himself with his left leg. Reuben watched him dragging his right leg and his right arm was cradled against his chest.

Reuben rushed out to help the poor fellow and it was only when he was standing there, towering over him, that their eyes met. He would have recognized those silver-gray eyes anywhere even though he looked nothing like the young man he'd last seen on the ship.

Nevertheless, it was Chad Morrow he was gazing down on. He quickly bent down to speak to him, for the young man seemed dazed. Reuben figured the pain he was enduring was enough to do that to him.

"Morrow, it's Reuben. Dear God, man—what happened to you? Can you tell me?" Reuben said, giving him a pat on his shoulders to let him know he was a friend hoping to comfort him.

In a faltering voice, Morrow mumbled, "Reuben? You—Reuben?"

"That's right, Morrow. Your friend, Reuben, and I am going to help you." Obviously, Chad couldn't walk and Reuben had no way to get him back to his place. Even if he could, there was no way he could climb two flights of steps. Reuben knew he had to get help.

He cradled Chad's head in his lap as he would have a small child. "I want to help you, son, but I have no way to get you back to my place even though it isn't very far from here."

Chad told Reuben his address. "My man, Simon, will come and get me. If you can just go there and get Simon to come here. Will you do that, Reuben?"

"Of course I will. Now, you listen to me, Morrow. Do you think you could make it with my help to the edge of this woods which is only some fifty feet away?"

"I've worked all night long to get this far so I think I could make another fifty feet," Chad told him.

326

"All right. I'd like to get you to the road so I can go back to my place and send my friend, Jacob, to stay with you while I go into London to get your man. I'll send Jacob with some whiskey to ease your pain until we can get you to a doctor."

"I'd be beholden to you, Reuben."

"All right! Let's get going, eh?"

"I've got a broken leg and I think every damned finger in my right hand is broken," Chad moaned in a faltering voice.

Reuben figured if he kept him talking he might not notice the pain so much. "This was no accident. Someone has a big hate for you, eh, Morrow?"

"Someone has a very big hate for me, Reuben, but when I get through with those responsible they are going to have a pain to last them the rest of their lives. I assure you of that."

They covered the fifty feet faster than Reuben had expected. He figured that his talking had helped.

When he had Morrow by the side of the road where Jacob could not possibly miss the sight of him, Reuben told him farewell. "Jacob will be here shortly with a flask of strong whiskey, Morrow."

Chad managed to nod.

Reuben moved hastily down the dirt road. Once he had Jacob awake and on his way back to Morrow, he started out for the street where Chad had directed him to his townhouse.

It was a rather fancy address that the shabbily dressed Grodin approached almost an hour later.

Chapter 44

Being a man of impulsive emotions, Reuben found himself amazed by the cool, calm demeanor the manservant Simon displayed when he told him about his master's dilemma. Without batting an eyelash, he turned away from Reuben to immediately prepare to go to Chad. His wife Delphia seemed to know exactly what to do to help him to speed his departure. Reuben stood watching them moving as a pair in their common cause. Morrow had himself a very devoted couple here at his townhouse. There was no doubt that they were very loyal to young Morrow.

In less than a half-hour, he and the tall, bald-headed Simon were in the carriage moving at a fast pace down the London street to go to the outskirts of the city.

Simon was not much for talking, Reuben found, but he was a man of action and the artist admired that.

Simon pushed the bays unmercifully to get to his master, and Reuben found himself liking Simon more and more as they reached the outskirts of the city and moved into the wooded area.

It was a welcoming sight to Morrow when he watched the familiar carriage approaching as he sat there beside Jacob. The flask was empty and he was pleasantly numbed, which was a divine feeling to Chad after the many hours of pain he'd endured.

As the carriage came to an abrupt halt, Simon wasted no time leaping down to rush to Chad.

No one had to tell Reuben the camaraderie that existed between Simon and Chad Morrow once the two of them were reunited. He watched as the manservant carefully examined his master. "Help me, Monsieur Reuben," Simon instructed him. "Hold his right leg as straight as you can."

The two of them lifted Chad's husky body into the carriage so that he sat as comfortably as he could. Reuben offered his services to help Simon get Chad into the townhouse, for there was no way that he could be carried up the long flight of winding stairs to the master suite.

Chad was placed on the oversized leather couch in his study before Simon sent the young stableboy to fetch the doctor. Delphia was already there to apply cloths of her special ointments to his swollen fingers.

"Mercy me, what a mess," she sighed, surveying Morrow's pathetic-looking hand. She needed no doctor to tell her that every finger on the young man's hand was broken except maybe his thumb. What kind of animal did this to him? It had to be some devil of a man, for Chad Morrow was one of the kindest, nicest men she'd ever known.

She watched him flinch at her slightest touch, although she tried to be as gentle as she could. "Sorry, Mister Chad—so sorry," she told him.

"That's all right, Delphia. Go ahead with your ointments. I'll—I'll just try to grit my teeth a little harder." He gave her a weak smile. He knew how those ointments could help a swelling, for she'd doctored him before.

"Can you move your thumb, sir?"

Chad found that he could. It seemed that had been spared at least. Delphia smiled and nodded her head, pleased to see him move it slightly.

She took out her scissors to open up the leg of his pants so as soon as the doctor did arrive, he could get to examining it.

"You just lie still, sir, and rest. Simon's gone to fetch the doctor so they should be getting here shortly. I'll be back in just a minute," she said as she stood up and began to gather up her pan and jars of ointments.

The matronly housekeeper left his room. She went to the kitchen to start a kettle of water steaming so she might fix some tea. The doctor always expected his cup of tea after he'd performed a service.

She was startled by the sight of Reuben sitting there staring out the window. She assured Grodin that Chad was resting a little better and she declared how grateful she was for him coming to Chad's aid.

Tucking a straying wisp of her graying hair back into the tight coil at the back of her head, she angrily declared, "Can't for the life of me believe this could happen to Mister Morrow in broad daylight. It's a sad time we live in for something like this to happen."

"This didn't just happen, ma'am. Someone was hellbent to even a score with Chad."

"Oh? Well, my goodness! I can't imagine him having any enemies that would hate him this bad."

Reuben couldn't enlighten her about that, but Chad had managed to tell him how he'd accepted a young man's offer of his carriage and when he entered the carriage he was faced with two fellows waiting for him. The young fellow had speedily run away, so Chad knew this had definitely been plotted.

All Chad had mentioned to Reuben as they'd made the drive from the woods to his townhouse was that he knew the bastard responsible for this and he'd even that score

330

with relish just as soon as his leg and hand healed.

"I think it would be safe to say that he surely has one very bad enemy, ma'am."

Delphia offered him another cup of coffee, which Reuben accepted.

By the time he had finished the second cup, Simon and the doctor had arrived, so Reuben figured that he'd done all he could for Morrow. He announced to Simon's wife that he was going to leave now. "Tell Chad I'll be back to see him in a day or two."

Reuben walked along the London street, thinking about how different his first day back home had been from the one he'd anticipated. He was sure Chad Morrow was feeling the same way.

By the time the doctor finished with him, Chad felt like an absolute prisoner and totally at the mercy of everyone around him. He could do nothing but lie in bed and obey.

The days were endless and the nights were even longer. Delphia took over the house completely while Chad kept Simon busy running errands for him. He sent him to the Penbrook Lines with all his reports so they could be informed about what had happened to him. There were three different trips to Chad's solicitor with the instructions that the last plot of land should be purchased immediately. More than ever, Chad was determined to own that land now. The Chadwicks were going to pay and pay dearly before he was through with them, he fervently vowed. There was no shadow of a doubt who had done this dastardly act. His uncle and his son were seeking their revenge against him for buying the Chadwick land.

As cleverly and shrewdly as he'd manipulated his purchases over the last few years through his solicitor when he'd been away from England, the family had managed to find out that it was he who was buying up their land.

Obviously, the oldest son of his uncle had hired the two ruffians to rough him up after they'd found out that he was arriving back in London. Well, Chad figured that his hand and his leg would heal but what he planned for the Chadwicks would haunt them forever. Never would they heal from the blow of revenge he'd seek against them!

He had plenty of time to think about his revenge in the next three weeks that he had to stay in bed. Lucky for him, that big thug had not succeeded in breaking his leg as he'd planned. The bone was slightly cracked, the doctor had told him, but with the support of a cane, Chad found that he could move around his bedroom by the end of the third week. His fingers were not healing so quickly but he had practiced constantly with his left hand to be able to sign his name.

Signing his name was the most important accomplishment to Chad, for he hoped to be able to sign the papers his solicitor submitted to him when he managed to get that last plot of land. It had been his desire to own this land, since he was denied it by his greedy uncle; he had always blamed his weak, spineless mother for allowing this to happen. He knew he was as deserving of it as was his uncle's wastrel son. Time had proven him right, Chad considered. It was a very gratifying feeling.

He was never so happy as he was the day the news came to him that he was the owner of that last plot. It had happened faster than he'd anticipated. He wondered if the reason it had happened so quickly had to do with the fee paid to have him battered and bruised, coupled with Chadwick's losses at one of the gaming tables.

He did not question why fate had played so favorably into his hands. He just accepted it gratefully!

Now, he was free to concentrate on his next plan for

the Chadwicks. But he was so preoccupied with this dilemma that he barely realized how many weeks had gone by since he'd left the ship and vowed to Tiffany that he would soon be in France.

As much as he yearned to rush to Paris and the woman he loved with all his heart, there were things he must do before he could leave London. But knowing his impetuous, impatient Tiffany as he did, he tried to sit at his desk to write a letter to her to explain why he would be late in arriving in Paris. But it was impossible. Signing his name was one thing, but writing a letter was another matter. This was something he could not ask Simon or Delphia to do for him.

Surely she had to know he loved her and he was going to have to gamble on that. Just thinking about her was enough to hasten his unfinished business with the Chadwick family.

Once more he tried to make his left hand work to write the message his heart was crying out to say, but his strong will was not enough. Dejected, he flung the paper across the room and admitted defeat.

He'd just have to hope that her love for him was as deep as his was for her.

Chapter 45

The first ten days after Tiffany arrived back home in Paris she had no time to miss Chad, for the days and nights were busy ones. She found it a divine pleasure just to roam the spacious rooms of her home after some of the miserable quarters she'd had to spend time in the last several months.

It was wonderful to see dear Noah and he was so happy to see her. "Missed you terribly, mademoiselle. It was lonely here without you around," he had told her. When she gave him the gift she'd purchased for him in New Orleans, he was overwhelmed with joy that she'd thought about him. "You're a sweet child, Mademoiselle Tiffany! I can't imagine you having time to think about old Noah with all the traveling you were doing. I thank you, missy. I truly thank you!"

Tiffany had given a soft giggle. "Oh, Noah—I was wishing that I was back here with you a lot of the time instead of where I was. It—it is so very good to be back. I'm so happy to be home!"

"Well, not half as much as I am." He smiled adoringly up at the young girl standing there by his chair. She had dashed up to his quarters shortly after she'd arrived back home.

Of course, the first place she rushed to was her pink

bedroom decorated with all the floral pastel ruffles around her canopy bed and piled with cuddly pillows. How wonderful it was going to be to sleep there tonight, she thought to herself as she rushed up the flight of steps.

The minute she stepped inside the room she thought to herself how beautiful it looked. She took in the pink floral luxury of the velvet chair and pink ceramic lamps on the nightstands on either side of her bed. She walked over to the tall, highly polished armoire to see the fancy gowns hanging there. She found herself eager to wear them again. Oh, it was like being alive again to be back in France!

She walked out the arched terrace doors into the small balcony and looked down below at the beautiful sight of their gardens. She smiled, thinking how much more she appreciated her home than she had before.

She was just turning to go back into her bedroom when she heard an excited shriek and she turned to see the tiny Magdelaine coming through the door with her basket of flowers. The little maid came rushing to greet her mistress.

They embraced as they cried and laughed together. Between sobs, Magdelaine stammered, "You take me with you next time, mademoiselle? I was so lonely I didn't know what to do with myself with you away."

Tiffany nodded. "I shall, for I was quite helpless without you, Magdelaine."

"I am glad you found you needed me, mademoiselle. You were gone forever, it seemed. I was beginning to think you were never coming back. But ah, now it will be the most wonderful holiday season!"

"I was thinking it might be forever too," Tiffany told her. For the next two hours the two of them talked and talked as the little maid moved around the room doing the simplest tasks for Tiffany.

Magdelaine was overcome with emotion when Tiffany gave her the package containing her gift from New

Orleans. "Mademoiselle, I don't know what to say," she confessed. It was rarely that the little maid was speechless, but that was one of the things that Tiffany had liked about her from the very first moment that she'd begun to work for her. The little chatterbox kept her entertained with stories about her life before she came to the Renaud household.

Tiffany indulged herself with unrestrained delight with a warm bath, fragrant with her favorite bath oils. Magdelaine was there with the huge towels when she was ready to step out of the tub. Tiffany had to admit that she suddenly realized just how much she had missed all this pampering.

As she sat in her soft silk wrapper, she completely relaxed as the maid's nimble fingers styled her hair in a most attractive fashion, high atop her head with a tiny wisp curling around her ears.

"Ah, mademoiselle—you look so lovely, but then you always do! You wish the pearls for your ears—oui?"

"The pearls will be perfect. I think I'll wear my crème-colored gown tonight, Magdelaine, for I feel like dressing up."

"The crème silk with the little pink rosettes?"

Tiffany nodded her head cautiously, for she didn't want all the lovely curls piled atop her head to fall down; but Magdelaine laughed, assuring her that they would not do that.

It was not only in Tiffany's bedroom that an air of gaiety seemed to be ringing out in the palatial house tonight. The servants were scurrying around the second floor to attend to the monsieur and madame as well as their guests, Tasha and her son, Etienne.

In the kitchen below, the cook and her helpers were preparing a feast to celebrate the return of the Renauds. The monsieur's favorite wines had been brought up from the cellar.

Charmaine too was pleased to be back home. While it

336

was a thrill to revisit the place where she and Pierre had shared an exciting part of their past, this was home. Back in New Madrid was the past and while there had been some wonderful memories, there were some horrible ones that haunted her like a nightmare. Charmaine had thought that she had put all that behind her long ago, but it was still vividly recalled, now that they'd returned to the place where it had all happened.

Pierre had lingered in his study after his wife went upstairs to their bedroom, because the mountain of papers and letters awaiting him was staggering. He realized that he had many hours of work ahead of him in the next weeks to make up for his long absence.

He sat at his desk for over an hour—long enough for him to make a very definite decision: Charmaine would have to take Tasha and Etienne to Cherbourg without him. He had to remain in Paris, for he could not take the time off.

He made no mention of this when he finally dimmed the lamp of his study to join her upstairs so he could dress for dinner.

Seeing all the opulence surrounding her in this mansion Charmaine lived in, Tasha loved her more for all the things she'd done for her in her humble cottage back in New Madrid. Why, she couldn't believe all the servants in this place! She'd never seen such beautiful furnishings as the ones in the fancy guest bedroom she'd been ushered to by one of the houseservants. She was sure that Etienne was thinking the same thing in his room directly across the hall from hers.

She felt that in this elegant setting she should wear the pretty berry-colored silk gown Charmaine had bought for her in New Orleans. When she was dressed and stood in front of the full-length mirror to survey herself, she was pleased with the way she looked in the rich wine gown with the white lace collar and cuffs. She added small pearl earrings. Reuben's gold chain was tucked inside her gown.

Tasha knew she was far too old to believe in fairy tales, but in a place like this, and dressed so elegantly, she felt like a princess. Maybe it was crazy for ladies as old as she was to indulge themselves in such foolishness, but she couldn't help herself. Her whole life had taken on a new excitement. Tasha felt young and adventurous again and the feeling was wonderful!

She dared not voice these private feelings to anyone, especially to Etienne. To Charmaine, she could, but there'd not been that right time to do so.

Unlike his mother, Etienne was feeling very ill at ease. Madame Renaud had told him that he would be meeting their oldest son, Charles, tonight at dinner. Etienne wondered how Charles would react to him and his mother. It certainly did not seem to make his mother nervous.

A few hours later he found himself sitting in the most elegant dining room that he'd ever dined in. He'd thought the Carrolls' home was a palace, but this mansion surpassed their fine country estate. He realized that he had no reason to feel ill at ease, for he was with the same people that had gathered around the simple rough-hewn table back in his home in New Madrid.

Their oldest son, Charles, was just as friendly and outgoing as his parents. It was obvious that he adored his young sister, Tiffany. He enjoyed teasing her by remarking, "Well, I guess we might as well prepare ourselves that all the nice peace and quiet is over, eh, Tiffany? However, it was a little dull, I have to admit." He turned to his mother and winked.

Pierre gave way to laughter as he thought to himself how grand it was to be sitting at the head of his table, listening to his son playfully taunting his younger sister.

Charmaine gently admonished him, "Charles, you are being the typical older brother, you know?"

He laughed good-naturedly, "Ah, Maman—Tiffany knows I adore her. Is that not true, ma petite?"

Tiffany turned her head in his direction and her sparkling blue eyes challenged him. "I'm not so sure of that, Charles. The truth of it is you always considered me your spoiled brat of a sister and you, dear Charles, were the oldest domineering brother. Phillipe and Jacques were always sweeter to me."

"Oh, Tiffany—you—you wound me!" he laughed.

As the two of them jested, Tasha and Étienne exchanged glances. The impact of the name Jacques had an effect on both of them. It pleased Tasha to think that Charmaine and Pierre had wished to name one of their sons Jacques. He was their youngest son and Tasha found herself most anxious to meet him too.

Étienne left the table with no qualms about his future here in France. He felt confident that he could adjust to this new way of life without any problems. In fact, he rather liked the sweet taste of all this elegance.

Never had he seen Tiffany looking more ravishingly lovely and he realized now that this was the way she was accustomed to living. He'd never seen a more beautiful gown than the one she wore tonight and the way her lovely black hair was styled made her look like a princess. She was enough to take his breath away every time he looked in her direction.

In a setting like this, he saw a different Tiffany than he'd known before. This Tiffany was even more exciting to Étienne! Étienne was glad he'd come to Paris.

There was only one person disturbed at the end of the evening and that was Pierre Renaud. He knew that he had to enlighten his sons and his daughter about the truth concerning Tasha and Étienne.

Grand-père Renaud was not going to be happy about this!

Chapter 46

Charmaine took full charge of showing her friends the spectacular sights of Paris. It was a pleasure for her to take them on the daily tours, and she always had Noah stop at one of her favorite sidewalk cafés so they could enjoy the coffee, chocolate or wine for a relaxing moment before they got back into the carriage to go somewhere else.

Some days, Tiffany accompanied them. Other times, she remained behind, for she was eager to pay a visit to her friends, especially Denise.

One afternoon while her mother, Tasha and Etienne were touring the city, Tiffany decided to pay a visit to her grandfather.

Magdelaine helped her dress in the new frock that she'd had no chance to wear when her father had abruptly announced that they were leaving Paris back last spring.

It was the new bobbed jacket ensemble in a brilliant blue wool that she'd intended to take with her when she visited Sabrina in London. It was most flattering and a perfect match for her deep blue eyes. She looked stunning as the maid tied the ribbons to the side of her face after placing the matching bonnet on her head.

After Magdelaine had left the room and Tiffany gave a final dab of the toilet water behind her ears and wrist, she decided she saw nothing wrong with flaunting her exquisite ring in front of her grand-père. He would appreciate such a magnificent piece of jewelry.

Before she went downstairs to board her carriage, she pulled out the chain to take the ring off and slipped it on her finger. For a moment, she stared at it and thoughts of the man who'd given it to her consumed her.

She had at least another two weeks to wait for him to come to Paris, she thought as she looked at the ring. Two weeks seemed forever!

Old Etienne sat in his study, reading his morning paper. Age and failing health had not dampened his effort to be the dapper gent he'd always been. He always wore his fine-tailored velvet morning coats to lounge around his palatial house whether he was expecting a visitor or not.

Tiffany could never recall a time when she'd seen Grand-père that he'd not been impeccably dressed, ever though he rarely went to the office anymore. She'd alway teased him about his curly hair which had become thinner and whiter.

"Why did Papa not inherit your pretty curls?" she'd often teased him.

He always retorted, "Took after his maman, ma petite!"

This kind of lighthearted repartee had always existed between old Etienne and Tiffany since she was a small tot, and he'd never been that way with his grandsons, even though he'd tried. With Tiffany, it had come easily. He'd never tried to disguise the fact that she was his favorite of all of Pierre's children. He was grateful that the brothers had never seemed to resent it. Not that it would have made one bit of difference to old Etienne. No one changed the old fellow's thinking on anything and his family was well aware of this.

At least, all the family accepted this except Tiffany. Often, she'd managed to do just that where her father had failed.

When she arrived at the stately old mansion, she insisted that the servant not announce her. She wanted to surprise him as he sat there in his comfortable brown leather chair by the hearth, reading his paper with his spectacles barely handing on the tip of his nose.

Quietly, she walked into the room with her reticule and the box with the bright plaid scarf she'd purchased for him. Never would she have thought about purchasing a vivid red and green scarf for her brothers, but Grand-père liked flamboyant, showy accessories.

She thought he looked very elegant sitting there in his rich bottle-green velvet jacket with the paisley ascot at his neck. On his feet he wore soft velvet slippers to match his morning coat. On the table by his chair was the cup of hot chocolate he always enjoyed while he read his paper.

While his sight might be going, there was nothing wrong with old Renaud's sense of smell. He recognized the special fragrance his granddaughter always wore.

"Tiffany, ma cherie," he asked, peering up from his paper, "is that you sneaking in on your grand-père?"

She gave a soft giggle. "You old rascal—how did you know?"

He extended his wrinkled hands up to her and declared, "Ah, you don't think I'm going to tell you all my little secrets, do you? Come here and give me a kiss! I've missed you! Missed you terribly."

She did as he requested. When they broke from their embrace he held her at arm's length to look at her. There was an admiring look on his wrinkled face as his piercing eyes surveyed his lovely granddaughter, but he saw

342

a different young lady from the one he'd last seen.

"You've changed, ma petite."

"What do you mean, Grand-père?" Tiffany took the seat beside him as she still held his hand.

"I don't know that I can put it into words but I can give you an example of what I mean." He related the change in her to the gardens that his wife took such pride in before her death. "You are like her roses. The last time I saw you, you were like the most perfect rosebud I'd seen in that garden. The promise was there of a most beautiful full-blossomed rose later. Now I see that rose—you, Tiffany."

"Oh, Grand-père—you are so sweet! I love you so much," she declared and moved over to hug him. "I just wish you weren't my grand-père; I'd just marry you, I think."

That brought forth a roar of laughter from old Etienne. She had some magic about her to lift his spirits. He patted her dainty hand. "Ah, Tiffany, you are like a tonic! I need you to come around just to make me feel better."

"I'll make a point of doing just that, Grand-père. You can't know how glad I am to be back in Paris. I never wanted to go to America. It was Papa's idea that I go."

"Can't understand Pierre's reasoning about that. Seems to me that he paid a high price for his friendship with these people he went to take care of. But then, that was his affair. Six months is a long time to take away from our own business."

As old Renaud had patted her hand, he had noticed the magnificent ring on her finger. "Ah, what is this? Now when did you get this, little Tiffany?"

She gave him a sly smile. "Is it not a beauty?"

"It is that and a lot more. It is a most valuable ring!"

She should have known his expert eye would recognize that. She told him about the young man she'd met on her trip and that he had given it to her.

"I must surmise that you and this Chad Morrow are more than just friends then. Are you in love with him, ma petite?"

"I think so, Grand-père."

"Well! Well! My little Tiffany is in love!" Old Etienne needed no other explanation as to why his little "rosebud" was a full-blossomed rose. She was a woman in love!

"You will get to meet him in a couple of weeks, Grand-père. He is coming to Paris."

"I shall look forward to that. He must be quite a man to have captured my Tiffany's heart. No ordinary man could manage that, I know."

Old Etienne asked Tiffany many questions about Chad Morrow. For the next half-hour, Tiffany found herself talking freely about the man she loved.

In her enthusiasm of singing Chad's praises, she told him about the incident in the park when he had rescued her from a scoundrel her father had fired from his office. Etienne was incensed. "Pierre never told me of this! Why, Charboneau, that cochon, should have been killed for doing that to you!"

She tried to soothe him by assuring him that she thought he was taken care of by the officials. "I know that Chad gave him quite a beating. Forget it, Grand-père . . . that was over months ago."

But when old Renaud got riled, it took him a long time to simmer down. When she finally managed to calm him, he found himself already approving of Chad. "I certainly want to meet this young man. Seems he's been there not once but twice when you needed him very badly," he declared after she'd told him about the similar incident that happened in New Madrid.

Now that she'd soothed the old man and the mood was lighter, Tiffany breathed a sigh of relief. But she also knew that he would mention what she'd told him to her

344

father the next time they met and this she regretted.

She could not believe that the clock was chiming five and that she'd already spent over three hours with her grandfather. Time went by so fast when she was with him! She rose to announce that she must be leaving. It was only then that she noticed she'd not given him the scarf.

He opened the package and pulled out the colorful scarf, declaring to her that he'd wear it only if she'd accompany him in a carriage ride around the city. She promised to do that.

"On a cold winter day, we shall take a jaunt about the city and have some hot chocolate at Le Pignon—oui?"

She bent down to gently kiss his face before she took her leave. "The winter will soon be here, Grand-père."

"I know! But you don't have to wait for that to come see me again," he told her.

"Oh, I won't. But I must leave now." She blew him a kiss as she walked out the door of his study and he gave her the same gesture in return. Tiffany was the golden joy of his life, he decided as he watched her leave him.

She gave him a reason to live! He damned well wanted to be around to see just what she was going to do with her life.

He struggled to get out of his chair to go over to his liquor chest to pour himself a brandy.

The old man gave a silent toast to his favorite grandchild before draining the cup.

Chapter 47

The first week in Paris had been thrilling for Etienne as he toured the city with Madame Renaud and his mother, but the busy Paris streets began to lose their luster after that. He found himself wishing for the quiet of New Madrid's country lanes.

It had also been fascinating to roam through the spacious mansion that Tiffany considered her home, but Etienne found all the grandeur tedious to live around daily. He was always fearful that he was going to bump into one of the fancy little tables and break something.

Etienne found himself ill at ease when the servants were always offering their services, for he was not accustomed to having things done for him.

He had finally met the Renauds' youngest son, Jacques, and found him just as friendly as Charles. But he had nothing to talk about with Charles or Jacques and he knew that they tried to encourage him to talk about himself. He could not fault any of the Renauds, for they tried to make him feel welcome in their home; but Etienne felt like an outsider. Quite to the contrary, his mother seemed to fit in easily.

Since they'd arrived in Paris, he'd had no moments alone with Tiffany at all. It seemed that she was constantly breezing away from the house to go somewhere. Monsieur Renaud spent long hours at his office and the only time Etienne saw him was at the evening meal. The rest of the evening he sequestered himself in his study to go over his business papers.

Two evenings, Tiffany had not shared dinner with the family because she'd had invitations to dine at friends' homes.

Some afternoons when Etienne found himself with time on his hands and nothing to do, he took long strolls around the spacious grounds. Sometimes he stopped to talk with the gardeners.

It was on one of these occasions, as he walked into a small section of the gardens near the house, that he heard a beautiful female voice singing a French song. Curious to see whom the voice belonged to, he strolled in that direction. He quickly spied the tiny miss with her basket swung over her arms. As she picked the clusters of asters, she sang her lively little tune and her body swayed in time to the music. As Etienne took in the sight of her, he came to the conclusion that his mother might have looked like this young French miss when she was young. The girl had naturally curly hair as black as the night, as Tasha had before it started to turn gray. The profile of her face and her golden skin were the same as Tasha's.

Magdelaine seemed to sense Etienne's dark eyes ogling her and she rose to look in his direction. A slow, warm smile creased her face. "Good afternoon, monsieur." She knew immediately that this must be the Renauds' house guest, but she'd not seen him except when she'd chanced to glance out the upstairs window when the group was getting in or out of the carriage.

"Good afternoon, mademoiselle. Lovely flowers." Etienne moved closer to where she stood.

"Ah, oui—for Mademoiselle Tiffany's room. She loves fresh flowers," Magdelaine remarked.

Remembering how often they'd roamed the woods when she was in New Madrid and he'd taken her for so many walks, Etienne smiled, "Oh yes, she does love flowers."

Suddenly, they were talking casually and Etienne found Magdelaine very easy to talk to and he was completely relaxed. It was nice to be around her as she suggested that they sit there on the thick carpet of grass. Etienne eagerly accepted. "I have plenty of time this afternoon because the mademoiselle is spending the afternoon with her grand-père. She will be returning late in the afternoon, I suspect."

She continued to call him monsieur as they talked and Etienne smiled as he requested that she just call him Etienne.

"But I am a servant—Mademoiselle Tiffany's maid. I fear that is not proper for me to call you Etienne."

"Now that is nobody's business but ours, is it, Magdelaine? I insist that you do this for me."

With a pleased twinkle in her black eyes, she grinned. "If you insist, mon—Etienne."

"See, that sounds better doesn't it?"

"Oui!" Magdelaine felt the heat of his eyes as they wandered over her. He'd sat down beside her, leaving a very small space to divide them. She tried to keep reminding herself that he was merely killing time. She dared not allow herself to think that he found her interesting or attractive. But he did, and that was why he lingered with her for a whole hour. It was a pleasant hour for Etienne and when they finally left to go their separate ways, he told her, "Perhaps, we might meet again, Magdelaine. I enjoyed talking with you."

Magdelaine swelled with excitement and told him that she was usually in the garden about this time of day.

As she went to the house she was glad that the part of the garden where they'd sat was a secluded one, concealed by huge flowering shrubs, so no one could have seen them. She didn't think she'd dare to mention this to the mademoiselle.

The next two afternoons they met in the same spot around the same time. Etienne found himself looking forward to keeping his rendezvous with Tiffany's maid.

Everything warned Magdelaine that she might be inviting trouble, but she looked forward to the brief period she spent with the handsome young guest. She didn't feel like a servant when she was with Etienne and he didn't treat her like one.

Today, he had reached over to take her hand in his and she liked the feel of his strong hand clasping hers. For one fleeting moment, she could have sworn that he was going to bend over and kiss her. She wanted him to but he didn't.

The next day it rained all day so no flowers could be gathered and Magdelaine missed seeing Etienne, for she had to stay inside all day. Mademoiselle Tiffany went shopping with her friend Denise, so it was a very long day.

Etienne did not expect to find Magdelaine in the garden, but he could not resist the urge to take the walk in the rain to see if she might be there. So he returned to the house with his thick hair dripping from the raindrops falling steadily over the area. Tasha had laughed at the sight of him. "My goodness, Etienne . . . it is not the day to be out walking."

He just laughed good-naturedly. "I found that out, Mama." He said no more as he turned to go on to his own room, but before Tasha continued on down the long hallway, she told her son that they would be leaving for Cherbourg at the end of the week.

A few days ago, he would have welcomed that news, but now that he'd met Magdelaine, all this had changed for him. He was not all that eager to leave the little maid behind, for he found himself very interested in knowing her better. She'd brightened his life the last few days.

That evening as Magdelaine was attending to the styling of Tiffany's hair which had also been dampened by the afternoon shower, Tiffany casually remarked about the trip she would be making with her mother. "I wouldn't go but I so want to see Phillipe."

"You will be taking your friends to Cherbourg at the end of this week, mademoiselle?" Magdelaine stammered. Tiffany did not seem to notice that the maid suddenly stopped combing her curls in place, nor did she notice the surprised look on Magdelaine's face.

"Yes, but this time I won't be gone so long," Tiffany assured her. She gave a girlish giggle, remembering her promise to the maid that the next time she left she would take her with her. "Shall I see if Maman will allow me to take you?"

Magdelaine smiled weakly at her mistress, for she knew in the past that Madame Renaud did not take her own personal maid when she went to their country estate outside Cherbourg. Tiffany would not be allowed to take her.

"Oh, please don't worry about that, mademoiselle. I—I am just glad that this will be a short journey." It was hard to disguise her feeling that Etienne would soon be leaving and that she might not ever see him again. It was foolish of her to have daydreamed as she had, but she could not stop herself.

For a few precious days, she'd gotten to know him. She knew that his handsome face would haunt her dreams for a long time to come, and she would have pleasant memories of the golden autumn days they'd spent that stolen hour or so in the gardens talking and enjoying each other's company.

When Tiffany left the room to go down to dinner, Magdelaine went about the bedroom, making it tidy, and

350

praying that tomorrow it would not rain.

After she had folded back the ruffled coverlet on her mistress's bed and laid out her gown, Magdelaine left to go to her own room. There, she allowed herself to think about Etienne Bernay. The next days would be very dear to her and she hoped she would know the sensation of his lips kissing hers just once before he left to go to Cherbourg.

Whether the sun was shining or the rains were coming down as they were today, she was going to that particular spot in the gardens where they had met in hopes that she would find him there waiting for her.

Tiffany had been so occupied with her own affairs that she had been neglecting poor Etienne. Tomorrow, she planned to pay another visit to her grandfather and it might be nice if she invited Etienne to go with her. After all, they shared the same name, so it seemed right that they should meet.

She'd make a point of inviting him tonight when they all gathered to share the evening meal. It seemed the evening meal was the only time the family was together since they'd arrived back in Paris. Poor Papa was surely paying the price of his many months of absence from his business. But she'd heard her mother tell Tasha yesterday that Pierre was so tenacious and determined to get everything in order before the holidays so he could enjoy that season to the fullest with his family. "He shall do it, too," Charmaine had told her friend. But then Tiffany had always known that her mother had an unwavering faith in her husband.

She wondered if she would ever have that kind of faith in Chad Morrow. She wanted to with all her heart but even now, she had to wonder if he would appear in Paris as he'd so fervently promised when he'd held her in his

351

arms the last time they were together. Oh, she would never forgive him if he failed her again!

It was always so easy for her to believe him when he was holding her close in his strong arms. Only today, she had realized that by the time she returned from Cherbourg he should be getting here.

In the meanwhile, Tiffany decided that she would enjoy herself as she waited for him to come to her and this was exactly what she had been doing. It was fun to see her friends and go to their special little haunts about the city. It had been wonderful to go to all her favorite shops, too, and she realized how much she had missed Paris.

It would be a pleasure to go back for a visit tomorrow to see her grandfather for the second time since she'd been back. Her family was very important to her and there was a pride instilled in her she had just recently begun to realize. She'd missed being around her oldest brother, Charles, and her youngest brother, Jacques. She was eagerly anticipating seeing dear Phillipe with his gentle nature. He loved the simple things of life and nothing excited him about the city of Paris. His land and his young wife were the loves of his life.

Very rarely did the family encourage him to leave his peaceful French countryside to venture into Paris for a visit. Usually, Tiffany and her parents went to see him but she knew it was her mother's plan to try to talk them into coming here during the holidays this year.

If anyone could persuade him, it was her mother! Phillipe adored her!

Part IV

Winter's Rapture

Chapter 48

Magdelaine was to be granted her wish that the sun would shine and she would have her meeting with Etienne Bernay. Before they would part company, she was also granted her other secret wish—that he would kiss her. Never had she known such happiness as he held her in his arms and told her how beautiful he thought she was.

He also told her that he would be leaving Paris to go to Cherbourg in a day or two. Of course, she already knew this, but it delighted her to hear him tell her that he would write her. "I want to keep in touch with you, Magdelaine, for I don't want you to forget me after I leave."

"Oh, Etienne. I—I could never do that."

"I hope not," Etienne told her. But as his arms were holding her, she looked up at him in wide-eyed innocence to ask, "I am curious about something. Are you and my mistress kin?"

She obviously did not notice the sudden tenseness of his muscled body, nor did she notice the bright flashing in his black eyes as he looked at her. For one brief moment he said nothing.

A forced smile came to his face as he asked her, "Why

would you ask that, Magdelaine?"

She gave a light laugh. "I guess I just assumed that you and your mother had to be relatives of the Renauds for them to travel so far and stay so long. Obviously, I was wrong—oui?"

"Oui, you were wrong."

Had she not noticed that two of the gardeners were coming in this direction, Magdelaine was not sure what might have happened if they had lingered there much longer. But they both hastily leaped up from the ground and she grabbed the handle of her basket to rush away. She gave Etienne a wave of her hand as she fled through the shrubbery and he ambled away in another direction.

Etienne was having the same thoughts as she was as they went their separate ways, for he was churning with desire to make love to Tiffany's pretty maid. If those two damned gardeners had not happened along when they did, he would have gotten to satisfy the ache of wanting her.

He soothed himself, telling himself there was tomorrow left before he left for Cherbourg. At least, he would get to be with her tomorrow for the last time.

But that hope was dashed during dinner when Madame Renaud announced that they would be leaving for Cherbourg the first thing in the morning.

"I must get back to Paris a few days sooner than I had planned to. Pierre wants me back to entertain guests coming to Paris to discuss some business with him. So we all better retire early this evening—oui?" she said and smiled.

Etienne found it hard to conceal his displeasure. Tiffany was pleased, for it meant that she could be back in Paris a day or two sooner than she'd expected. She wanted to be in Paris when Chad arrived.

There was no point now of speaking to Etienne about the visit tomorrow to Grand-père's and she excused

356

herself right after dinner to attend to her last-minute packing. She wanted to be sure that Phillipe's gift and the lovely shawl she'd bought for his wife were in the valise.

The minute she bounced into the room to announce the change of plans to Magdelaine, she noticed the maid's crestfallen air. "Oh, Magdelaine . . . don't be sad, for I will be getting back sooner than I'd expected."

"Oui, I will try not to be so sad," the maid mumbled as she aimlessly paced around the room, her thoughts on Etienne. She saw that the presents for Tiffany's brother and sister-in-law were put in the luggage as requested.

"What will Mademoiselle wish to wear in the morning? Shall I get it out tonight or wait until morning?"

Tiffany suggested that she wait. "Why don't you go on to your room, Magdelaine? You look tired tonight and I can attend to my hair. After all, I did it every night when I was in New Madrid. I'll see you in the morning."

Tiffany watched the maid leave the room. She hoped that she wasn't coming down with something, for it was rarely that Magdelaine looked so downcast. She had certainly acted in fine spirits as she'd styled her hair and helped her dress for dinner, Tiffany recalled as she sat at her dressing table taking the pins out of her hair.

Magdelaine watched the party leave the next morning in the Renauds' fancy brougham drawn by the fine bays. Tears streamed down her face, for she knew that she'd never see the handsome Etienne Bernay again. Someone like her could not expect to hold him as she yearned to do. A simple little servant girl could not expect to have a beau like Etienne.

She took her apron up to dab her eyes and admonished herself harshly as she stood there. All right, she'd given way to a few days of foolish folly. So be it! It was over now and he was gone. She would never lay eyes on him again and she knew it. When she married it would be to a simple fellow with a background similar to hers. This was the way life was and she must accept it.

The rest of the day she tried to put her thoughts about Etienne behind her and forget him, but she realized that it was not going to be easy.

Across the English Channel from his ladylove, Chad Morrow brooded, still confined to his townhouse. As desperately as he tried he could only pull so much movement out of that damned leg of his. His doctor kept telling him that he was asking the impossible, for it had only been three weeks. "You're just going to have to be more patient, young man, whether you like it or not!"

His patience had run out! He still could not make his right hand work well enough to write Tiffany a letter explaining why he'd not be able to meet her in Paris as he'd promised. He knew his frivolous, flighty Tiffany; she would assume he had not taken his vow seriously. She could not possibly know his frustration that he could not keep that vow.

At least, the last three weeks had not been idle as he'd recuperated, trying desperately to restore his health and vigor. He could hire blokes just as easily as his uncle and his son had done. All one had to do was have the money and a few contacts and Chad had that. Simon ran those errands for him.

Simon hired two men to keep their ears and eyes open down at the pubs on Fleet Street for two men who fit the description of the two who'd waylaid Morrow. It wasn't long before they were spotted. The big giant, Ural, and his friend, Willie, were generously spending their bounty and bragging about their easy money. The only thing that galled Chad was that he had to hire the deed done that he would have taken a great delight in doing personally. But these two stupid blokes were really not the ones Chad sought his revenge on. It was his uncle and his oldest wastrel son, Henry.

There was no more property Henry could lose to the gaming tables because Chad had acquired that last plot of land, so any debts Henry had now had to fall back on his greedy uncle. Chad pondered just how long his Uncle Elbert Chadwick would allow this.

There was some degree of gratification to Chad that he'd managed to see that the two bastards that had injured him had gotten their due justice.

He had many hours to think about how he would play Henry. Knowing his weak, spineless character, Chad figured it would be poetic justice to let him destroy himself.

But Chad did not expect the surprise visit from his Uncle Elbert one early morning, with Simon trailing behind him. "I could not stop him, sir," Simon apologized as the frenzied elderly Chadwick bolted into Chad's bedroom.

"What are you trying to do the family, boy? You are a devil and I've always known that!" His eyes were wild and his mouth twitched as he stammered out his words.

Chad propped himself up in the bed and looked at his uncle. "I've done no more to you than you and Henry tried to do to me. You tried to cheat me out of the land that rightfully belonged to me after my mother died, so I simply got it back because your stupid son put it up for his gambling debts."

"You—you killed Henry! That's what you did!" Elbert Chadwick shrieked at him.

"I've not laid a hand on Henry. As you can see, I'm hardly in a position to kill anyone. You tried to blame my mother's death on me—remember? I was just a young lad when you tried to put that on my back. Now your son is dead and I'm at fault. Admit it, Uncle Elbert—you Chadwicks are a weak lot! It's always easy to lay the blame for your frailty on someone's else's doorstep. Well, forget it! If Henry is dead, it isn't my fault!"

Elbert Chadwick turned ghostly pale and he could not speak as he stood there staring at Morrow. He'd known even before he came to Chad's townhouse what had happened the night before. Henry had gone to the gambling hall and lost as he always did. The gents he'd lost to had made grave threats and Henry had proceeded to get very drunk.

He'd stumbled off a bridge into the water, and in his drunken stupor he'd not tried to fight to save his life. But Elbert had to have someone to blame, so in his frenzied state he sought out Chad. He could not allow himself to shoulder the blame nor could he admit that his son was a weakling.

Chad watched the man leave his room without saying another word and no one had to tell him that his uncle was in the pits of hell. Morrow knew that Elbert Chadwick was feeling his own damnation and he had no reason to seek any more revenge. That had been taken care of by a higher power than his.

Chad was hardly expecting to read in the London paper two days later that Elbert Chadwick had died in his sleep. There was no feeling one way or the other when he read the article and tossed it aside.

Instead, he turned his attention and energy toward making himself move up and down the length of his room to exercise his injured leg. Each day it seemed a little easier to walk.

Today, he was very demanding on himself. At the end of the day he felt drained and exhausted. By the time he'd eaten his dinner from the tray that Delphia had brought up to his bedroom, he found that he was ready to go to sleep.

Almost as soon as he sank deep into his bed and pulled the coverlet up over him, he fell into a deep sleep. Suddenly, Chad found himself caught up in a most realistic dream. He smelled the sweet fragrance that only belonged to one beautiful woman.

He knew it was Tiffany lying in bed beside him, and his whole being was aflame with desire. All he had to do was reach out to bring her close to him so his body could press against her.

He could hear the echoes of her soft, sweet sighs there in the darkness of his dreams. His arm flung out, his one strong arm, to grasp her. But his arm touched nothing but emptiness and frantically his hand patted the bed to find nothing.

Wide awake now, he sat up straight in bed. He felt damp all over with his own sweat. Quickly, he reached over to the lamp by the side of his bed. He had to know that the darkness was not concealing her somewhere.

It was only after the room was bright with lamplight that he accepted the fact that he had been dreaming. For a while, he sat there propped up on the pillows so he could sort out reality from the dreamlike state he'd been in.

He didn't care what his doctor said, he was damned if he was going to postpone making the trip to Paris for another three or four weeks.

Instinct told him he needed to get to Tiffany as soon as possible!

Chapter 49

Pierre Renaud decided to finally have an audience with his father the night after his wife had left to take Tasha and Etienne to their country estate outside Cherbourg. He had purposely planned not to speak to his father about the guests brought back from New Madrid until they were away from Paris. Pierre could not predict how this old rascal would react when he told him the truth about Tasha and Etienne.

Pierre was not looking forward to this visit as he traveled down the Paris street at twilight time. He had cut his day an hour short so he might have the extra time to spend with his father.

His father's devoted manservant ushered Pierre into the elegant parlor where Etienne was enjoying his favorite brandy. Pierre sauntered in to greet his father. He admired this aristocratic, arrogant gentleman. He had always envied that shrewd intelligence he possessed to have built his mining industry into such a wealthy empire. It had been a challenge to Pierre to do as well as his father once he had returned to Paris from New Madrid with his young bride, Charmaine.

"Well, Pierre—I finally have the privilege of seeing you. Six months is a long time," Etienne declared with a touch of sarcasm.

"Six months *is* a long tme, Papa, and that is what has been occupying my time. I'm trying to make up the lost time."

"You have your work cut out for you, I'd say. And why am I not being graced by that beautiful wife of yours?"

"Charmaine has gone to Cherbourg. She was anxious to see her son, Papa. It was a long time for her to be away from her family and you know Charmaine."

"Tiffany go with her?"

Pierre told him that she had. "You are looking very fit, sir."

Etienne opened the door for the discussion Pierre sought to have with him when he insisted on knowing, "I've yet to figure that impulsive venture of yours, Pierre. You're usually so level-headed, but to cross an ocean and stay so long! I found it unlike you."

"Then you surely had to know it was for a worthy cause, sir. At least, I considered it my duty."

Etienne gave a grunt. "Well, these people are exceedingly lucky to have you for a friend, my son." The old Frenchman went on grumbling that Pierre had certainly asked a lot of his beautiful wife and daughter.

"My wife agreed that we must go, but my daughter did resent the trip, I'll have to admit. To Charmaine, Tasha and Jacques Bernay were as dear as they were to me, so naturally when I received the letter from her son that his mother was seriously ill and his father had died, she felt we should go to Tasha."

Pierre enlightened his father of the many months they'd shared in the small hamlet of New Madrid and how they'd all endured the terrible earthquake and the aftermath that December night in 1811. The month afterwards was just as bad. "Something like that binds people together, Papa."

Etienne nodded his balding, curly head and admitted,

"I guess it would at that."

There was not going to be an easy way to tell his father what he knew he must tell him, so he declared, "But there was more tie binding me to Jacques Bernay, Papa."

"Oh?" Old Etienne looked up, for the tone of his son's voice sounded so serious.

"Yes, sir. It happened quite by chance. Jacques and I just happened to join up when I was in the Channel Islands. You'll remember you'd sent me from Paris to go to the States to see about your interests there. Jacques was a seaman. It seemed our paths were to go in the same direction. By that time my life had joined with Charmaine and his had joined with Tasha Weer. What we discovered came as a shock to both of us."

Old Etienne was as impatient as his granddaughter, Tiffany, and he was fidgeting with curiosity.

Pierre did not leave his curiosity waiting long as he continued his revelation. "Jacques happened to show me a miniature of his mother and I told him I thought that she was a very attractive lady. He told me that she was dead and how she'd raised him alone. His father had not married his mother. So I asked him if he knew about his father and he pulled out another miniature."

"A picture of his father?" Etienne asked in a hesitating voice. His expressionless face gave Pierre no inkling that he was already going back a lifetime in his memories and the name Bernay sounded familiar.

"You, Papa. You were Jacques's father."

Pierre was not prepared for the frozen expression on his father's face, and he was stunned by his cool, calm demeanor. The old man's face looked as if it was set in granite.

"Pour us another glass of brandy, Pierre, and we shall talk a little longer." As Pierre poured the brandy, Etienne lit up a cheroot.

"I would never claim myself to be a saint. In fact, I was

just as randy as you were when you got yourself involved with a married lady here in Paris and I shipped you to my brother's across the ocean to avoid a scandal. I had myself a little belle or two after your mother and I were married, but I was always very discreet. At least I was until I met Mademoiselle Bernay. The affair lasted a month and I did give her a miniature of me. She—she kept me from being lonely during a time I needed company. You were just a babe and your mother was a very fragile lady."

There was a mellow warmth in the old man's eyes as he spoke of this time when his wife was so happy and content that she'd finally given him an heir.

"But suddenly this lady became demanding of me, saying she was pregnant and I must leave my wife and marry her. This was out of the question. I left her that night in a rage. But when I was halfway home, I decided to turn the carriage around to make her the offer of a generous sum of money to take care of her and the baby. When I returned to her cottage and chanced to look through the window, I saw her in the amorous embrace of another young gent. I turned and walked away, having grave doubts that she might know who the father of her child was. It crossed my mind that she was not even pregnant. I never had any qualm of conscience about her and I don't now!"

"So you are saying that you don't consider yourself to be Jacques's father?" Pierre asked.

"I could have been but then I might not have been. She might have shown her son that picture and appointed me the figure, but I ask you, Pierre—how would you have reacted in a similar circumstance? A young woman who'd just made love to me and told me she carried my child was in another man's arms, ardently kissing him, a short time after I'd left her. I had a name for her and I think you have the same name. What would you

365

have done?"

It took Pierre a moment to speak. But when he did, he answered his father quite candidly, "I would have probably done exactly what you did, Papa." He realized at the same time that he had harbored false feelings about the old man that were not justified. It wasn't Jacques's fault or his. It was a woman's lies of a long time ago.

Pierre had much on his mind as he left his father's house that night. The possibility now existed that he and Jacques were not half-brothers as they'd thought all this time.

There was no denying that old Etienne's revelation put a different slant on things. He did not doubt for a minute the old man was telling him the absolute truth.

Pierre realized that there would never be a way to unravel all this insanity. Jacques's mother was dead and if what old Etienne said was true, she could not have been sure of who the father was.

There would never be an answer!

The country estate was situated in the rolling countryside, remote from the busy streets of Cherbourg. The moment the carriage got to the outskirts of the city it seemed to Tasha a magnificent quiet settled all around them. She could hear the birds singing and smell the wildflowers still blooming in the vast meadows even though summer was long gone. She thought about the magnificent landscapes Reuben could capture on his canvas if he did come to see her as he'd promised.

Everything seemed so beautifully green and alive here when she compared it to New Madrid at this time of the year, when the golds and rusts appeared in the woods surrounding her home, but then autumn was a most beautiful season back there too. Her thoughts were very much on dear Reuben and how he would appreciate this beauty for as far as the eyes could see.

She'd never known a man like him before. What fascinated her so much about him was how he seemed to absorb everything around him. It must be wonderful to be able to do that, she thought to herself.

Finally, she declared to Charmaine how beautiful she thought this part of France was. "No wonder you like to come here on visits from time to time." She turned to her son to say, "Isn't it wonderful, Etienne?"

"Yes, Mama—it is," he replied with a smile. Tasha could not figure out what had her son so preoccupied. He was hard to figure out lately. She had also noticed that Tiffany was very quiet and thoughtful as well. Charmaine had not seemed to let it concern her, so Tasha figured that she shouldn't either.

"We love it, Tasha. Pierre and I try to come here as often as we can and when Phillipe married Arabelle he requested that this could be their home, for he yearned to tend to the land and small vineyards. Of course, Pierre allowed it. Phillipe has loved the country ever since he was a small boy."

"And Charles or Jacques would be bored to death to live out here all the time," Tiffany quickly added.

Charmaine laughed. "You are right about that, ma petite, and neither would you like living here all year long as Phillipe and Arabelle do."

"Charles is like Papa and I've yet to figure out Jacques and his love of the sea and ships," Tiffany remarked.

"Jacques is just himself, Tiffany. He doesn't have to be like me or his father. I don't think Jacques has decided exactly what he wants to do with his life as Charles and Phillipe have. But then you, Tiffany, and Jacques are the youngest of my brood," Madame Renaud pointed out to her daughter. Tiffany saw the teasing twinkle in her mother's blue eyes as they looked at her.

Tiffany tilted her pretty head to the side with a

quizzical look on her face. "Are you saying that I don't know what I want out of life, Maman?"

"I think it is very possible, cherie."

"Ah, Maman—I will surprise you, I think. I know exactly what I want."

She wanted to love and be loved by Chad Morrow the rest of her life!

Chapter 50

Charmaine could see that Tasha was completely pleased with her new home. The spacious chateau had enough rooms to comfortably house Tasha and Etienne, as well as Phillipe and his wife. There were still rooms to spare any time the Renaud family decided to come for a visit.

The first thing Tasha noticed about the two-story structure with its numerous railed porches was how different it was from Pierre and Charmaine's elegant, palatial mansion in the city of Paris, with its delicate pastel furnishings and decor. There was a quaint, rustic atmosphere here with high-beamed ceilings and earthy colors of golds, rusts, and rich, brilliant greens.

Phillipe's wife had a tall, willowy figure and brilliant auburn hair hanging in long braids down her back. Phillipe had inherited his mother's fair hair and bright blue eyes but towering height was his father's. He looked like neither of his two brothers.

There were no servants here as there were in Paris. It was Arabelle who went to the kitchen to prepare spicy tea with a cinnamon stick in each cup. She also brought out a tray of delectable iced cakes.

After Tiffany had finished her tea, she gave her

brother and his wife a breezy farewell to go to her room. "I've some gifts for you two, but I've got to get my luggage unpacked to get to them," she said laughingly as she bounced out of the room.

Charmaine knew her way to the suite of rooms she and Pierre always occupied when they visited the chateau. Phillipe and Arabelle had been preparing quarters for Etienne and Tasha, too. The rooms afforded them a complete private entrance on two levels of steps going up to a railed porch of their own. The little sitting room with its numerous windows had a picturesque view of the rolling green countryside. There were two spacious bedrooms and a roomy kitchen so Tasha could putter around as she had in her own home. This had been his mother's request and Phillipe had done everything as she'd asked him to do.

Accompanying her friend and Etienne to their new quarters, Charmaine was delighted to see what her son and his wife had done with all this empty space. She would certainly make a point of thanking them for all the hours of work they'd done in such a short time.

After they had left Tasha and Etienne alone in their new home, Charmaine asked her son how he'd managed to make it so nice and comfortable.

Phillipe laughed. "One of my men moved furniture from some of the other rooms and Arabelle sewed long into the night to make the curtains and the coverlets for the beds."

Charmaine reached out to embrace her son and her daughter-in-law. "You are so very dear to me. I thank you for what you did."

As they walked back to the other section of the huge, sprawling house, Charmaine urged her son, "Put Etienne to work around your farm or your vineyard, Phillipe. It is not good for a young man to be idle. He is a robust, healthy fellow so he must earn his keep around here."

370

"Oh, I shall do that, Maman. Never you fret. No one stands idle around here, do they, Arabelle?"

"No, we don't allow that, Mother Renaud."

Charmaine saw a wonderful harmony between the two of them. This pleased her very much. She would hope that all her children found such bliss in their marriages as these two did. Arabelle was the perfect wife for her son.

It amazed her that there was not a babe in the beautiful wood-carved cradle they had up in their bedroom.

True to his word to his mother, Phillipe assigned some chores around the farm the very next day. Etienne was taken by surprise by his rather authoritative manner, and the perceptive Phillipe noticed it immediately. But he mentioned nothing about it to his mother all day.

At the end of the first day, Phillipe remarked to Etienne, "I'll never ask you to do anything I don't do myself around here, Etienne, but I will expect you to do your part. This is a working farm. My father works hard back in Paris and I work hard out here. This was the way we were brought up."

Etienne halfheartedly nodded his head to let Phillipe know he understood what he was talking about, but Phillipe rather doubted that he was absorbing what he was saying. That evening he considered telling Arabelle the misgivings he was feeling about young Bernay. But he did not plan to say anything to her just yet. Maybe in a day or two the young man would come around.

Etienne was uncertain about so many things. He was feeling resentment about Tiffany and all the Renauds. Tiffany was like a chameleon since they'd arrived in Paris. She'd absolutely deserted him to seek out her old friends. Not once had she invited him to accompany her on any of the jaunts she'd taken with her acquaintances. Etienne had wondered if it was because she was embarrassed to have him by her side now that she was back home.

His company had been welcome when they were aboard the ship, at least until Chad Morrow came back into Tiffany's life. He resented that and how the Renauds seemed to be ruling his life. He'd not wished to leave Magdelaine after they'd found each other, but he was forced to do it.

Today when Tiffany had asked him to saddle up Duke so that she could go for a ride in the countryside, he desperately wanted to tell the saucy little miss to do it herself.

He was not going to be one of the Renauds' servants. That was not the impression he'd gotten from his mother when she'd told him of their plans to come to France.

All the things weighing heavily on Etienne were not helped by the unexpected appearance at the chateau of Tiffany's youngest brother, Jacques. His mother might have thought it wonderful that her friends named their youngest son after his father, Jacques, but Etienne didn't like the cocky, conceited young man who graced the table that night. Jacques was nothing like his other brothers, and Etienne certainly saw nothing about him that resembled his father.

He was a typical rich man's son. But all the members of his family obviously adored him as they listened to his lighthearted stories about his trip from Le Havre to the port in Cherbourg.

"That's why I thought I might as well come on out here to spend the next couple of days before I leave Cherbourg," he told his family.

Phillipe and his wife assured him that they were happy about his unexpected visit, but Etienne could not wait to excuse himself. As soon as he could do it without embarrassing his mother, he did so.

As he strolled around the grounds in the darkness by himself, he realized that it didn't matter that Renaud blood flowed in his veins as he'd been told. He would never be a Renaud. He would be a fool to think so.

Could his mother not see why they had been shipped out of Paris to this remote country estate? It was she who was living in a fool's paradise, but he'd let her enjoy it. It didn't mean that he had to live here indefinitely though, and he wasn't going to!

He didn't intend to be under obligation and authority of the Renaud family for the rest of his life. Maybe his mother didn't know what gnawed away at his father the last years of his life, but Etienne did. He felt cheated that he didn't share the wealth of his father's empire as Pierre did.

Over twenty-odd years, he labored in New Madrid after Pierre left to go back to France to enjoy the luxury of that wealth. Jacques Bernay had nothing to show for it but a day-by-day existence. There was no empire he could build on the meager wages he made.

The Renaud blood in his veins had killed Jacques Bernay, Etienne had decided. Well, it wasn't going to do that to him. He was going to rid himself of the poison and the fever in his blood. There was only one way to be rid of that fever and Etienne knew the answer to that.

Tiffany Renaud was the fever in his blood!

The next day, Etienne had to watch Tiffany go off for her daily ride with her brother Jacques, so he had to quiet the fury burning inside him. Tomorrow, Jacques would be gone, according to what he had said at the table the night before. He comforted himself with those thoughts.

What Etienne could not know was how those scrutinizing eyes of Madame Renaud had been carefully watching and weighing him. She had to have a talk with Pierre and very soon. Tiffany had to be told the truth just as soon as they returned to Paris. She didn't like the way Etienne looked at her daughter when he didn't think anyone was observing him. There were other things she felt that she couldn't put into words, but she felt them most intensely.

Charmaine was never one to dismiss such feelings. As dear as her friend Tasha was to her, her daughter was far more precious. Something about Etienne's manner had disturbed her after they'd been back in New Madrid a few weeks.

She'd never mentioned this to Pierre for she figured that he had too much on his mind; and since they'd been back in Paris, Tiffany had been too busy spending time with her old friends for her to be disturbed about it.

Since they'd returned to France, she'd noticed a very definite change in the young man. She knew that her husband had talked with him about the path he wished to choose and he would help him. This, he had done with his own sons, for he had made it perfectly clear to each of them that they would work to carve a place for themselves in life just as his father had demanded that he did when he was a young man.

He felt the same way old Etienne did about this issue. Charmaine intended to pass her observations on to her husband when she returned to Paris. Etienne did not seem to be interested in the farm and the vineyard. Perhaps he should consider a seafaring life like his father had. Her son Jacques could help him get assigned to a ship if that was what he enjoyed. She knew her happy-go-lucky Jacques would be most obliging if Etienne would accept his help.

What a magnificent family she had, she thought.

*　　*　　*

Etienne watched Tiffany and Jacques gallop out of the barnyard. His thoughts were brooding and gloomy. They were an arrogant pair with their haughty, conceited airs. He was beginning to think that he hated them all, especially Tiffany.

She'd used him as if he were a puppet on a string and he'd allowed her to pull the strings!

Chapter 51

The others at the chateau might have been sorry to see Jacques Renaud leave, but Etienne was glad to see him go. He was caught off guard when Tiffany invited him to take a stroll with her. He should have figured that it was because she did not have the entertaining company of her brother there tonight.

Yes, he was a puppet on a string, helpless to refuse her! She was standing there, devastatingly beautiful in a mauve-colored gown showing off the softness of her throat by the low scoop of the neckline.

"Shouldn't you have a shawl, Tiffany? The night air is getting cooler," he pointed out to her.

"Oh, I will be fine, Etienne. Besides, I have long sleeves. If I start getting chilled, we can come inside. I won't keep you out too long."

As they went out on the porch which extended along the entire side of the house, she took his arm. He guided her slowly down the length of the porch. Just the mere touch of her dainty hand against his arm aroused Etienne. He tried to convince himself that if he hadn't had to leave Paris and Magdelaine, he wouldn't be consumed by this fever Tiffany flamed in him. But Magdelaine was miles away, Tiffany was here.

"Isn't it glorious here? You do like it, don't you, Etienne?" She sighed as they paused by the railing.

"Oh, it is a wonderful place and your brother has obviously worked very hard to make it so," Etienne told her.

"He and Arabelle. Don't forget her. Did you know that there are still rooms here that stand empty?"

"No, I didn't know that."

"They will be empty until Phillipe and Arabelle have a family to fill them," she laughed.

"When will you and your mother be going back to Paris, Tiffany?" Etienne asked her.

"Tomorrow is our last day. Shall you miss me, Etienne?"

"Of course I will, Tiffany," he confessed.

"Well, Paris isn't that far away. I suspect that you and your mother will be coming to Paris quite often."

She was hardly prepared for his next remark. "I imagine that Chad Morrow will be coming to Paris before too long."

For a second, she made no reply. Maybe it was the tone in his voice that prompted her to reply, "Yes, I expect he will."

A chilling stiffness washed over both of them, and it was Tiffany who suggested that they go inside.

There was a brisk breeze flowing in over the port city of Cherbourg and its chill could be felt in the countryside. Arabelle had had Phillipe bank up the massive fireplace in her spacious kitchen and the sparking, flaming logs gave a cozy warmth to the room as she busily prepared breakfast. She and Phillipe liked hot chocolate in the morning but she knew her mother-in-law and Tiffany preferred strong black coffee.

She and Phillipe had had their breakfast before Tiffany

came bouncing down the steps to the kitchen area.

"Good morning, you two," Tiffany greeted. "Bet you'll be glad to see tomorrow come and all of us gone."

"That's not true at all, Tiffany," Phillipe corrected her. "You know we always look forward to seeing our family."

"I want to take one more ride on that magnificent Duke before I leave in the morning," Tiffany said.

"Best you wear a jacket, then. It's going to be a little chilly out there this morning," Phillipe urged her. She assured him that she had come downstairs prepared for the brisk morning.

The two of them left the kitchen together. His hired man saddled up the stallion for Tiffany, then he and Phillipe left for the vineyards. The stables were left for Etienne to attend to, along with other chores around the barn. Arabelle did the feeding of her chickens and the geese, but Etienne had been assigned the duty of feeding the milk cow.

He didn't realize that Tiffany had been out for a ride until he heard the stallion galloping up to the barnyard gate. The jet-black horse with Tiffany astride, her black hair flying wildly in the breeze, made an enchanting sight. He stopped what he was doing to watch her as she approached the gate, and then he went out to open it so she could ride the horse on into the barnyard.

Helping her down from the huge horse, he felt the soft curves of her body under the attractive deep green riding habit. He would have had to be dead not to have been stirred by the pressing of her body next to his. Surely, she must have felt the heat of his body so close to her; she certainly didn't shy away from him.

They strolled on into the barn as he took charge of the reins, leading Duke toward his stall.

As Tiffany leaned up against the planks of the stall and took off her jacket, which seemed too heavy now that she

378

was inside the barn, she had no inkling about the thoughts obsessing Etienne as he ambled around to stand in front of her. He was recalling the day when they'd taken refuge in the cave back in New Madrid. That day the sheer blouse she wore molded to the full mounds of her breasts. The same was true now that she'd removed the heavy twill green jacket of her riding ensemble.

Before she realized what he was about, his hands were taking her waist to pull her next to his chest. His dark head was bending close to her face and his lips were claiming her lips in a kiss. It was a kiss of flaming passion that demanded Tiffany surrender to him. Tiffany could not deny for a moment that his sensuous mouth was persuading her to submit.

But something in those black eyes suggested something else besides passion and desire. She knew not what it was.

She pushed against his chest with her hands, knowing that he was far stronger than she. But her head moved back and forth until he was forced to release her.

"No, Etienne! No! Let me go!" she shouted at him.

Finally Etienne removed his arms from her waist and stood back to take a deep breath.

"You had no right to do that, Etienne!" she said.

"Why, Tiffany? Because I'm not Chad Morrow or one of your little French dandies?"

"You're right about one thing. You're not Chad Morrow. And as for my French dandies, they don't take the liberties you seem to think you've the right to take!" She whirled around to leave him standing there, watching her angrily march out of the barn.

Tiffany was glad that she didn't meet anyone as she entered the house and immediately went to her room. She would have been most embarrassed if she'd met her mother, Tasha, or Arabelle.

She welcomed the privacy of her room to gather her

thoughts and gain control of herself. What was the matter with Etienne? He was not the same gentle person she'd known back in New Madrid when his sweet persuasion had tempted her to submit to his ardent, romantic kisses. But never had his romantic overtures carried her to that lofty peak as Chad's had that first time their lips met.

Nothing about Etienne Bernay excited her as Chad Morrow did, and she knew he never could. But then she had decided that there was probably no man that would ever affect her the way Morrow did!

More than ever, she was now ready to leave here and get back to Paris. She was glad they would be leaving the first thing in the morning. The only reason she'd wanted to come in the first place was to see her brother and his sweet wife. Now, she was ready to go home.

A light misting rain was falling over Paris as the brougham carried Tiffany and her mother toward their home. The familiar street they traveled down was enough to gladden her heart. Charmaine glanced over to see Tiffany's bright, flashing eyes. This was truly where she belonged, she realized. Tiffany could never find contentment on the isolated country estate outside Cherbourg. No, not her Tiffany! She liked the glamour and glitter of the city!

"It is good to be getting home again, cherie," she remarked as they rode down the wide boulevard.

Charmaine was anxious to get settled once again in her own home, and she was very pleased that Tiffany was, too. But she was returning to Paris with some apprehensions about the plans they'd made for Tasha and Etienne's future. It might not just work out as they expected, so she figured that she might as well prepare Pierre about this.

It was a most festive evening at the Renaud household, for Pierre eagerly welcomed his wife and his daughter back home. Tiffany excused herself shortly after the evening meal to go to her room to look over all the messages left for her while she was away. There was nothing there from Chad Morrow.

She checked the calendar: three weeks and three days had passed since they'd last seen each other and said goodbye.

Four more days, she told herself and Chad would not be keeping the vow he so fervently made to her that day aboard the ship. Damn him if he disappointed her again! How many times could she be expected to forgive him for promises not kept?

Those next four days, Tiffany stayed home, daring not to leave in case she would miss him. Charmaine had to conclude that she was just happy to be back in Paris. She had no inkling that Tiffany spent hours in her room looking out the window to see if a carriage was coming up the long drive. She never noticed the alive look on Tiffany's face when the servant answered the door if they were all sitting in the parlor, and then the crestfallen look when the caller wasn't Morrow.

The sixth day of waiting was enough to convince Tiffany that Morrow was not going to keep his promise, so she accepted the invitation to a soiree and allowed Emile Rapheal to escort her.

Emile could not believe his good fortune when Tiffany Renaud finally accepted his invitation. Several times, she had declined his offers.

Tiffany knew he was one of the most sought-after bachelors of Paris, but she found him very unattractive. She was tired of twiddling her thumbs at home, however, waiting for the arrival of the man she loved.

For someone like Tiffany who'd never been denied anything she wanted in her whole life, it was inconceivable to her that she would not have the man she wanted.

Chad *had* to love her as she loved him. She wouldn't have given herself so freely to this man if she had not believed that. But a troubling little voice had been prodding her the last two days since four weeks had now gone by and he'd not appeared. What if he didn't? What if he'd played her false and used her for his own moment of pleasure?

Her fierce Renaud pride could not accept that. She rebelled at the very thought!

Chapter 52

Magdelaine told her she looked stunning in her pale pink gown as she dressed and fashioned her black hair in an upsweep hairdo. The maid pinned a garland of pink velvet rosettes in the cluster of the curls atop her head. Pearl teardrop earrings dangled from her ears and a choker of matching pearls draped her throat. Magdelaine thought she looked like a princess as she left the room with the rich wine-colored cape lined in pale pink satin flung over her arm. But as beautiful as she looked, Magdelaine thought Mademoiselle Tiffany did not seem her vivacious self tonight. She wondered why.

The little maid felt so desperately sad and lonely. She was missing the company of the handsome Etienne. In a most discreet way, she'd questioned Tiffany about the trip to Cherbourg, and she was smugly pleased to hear that Etienne was none too happy there. Magdelaine wanted to think that it was because he was missing her.

That was enough to give her something to cling to and hope that he might return to Paris and to her.

As she put the mademoiselle's room in order she noticed the exquisite ring on the dressing table. She wondered why she'd not wished to wear such a magnificent gem tonight.

Magdelaine went about the room, putting things in place, but her thoughts kept going back to that ring she'd put in the jewelry chest. Mademoiselle Tiffany had never told her about the ring.

When all her chores were done, Magdelaine sat down to wait for Tiffany to return from the fancy soiree. It was going to be midnight or later.

But the clock was not striking midnight when Tiffany dejectedly climbed the steps. She'd be a spinster all her life, she swore, before she'd marry such a bore as Emile.

Let him be the most sought-after bachelor in Paris, as far as she was concerned, for she didn't intend to settle for that. Wealth did not mean that much to her! Social position did not concern her at all.

She'd watched the ladies fawning over him tonight and it sickened her. It certainly wasn't his good looks; that was obvious. When she had reached the limit of boredom, she'd pleaded a headache and asked to be brought home. Should she never have another invitation from him the rest of her life, she could not care less.

After she crawled into bed, she moaned out her agony to the emptiness of her room, "Oh, Chad, why did you do this to me? Why did you spoil me for any other man, you devil! I hate you for this!"

She felt her bare finger and realized she had not worn his ring tonight. Something urged her to leap out of the bed to take it from the chest and slip it on her finger. Once the ring was on her finger, she could almost feel the heat of the forceful Chad Morrow there with her.

That was more exciting than the evening had been with Emile!

Stubbornly, Chad Morrow had refused to believe what his doctor had tried to tell him, but when he insisted that Simon help him down that long winding stairway from his bedroom to the lower level of his townhouse, he had

384

to admit that the doctor was right. It was an ordeal that Chad had not expected.

It also made him more determined to conquer that damned stairway and the sooner the better. But he also noted by his calendar that he was already a week late on his promise to Tiffany. His pride kept him from sending the missive he struggled so hard to write. He looked at the letter and angrily tore it up. His writing looked like that of an old man with a trembling hand and he refused to send it.

Delphia found his letters as she cleaned his room and knew of his frustration. She saw the pained look on his face. She wanted to offer to write this young lady in France that he was so obviously in love with, but she knew he would not allow it. It was something he must do.

Chad had too many hours to lie in his room and brood. There was a time when he would have been elated about what he had accomplished by acquiring each and every plot of land that he'd felt he'd been cheated out of by the Chadwick family. Now, this meant nothing to him if he could not have Tiffany Renaud, who meant more to him than all of these long-range plans that had encompassed some five years of his life.

Never would he have believed that a woman could so possess him, but damn it, she did!

But it did not surprise Simon or Delphia the morning he announced to them that he was leaving London to go to France. He gave Simon instructions to buy his passage across the channel, along with arrangements to go on to Paris. He saw the protest in Simon's eyes but he quieted him, "No, Simon—I'm going! Nothing you can say will change my mind. I'm long overdue in Paris. I must go!"

When Simon saw that determined look in his eyes he knew that it was useless to argue with Chad Morrow. While it was against his better judgment, Simon obeyed Chad's request to make arrangements to go to Paris as soon as possible.

Chad spent the next few days preparing himself by going up and down the stairway without the aid of Simon or Delphia. He roamed the entire townhouse to test his leg, and when he was satisfied with his progress on his leg, he put his hand through the same vigorous pace.

Delphia observed him working so tirelessly and shook her head. She hoped this young lady was as in love with him as he must be with her.

She packed his luggage with the clothing he'd requested and casually inquired, "How long will you be in Paris, sir?"

"I can only be gone eight days—nine at the most, Delphia."

"I'm happy to know that you'll be back home for the holidays, sir. Simon and I would be lonely without you here."

He smiled warmly at her. "Thank you—thank you, Delphia."

Charmaine appreciated Tiffany excusing herself after the evening meal so that she and Pierre could enjoy the rest of the evening together. She felt the need to discuss the thoughts that had been on her mind.

Pierre's first questions were about Tasha and Etienne, after he declared how lonely he'd been without her in Paris.

"I still feel the need of you by my side to be happy, cherie, and I guess I shall always feel that way," he told her as his hand clasped hers.

"Ah, Pierre, my feeling is the same. When we're apart I always think about that horrible moment that the earthquake separated us back in New Madrid and I saw that horrible gorge grow wider and wider. There are times when it seems like yesterday and I can recall every detail of that miserable night." Her face suddenly took on a somber expression.

386

"I know, ma petite. It is that way for me, too, and I've never sought to be away from you too long since the moment we finally found each other after all those weeks of being apart."

"And we haven't," she smiled as she bent over to kiss him.

"And we won't if I can help it! But you are home with me and I am happy the trip to Cherbourg is over. We can get on with our lives and Tasha and Etienne must now take charge of theirs. Did they seem to like their new home, Charmaine?"

"I am sure Tasha loves it there. As for Etienne, I find him a very complicated young man with a very moody nature, Pierre. Oh, Phillipe immediately gave him duties to perform around the estate but I got the impression that Etienne was not too happy about his job."

She noticed her husband bristle and sit up straight in the chair. "Who does this young pup think he is? He was working from sunup to sundown back in New Madrid. We took him away from that and brought him back here to a fine home and good job."

"Could we have been too generous, Pierre? Is that a possibility?"

"That might be, but generosity stops for Etienne as of now if he does not wish to earn his keep. I will hope that I never have to talk to Tasha about her son but I will if I have to. Tasha has a home as long as she wishes but Etienne is a healthy young man and I'll not carry him. He'd best realize that. I shall write Phillipe tomorrow about what I expect from this young man. I want there to be no misunderstanding."

"I think that is a wise idea, Pierre. However, Phillipe immediately assigned him chores to do," Charmaine said. She told Pierre of Jacques's unexpected visit and what a delightful time Tiffany had shared with him.

"But that was another strange thing I observed, Pierre. Etienne did not like our son Jacques and you know Jacques is always adored by everyone. He truly tried his best to be friendly with Etienne." But she confessed that the thing that really bothered her the most was the strange way she observed Etienne looking at Tiffany. "It was as though he resented Tiffany's attention to Jacques."

Pierre listened to his wife and said nothing but he knew exactly what she was talking about, for he had observed the same thing from Etienne on a couple of occasions when they were aboard the ship and Chad Morrow was with Tiffany.

When his wife's deep blue eyes searched his face with a serious expression, he knew she thought it was time to tell Tiffany that Etienne's father was his half-brother.

But since he'd talked with his father, there was that shadow of doubt now in Pierre's mind that Jacques Bernay *was* his half-brother, as he'd thought all these years. If Bernay's mother had lied to Jacques when he was a youth, then he had considered the wrong man as his father. So they both had believed a lie for many, many years.

Pierre did not wish to go into this tonight, so he merely shrugged the suggestion aside by telling her that he would take care of everything.

Other thoughts were occupying his mind and those were most pleasant thoughts. Charmaine's soft body and sweet lips had not been with him for over seven nights and he missed her kisses and lying by her warm side at night.

"Shall we go upstairs, ma petite?" he suggested.

She saw that familiar glint in his black eyes that age had not changed at all. She did not answer him but merely rose from the chair with a smile on her face.

Together, they mounted the stairway, holding hands as they had when they were young lovers.

Chapter 53

The light rain shower did not seem to dampen the spirits of the young lovers strolling down the street. Afternoon showers came on quite suddenly and disappeared as swiftly.

Pretty young French ladies always took their colorful parasols with them when they went shopping or to the tearooms. Tiffany and her friend Denise were among this passing parade this rainy afternoon. But to their delight when they emerged from Madame Tourneau's Boutique, the rains had ceased so they did not have to open their parasols.

Lightheartedly gay, they strolled to the sidewalk cafe where they planned to enjoy a cup of hot chocolate.

They found a table under the striped canopy. Being a very popular place for people to gather by midafternoon, most of the tables were occupied by the time that Denise and Tiffany arrived. Both young ladies were elated over the beautiful chapeaux they'd just purchased.

No one was more fun to spend time with than Tiffany, Denise felt, and no other friend she had was dearer to her than Tiffany. In fact, she and Tiffany had been close friends for over ten years. Knowing her all this time and seeing her so often, Denise was quick to notice changes in her friend.

This afternoon, Tiffany appeared to be her vivacious self, but Denise had noticed that Tiffany was not enjoying herself at the gala soiree the other night. It was not just because she was bored with Emile. None of the young men there seemed to catch her roving eyes as they used to do. Ah yes, there were changes in Tiffany!

Becuse she was so very fond of Tiffany, Denise dared to ask her as they sat there sipping the hot chocolate, "Tiffany, are you unhappy? You seem to be at times, I've noticed."

"Now how did you guess that, Denise?"

"Because I feel like the two of us know each other so well, Tiffany. We've been friends since we were seven years old. That's a long time."

Tiffany saw no reason why she should keep the truth from her closest friend. After all, it was obvious that she had sensed it or she would not have said anything.

Tiffany nodded her head. "It's Chad Morrow. I love him, Denise. I love him as I never believed it possible to love a man. Remember when we first got back to Paris how happy I was? I've waited for him to come to Paris as he'd promised he would do.

"But three weeks have gone by and now four. He's not coming as he promised, Denise. I swore that if he didn't keep this promise to me I'd never forgive him again as I have in the past."

"But he gave you that exquisite ring, Tiffany. A man doesn't give a ring like that to any girl."

"Well, that was what I've kept telling myself until lately."

"Something could have happened to prevent him from keeping his promise."

"I thought of that too, but he could have written me a letter, Denise. But I've not even had a letter from him."

"Then just try being patient, Tiffany—just for a while

390

longer. Maybe all your concern is for nothing and he will come."

Tiffany's deep blue eyes flashed as she lowered her voice and told her friend, "I can't afford patience, Denise. I—I think I may be carrying his child. I've been wondering about this for the last three weeks, to be honest with you."

"You mean, Tiffany—you mean—"

"I mean exactly that! I mean that I could be a few weeks pregnant. I will not bring that shame to the Renaud family if I have to marry someone I don't love. I have my pride to consider. I was a fool to gamble as I did but I did."

"Mon Dieu!" Denise whispered softly as she stared at Tiffany.

"Now, you see what I mean."

Denise had not even considered that possibility. Poor Tiffany! She could not imagine being in her shoes right now. For the first time in her life, she did not envy Tiffany Renaud.

As they left the cafe to go their separate ways, Tiffany told her friend, "I appreciate your listening to all my woes. I needed to talk to someone and I had no one else to confide in but you."

Denise gave her a warm embrace and assured her, "Oh, Tiffany—you know you can tell me anything. We're friends and I care! That's what friends are all about, n'est-ce pas?"

"Oui, Denise—that is what friends are all about." Tiffany managed a smile as she broke from their embrace to go to her own carriage.

As she traveled toward her home, the burden she'd been carrying alone seemed lighter now that she'd talked with Denise. But Denise had no inkling of how frightened she was feeling right now.

Just as the carriage was turning the corner to go down

the street, another heavy downpour began to fall. Out of the corner of her eye, Tiffany noticed a dashing figure fleeing through the gate just before the carriage was about to roll through the double iron gate leading into the Renaud property. It was true the heavy rains blurred her sight but she could have sworn that that black-haired fellow looked like Etienne Bernay. Yet, logic told her it could not have been Etienne. He was miles away in Cherbourg! It had to be a new man her father had hired to tend the vast grounds or a new house servant.

She gave no more thought to it as she left the carriage and rushed through the house to her room. She hoped that Magdelaine would like the black velvet reticule she'd purchased for her which was an exact match to the one she'd bought for herself.

She could not resist the reticule because it matched the magnificent black velvet chapeau with its brilliant blue plumes at the band of the hat. She thought it was perfect for the black velvet gown she'd had made when she'd planned to go to Sabrina's for the theatre season in London.

Magdelaine was always amazed by her mistress's generosity and to think that she'd purchased her an identical beautiful velvet reticule left the little maid dumbfounded. All she could say was, "Ah, mademoiselle —you are so very kind to me!" She smiled when her mistress pulled out the attractive hat she'd purchased for herself. "Oh, mademoiselle—mademoiselle, it is beautiful! You will look like a dream!"

"Is it not perfect for that black velvet gown?"

"It is!"

Tiffany's thoughtful gift was enough to lift Magdelaine's spirits for the rest of the evening, so she was feeling very cheerful and gay by the time she gathered in the kitchen with the other house servants. She eagerly displayed the exquisite velvet reticule that mademoiselle had bought for her when she sat at the table with Madame Renaud's maid.

"We are both lucky, Magdelaine, to work for people like the Renauds. My friend is not so lucky," Madame Renaud's maid told her. Magdelaine did not push her to tell the sad story of her friend's plight, for she was happy tonight and she wanted to stay that way.

Magdelaine had decided that happiness was an elusive delight for people like her and she wanted to grasp and hold it when it came along.

Never did it seem to remain too long!

From the minute her maid come to her room the next morning until the late afternoon, Tiffany sensed something was troubling Magdelaine even though she denied it. She did not believe her for one minute, for she knew Magdelaine too well.

"Now, you tell me, Magdelaine! I insist that you do! We are friends," Tiffany demanded of her maid.

"I fear you will be angry, mademoiselle, and I would not wish this."

"Trust me, Magdelaine! Tell me!" Tiffany insisted on knowing what sort of dilemma had made her so upset.

Because she trusted the good-hearted little mistress, she confessed the truth about Etienne. "He was unhappy in Cherbourg, mademoiselle, he said. So he left there a couple of days ago to come back to Paris. I—I don't know what to do, for I don't wish to get in trouble with Monsieur and Madame Renaud."

"Where is he now, Magdelaine?" Tiffany asked her.

"He is in the carriage house and I've slipped him food out there. I have been so very upset all day and poor Etienne does not know what to do or where to turn."

Tiffany fidgeted and paced back and forth for a few minutes as her pretty head whirled with ideas about how she could help these two young lovers.

"Take him blankets to keep him comfortable tonight, and there is plenty of food so he will be free of hunger," she told her and smiled. She informed her maid that she would not need her services the rest of the night as she gave her a wink of her eye. "Tell Etienne that I will find him a place to stay and I will take him there in the morning, Magdelaine."

Magdelaine had never expected such generosity from her mistress when she confessed the truth to her. There could not be anyone like her Mademoiselle Tiffany, Magdelaine knew.

All during the evening she shared with her parents Tiffany gave no hint that she was preoccupied with the plans spinning around in her head about what she was going to do the next morning. Her father would be furious if he knew that Etienne was here in Paris, she realized. But now she understood why he was so quiet and withdrawn after they'd arrived at the country house just outside Cherbourg. He had not wanted to leave Paris after he'd fallen in love with Magdelaine.

True to her promise to Magdelaine, the next morning she ordered her carriage brought around. She asked the new driver to fetch the parasol she'd arranged to leave behind so she might summon Etienne to leave the carriage house. It mattered not to her that the driver would see him leave the carriage with her once they arrived at her grand-père's house. She was only concerned with getting him away from her house.

Tiffany knew that Grand-père could be enticed to go along with her plan once she got Etienne to his house. He had never refused her anything in his whole life so she never doubted for a minute that he would disappoint her now.

But old Etienne's senses came vitally alive the minute he entered the room where his granddaughter sat with

394

the young stranger. He looked at the young man with his curly hair and the same eyes he saw in his own reflection when he looked into a mirror.

"Grand-père, I'd like you to meet Etienne Bernay. Etienne, this is my beloved grand-père, Etienne Renaud. I think it is time the two of you met."

Etienne rose to extend his hand to the elderly gentleman as he declared, "It is a great honor for me to meet you, sir."

"My pleasure too, young man. Now sit down, for that is what I intend to do." Old Etienne was shaken to the core of his being. The young man could have been himself when he was in his twenties!

Tiffany wasted no time in telling her grandfather why she had brought Etienne there and the old man admired her spirit and spunk. Besides, he was just a little out of sorts with Pierre. He'd have himself some sweet revenge.

"He can stay here with me, Tiffany. Is that what you wish?"

"It is. But Papa will be furious that Etienne left Cherbourg," she told him.

Later, he asked his butler to show Etienne to his room. "I've got a discussion to have with my granddaughter."

When the door was closed, he turned to Tiffany. "Are you telling me that your father has no knowledge that the young man came here after he'd settled him and his mother in Cherbourg? He obviously doesn't wish to stay there as Pierre had expected him to do."

"That is right, Grand-père, so I agreed to help him," Tiffany said.

"Then I will help you help him," Etienne Renaud smiled. It pleased him to play this deceptive game with his granddaughter. Pierre might as well learn that it was impossible to plan other people's lives, as he'd decided to to do with the Bernays.

"What about the young man's mother? Is she happy

where she is, Tiffany?"

"Oh yes, I think she is very happy. She loves the country and the peaceful atmosphere out there on the estate."

"Well, don't worry about me and young Etienne. We'll spend the next day or two becoming acquainted. I—I might just have something in mind that might whet his interest," old Etienne slyly smiled at his granddaughter.

She rushed over to embrace him warmly, declaring, "Oh, Grand-père—you are absolutely wonderful! I adore you!"

"And I adore you, too, ma petite. Now don't worry your pretty head about a thing and leave it in my hands. Everything will be just fine."

Tiffany left, knowing he'd take care of everything!

Old Etienne had not felt so alive in a long time. Ideas were whirling around in his mind about this young man who was his namesake.

To be in this little conspiracy with his beloved Tiffany was enough to please the old Frenchman. They'd show Pierre he could be outfoxed.

Besides, old Etienne had decided that this young man was truly his grandson! That was enough to make the decision for him.

Chapter 54

Magdelaine spent an uneasy, restless morning as she awaited Tiffany's return. She finally came bouncing into the room with a broad grin on her face.

"He is in a nice place with a fine man, Magdelaine, and he told me to tell you that he would see you soon."

"Oh, I am so grateful to you, mademoiselle! Poor Etienne—I think he was very worried. He didn't want to be in disfavor with your father but he said he just could not remain there. He was going crazy," the little maid confided.

"Oh, Father will not be pleased at first but he will have to accept Etienne's decision," Tiffany told her, omitting to tell her that he could hardly argue about Etienne staying under his father's roof. It had been Grand-père's idea that he remain there.

Tiffany was so pleased about her good deed for Magdelaine and Etienne that she forgot about her own dilemma. It was not until the end of the day that she thought about Chad and the fact that another day had to be crossed off the calendar.

As she sat at her desk staring at the calendar, she thought that she might as well accept Paul Boyer's invitation to the ball. Denise and Angelique would be going with their escorts, and she would enjoy their company. Perhaps if she wore one of her new gowns and danced the evening away, she would not be in her room nursing her aching heart over that rake Morrow!

She'd send the message in the morning to Paul that she would be delighted to go to the ball with him. Why not! She'd wager that Chad Morrow was not sitting in a lonely room thinking about her.

Before she went to bed, she wrote the message so she could send it the first thing in the morning.

While Tiffany wrote her message to Paul Boyer, her grandfather sat at his desk jotting some notes to himself, for he had done this for years when he didn't want to forget something.

His faithful manservant, Jean, had checked the light under the old man's door as he often did when the monsieur stayed up late as he did from time to time. There was no set routine to the old man's hours. Some nights he would retire immediately after he finished dining, but then there were those nights when the hour was long after midnight.

The young man who was their guest was obviously weary, for his light had been out for a long time, Jean had noticed. He had also noticed that the old man seemed to genuinely warm to the young man Mademoiselle Tiffany had brought here. After years of serving Etienne Renaud, Jean knew he was very discriminating in whom he warmed to. Rarely was he as friendly as he was with this young man. Jean found that most interesting.

As he always did before he finally went to his own quarters, he made a point of checking with the elderly gentleman to see if there was anything he could do for him.

"Not a thing, Jean, but I would like to talk to you for a minute. I'm thinking about lightening the load you have carried for so long. I may have young Etienne be my driver and save you that duty."

"Your driver, sir?" Jean knew that he rarely left

the house.

"That's right, Jean. I've decided that I've been staying too close to this place. I need to get out more. What would you think about that?"

"Why, I think that if you are feeling that good, you should get out more, sir," he smiled at the elderly man, knowing that there was much more to it than that.

"Well, it wouldn't hurt you to have an afternoon and evening free once in a while. After all, Jean . . . you are still a young man and I bury you here in the house with me."

"I've no complaints, sir," Jean told him.

"I know this, but Etienne could take some of the load away from you and give you the chance to enjoy a few hours of freedom and fresh air. Let me assure you, Jean—no one could ever take your place with me. I could never have wanted a more devoted man serving me as you have the last few years."

Jean expressed his sincere gratitude. He knew most people thought the old man overbearing and cantankerous, but Jean had never found him to be that way with him.

"Well, go to bed and get some rest, Jean. Tomorrow I will approach this young man with my idea."

"Sleep well, sir," Jean bade him as he turned to go out the door.

"You, too, Jean."

Jean thought about everything the elderly Renaud had said to him. Now, he'd always known how Mademoiselle Tiffany could mellow the old man, but there was something about this young stranger that had also had a similar effect on him.

Jean was curious about what it could be!

For the first time in many months, Tasha Bernay was distraught and completely confused by her son's irresponsible behavior. What would Pierre and Charmaine think of her and him after all they'd done for them?

She'd read Etienne's note and she felt absolutely numb. Surely she read it wrong, she tried to tell herself so she sat in the chair and read it a second time.

She asked herself what was the matter with that young man. Most people would give anything to live in a place like this with such nice people around as Phillipe and Arabelle. She wondered how she was ever going to face them.

Perhaps, she could prolong the agony for a day but that was about as long as that would be possible. Phillipe would be coming to see why Etienne had not been attending to his chores.

After Charmaine and Tiffany had left the chateau, Tasha had settled into her own quarters and cooked her own meals so that the young Renauds could enjoy their privacy. But she knew that she could not conceal Etienne's departure too many hours.

The next few hours she sat and thought about the time they'd been here and why she'd not noticed this feeling of discontent. The truth was she had, but she thought it might pass with time when he adjusted to his surroundings or met some people his own age. Oh, she did not expect that he would be content to spend his evenings around her. But how very impatient young people were, she thought to herself. He didn't give himself a chance to fall in love with this beautiful countryside. Never did she suspect what was really gnawing at Etienne.

Finally, she approached the young Renauds and showed them the letter Etienne had left for her. She saw no point in prolonging the agony.

Phillipe was not really shocked about Etienne's sudden disappearance. He dared not mention to Tasha that he'd received a very long letter from his father and his grave apprehensions about Etienne. His only concern was for Tasha, and he sought to ease her mind.

It was his gentle, kindhearted Arabelle who gave Tasha comfort. "He is a good man, Tasha. Maybe, he just wishes to explore the world a little. He will be fine. He knows he has people who love him. That is what really matters. Don't worry."

"I'll try not to worry, Arabelle. I really will."

"Good! Besides, I'm going to ask you to help me make my herb wreaths, and that should keep you so busy you won't have time to fret and worry," Arabelle laughed.

"Oh, Arabelle—I'll be happy to help you! You've already made me feel so much better. I dreaded facing you and Phillipe this afternoon," Tasha candidly confessed to her and her husband.

"Well, you need never feel that way again, Tasha, and I insist that you share our dinner tonight and one of Phillipe's own wines. I have a huge pot of bouillabaisse simmering right now that we shall all enjoy later. Say you will join us!"

Tasha smiled. "How could I possibly refuse, Arabelle?"

"Wonderful! Now I will go to see about my bread. We will have a wonderful evening, Tasha," Arabelle said, and patted her shoulder as she scurried out of the room.

Tasha turned to Pierre's son to declare, "She is a wonderful girl, Phillipe."

"She has made my life complete. I have everything I ever wanted. I was not like my father or my grandfather and I will always be glad that they didn't expect me to follow them in the business world. I would have been most unhappy."

"Are you trying to tell me that I should let Etienne do as he wishes and not stand in his way, Phillipe?" she asked as her black eyes searched his face.

"It's the only way he'd be a happy man, Tasha."

"Then I shall do it."

As the two of them parted and Tasha went her own way nothing was troubling her. All her worries had now been swept away.

The next week passed pleasantly for Tasha. She was kept busy helping Arabelle make her holiday wreaths of herbs tied with colorful ribbons. She thoroughly enjoyed herself and only rarely did her thoughts wander to her son.

Had she known how much he was enjoying himself and his new surroundings, she would have known that what Phillipe had told her was correct. Etienne would be all right.

The elderly Renaud had kept him so occupied that he'd had no time to be bored. In fact, he found himself entranced just sitting and listening to the old man's stories about his long, adventuresome life. He'd only slipped out of the house once to see the pretty Magdelaine.

Etienne found Etienne Renaud to be a paradoxical gentleman. At times, he was the perfect image of the French aristocrat in his elegant attire and genteel manners. The young man was very impressed by the old man's sharp intelligence. His aging body might be frail, but there was nothing feeble about his mind.

Then there was another side of this old man that intrigued Etienne and drew him to Renaud as he'd never expected. There was the trait of the common man within him that made Etienne feel at ease when he was around him.

He told Etienne of the humble beginnings he'd never forgotten even after he'd become a wealthy French industrialist. He never forgot the sage wisdom passed on to him by his hard-working parents. He told Etienne how he'd been a very stern, demanding father when Pierre was young.

"Pierre was a very handsome young man by the time he was eighteen and so it was only natural that ladies, single and married, flaunted themselves at him. By the time he was twenty, he got himself involved in a scandal with a married lady—so I shipped him out of Paris to my brother's in the Missouri region across the ocean. I figured that he would come back a man after living in that backwoods country, where living was not soft and easy, or he'd continue to get himself in more trouble. At least, his troubles would not break his mother's heart. She was always so frail."

"You speak about Monsieur Renaud going to New Madrid, sir?"

"This is what I speak about, Etienne," Renaud confirmed.

A smug smile came on the old man's face as he told Etienne pridefully that he was delighted to see his son when he returned to France, for he had become a fine young man. "He brought with him a beautiful, fine lady as his wife. I could not have picked a more perfect lady to be my son's wife. Charmaine is a jewel!"

Etienne listened to the old man's praises of Madame Renaud and he had to agree that she was a most magnificent lady. Never could he forget how she'd rolled up her sleeves and gone to work to nurse his mother back to health.

Etienne told the old man about this and his reply was, "That sounds like Charmaine. I would expect her to do just that." Pierre had not told him about any of this, so this was the first he'd heard about the New Madrid venture.

By the end of the evening, each of them had learned more about the other, and felt much closer.

When Tiffany paid a visit to her grand-père two days after she'd left Etienne there, she left in high spirits, for they were getting along fabulously.

She left in a lighthearted mood, ready to go to the grand ball with Paul. Tonight, she was going to forget Chad Morrow and enjoy herself.

She was going to be that young, carefree girl who'd not been wounded by love!

Chapter 55

A haze of fog shrouded the channel separating England from France. The thick gray mist made it impossible to see approaching passengers strolling along the deck of the small ship making the crossing, and Chad almost collided with a couple of them.

But even the fog could not conceal that next passenger Chad came face to face with. "What the bloody hell are you doing here, Reuben? Never expected to see you," Chad laughed as the two of them gave each other a warm embrace.

"Now, I could say the same thing, Morrow, as I recall the miserable mess you were in the last time I saw you," Grodin chuckled.

"Well, I'm in much better shape now, I'm happy to say."

Chad told him how he had gotten a harsh lecture that he should not make the trip by both Delphia and Simon. Reuben laughed, "That Madame Delphia is one fine, bossy lady. She takes very good care of you, though, and that Simon is pure gold."

"They are that, and I think that the only way I was allowed to leave the townhouse was my fervent promise to come back before the holidays. Delphia flatly refused to fix her Christmas goose if I wasn't going to be there, so I swore I would."

"So it is Paris you are going to, eh?"

"Yes. And you—where are you headed, Reuben?"

"To Cherbourg, my friend. I am going to Cherbourg."

Chad gave him a crooked grin, knowing that it must be Tasha Bernay he was going to see. Reuben saw that taunting smile on his face and was quick to inform him that his old friend, Anton Belleau, lived in Cherbourg. But he quickly added, "Now, I might just have to pay a visit to Tasha and see how she is doing."

"Just figured that you might have that in mind, Reuben."

They both laughed and agreed that they should sit down and share a drink before they would soon part company. Chad was leaving the ship at Le Havre while Reuben would travel on up the coast to Cherbourg.

An hour later, the two were saying farewell and wishing one another good luck. Reuben watched the young man leave the ship to make his way to the docks below. He could tell that his powerful body was not back to normal by the slowness of his gait.

He hoped Chad would find in Paris what he was hoping to find in Cherbourg. The truth was Tasha had made him change some ideas he'd harbored for years. He had been terribly lonely since she'd departed from his life.

Oh, he would seek out his old, dear friend, Anton, but it was really Tasha who had ignited the desire to go to France. He had to know if she felt as strongly about him as he'd realized he did about her.

Reuben knew that he was going to be a most unhappy man if she didn't welcome him with open arms. In fact, he was going to be shattered! Feeling like this was a new experience to him, for he'd never allowed any woman to dominate his thoughts or his time. Tasha had accomplished this and she didn't even realize it.

By the time the ship made it the several miles up the coastline of France to Cherbourg, the fog had lifted and the sun was shining brightly. Reuben hoped it was a good omen as he disembarked from the ship.

Chad found the thick mist had turned into a light shower of rain as he rode in the carriage to the hotel where he had lodgings for his stay in Paris. The clouds were thick and heavy as if the rains could last for hours.

Once he was settled in his room in the hotel, the first thing he sought was a warm bath to hope to ease the discomfort in his leg. It did seem to help.

Noticing the hands of the clock there in his room, he realized that it was not a time when he wished to make his arrival at the Renaud residence. So he fought the urge to immediately dress and rush to the door of her home.

He had dinner in his room before he summoned a carriage to take him to his beloved Tiffany. A light mist was still falling as he emerged from the hotel entrance to get into the carriage. A little old woman was standing there with her last flowers in her basket in hopes of selling them before she called it a day to go home. Feeling in such high spirits that he would soon be seeing his beautiful Tiffany, he bought all the lovely pink, purple, and white asters left in her basket.

The driver of his carriage recognized the address Chad had given him. Chad sensed that instantly as he settled back in the seat with the huge bouquet in his hand.

As Chad dismounted from the carriage, the driver inquired if he should wait and Chad advised him that he should. After all, Tiffany had no knowledge that he was arriving. While the spacious house was ablaze with lights, Chad did not wish to have to walk back to his hotel.

It was not Tiffany he was to greet as he was ushered into the entrance. Madame Renaud was descending the stairway, thinking that it was her husband coming home when she'd heard the carriage rolling up the drive.

Chad stood there with the massive bouquet in his hand and observed her coming down the steps.

A warm, welcoming smile creased her face as she saw him. "Chad—how wonderful to see you again. I thought you were Pierre coming home." She descended the stairs to take his hand while the other hand clutched the bouquet.

"It's good to see you again, Madame Renaud."

Charmaine knew the flowers were for Tiffany and not for her but she sensed that he was having a struggle holding the big bouquet. "Ah, how beautiful they are, Chad." She called out for the servant to take them.

Taking his arm, she told him that neither Tiffany nor Pierre was home. "You are stuck with me, I fear. But we can have a glass of wine and talk—oui?"

"I would enjoy that very much, Madame Renaud."

"And so would I!" She instructed the servant to serve them her favorite wine in her sitting room as she guided Chad down the long hallway.

As they entered the small, cozy sitting room, the smoldering embers of the logs in the fireplace were still flaming. She told him that this was the room she usually spent her time in when she was waiting for Pierre to come home in the evening. "I fear he is still having to work very long hours to make up for our long absence away from Paris."

"I know, for I have had to do the same thing," Chad confessed to her.

"Tiffany will be very disappointed that she was not here when you arrived."

Chad shrugged his shoulders as he explained that he was unable to write. Before he realized it, he was telling her about the incident that had happened from the moment he'd left the ship and gone down the wharf.

Charmaine listened as he told about the ruffians who'd attacked him. Chad had not planned on revealing all the things he suddenly found himself telling her, but she was easy to talk with.

They were now drinking their second glass of wine. She seemed intensely interested in what he was saying.

"Oh, madame—forgive me for rambling on so. Besides, I—I should be going. I'll hope to catch Tiffany home tomorrow."

"Oh, you are not boring me at all, Chad. I've enjoyed your company very much and I know that Tiffany will be disappointed that she missed seeing you tonight. Please come back tomorrow."

Chad rose up from the chair and assured her that he would. She escorted him to the door and bade him farewell. Chad found that his driver was sound asleep and had to wake him up.

But they had only traveled a short distance from the spacious grounds when Chad ordered him to pull up and stop.

"You wish to get out here, sir?" the driver inquired with a frown on his face.

"No, I merely wish you to stop the carriage. I wish to linger here for a while. Go back to sleep if you want. I'll pay for your time," Chad told him.

"As you say, monsieur." The driver allowed himself to get comfortable after he'd stopped the carriage.

The hour was getting late and he grew angry when he looked at his pocket watch. Madame Renaud had made no mention as to where her lovely daughter might be for the entire evening. He had not expected to make this long trip and be greeted with the news that she was not home. The woman he loved had no business sharing an evening with another gentleman. The very thought of this riled him as he sat in the dark, waiting to see a carriage entering the drive leading up to her home. He wasn't sure what kind of ruthless urge might seize him if he did see her returning home accompanied by some Frenchman.

Having to listen to the driver's snoring did not help the waiting. His impatient nature could not endure more than an hour's waiting so he shook the driver's shoulder and ordered him to take him on to his hotel. He was weary from a long day of traveling.

He'd just mark this night off as one night lost here in Paris. When they arrived back at the hotel, he gave the driver a generous fee and leaped out of the carriage to go inside the hotel.

He entered his room, giving the door a mighty slam, and flung off his coat. It was hardly the night he'd lain awake thinking about with wild anticipation for weeks.

Obviously, Tiffany had not been pining away for him or waiting for him to come to her, as they'd talked about as they clung together the last time they'd been with each other.

With angry jerks and yanks he removed his clothes and stretched his tired, aching body out on the soft bed. He suddenly realized just how long his day had been.

Just as he was about to fall asleep, a troublesome voice prodded at him, "You didn't keep your promise to Tiffany and get to Paris in three weeks. What did you expect of her—to wait at home week after week not knowing whether you were going to come or not?"

He flung his body over on his side and muttered to himself he knew it and that was what disturbed him.

Tiffany was as impatient and impulsive as he was!

Chapter 56

Reuben's arrival in Cherbourg was a much happier occasion than Chad Morrow's in Paris. To find that his old friend, Anton, had suddenly moved away from Cherbourg had not devastated him. He just started walking down the cobblestone street, following the directions that a local citizen had given him to get to the country estate of the Renaud family.

By the time he'd reached the outskirts of the city, a farmer stopped his wagon and offered Reuben a ride to the estate. Reuben couldn't believe his good fortune, for he was arriving at the gate of the property about an hour after he'd disembarked on the wharf in Cherbourg.

Arabelle responded to the rapping on the door but once the door was opened, the face Reuben saw was Tasha's. Tasha was a picture, sitting with clusters of dried flowers and grapevine wreaths on her lap. But all this fell to the floor as she leaped up from the rocker and rushed to the door, exclaiming, "Oh, Reuben! Reuben!"

Arabelle stood there, a little befuddled, for a second or two, until they broke from their warm embrace to apologize to her. "Arabelle, I'd like you to meet Reuben Grodin. Reuben, this is Arabelle Renaud." She hastily added that Arabelle's husband, Phillipe, was Pierre and

Charmaine Renaud's son.

"Well, it is a pleasure to meet you, Madame Renaud, as it was to meet your mother-in-law and father-in-law when we crossed the ocean on the same ship."

"Thank you, Monsieur Grodin. Please—come into the parlor. Tasha and I were busy preparing our wreaths for the holidays but we were just about to stop to enjoy some tea."

"That sounds good to me, madame." The atmosphere of this quaint, wonderful house intrigued Reuben. The magnificent high ceiling and the massive windows that allowed the bright sun to flow through impressed him. Its sturdy furnishings of dark wood were made to endure and Reuben found them far more to his taste than the fancy delicate gilt furnishings that looked as if they'd shatter if they were touched or sat upon.

The aromatic sweet odors of the dried flowers and herbs were pleasant as Reuben inhaled deeply.

"You have a charming house here, madame," he told the young woman as she motioned him to have a seat.

"We love this place," Arabelle said smilingly.

"It shows," Reuben told her. His artist's eyes admired the perfection of the blending colors she assembled. Varied shades of rust, gold, and deep greens dominated the room. He let his eyes roam over the room, noting that she obviously had a fondness for baskets which she used for her dried flowers, yarns, and kindling for her fireplace.

He glanced over to smile at Tasha and he saw why she must be so very happy and content here. It was a serene, wonderful place.

When Arabelle went into her kitchen, Reuben leaned over to kiss Tasha's cheek and whisper, "It is good to see you again, Tasha dear. I—I have missed you."

"Oh, Reuben—I've missed you too," she confessed.

Arabelle purposely lingered a little longer in the

411

kitchen than was necessary to give the couple some extra moments of privacy.

When she returned with a tray bearing their cups of tea, she graciously invited him to be their guest. "You must enjoy our beautiful countryside, for this is one of the nicest seasons of the year. Phillipe and I would love to have you stay and I know you two have a lot to catch up on."

Reuben smiled and thanked her. But he was also thinking how he'd like to capture that face of hers on canvas. She was not a beauty in the true sense of the word, but there was a remarkable quality about her face, a glowing radiance. The simple hairdo she wore, with a single long braid hanging around her shoulder and her plain frock decorated with a frosty white apron, told him so much about this young lady. She lacked sophistication but that was what made her so interesting to Reuben.

Tasha was elated to hear Arabelle invite Reuben to stay. There could not be a kinder soul in all the world than Arabelle Renaud, she knew.

By the time the evening meal was over and Reuben had met Phillipe, he found himself as impressed by the young man as he had been by his wife. When he and Tasha were finally alone and he was escorting her to her quarters before returning to the guest room, he told her, "This surely has to be paradise, Tasha. This is a place I've always imagined finding but never have."

"To me, that is a perfect description of this place. Wait until you see the picturesque countryside in the morning. It is breathtaking!"

"Oh, Tasha—I'm glad I came!"

Tasha reached up to kiss his cheek and declare that she could not be happier. "I didn't know if I'd ever see you again, Reuben."

Reuben's arms went around her waist and he held her close to him. His bushy gray head bent down to kiss her

412

tenderly before he allowed her to leave him. "I didn't know either, Tasha, until I was in London alone without you. It was then I realized just how much you meant to me—to my life!"

He yearned to insist on going through the door with her but he fought that urge. Not with Tasha! It was different with Tasha and he would not do anything to change that. He wanted a lifetime to share with her. At least, he wanted the years the two of them had left to share together.

The next few days, Reuben enjoyed all the daylight hours absorbing the beautiful countryside. He was overjoyed that Arabelle Renaud had agreed to sit for him to paint her. She was flattered to think that an artist would wish to capture her on his canvas and Reuben had told her that it would be his gift to her and her husband.

Excitedly, Arabelle exclaimed, "Oh, monsieur—let it be our secret and I shall present it to Phillipe at the holiday. Oh, that would be magnifique!"

"You are right, madame! So it shall be!"

Each day she arranged the routine of her chores so that she could sit for Reuben for one hour. He found her a wonderful subject, for there was a most relaxed, calm about this young woman.

Tasha was in on their little secret but Phillipe was busy all day long toiling his land, so he had no inkling when he returned to the chateau at sunset what was going on.

When Reuben was not occupied with the canvas, creating the likeness of Arabelle, he went into the countryside to capture the beauty there. No one had to tell Reuben that he was doing some of the best work he'd ever done, and he knew why. He was a happy, contented man!

Never did he want to leave this place—but then he

knew that nothing lasted forever!

It was late when Tiffany returned home from the ball and she had done exactly what she'd intended to do. She enjoyed every dance and she even allowed Paul a kiss or two during the evening. By the time she'd stumbled exhaustedly into her bed, she was convinced that there were exciting times for her to enjoy with other men. Chad Morrow was not the only man who could spark excitement in her. She'd had herself a grand and glorious time tonight. Paul was a good-looking young man, and there were many other men she'd danced and laughed with during the evening. She'd drunk generously of the champagne so her mood was gay and lighthearted.

Her pretty head was whirling by the end of the evening, but she knew that she had been the belle of the ball. Her dainty feet were aching because she'd danced so much. Everyone had raved about her gorgeous gown that seductively displayed her bare shoulders. The shade of blue of the gown was a perfect match to her deep blue eyes. She could not resist wearing Chad's magnificent ring so all her friends could admire it.

When she was asked about it, a mischievous twinkle sparked in her eyes as she replied, "An admirer gave it to me."

She watched as her friends exchanged glances, pondering which of her admirers had given the ring to her. She'd hastily turned to leave them there to speculate as she moved graciously across the huge ballroom. If she wasn't holding onto Paul's arm, there was always another man there eager to be her escort.

Just before the ball was coming to an end, her friend Denise came to her side to whisper in her ear, "Tiffany, you had every man in this huge ballroom vying for your attention. My own escort could not keep his eyes off you all night." Denise felt no jealousy about this, for the young man escorting her tonight was just a good friend and there was no romance in their relationship.

For one brief moment, the smile on Tiffany's face faded as she whispered back to her friend, "I can attract all the men except the one I want, I guess."

Denise saw that sad expression on her friend's face, but that expression didn't last long. She forced herself to smile and be gay. Denise felt sorry for her pretty friend. Neither her wealth nor her beauty gave her what she was yearning for.

It was the last time the two of them talked before they boarded separate carriages to go home.

Madame Renaud had retired to her boudoir long before Tiffany returned home; the next morning when she had intended to tell her about Chad Morrow's arrival in Paris, Magdelaine informed her that Tiffany was still asleep. So she sought not to disturb her until later that morning.

It was past the noon hour when Tiffany finally raised her head from the pillow. Her lovely head felt heavy and throbbed from all the champagne she'd consumed the night before, and she immediately requested Magdelaine go to the kitchen to fetch her a carafe of coffee.

Magdelaine suspected that the mistress must have had a fine time the night before. When she returned to the room, Tiffany slowly sat up in the bed, propped herself up against the pillows, and brushed her hair away from her face.

"A grand evening, mademoiselle?" Magdelaine asked.

"A very festive evening, Magdelaine, and I fear that I am paying for it this morning." Tiffany gave a weak smile to her maid.

"Then this hot coffee should help that, we'll hope." Magdelaine poured the coffee into the cup, handing it to Tiffany. She inquired of her mistress if she would be going out this afternoon or staying home.

415

"I wish I was staying home, but I do have an engagement with Clarise at three. Mon Dieu, I wish I had not made it now. I feel like I'd just like to stay in this bed for another hour or two!"

"What shall I take out for you to wear this afternoon?"

"The pink gown with the striped jacket, I think."

Two hours later, Noah was waiting in the carriage at the front entrance for her to come out the door. The sight of her sweet, pretty face always seemed to heighten his spirits. Her youth and vitality seemed to rub off on him, he'd decided long ago.

Old Noah left her at her friend's house and Tiffany instructed him to pick her up at five. As she mounted the steps, Tiffany was hardly in the mood to help Clarise plan the party she wanted to give during the holidays. Tiffany wished she had not offered to help her now. A party did not even appeal to her this afternoon.

By the time she was sitting with Clarise in her mother's colorful, bright sitting room, Tiffany was wondering why she was queasy. Something did not seem to have set well with her and she found it hard to believe that it was the light lunch she had eaten.

Clarise mentioned that she looked pale as they sipped the tea the servant had just served. Tiffany excused it by blaming the champagne the night before.

But she knew it was hardly the champagne. If it had been only the champagne, she would not have been so concerned. From all the things she'd heard, she had all the symptoms of a lady expecting a child.

Here she was in Paris—and the man who'd sired this child was across the channel in London. She was damned if she'd humble herself to cross that channel and throw herself at his feet to ask him to marry her.

Not even for the Renaud honor could she bring herself to do that!

416

Chapter 57

Charmaine had just returned from a luncheon and was removing her bonnet when she heard a servant informing someone at the door that Mademoiselle Tiffany was not home.

Tossing her reticule and bonnet on the chair in her sitting room, she rushed down the long hallway to see if the caller might be Chad Morrow. She felt very bad that she'd not told Tiffany about him coming to call last night as she'd promised to do.

She saw immediately that it was the tall Englishman standing there at the door with a bouquet of pink rosebuds in his hand.

"Please, Monsieur Morrow—please come in." She had only to look at his face to see that he was profoundly disturbed about the servant telling him that Tiffany was not here on his second visit. She understood the young man's feelings, but then her daughter had no knowledge of his being in Paris and that was her fault. She must confess to him that the blame was hers, not Tiffany's.

She took his arm and led him back into her sitting room. As they walked down the hallway, she told him that she was to blame, for she'd left the house before Tiffany was awake.

417

He tried his best to conceal his rage in the presence of this gracious lady. How could he blame Tiffany if she did not know? he tried to convince himself. Well, it wasn't that easy to accept! He did blame her for being gone.

But Madame Renaud had a way about her that made it impossible for a man to be upset too long when he was around her. So once again, he found himself being entertained by Tiffany's mother instead of Tiffany herself.

They shared a glass of wine and she had the servant take the beautiful pink roses to Tiffany's room. "That is her favorite color, you know. She will love them, Chad."

"She told me," he informed her.

"I'm so sorry that everything has been so badly arranged, Chad, when you've traveled from London, but I guess we have all been trying to catch up with our lives since we've been back in Paris. Tiffany has been trying to catch up for all the time she was away from her friends."

Chad said nothing but he was glad Charmaine could not read his thoughts. He was wondering if, now that she was back in Paris, Tiffany had forgotten all about him and the love they'd shared the last months of the spring and summer.

She noted a tautness on Chad's tanned face as he sat there saying nothing and she quickly added, "Tiffany gave up a lot of her plans when we forced her to make this journey with us. It was a sentimental trip for Pierre and me as well as an opportunity to help our friends. But our daughter did not feel this way."

"Yes, I realize this, Madame Renaud. My father's journals relate all that time when you and the Bernay family were in New Madrid," Chad declared to her.

"Your father's journals, Chad?" Her deep blue eyes were staring strangely and she seemed to be carefully searching his face.

"Yes, Madame Renaud. My father knew you and the Bernays. Guess you could say he found you to be the most fascinating lady he'd ever met."

She knew young Morrow reminded her of someone from her past, and now she was certain she knew who it was. It was that tall, lanky riverboat captain.

"Your father was Cat Morrow, wasn't he, Chad?"

"Yes, madame. He married an English lady who chanced to be in the area when the earthquake struck, after you disappeared from the cabin where the two of you sought refuge. But he was always in love with you even though he knew that it was Pierre Renaud you loved."

"Cat was a wonderful man and he certainly was a dear friend to me. I don't know what I would have done without him during those days. It was a time of panic and madness, and I fear I would not have had the strength to have made it without Cat when I was separated from Pierre and the Bernays when that horrible gorge opened up in the earth."

He watched her face as she spoke and he saw the intensity of pain etched there as she recalled the disaster. "To this day, I still have the small gold nugget Cat slipped into my reticule; he considered it a good luck charm. Perhaps he was right."

"I agree with you that he was a wonderful man. That was why I went to New Madrid—to do something I thought he would approve of." He explained how he had restored the old riverboat and hired Cat's old friend, Bickford, to run it.

"I think that is remarkable and Cat would certainly be proud of you doing that."

"Oh, I know it is a relic and a thing of the past but there are those who will enjoy a little sentimentality. Maybe that old riverboat will provide that."

The young man impressed Charmaine more and more

as she was around him and listened to him talk. She could see why her beautiful Tiffany lost her heart to him.

Once again, Chad felt that he had taken up enough of Madame Renaud's time as he waited for her wandering daughter to return home, so he thanked her graciously. "But I must tell you that I'm glad I've had the opportunity to talk to you about my father and the past."

"It was my pleasure, Chad, and I vow that I shall tell Tiffany that you've been here to see her the minute she returns. I wish you would just stay and dine with us this evening," Madame Renaud requested.

"I wish that was possible but I have an engagement this evening, madame," he lied. "I've some business to attend to while I'm here in the city." He wanted a private time for his and Tiffany's reunion. The idea of sharing their first evening with her parents did not appeal to Morrow.

Leaving the mansion once again without seeing Tiffany was enough to tax Morrow's patience to the limit and he was in a miserable mood. Two days had yielded him no moments of joy and pleasure.

He had to believe that Madame Renaud was telling him the truth; she had really spoken sincerely. If he returned to the Renauds' residence tomorrow and Tiffany was gone again, he would have to wonder if Tiffany was purposely not being told that he'd called on her, not once but twice.

That thought didn't please him but he was smart enough to know that something was not right. There was also the possibility that Tiffany did not wish to see him, but he found that hard to accept.

But a man's imagination can play cruel tricks on him and the most repulsive thoughts invaded his mind as he left the house to return to his hotel.

Could it be possible that Etienne Bernay had captured Tiffany's impulsive heart, since the two of them had been together so constantly after he left the ship in London? He didn't exactly go along with the theory that absence enhanced romance. Two lovers divided by many miles were too often enticed into another's arms. Had this happened to Tiffany? Had she rushed into Etienne's waiting arms when Chad had not come to Paris as soon as he'd intended?

One thing was for sure and that was he'd get his answer tomorrow. If he had to camp outside the Renauds' grounds, he'd see Tiffany if she emerged from that house.

He did not look forward to another night of dining alone but he vowed that he'd not be alone tomorrow night.

Madame Renaud did not hear Tiffany as she returned to the house and rushed upstairs to her room. Tiffany was grateful that her mother was not roaming down the hallway from her sitting room nor that she encountered anyone. It was all she could do to hide her attack of nausea from Noah as they were coming home.

She was so glad that Magdelaine was away from the room when she closed the door and flung herself across the bed. But after she'd lain on the bed a while, the feeling faded and she slowly roused to untie the ribbons of her bonnet which she'd not taken the time to remove when she'd first lain down.

Suddenly her dark blue eyes looked over on her desk to see the mammoth bouquet of pink rosebuds in a cut crystal vase. She came instantly alive to go over to the desk. Wild excitement exploded within her. Could it be that Chad had finally come to her? There was no card by the base of the vase as there usually was when someone had sent her flowers.

As she was standing there, staring down at the rosebuds, Magdelaine rushed into the room. "Oh, you have returned, mademoiselle!"

"Yes—tell me, where did these come from, Magdelaine?" she inquired impatiently.

"I cannot say, mademoiselle—another servant must have brought them to the room and there was no card," the little maid told her.

"Go downstairs and find out for me who brought the roses, Magdelaine. Someone must know," she instructed her maid. Magdelaine saw the anxiety in her eyes and on her face.

"Oui, I will see what I can find out, mademoiselle." She rushed out the door.

Tiffany sank down on her bed and slowly removed her jacket. Surely if it was Chad who'd brought these beautiful roses, he would have waited for her to return, she reasoned with herself. After all these long weeks that they'd been apart and if he was as anxious to see her as she was to see him, he would have waited.

If they had been any other color, she would have thought that they might have been from Paul, but they were pink. Tiffany's romantic heart knew that meant they were from Chad. But then it might just be possible that another man would choose pink roses for her, she had to force herself to admit.

Magdelaine came rushing through the door with her black eyes blazing brightly. "I found out, mademoiselle. It was your Monsieur Chad Morrow. He was here this afternoon while you were visiting your friend."

A lovely smile creased her face as she sighed, "Oh, I knew it was Chad! I just knew it was!"

Magdelaine laughed. "Mademoiselle is happy; I—I can see!"

Tiffany gave a soft gale of laughter. "Ah, I am most happy! He is the man I love, Magdelaine! I thought he was never coming to Paris." She was so overcome with elation she danced around the room, grabbing the little

422

maid's hand to join her as she whirled merrily around in a circle.

The two of them finally collapsed on the bed, laughing and giggling like two schoolgirls. Magdelaine was the first to rise to declare to Tiffany, "Oh, I almost forgot to give you madame's message to join her in the sitting room."

Tiffany rose from the bed to give her gown a straightening and brushed back her tousled hair from her face. "In her sitting room, you said?"

"Yes, mademoiselle."

Tiffany wasted no time leaving the room to see what her mother wanted to see her about, for she was certain that it had to do with Chad.

She flew down the steps swiftly and dashed down the long hallway to her mother's sitting room. Her heart was pounding wildly as she came to the door. Her mother sat with her little dog nestled in her lap, stroking his soft white thick coat of hair. Gently, she placed little Fancy down on the carpet and greeted her daughter.

"You look very radiant, cherie. Do I dare to assume that the lovely roses brought the glow on your face and the news that Chad has arrived?" Charmaine grinned as Tiffany came on into the room to take the chair next to hers.

"He's here? Did you—did you talk to him?"

"I did, and he will be back tomorrow. I invited him for dinner tonight but he had a business engagement."

"Business engagement?" A disgruntled look broke on Tiffany's face. So it was not just to see her that he'd come to Paris. Well, what could she have expected from Chad Morrow!

"Yes, my dear. But then I shall be dining by myself tonight, for your father also has an engagement this evening. So you and I will be having dinner without him, Tiffany." She was hoping to make a point with her darling daughter who must surely realize that everything

423

could not revolve around her.

But Charmaine could not stand to see the disappointment on Tiffany's face so she quickly added, "But he will be coming back tomorrow. He told me to tell you, Tiffany."

She also told Tiffany that this was the second time he'd come to the house. She explained that she'd had to leave the house this morning while Tiffany was still asleep, so she'd been unable to let her know that Chad had called on her the afternoon before.

"He's been in Paris for two days and I didn't know?"

"I'm afraid that is the way it happened, Tiffany, but such is life. My darling daughter, he is here and you shall see him tomorrow, I'm sure."

But for all her words, Madame Renaud sensed the impatience churning in Tiffany and she found it hard to conceal an amused smile coming to her face.

But she could also sympathize with her young daughter, for she well recalled a time when she was just as impatient for Pierre to come to her.

Each day had seemed endless!

Chapter 58

Tiffany was not very good company for her mother as they dined that evening at the long dining room table, all alone. Charmaine understood her daughter's quiet, thoughtful mood and did not try to engage her in conversation.

When the meal was finished, Charmaine asked Tiffany to excuse her for the rest of the evening because she had some letters to write. "I can get all caught up while your father is gone for the evening. You don't mind do you, cherie?"

"Not at all, Maman. I've some things to do myself so we might as well go upstairs together," Tiffany suggested. She felt delighted that they were not going into the parlor, for she was in no mood for casual chatter.

"Goodnight, Maman," Tiffany said as she walked down the hallway to her room.

Two hours later, when Pierre returned, he found himself being greeted by the ghostly quiet downstairs. Charmaine rarely went upstairs this early and he'd expected to find her in the parlor or her sitting room.

He wasted no time before going upstairs. When he saw the light under their bedroom door, the thought rushed through his mind that she might be ill.

The vision of her sitting in bed reading swept any thought away. "Ah, mon cher—you are home!" she greeted him.

As he took off his coat, she quickly explained to him everything that had gone on in the household since he'd left for his office early this morning.

"You mean to tell me Tiffany has not seen Morrow after two days? I had the impression that he was not a man to take no for an answer."

But Charmaine explained how it had happened that she did not get to speak to Tiffany today before she left for her appointment, so her daughter had no way of knowing that Chad had come to see her yesterday. "I told her as soon as she returned from Clarise's this afternoon. She seemed very displeased that he did not wait for her return."

Pierre laughed. "Oh, she did, did she? Well, Tiffany should have gathered by now that Chad Morrow is not a man to wait for anything. If she wants to see him she'd better make a point to stay home for the day."

Charmaine laughed. "Oh, I expect she will do just that."

Now that she had told him about the happenings around their house today, he told her about his father paying a visit to his office. "He has himself a new driver."

"You mean Jean is no longer with him?" Charmaine sat up straight in bed, finding it hard to believe that the devoted, loyal Jean would leave her father-in-law.

"Oh, no. Jean is still there. Father just felt he needed to lighten his duties, so he has hired a younger man." He was glad his lovely wife was already lying down so she wouldn't faint when he told her who the young driver was.

Charmaine was hardly the fainting type but she was so startled she couldn't speak. "He's—he's back here in Paris and not in Cherbourg!"

"That's right. Didn't stay there a week after you and

426

Tiffany returned to Paris. Now, I still don't know just how the two of them met, and Father did not seek to enlighten me. In fact he just shrugged it off, telling me that it really didn't matter. Told me that he and the young man were getting along just fine. Now what do you think about that?"

"I find I am in a state of shock. I—I wonder how Tasha feels about all this. I hope Etienne did not leave without letting her know what he was about." She had suspected that Etienne was not too content in Cherbourg. That was obvious now.

So the two Etiennes had finally met, she thought to herself. Maybe this was how it should be. Maybe fate had planned it.

She'd learned a long time ago that old Etienne Renaud was an unpredictable, perplexing gentleman who liked to shock and surprise you on occasion. But she had adored him from the first moment they'd met, when Pierre had brought her to Paris as his young bride. She also knew that he had instantly warmed to her that day.

All through the years he'd taken great delight in telling his son that if he was just a little younger he'd take her away from Pierre. By the time she'd presented Pierre with three healthy sons old Etienne sang her praises to everyone.

Pierre had always teased her that she had to possess magical powers to have charmed that old man so quickly.

Charmaine urged her husband to make his day shorter tomorrow, for he looked tired. He promised her that he was planning on getting home very early. "I missed having dinner with you and Tiffany tonight," he said.

"And we missed you too, mon cher." She wondered if he even heard her, for he seemed to fall asleep as soon as his head hit the pillow.

Two days of exasperation had left Chad with a short

temper. He realized this when he snapped at the young waiter who brought his breakfast tray to his room. Neither did he take the time to buy fresh flowers from the lady who stood daily just outside the hotel entrance. He walked right past her to get into his waiting carriage, and it was only when he happened to glance out the window and see her crestfallen expression that he was sorry he had not purchased a bunch of colorful flowers.

But the day greeting him outside the hotel was not the most cheerful one. A heavy rain was pelting him as he made his mad dash to the carriage and a rivulet of rain streamed down his forehead. He swiped his face and pushed back his damp hair that was falling to one side.

He wondered if this dark, dismal day was a foreboding. As he looked out the window, he wondered how the driver was able to guide the carriage, for the rain was coming down furiously.

Tiffany's thoughts were much the same as Chad's when she got out of bed to see the torrents of rain hitting her windows. If he did not come today, she'd just die. Magdelaine saw how nervous she was as she helped her dress. After Tiffany had confessed her love for this Englishman to her yesterday, she was hoping for Tiffany's sake that he would come back again today.

The young man Magdelaine loved was coming to see her today. Etienne had sent her a message yesterday and Magdelaine was trembling with excitement. She felt a little guilty about the way she was rushing to finish up Tiffany's hair so she might ask her mistress if she could be free for the next couple of hours.

When the last pin was placed in her hair, Magdelaine inquired if there was anything else she could do. Tiffany told her she might go to her own quarters if she wished.

"Etienne is coming to see me, mademoiselle. Monsieur Renaud gave him the day off and he sent me a message to meet him in the stables. Old Noah will say nothing, and the other driver is gone today since you or Madame Renaud were not going anywhere."

Tiffany saw her face, so flushed and glowing about the prospects of seeing Etienne again, and she told her to take as much of the rest of the day as she wished with him. But as the excited Magdelaine was about to rush out of the room, Tiffany called out to her, "You will be drenched, Magdelaine, without a wrap. Don't you have your shawl?"

"No, mademoiselle . . . I forgot it this morning."

"Then take my cape. Mon Dieu, I don't want you wet to the skin running from the house to the stable. That rain is coming down in sheets."

"Thank you, mademoiselle. Thank you so much!" She dashed out the door as she flung the lovely berry-colored cape around her tiny shoulders.

Tiffany ambled over to the window to look out on the grounds below. She smiled when she caught sight of her petite maid rushing across the garden toward the stables. The truth was she and the black-haired Magdelaine were about the same size and height. Seeing her now with the brilliant colored cape draped around her shoulder, she realized the similarity. Through the clouded haze of rain, she watched Etienne's tall, slim figure coming in sight and the two of them rushing into each other's arms. The sight of them made her envy Magdelaine. She wished that she herself was rushing into Chad's arms. She watched the two as they clung together, then moved toward the area of the stables and the carriage house.

Tiffany could not decide whether she should stay here in her room or go downstairs. Wherever she was, the day was going to move slowly as she waited for Chad to appear.

She finally decided to leave her room to go downstairs. Madame Renaud saw her go into the parlor but she did not join her. Instead, she went into her sitting room where Fancy eagerly waited for her company. She figured that Tiffany might prefer to be alone. After all, she had been the one to greet Morrow the last two days. It was time that Tiffany had a chance to greet him.

Charmaine quietly closed her door so that her little rascal of a pup would not run out the door. She decided to write a long letter to Tasha. She wanted to invite her to spend some of the holiday season with them. Paris was a magnificent sight at holiday time. Besides, she could enlighten Tasha to the whereabouts of her son if she didn't know.

Tiffany was not the only one to observe the meeting of Magdelaine and Etienne. Chad was just leaping out of the door to the carriage to take the few steps to the front entrance of the house, when he chanced to glance over at the garden area. He caught sight of the flowing woolen cape of deep wine and the mass of thick black hair cascading down the back of the cape.

He froze on the spot where he stood, caring not that the rains were soaking his coat and his hair. There was no shadow of a doubt who the tall, black-haired man was. He watched as Etienne's arms claimed her possessively and they walked out of sight.

Briskly, he turned on his booted heels and marched back to his carriage. His first inclination was to order the driver to take him back to his hotel and not even enter the house, but by the time he'd raked the wet hair out of his face and calmed some of the rage smoldering within him, he decided that he was going to march into that house to see just what kind of outrageous story he would be told on this third trip.

Tiffany was not in the parlor or staring out the window as she'd been doing just moments before Chad's carriage pulled up. She had gone into the kitchen to get one of the cook's fresh-baked iced rolls in the hopes that it might ease the churning of her stomach.

She was finishing the last bit of the roll and coming down the far end of the long hallway as she heard voices—and that deep, husky voice could only belong to Chad. She rushed down the hallway as fast as her dainty feet could carry her. The sight of her coming toward him with her long hair streaming around her shoulders and her deep blue eyes sparkling brilliantly made Morrow's mind go blank to the sight he'd seen some few minutes ago. His arms had a will of their own as they reached out to grab her as she eagerly rushed into them.

All he could think of as he held her like this was that those half-parted rosy lips were inviting him to kiss them and he did in a long, lingering kiss. That wild, wonderful desire that always flamed in him when he held Tiffany in his arms flamed now as his huge body felt her pressing close against him. This little enchantress could render him so damned helpless that he could not control his feelings.

He felt her sweet lips respond to him as they always had in the past and he asked himself what kind of wicked little vixen hid behind that sweet angel face of hers?

When he finally released her from his strong arms, she looked up at him, her long thick lashes fluttering, to exclaim breathlessly, "Oh Chad, I thought you were never coming!"

A crooked grin came on his face and he masked his private thoughts very well as he remarked, "Now, did you, love? You mean you were lonely for me, Tiffany?"

She pushed away from him to search those cold gray eyes staring down at her. There was an offensive, haughty tone in his voice.

There was no smile on her face as her eyes locked with his eyes as she frankly admitted, "Yes, I was lonely, Chad. And I did miss you!"

"You missed me so very much, eh? Did you have someone to keep you company, love?"

431

Why was he being so mean and cruel after he'd just kissed her so passionately?

"Wha—what's the matter with you, Chad?"

"I'll tell you what's the matter with me. One of the things I loved about you was that beautiful honesty of yours. It made you a rare, magnificent lady to me. There was no deception between us and for the first time I found myself in love!"

"And I found myself in love with you, too."

Every fiber in his being tensed as his cold gray eyes danced over her face. "Maybe we measure our affections differently, love. The woman I love can love only me and no other. I'm very selfish that way."

She shook her head, for she did not understand his angry words and she saw the furor on his rugged face. "What are you saying, Chad? Suppose you try being honest with me. Say what you mean, for heaven's sake!"

"What I mean, Tiffany, is this. Etienne Bernay has no right ever to kiss your lips. I'll allow your parents to tell you why he shouldn't." He backed up a couple of paces to free himself from her and her nearness. A pained expression was etched on his face as his deep voice declared to her, "I've only five days left here in Paris, love, and I'll not come here again. The decision must be yours. Come to me in the park on Saturday afternoon if you truly love me as I have loved you. Come to me by three in the afternoon, for that was the time we first saw each other. You remember, Tiffany?"

She watched him turn and walk away from her, but somehow she knew that he was as pained as she was. But the things he'd said had completely puzzled her.

Chad Morrow had always been so different from any other man she'd known. That was what had so completely captured her interest and her heart.

More than ever, she was convinced that he was like no other man she'd ever meet!

432

Chapter 59

Tiffany rushed up the stairs to her room, glad that Magdelaine would not be there for the rest of the afternoon. As soon as she slammed the door, she marched over to her desk and angrily yanked the pink roses from the vase. She didn't wish to look at his roses and be reminded of him. Right now, she almost hated him!

She felt as if her whole world was shattered; all her romantic dreams about Chad had been swept away as hastily as he had turned to walk out the door into the rainy afternoon.

She flung herself across the bed and gave way to the tears welling up in her since Chad's voice had turned so suddenly cruel. She didn't understand this stranger she encountered this afternoon. What was the snide innuendo he was tossing at her? As soon as she gained control of her distraught emotions, she intended to demand of her mother and father just what Chad Morrow was insinuating.

The way he uttered Etienne's name it was obvious he must hate him, but why? When she looked at Chad's gray eyes, she thought she saw raging jealousy sparking there, but he had no cause for jealousy where Etienne

433

was concerned.

Downstairs, Charmaine kept waiting anxiously in her sitting room for her daughter to come to her after Morrow left. She would have expected her to come into the room with her face glowing with happiness because the two of them had finally gotten together. But no such thing happened, and more than an hour passed. Madame Renaud was beside herself with curiosity. What had happened to make Tiffany rush up to her room?

Quietly she mounted the stairs and walked down the hallway to stand outside Tiffany's door. She had only to listen to her daughter's sobs to know that there had obviously been a lover's quarrel. Oh, how she yearned to go into the room and comfort her as she had when Tiffany was a child, but the hurt she was feeling now was different, and she knew Tiffany wanted to be alone.

Charmaine knew so well that the comfort she could give Tiffany was not what she needed. Only Chad Morrow could ease the pain she was feeling, so her mother walked down the hallway to her own bedroom.

Oh, she was so very glad that Pierre was planning on being home early tonight! He would know how to handle the situation far better than she could.

She sat in her room, silently staring out the window to watch the miserable weather outside. Darkness was already shrouding the grounds outside as the days grew shorter now and the nights were longer.

She finally urged herself to go to her dressing table to attend to her toilette, since she had given her own maid the day off.

She could not have been happier to see the door fly open and her dear husband come through it. She eagerly got up from the velvet stool and rushed to greet him.

"Mon Dieu, I shall start coming home every night this early if this is the response I'll get," he laughed as he held her in his arms.

434

Charmaine gave him a smile as she looked up at him. "I would love that, Pierre, but I am especially glad you are here tonight."

A frown wrinkled his brow as he asked her what was troubling her. She told him about what had happened this afternoon. "It had to be a lovers' quarrel for Tiffany to have retreated to her bedroom for the rest of the afternoon."

He gave her a kiss on the cheek and remarked, "We know all about that, don't we, cherie? If their love is strong—as strong as ours was—then everything will be just fine."

Charmaine sighed and shook her head. "But Tiffany is so headstrong and stubborn, even though I feel sure that she adores Morrow with all her heart. Why else would she have been in her room sobbing so?"

Her husband laughed and reminded her just how unyielding she'd been once with him when they were young lovers. Pierre pointed out to Charmaine that if Chad loved Tiffany the way he had loved her, a mere lovers' quarrel would not cause him to leave Paris.

"I told you I was glad you are home. You're already making me feel better," she told him.

"Maybe I can do the same thing for Tiffany before this evening is over," he told his wife.

The two of them finished dressing before going down the stairs together; both of them were wondering what kind of mood their daughter would be in when she joined them for dinner.

Nothing she or Magdelaine could do hid her red-streaked eyes, Tiffany saw as she looked at her reflection in the mirror. She asked the maid to bring her dressing gown after her hair was all in place. "Please fetch a tray for me and inform my parents that I am feeling a little under the weather—nothing serious so they won't rush up to see about me, you understand?"

"I understand, mademoiselle," Magdelaine said, feeling helpless that she could not cheer up her mistress. She'd felt terrible that when she'd come to Tiffany's rooms so aglow with the time she'd spent with Etienne and had seen the unhappiness on Tiffany's face. She'd mentioned to Tiffany that she'd seen Monsieur Morrow's carriage arrive as she was running to meet Etienne in the rain shower. All she could think to say to her mistress was she was hoping her reunion with Monsieur Morrow had been as happy as hers was with Etienne. As soon as she'd said it she was wishing she hadn't from the look on Tiffany's face.

In faltering voice, Tiffany had remarked, "I wish it had been, too, Magdelaine, but it wasn't. Oh, God, it certainly wasn't."

But for the last hour since Magdelaine had returned, the maid's words kept coming back to her: she'd seen Chad's carriage arrive. Was it remotely possible that he had also seen Magdelaine meeting with Etienne and thought it was she? Was that the reason for the venom in his voice and the sparking jealousy in his eyes when he spoke about Etienne?

When dinner was finished, Pierre and Charmaine left the dining room together. Charmaine turned down the hallway to her sitting room to gather up her little lap dog, Fancy, before going upstairs to their bedroom to wait for Pierre to come to her. She knew that he was on his way to Tiffany's room to try to comfort her.

Tiffany recognized his rap on her door and sighed, "Oh, no!" But she motioned to her maid to open the door.

Pierre walked in with his usual air of authority and asked Magdelaine to excuse them. "I wish to speak to my

436

daughter," he graciously told the maid as he dismissed her.

Magdelaine obeyed his request and left the two of them alone, but she knew that her mistress did not wish an audience with her father tonight.

For the first few minutes, Pierre asked his daughter the questions any father would ask of a daughter who'd not joined her family for dinner, but as his dark eyes searched Tiffany's face it pained him to see how sad she was tonight. He also realized that his pampered daughter was no different from any other lady, so if she was to know the ultimate joys and passions of life, she must also know the hurt and pain. This was life! All his wealth or influence could not spare her. Neither could his doting devotion shield her.

He sat down on the side of her bed, took her hand in his, and told her that he was sorry that her meeting with Chad had not been the happy occasion she'd anticipated. "Love is an insane thing sometimes," he said softly.

"And who is saying that I am in love with Chad Morrow?" She sat up in the bed with an indignant look on her face. He knew that her fierce pride must be terribly wounded.

To look into her deep blue eyes was like looking into Charmaine's. "There has to be deep love for deep hurt, ma petite."

"I—I can't imagine that you could ever say the cruel things to Maman that Chad said to me this afternoon!"

"I was no paragon, Tiffany—especially when I was a young, reckless rascal. Ask your maman," he told her.

"I shall, Papa, and I shall ask you to explain to me what Chad meant when he told me to ask you and Maman why Etienne Bernay had no right to kiss my lips. That's the way he put it. Tell me, Papa, what he meant by that! I have the right to know what he was talking about."

Her sharp words stabbed at him like a knife and they found him completely unprepared as he faced his daughter. He remembered how Charmaine had told him that they should tell Tiffany the truth and he had intended to do just that as soon as they arrived back in Paris. But then he'd had his talk with his father and old Etienne had put some shadows of doubt in his mind. So he'd questioned if it was even necessary. Since they'd returned to Paris, Etienne had played no part in Tiffany's life, as he had back in New Madrid.

As he gathered control of himself from the stunning blow Tiffany had handed him, he thought about Chad Morrow and the overwhelming fury of jealousy that must have been consuming him this afternoon. Mon Dieu, he knew what it was like for a man to be jealous! It was a gnawing in a man's gut.

"All right, Tiffany—I'll tell you what Chad was talking about. I'll tell you the whole story and then you will know why I felt I had an obligation to do what I did for Tasha and Etienne." He left no detail untold and Tiffany listened attentively.

As she heard what her father was saying, she shuddered to recall a time in New Madrid when she and Etienne had amorously embraced and kissed in the cave during the storm. There had been other times that their lips had met, but somehow, their love-making had never reached a peak where there was no stopping it. Dear Lord, she was glad it had not!

But then he explained to his daughter how and why his plans to tell her had changed after his talk with her grand-père.

"Now, you know the entire story. There is no mystery about anything. The only mystery left for me to wonder about is how Chad Morrow was privy to this carefully guarded secret, for Jacques Bernay and I were the only ones to know this and later on, we both told our wives."

438

"Well, I can't tell you that, Papa, but it is obvious he does know."

Pierre bent down to kiss her cheek. His only daughter was very special to him. She always had been and she always would be. He had answered her questions as honestly as he could and cleared up the mystery Chad had stirred in her.

The rest he had to leave in Chad's hands. But he felt that he knew Tiffany well enough to know that the desires of her heart would lead her to the man she loved.

If Chad Morrow was half the man he'd sized him up to be, he'd eagerly take her in his arms and their strong love would conquer everything standing in their way.

He moved to leave her room and bid her goodnight. "Forget today, Tiffany. It is the past. Think about tomorrow, for that is all that matters."

Chapter 60

Disillusionment consumed Chad about this ill-fated trip to Paris. Perhaps he should have listened to his two devoted servants, Delphia and Simon, and not attempted to come. It had certainly given him no pleasure for the special effort he'd made to travel here. Now as he rode in the carriage back to his lonely hotel room, he wished that he had the illusion to cling to. He didn't even have that anymore!

Maybe that was all Tiffany Renaud was ever meant to be in his life, for all men have their special fantasy of their ideal woman. From the minute his eyes had seen her, he saw that vision was a flesh and blood woman with the most astonishing, beguiling beauty. It was not merely a dream he'd often dreamed, for that spring day in a Paris park he had actually seen her.

Once he'd tasted the sweet nectar of her lips he had been carried to a height of rapture he'd never known with any other woman.

Never had he had the desire to kill any man until the times he was faced with the lusting men who'd tried to have their way with Tiffany. Having had his fair share of fights, he knew his powerful fists could be a fatal weapon. Twice since he'd met Tiffany he'd come close to killing.

Right now, the way he was feeling, it would not do for him to come face to face with Etienne Bernay, for this might be the time he'd not stop himself in time. But then, he was reminded that he did not have two strong fists to render that kind of havoc right now.

All the way back to his hotel, he asked himself how she could have possibly rushed into his arms with her lovely face smiling as though she was so happy to see him, when he'd just spied her out there in the gardens enjoying the embrace of Etienne Bernay. What kind of wicked little wanton was she?

Why had he punished himself by even making the effort to enter the house and come face to face with her? he wondered. What a bloody fool he was! But then he had been a bloody fool since the minute he'd met her. Nothing or no one had ever distracted him from his job and the very strict rules he'd laid down for himself the last five years, until that little temptress came along.

The truth was, everything about his life had changed since she'd paraded by him that day in a carriage.

Another young man walking jauntily down the street that rainy day in Paris was thinking how a certain little black-eyed girl had changed everything about his life. The sweet warmth of her still lingered with him as he walked in the chilling rains.

He already missed his sweet Magdelaine, and especially so since they'd made love this afternoon in the cozy warmth and seclusion of the stable. By the time he'd taken a farewell kiss from her sweet, rosy lips when he'd said goodbye to her, he knew that he was finally cured of the fever of Tiffany Renaud. Etienne Bernay had never been happier as he walked the long distance to Etienne Renaud's home.

He knew that meeting Magdelaine by chance there in

the gardens had changed his whole life and it was the reason for his discontent when he was so far away in Cherbourg. He had to come back to Paris so he could be near her.

He had Tiffany to thank for introducing him to old Etienne Renaud. He genuinely liked the old man whom he'd found to have a generous heart during the few weeks he'd been living under his roof.

With his food and lodgings furnished, Etienne was able to save all the generous wages old Etienne paid him. He'd written his mother a long letter to tell her about his good fortune and he asked her understanding about his leaving Cherbourg as he'd done.

As he neared the stately old mansion, he was consumed by his dreams of the future he hoped to share with his pretty Magdelaine. He had not asked her to marry him this afternoon but he planned to the next time he saw her, he'd decided as he was walking back to the Renaud mansion.

Etienne's cheerful mood was obvious to old Etienne that evening. When they were in the study together, old Etienne teased him playfully, "Only know one thing that makes a fellow as jovial as you are tonight, son, and that's a pretty little mademoiselle."

Etienne laughed. "You're far too wise for me to try to fool, so I wouldn't dare to lie to you, sir."

Old Etienne laughed. "You see—I"m not too old yet that I can't recall my youth."

Etienne confessed to the elderly Renaud that it was Tiffany's maid, Magdelaine, that he'd lost his heart to after arriving in Paris.

"Tiffany's maid, eh?"

"Yes, monsieur. I think I loved her the first day we met!"

"And does she feel the same way about you?"

"I think she does. She swears she does," Etienne

told him.

The old man's head was already whirling with ideas of his own about this new development. But that could take some doing, for old Etienne would never do anything to offend his beloved granddaughter. Nothing was more precious to him than Tiffany!

"If the two of you really love each other, then it will all work out," he told Etienne as he prepared to go upstairs to bed.

"I know it will, sir. I've no doubt about that at all!"

Old Etienne liked his attitude. He knew he'd been right about his first impression of the young man the day Tiffany had brought him here.

Never been wrong on my first impressions yet, old Etienne told himself as he tucked the coverlet around himself and got into his bed.

He wasn't wrong this time!

Reuben Grodin knew he wasn't wrong about his feelings for Tasha Bernay. It was not merely a moment's attraction aboard the ship, either. The weeks he'd been in London and she'd gone on to France he had plenty of time to sort out his feelings and he'd been left wanting desperately to see her again.

He'd decided to come to Cherbourg and the few weeks he'd been in this divine place had convinced Reuben that he was in love. It had been a long time coming, but it had finally happened and he'd never felt more alive in his whole life. His paintings were reflecting his serene contentment and happiness.

Those sweet stolen moments of ecstasy that he and Tasha shared were more than he'd ever dreamed of experiencing at this time of his life. If it was any woman other than Tasha, he would not have been plagued with such serious concern. But Tasha was no ordinary woman. She was a gracious, loving lady whom Reuben loved and respected. He thought about their love for a few days before he approached her with what had been on his mind for a quite a while.

They'd dined with the young Renaud couple and he accompanied Tasha back to her private quarters. She'd invited him in to share a glass of Phillipe's fine red wine as she'd done often lately.

"We make a good pair I think, Tasha dear. What's your opinion?" Reuben remarked as he took the glass of wine she offered him.

She gave one of her little laughs. "We make a very fine pair."

"Glad you feel that way," he smiled, brushing aside his straying mop of gray hair.

Tasha sensed that Reuben's whole manner was about to turn serious from the look in his eyes. The first thought that came to her was that he had done a number of magnificent paintings of the beautiful countryside and the portrait of Arabelle was almost done. Arabelle was elated about the wonderful gift that she was going to present to Phillipe during the holidays. The thought prodding at her was he was getting ready to announce that he must leave for London in a few days.

"Damn it, Tasha, I know I'm going to make a mess of this, for to be honest I've never done it before, but I do love you, and to me that's what counts, so I'm going to ask you to marry me," he said as fast as he could utter the words for fear if he didn't he'd not get them all out. In a dramatic gesture he threw up his hands as he hastened to add, "Now before you answer me, let me tell you that I could take care of you very comfortably. I've just never had the need to spend any of my money on myself all these years. I didn't need a fine house, for an attic room was good enough for me, nor did I feel the need for fine clothes. I merely enjoyed being comfortable in my

444

old baggy trousers and shirts."

"Oh, Reuben! Reuben!" Tasha's hand reached over to cover his and her black eyes were so warm with the great love she felt for this unusual, talented man. "I—I found you the most interesting, exciting man I'd ever met even in those old baggy pants that first day we met on the ship. But the more I was around you, Reuben, the more I came to know a man who was so loving and kind, a man who enjoyed the simple things of life as I do. Oh, yes, Reuben, I'll be happy to marry you and share your life. I can't think of anything more wonderful or exciting."

The bushy-haired artist reached across the table to ksis her. When he released her from his huge arms, he still had an apprehensive look on his face. "You really . . . you really mean to tell me you love me too?"

She gave a lighthearted laugh. "I really mean it, Reuben Grodin, with all my heart."

He was like a young man who had just wooed and won the young maiden he'd been courting. "I'll buy us a little cottage right here in Cherbourg because I've come to love it so, and I'll paint my paintings. God, Tasha, we will have ourselves one hell of a good life. You shall go with me when I have to go to my exhibits back in London and Paris. Wherever I go, you'll go with me."

"Of course I will, Reuben. I'd let you go nowhere without me if I married you."

Reuben felt the same exultation he experienced when he had put the final stroke on one of his canvases; he was overwhelmed with joy. Never had he been a happier man than he was this night.

"Oh, Tasha—let's not wait. Let us be married quickly. I find myself most impatient to be your husband. We've no time to waste, for I've already had my fiftieth birthday."

"And so have I, Reuben, so I agree with you. I see no reason why we should wait."

Once again he eagerly embraced her and declared to her that he knew he had to be the happiest man in the whole wide world tonight.

"Might I impose on the Renauds for the use of their buggy tomorrow so that we might go into Cherbourg, Tasha?" he asked her.

"I—I suppose you could. What are we going into Cherbourg for, Reuben?"

A broad grin came on his face as he took her small hand in his and said, "Why, I've a ring to buy for my little bride."

It seemed strange to hear herself being called a bride at her age, for she'd never expected to marry again after Jacques had died. But then she'd never expected to fall in love again the way she had with Jacques Bernay. By a strange coincidence, she'd met both men when she'd least expected to.

But she knew that there were many kinds of love a woman could feel, and what she felt for her dear Reuben Grodin was just as deep and intense as the young reckless love she'd known with Jacques Bernay—the first man she'd made love with.

She had never felt so serene and secure in her life as she did now with Reuben. It amazed her that she could have fallen in love with two such different men as Jacques and Reuben.

All she knew was she'd never been happier in her whole life!

Chapter 61

A magnificent fragrance wafted through the house from the drying herbs hanging from the beams of Arabelle's kitchen. She had already hung the garland up the railing of the stairs leading to the second landing of the house, and its pungent aroma permeated her parlor. The huge grapevine wreath decorated with colorful dried flowers hung over her mantel. Along the mantel were sprigs of rich red berries and cones amid branches of evergreens. The sparkling light of the candles gave a festive air to the room.

Tasha could not have wanted a more perfect setting for her wedding than she'd had as she and Reuben had stood in front of the fireplace to exchange their wedding vows.

The grand feast Arabelle had prepared for them after the wedding was fit for a king and queen. She and Reuben felt like royalty tonight.

Arabelle had fixed a roasted goose with herbed potatoes on a huge platter. Bowls of fresh vegetables from their gardens lined the tables, along with fresh baked bread. Tasha was overcome with emotion by all the effort Arabelle had put into the feast she'd prepared, when the wedding cake was brought out and placed in front of her and Reuben. There were bottles of wine from Phillipe's own vineyard.

No bride could have asked for a lovelier wedding than Tasha had. Dressed in the pretty berry-colored gown that Charmaine had bought for her when they were in New Orleans and the beautiful gold ring with a single diamond on the band, she felt like a queen. But Reuben was not satisfied that she should have only a ring, and he'd insisted that he buy her a pair of diamond earrings. When she sought to protest his extravagance, he quieted her by reminding her that he was not exactly a poor man and could well afford the particular earrings he thought were perfect for Tasha's tiny ears.

It seemed that Arabelle and Phillipe had forgotten nothing to make the night a special occasion for the two older people they'd become most fond of. When the festivities had finally ended and Tasha and Reuben left to go to her quarters, they found a beautiful wreath hanging on Tasha's door. Inside, a fire was already burning in the small fireplace. Tasha's settee was lined with pretty new pillows which she knew Arabelle had made, and on the table was a wicker basket filled with cheeses and muffins, along with two bottles of wine. A tray held a variety of the special little iced cakes Arabelle was always fixing.

"There are surely no nicer people than those two, Reuben," Tasha declared. "I've only one regret and that is that Charmaine and Pierre could not have been here. I would have wished for Etienne to have been here too."

"I know, Tasha. I know, but maybe this was the way it was meant to be. Just maybe, we shall go to Paris during the holiday season. Would that please you, dear?"

A radiant smile came to her face as she exclaimed, "Oh, Reuben—how could—how would we manage that?"

He broke into laughter. "I told you, Tasha dear, and I guess I will have to keep reminding you for a while, that I can afford to do many things I've never sought to do in

448

the past. I found myself rather enjoying spending some of that money the other day, especially when it is on my pretty wife. Yes, I think I shall enjoy doing that from now on."

"Oh, Reuben—how could I have ever been so lucky?" she sighed as her hand reached up to pat his bearded face.

"Ah, I am the lucky one and I will never forget it, Tasha. I waited my whole lifetime for such a magnificent lady as you to come into my life. May I tell you it was well worth the wait?"

The iced cakes, wine and cheese were not touched that night, for the lamps were dimmed as the two of them sat there on the settee in front of the glowing fireplace in a warm embrace.

Each of them dwelled quietly on their private musings about how happy and content they felt for the first time in many months. Both vowed that they would never let anything take this happiness away from them.

Reuben knew that never would he be a happy man if he had to live his bachelor's life again. He needed Tasha. She was the inspiration he'd always searched for and never found.

Tasha knew that whether her marriage met with her son's approval or not, she did not care, for she was happy. She doubted that Etienne would seek her approval of the young lady he sought to marry.

As she sat close to the husky Reuben and his arm held her close to him, she knew that by his side was where she wanted to be for the rest of her life.

Those first two days after Chad had walked out the door and left her were like a nightmare lived over and over. On the third day, Tiffany knew she had to get out of the house or she would go crazy, so she summoned her carriage to be brought around. As it would chance to be,

449

it was old Noah who was to drive her to Denise's house.

Noah found her unusually quiet this afternoon. She was not the vivacious Mademoiselle Tiffany he took around Paris. This young miss was very precious to the old man, for he'd watched her grow into a lovely young lady from a tot. What was troubling her so? he wondered.

"You are not feeling well, mademoiselle?" he asked, turning back to glance at her.

"I've felt better, Noah," she mumbled with her eyes cast down at her lap, for she dared not look the old man in the eye. He knew her all too well and she feared that she might burst into tears, as she'd done so often the last two days.

"Anything I can do to help you, mademoiselle? Known you since you were a babe in your mother's arms. Feel like you almost mine. You tell Noah what troubles you!"

He turned his back to her to look back at the street they were traveling along. Crazy as it might seem, she found Noah easy to talk to and her pride did not have to stand in the way with him. "What do you do about a man you love and hate at the same time?"

"Well, mademoiselle . . . it depends on if you hate him more than you love him or if you love him more than you hate him. Some man hurt you, mademoiselle? You tell Noah and Noah will have a talk with that rascal!"

She smiled as she glanced at him with his graying fuzz of hair and his humped, feeble body. How dear he was to her! And to think that he was willing to do battle with anyone who had hurt her.

"No, Noah—I'll take care of Chad Morrow in my own way. He's just a hardheaded Englishman with a stubborn streak in him that matches mine."

"You speak of the man who rescued you in the park back in the springtime?"

"The same man, Noah."

Noah made no comment, for he found this man to his

liking. He found it hard to believe that he could do anything to hurt her. Noah remembered that day vividly; he had been left with a high opinion of that Englishman. Living as long as he had, Noah always figured himself to be able to size a man up. Chad Morrow had received a high score on his card.

"He's here in Paris?"

"Yes, Noah, he is here in Paris. At least, he is here until Saturday."

Noah said no more, but the old man knew what he was going to do to help these two young people to get back together.

When he left Tiffany at the doorstep of her friend's house, he asked if he should wait or return in a few hours' time as he often did.

"Come back in three hours for me, Noah. There is no point in your waiting all that time for me to have lunch with Denise and have my visit. Come for me at four."

"I'll be here at four, mademoiselle," Noah promised before he spurred the bays to move on down the drive.

But it was not back to the Renauds' residence that Noah guided the carriage. He figured he knew which of the city's hotels young Morrow would be staying in. This was the direction he guided the bays.

When he arrived at the hotel, Noah secured the carriage and walked into the lobby and up to the desk to inquire about a Monsieur Chad Morrow.

As Noah had expected, he was staying in this hotel and the desk clerk was obliging to the old black man when he requested that a message be sent to Morrow's room to join him in the lobby. The young desk clerk was clever enough to observe that such a livery as this black man wore denoted some very wealthy French family here in Paris. There was a certain dignity about Noah that urged the clerk to oblige the old black man. Noah did not wait long in the lobby before he saw the tall Englishman

451

trotting down the stairway. He recognized him immediately even though he'd only seen him that one day in the park.

Noah watched that towering figure of Morrow ambling toward him with a broad, friendly grin on his face and Noah knew that he also remembered him warmly. He liked this young man, so he knew that whatever was troubling the little mademoiselle could surely be worked out. He knew Mademoiselle Tiffany had a very explosive temper when she got riled. He rather suspected that Morrow was a hot-blooded gent himself.

"Noah, what a bloody good sight to see! What brings you here?" Chad greeted him, extending his hand to shake Noah's.

"Good to see you again, monsieur. Surely is! Could we sit down for a while to talk, monsieur?"

"Of course, Noah!" Chad saw how the old man's health had failed since he'd last seen him.

Chad took his arm to lead him over to one of the comfortable chairs. "Now tell me, Noah—how did you know that I was here at this hotel?" He did not recall mentioning to the Renauds or Tiffany which hotel he was staying at while he was in Paris.

"Mademoiselle Tiffany told me you were in Paris, but I figured this might be where you were staying."

Chad wondered if he dared hope that Tiffany had sent a message to him by Noah. "And how is Tiffany?" he asked the black man.

The old fellow did not mince words with the Englishman. "Mademoiselle is not happy and I think you are the reason for her unhappiness."

Morrow was taken aback by the man's blunt words, but he recalled the great devotion between Noah and Tiffany.

"What you say is probably true, Noah, and I don't like it any better than you do. I have not been too happy myself since I've been here in Paris, and if it's any consolation I will tell you that my only reason for coming here was to see Tiffany."

"It is consoling to hear that, sir. I—I know I'm out of order and the little mistress would feel like skinning me alive if she knew I'd done what I've done, but I—I just had to," Noah told Morrow.

"She'll never know it as far as I'm concerned, so rest easy."

"I appreciate that, Monsieur Morrow. But then I always had a high opinion of you since you saved Mademoiselle Tiffany from those rascals."

There was a gentle tone in Chad's deep voice as he told Noah, "I love her too, Noah. I love her more than anything in the world, but I must tell you that I am a very selfish, possessive man where Tiffany is concerned. I won't share her with any other man and especially Etienne Bernay!"

"Etienne Bernay, monsieur? Why would you think that she has any interest in him, may I ask?"

Chad told him how he'd come to the house two afternoons and each day Tiffany had not been home. Yesterday when he'd come for the third time, he happened to see her out in the gardens where she was rushing to meet Etienne during the heavy rain.

When the black man burst into laughter, Chad frowned, for he saw nothing amusing about what he was saying. It took Noah a few moments to quit laughing, for if this was what this senseless lovers' quarrel was all about, he could quickly clear it up.

"Oh, Monsieur Morrow—it was not Mademoiselle Tiffany you saw with Etienne. It was her maid, Magdelaine! She is as tiny as her mistress and she has hair as black as her mistress's. I'll wager you did not see her face, for then you would have not made such a mistake as you obviously have."

He knew the man was not lying to him. It was true that

he had not seen the face of the young woman in the garden. So what could he say but that he had been a bloody jealous fool! He made this confession to old Noah.

Noah was feeling much better by the time he noticed the hands of the clock in the lobby, and knew he must take his leave so he could pick up Tiffany. He was urged to ask Chad Morrow to get in the carriage and come with him, but he didn't figure that he would, for Morrow was a proud man.

Chad patted the man's shoulder as they said goodbye and he told Noah, "I'll be hoping you will be bringing Tiffany to me in the park. I've told her that I'll be waiting there for her Saturday afternoon. I'm counting on her love for me, Noah. I'm counting on that very much!"

Knowing what a proud, stubborn miss she could be, Noah gave him a nod of his graying head and declared, "I'll be hoping so too, monsieur."

Chad threw his hand up and gave a final wave to the driver as he put the carriage into motion.

Chapter 62

Noah had expected to come away from his meeting with Chad Morrow not feeling too kindly toward him. This had not been the case at all. In fact, he felt about him as he had the first afternoon he'd met him. More than ever he was convinced that he was the right man for Tiffany Renaud. She had to realize this before it was too late, for if he left Paris without her this time, there might never be another chance for them.

Oh, he wished he had the right to talk to her as he yearned to, but he knew he couldn't. But he was surely going to say a few prayers for those two young people. This, he could do!

She looked no happier when he picked her up than she had when he'd left her. The trip back home found her just as quiet and withdrawn as she had been a few hours earlier.

After Noah left him, Chad gave way to an impulse to pay a visit on Madame St. Clair. Maybe it would take his mind off Tiffany and how falsely he'd judged her yesterday. Now, he understood the perplexed look on her lovely face and the bewildered look in those blue eyes when he'd flung his jealous accusations at her. He cussed himself for his hot temper and jealousy that had gone out of control. Every fiber in his body urged him to rush to her but he knew he must not. He had to have the satisfaction of knowing that she loved him enough to come to him.

So he went to the residence of Madame St. Clair instead and she eagerly greeted him. They enjoyed each other's company for over two hours; she spoke of his mother and frankly admitted to Chad that she rather doubted that her friend Elizabeth could have found happiness with any man.

"It was the very strict upbringing of her family, Chad. She never gave herself a chance to find happiness with your father, so she rushed back here to the folds of her family. It was the only place she felt safe. It was sad, but that was the way it was." Chad told her how he had discovered in his father's journals that the opal ring had been a gift from Cat to young Elizabeth.

Madame St. Clair was not a lady who enjoyed lingering in the past, especially when it was a sad one, so she inquired of the young man if he'd given that magnificent black opal ring to any young lady.

He gave her a sheepish grin as he declared, "Well, I have the young lady picked out, but I intend that the ring you are talking about shall be given to her after we are married and not before."

"I see. So you do have the young lady picked out?"

"I do, and if all my plans work out, I will be leaving Paris with her this Saturday."

With a twinkle in her eye, Madame St. Clair dared to inquire of him, "And are you going to tell me who this young lady is, or am I to have to wonder about this for days and nights to come?"

"I would not do that to you, madame. The lady I speak about is Tiffany Renaud."

She broke into a gale of laughter and gave him an

approving nod of her gray head. "Ah, she is the perfect lady to wear such a ring. I shall be hoping all your plans work out, Chad."

When Morrow bade her farewell a short time later, he was glad he'd obeyed his impulse to visit her. Somehow, he felt in better spirits. But he was also ready to get to the comfort of his room, for the damp rainy days here in Paris had not helped the condition of his leg and hand.

Once he was back in his room, he decided that a little whiskey would ease the pain in his heart and his body. Once again, he ordered his dinner brought to his room on a tray instead of going downstairs to the dining room.

After a few shots of whiskey, he sat wondering what old Cat would have done if he was in his shoes. Damn, he'd like to have him there with him tonight to talk with about this woman who was driving him crazy!

Tiffany knew she had to join her family for dinner this evening but she didn't relish the idea. The meal seemed endless and as delicious as the food was, she could hardly swallow a bite. She sensed that her parents were scrutinizing her when they thought she was not aware of their eyes upon her.

She welcomed the sight of her father finally getting up from the table. She was more than ready to retreat to her room. But her father casually announced as they left the dining room, "Keep your maman company, ma petite. I've some papers to go over in my study."

Charmaine turned to Tiffany and suggested, "Let us go to my sitting room instead of the parlor, cherie. My little Fancy has been ailing today and I would like to see about him."

Tiffany could not bring herself to be excused. "I'm sorry to hear that poor little Fancy's not feeling well. But he is very old, Maman."

"I know, Tiffany. I got him as a pup right after my dear

457

White Wolf died. I'd brought him all the way from New Madrid with me. He lived a wonderful sixteen years."

The sitting room glowed with the flames of the burning logs in the fireplace and Charmaine found the little lap dog curled up there on the rug by the hearth, sleeping peacefully. Seeing this, Charmaine was satisfied. So she invited Tiffany to sit down and the two of them would share a glass of wine.

"Some would think me crazy, Tiffany," she remarked. "Your dear father has given me many exquisite jewels during the years we've been married and I have enjoyed their beauty and wearing them. But nothing ever thrilled me as much as the gift he brought home to me that afternoon when he knew I was so lonely about losing my dear White Wolf."

Tiffany found that hard to understand, for she'd never felt that way about any pet she'd ever had. But she did admire all the magnificent gems her father had bought her mother.

Charmaine gave a soft little laugh. "I see by your face that you find me ridiculous—oui?"

"I guess I just remember all those beautiful jewels, Maman."

Charmaine sat down and took a sip of wine. "Ah, they are, but they give you back no love, Tiffany. I never expected the life I've led. It has gone beyond the bounds of anything I could have possibly imagined as a young girl. But I will tell you this, that love has no boundary. I was just as happy when your father and I were in New Madrid in those humble surroundings as I have been in my palace here in Paris, shall we say."

"I—I find that very hard to believe, Maman," Tiffany retorted as she raised a skeptical bow.

"I thought you might, ma petite, but there will come a day when you will tell me that you see what I was talking about tonight." Charmaine's deep blue eyes locked with her daughter's eyes that were that same deep blue-violet shade. "Nothing matters, Tiffany, if the man you love also loves you more than anything else in the world. I found such a man in your father. When you find such a man, don't let him go, or you'll regret it the rest of your life."

She watched the expression on Tiffany's face as she spoke and she knew her daughter had been absorbing what she'd said. Mon Dieu, she prayed she had!

"It seems your papa will be lingering in his study longer than he thought," Charmaine said. "Shall we call it a night? I think I am ready to go upstairs and get Fancy settled. How about you, cherie?" Charmaine stood up and set her glass on the small chest by the side of the settee. She walked over to the hearth to scoop up her little lap dog in her arms and dim the lamp.

Tiffany stood quietly, saying nothing. It was not until they had climbed the stairs side by side and were going down the carpeted hallway that Tiffany turned to face her mother and say, "Maman, I must tell you something before we say goodnight. I will hope someday that my daughter will feel as I feel tonight. I will hope that I can be just half the lady you are. I can see why Papa adores you so and my brothers idolize you. Grand-père considers you the grandest lady he has ever known and tells me so from time to time. I've often thought he fears desperately I won't measure up to you." She laughed, as she leaned around to kiss her mother's cheek. Charmaine's arms went around her to hold her warmly in an embrace. "Ah, ma cherie—never you worry. You will be as much woman, and maybe more! I've no doubt about that!"

Both women were overwhelmed with the emotions consuming them. Both were close to tears when they broke the embrace to rush into their bedrooms and close the doors.

Charmaine was overcome with the grand tribute her daughter had paid her. Her words meant so much to Charmaine! She knew that what she'd said to Tiffany had surely had some impact. She had only to look at her daughter's face to realize that.

God forbid that she might be wrong, but she knew Chad Morrow loved her daughter and she would swear that Tiffany loved him, too. She could not stand to see stubborn pride deny those two young people a glorious happiness they could share.

Being a romantic, she knew that it took such two eyes meeting to lose one's heart. She'd experienced it!

Her mother had given her much to think about so Tiffany quickly dismissed Magdelaine as soon as she entered the room. Once she was alone, it didn't take her long to make the decision that her stupid pride was not going to deny what her heart desired. She was going to the park tomorrow afternoon to meet Chad.

There was more to think about besides herself, Tiffany realized. No longer could she allow herself to ignore the fact that she was carrying Chad's baby.

Nothing in her pampered, spoiled life had prepared her for this and she knew that this was something she would have to bear alone. She'd told herself she was too young to have a baby but nevertheless, she was going to have one, she was certain. That possibility had never dawned on her when she'd given herself in the sweet surrender of Morrow's demanding arms.

Well, it was Chad's responsibility too, she thought to herself as she finished undressing and slipped between the sheets. She planned to tell him exactly that tomorrow when she met him in the park.

With her plans set in her mind, she drifted off into a most peaceful sleep.

The opposite was true for Chad Morrow, for he had many thoughts disturbing his sleep. Restlessly, he lay there in his bed, wondering if Tiffany would come to the park to keep the rendezvous with him.

He could not be sure, for she was so unpredictable! Every time he'd felt sure of her affection and love for him, she'd quickly flared out with that cool aloofness that chilled him. He'd wondered if he would ever conquer her fickle heart.

Tomorrow he would have his answer, but would it be the answer he hoped to have? In the meanwhile, he lay there in the darkness, alone.

He had no idea how many hours passed before he finally fell to sleep. But the dawn was soon to break when he did close his eyes and yet, he was wide awake some four hours later.

Once again after he was shaved and dressed, he found that time was hanging heavily on his hands, for he still had hours to wait for the appointed time.

He decided to go downstairs to see if the flower vendor was in front of the hotel entrance.

The splendor of the day greeting him was enough to lift his spirits. There were no dismal clouds hovering over the city and no rain falling. It was a delight to see the old lady there with her flower cart and a glorious amount of pink rosebuds in the bucket. He bought all of them, which made it a joyous day for the flower vendor.

After he took the huge bouquet of roses up to his room, he suddenly felt the need for something to eat, so he went down to the dining room to satisfy his sudden surge of hunger. Whatever apprehensions he'd been plagued by were swept away, it seemed. Everything was going to go his way. He felt it deep inside.

Maybe it was the glorious day outside, he thought as he went back up to his room. At least the last two hours had gone by faster.

He didn't have much longer to wait now, so he could not be happier!

Chapter 63

Being the mother of a daughter was a different experience from being the mother of three sons, Charmaine could honestly say. Never had she realized that more than she had this long day. Would it end happily for Tiffany or would she be devastated by sadness? Oh, she prayed that her daughter would have what her young heart desired!

Tiffany's maid came rushing down the steps and almost collided with Charmaine. "She is ordering the carriage, madame. She wishes Noah to drive her to the park," Magdelaine exclaimed.

"To meet Chad Morrow, Magdelaine?"

"Oui, Madame Reynaud!"

"Ah, I am so glad!" She felt that once the two would meet that their love would take care of the rest. A very happy Charmaine Renaud urged the little maid to go on her way to inform Noah that his services were needed.

Magdelaine dashed away to do as the madame had requested. Charmaine turned to her sitting room with a happy smile on her lovely face.

But she made a point of watching Tiffany leave the house a little later from a concealed spot in the hallway as she came down the stairway.

She was close enough that she could see the expression on Tiffany's face. There was a certain look of determination in those deep blue eyes and set of her mouth, as she descended the steps. But there was more that Charmaine saw. It was no carefree, frivolous girl she viewed. It was a strikingly beautiful woman who was going to her lover.

Her mother observed the special effort she'd given to toilette and the stunning outfit she'd picked to wear to meet Chad. She had never looked more enchanting!

When Old Noah put the carriage into motion, Charmaine turned to walk down the hallway once again to go to her sitting room. Anticipating that it would be a long afternoon for her, she decided that it would be a perfect time to finish her letter to Tasha.

But she found herself reflecting about her past as she tried to write her letter. Memories paraded through her mind of the time when she was Tiffany's age, and she relived the pleasures of the ecstasy as well as the heartbreak. Only with Tiffany could she share these feelings. That was the difference between sons and daughters, she concluded as she sat at her desk.

At the park, Chad dismissed the driver and his carriage after he'd leaped down with the bouquet of pink roses. He made for the exact spot where he'd first set eyes on Tiffany.

No longer were the trees flourishing with bright green leaves. Now they had turned to a rich gold and rust color. Some were a most vivid scarlet hue. The verdant carpet of grass was beginning to be covered by layers of falling leaves.

There was no band playing today in the park but the young couples were there, strolling hand in hand. Older couples were taking an afternoon walk down the stoned pathway to enjoy the glorious sunny day. Each time a carriage rolled down the trail winding around the park, Chad turned to see if it might be the Renaud carriage.

After a few minutes, he found the bouquet of roses to be cumbersome and he also noticed how the strollers glanced his way as he paced back and forth with the flowers cradled in his arms. Amused smiles were on their faces and Chad was beginning to feel embarrassed when they stared in his direction.

He walked over to sit down on one of the wooden benches so he could lay the huge mountain of roses on the seat beside him. By now he was getting a good case of nerves, so he took the gold case holding his cheroots out of his inside pocket of his coat and took one out to smoke.

He also pulled out his pocket watch to see what time it was. Oh, Tiffany, you little minx—don't you disappoint me! he sighed silently.

Sitting there puffing on the cheroot did ease his impatience. He still had a clear view of the carriages as they rolled down the lane some three hundred feet away from where he sat on the bench.

Never would he have expected to be in Paris for almost a week without knowing the bliss of one sweet kiss from Tiffany's lips! He had certainly not anticipated that he would arrive in Paris to spend all his days and nights alone as he'd ended up doing. It had not been the paradise he'd dreamed about back in London while he was working so hard to strengthen his leg and arm so he could travel here.

Well, he'd made it to Paris for what good it had done him. Today was the day of decision and it was in Tiffany's hands. He would never darken the doorstep of the Renauds' house again, he'd vowed. Tiffany had to come to him!

Old Noah was apprehensive as he guided the carriage

along the lane. His eyes darted from one side to the other. He asked Tiffany, "Where do you wish to go in the park, mademoiselle?"

"I'm—I'm not sure, Noah. Just drive around," she told him. Chad had been very vague, now that she thought about it, when he'd told her to meet him, but that was Chad Morrow!

Ironically, the carriage had gone past the spot where Chad was sitting. But Tiffany had not spotted him nor had he glanced up to see old Noah sitting on the driver's perch of the carriage as they'd gone by.

Chad had the need to stretch his long legs, so he tossed his cheroot to the ground and ambled back to the spot where he'd been standing when Tiffany and her mother had passed by that first day they saw each other.

As Tiffany's carriage turned the bend of the lane, she spotted the tall, towering figure standing in that same place where she'd first seen him. Her heart started pounding wildly. He was hatless and his dark brown hair was unruly, with wisps falling over his forehead.

"Stop the carriage, Noah!" she cried excitedly.

Noah had also spied Chad by now, and he did as she requested. A broad grin came to his face as he watched her leap out of the carriage and race like a gazelle toward the young man who was also running to meet her. The lovely roses fell to the ground.

Old Noah figured that he would be returning home with an empty carriage.

There was no more beautiful sight to Chad's gray eyes than the one of Tiffany with her skirts held high as she ran toward him. His strong, outstretched arms caught her lovingly to him. "Oh, love—you came to me! You came to me!" He held her to him so close that she could hardly breathe but she didn't mind, for this was where she wanted to be—in the circle of his arms.

Chad knew that he would never let her go. He intended

to keep her close to him forever.

All his lips had to do was claim hers and Tiffany knew that she would have been a fool not to have come to the park. To deny herself this ecstasy for the sake of pride would have been insanity!

When they finally broke the long, passionate kiss, Tiffany found herself weak and trembling as she glanced up into Chad's adoring gray eyes.

In his deep, husky voice he told her that Noah had left. She slyly smiled. "He probably knew that I was not going back home with him." Chad said nothing for a moment as he just allowed himself to savor the loveliness of her face. "I'm not going home, am I, Chad?" she asked him with her thick-lashed eyes fluttering nervously. He saw the face of sweet innocence there with those blue eyes gazing up at him.

"What do you think, love? You must know that I'm never going to let you go now that I've got you again. No, my darling Tiffany—you're not going home!" Chad was fired with wild desires that had been waiting far too long to be fulfilled.

Together they started to walk down the lane with Chad's arm around her waist. Surely an empty carriage would come along, Chad figured.

But it would not bother Chad if they had to walk all the way to the hotel, for he was with the woman he loved and the way she was clinging to him it would seem to him that she was as happy as he was.

As it would happen, they had only a short distance to walk before an empty carriage rolled down the lane. Chad quickly threw up his arm and the carriage halted. He assisted Tiffany inside and leaped up to sit by her side.

She asked not where they were headed for she didn't care as long as she was with him. By the time they reached his hotel and ascended the steps to the second landing, the huge clock in the lobby was striking five. Chad pressed her closer to him.

As they walked through the door, he glanced down at her. She wore a thoughtful expression and he noticed how very quiet she'd been for several moments. He turned her around to face him and his gray eyes locked with hers as he asked her, "Is something wrong, love? Is this my talkative Tiffany?"

She smiled sweetly up at him. "Nothing is wrong, Chad. I was just thinking about things . . . many things. I was thinking that finally everything is right."

"Ah, love . . . that makes me happy to hear you say that. I'd say we've a reason to celebrate, Tiffany love. Champagne is in order, wouldn't you say?" He gave a boyish laugh as he picked her up in his arms and whirled around the room. He was quickly reminded that his one hand was still not up to full force yet.

He gently lowered her back to the floor and left her only long enough to order some champagne to be sent to his room.

As they sat there sipping their champagne and enjoying just gazing at each other, Chad turned serious as he told her, "Tiffany, it was not a matter of me not keeping my promise to you. I was forced to delay the trip." He explained what had happened to him and the weeks he'd been confined to his bedroom.

"Oh, Chad, if only I'd known that, what a lot of misery both of us would have been spared! Mon Dieu, why didn't you write me?"

"Couldn't, love, and damned if anyone else was going to write my love letter to you. Couldn't have done that!" he grinned.

She bent over to kiss him as she softly laughed. "Oh, you adorable devil! I love you, Chad Morrow! I love you madly but then you know that!"

He parted from her just enough to whisper against her cheek, "Keep telling me that over and over again, Tiffany!"

How much precious time they'd wasted, Tiffany thought to herself as she sat there so close to him. She thought how she'd gone through sheer hell yesterday and now she felt she must be in heaven.

"I'll tell you as many times as you want me to, Chad," she declared.

"I'll want it the rest of my life, love. I figure it will take that long to get my fill of you, Tiffany Renaud."

A teasing twinkle sparked in her blue eyes as she asked him, "Are you asking me to marry you, Chad Morrow? You've never mentioned marriage before, you know."

"Are you sure of that? I could have sworn I had. Well, I'm asking now," he told her with a grin on his face.

A soft, lilting laugh broke from her as she quickly responded, "And I'm accepting before you change your mind or disappear again."

"Never fear! I don't intend to let you out of my sight again until we're married. I hope you'll agree to that."

But before she could answer him his lips had captured hers.

Her kiss was her answer so she had no reason to reply!

Chapter 64

Two glasses of champagne were enough to make her head whirl, for she'd eaten no breakfast or lunch before she'd left to keep her rendezvous at three in the afternoon. But it was the intoxicating effect of Chad's love-making that dazzled her as she abandoned herself to his forceful male body towering over her.

Yet, she'd never known such tenderness in his kisses and caresses as they consumed her. No deceptions plagued them now. The love they both felt had conquered all this and in its place was the overwhelming desire for each other. Both knew that nothing was ever going to come between them again.

Chad's hands had missed the feel of her soft, velvety flesh and his lips had hungered for the sweet nectar of those lips. He greedily took his fill.

It was sweet music to his ears as he heard her soft gasps of pleasure as his flushed body pressed down against hers to burrow deep within her. A searing liquid heat was rushing through him as her flaming heat washed over him.

"Oh, God, Tiffany! I—I wish I never had to stop loving you like this." He could feel the effects of the torrid passion swelling within him.

Her soft sensuous lips responded to him, letting him know that she was feeling the same way as he did. He felt the eager arching of her body against his. A new ecstasy mounted their passions like a wildfire out of control.

Neither of them could stop it so they gave themselves up to it. Tiffany felt the giant quaking of Chad's body which left her breathless as she clung to him, her fingernails digging into his back.

With a husky gasp, he whispered just how much he loved her. Now, that she was filled with Chad's love, a divine calm settled over her as she snuggled in the circle of his arms.

Chad had been so completely absorbed by Tiffany when they'd entered his room that he'd not closed the drapes at the window. Neither of them had taken notice that the bright sunshine was no longer gleaming through the windows. A light shower was pelting the city streets below, but it was a cozy, gentle rain.

The two young lovers contentedly fell asleep in each other's arms. After all the restless nights both of them had gone through lately, they both slept for many hours.

Tiffany gave no thought about her parents or what they would be thinking!

It was a happy Noah who'd returned to the Renaud home that afternoon. But he felt it his duty to report to Madame Charmaine, so he did.

"She may be late in coming home, madame," he said.

"So she did meet with Chad?"

Noah nodded his gray head. "She did that, madame, and if I may say so I think it was a very happy reunion." He saw a pleased smile brighten the madame's lovely face. He knew that she was as happy about them as he was.

"I am grateful to you for telling me this, Noah. I would

imagine your services will not be needed for the rest of the afternon or evening," she slyly smiled.

"I figure it that way, too. So I'll bid you a nice afternoon and evening before I go."

"The same to you, Noah. Cook's fixing a nice fat hen so I'll have some sent to you this evening," Charmaine told him.

"That is mighty kind of you, madame. Always enjoy that."

Leisurely, Charmaine strolled back to her sitting room. She thought about old Noah's remarks that it might be late when Mademoiselle Tiffany returned home. She sat down in her favorite chair and gathered up Fancy in her lap to stroke his fur. If she was to wager, she would bet that Tiffany just might not be returning home tonight. If Chad Morrow was the ardent lover her Pierre had been, then she was certain that Tiffany would not be coming home this night!

Late in the afternoon when she went up to her boudoir to refresh her toilette before Pierre arrived home, she broke the news to Magdelaine about her mistress. Madame Renaud was certain that Tiffany would have no need of the little maid's services tonight.

All the time Charmaine waited for her husband to come through the door of their bedroom, she wondered how he would react to her news. Would he be outraged and fly into a fury of temper?

When he did appear, his face looked so weary and tired that Charmaine said nothing, since he seemed to have other things on his mind besides Tiffany.

It was not until they'd gone down to the parlor and Tiffany had not appeared to join them for dinner that he inquired about their daughter.

Rarely did she keep the truth from her husband, but tonight she did not tell him the whole truth. She justified her reasoning because she felt he should have a pleasant

471

meal before she mentioned anything that might upset him.

"Tiffany had an engagement tonight with Chad Morrow," she casually replied.

"I see." He said nothing more and Charmaine was more than pleased that he did not seem to be concerned. Instead, he complimented her about how beautiful she looked.

The two of them enjoyed a fine meal of roasted chicken with all the trimmings. Charmaine had not forgotten to instruct one of the serving girls to take old Noah a generous portion.

"Come into the study with me, cherie, and share a brandy. I've something to tell you," Pierre suggested to her as their meal was finished. Knowing her husband as well as she did, Charmaine instantly sensed something had happened today that he was about to announce to her.

As his wife had suspected when he first arrived home, Pierre had had a very busy day. His father had visited his office with some most surprising news.

In addition, the jeweler he commissioned to find him a most magnificent ring to present to his wife had finally found one that surpassed the one Chad Morrow had deprived him of acquiring back in New Orleans. The moment he'd arrived back in Paris, he'd decided to find a ring for Charmaine that would match the beauty of the one his daughter wore on her finger.

Today, he had viewed it and purchased it. The huge canary diamond had cost him a fortune, but he was thrilled to find it just in time for her birthday.

When they were settled in the study and Pierre went to the liquor chest to pour them some brandy, she noted that particular twinkle in his black eyes.

472

As he stood in front of her to hand her the glass of brandy, she looked up into his face to declare, "Pierre, will you please tell me what's on your mind? My curiosity is killing me and you know it!"

An amused grin was on his face. Some things never changed about his beautiful Charmaine and this was what he adored about her.

"All right, ma petite—I shall tell you and then we will raise a toast with our brandy. My father came by the office this afternoon and Etienne had had a letter from his mother. It seems Tasha and Reuben were married just recently. Our Phillipe and Arabelle gave them a beautiful, simple wedding there at the chateau and they are going to remain there for a while. It seems Reuben loves the Cherbourg countryside and wants to live there."

Tears of joy streamed down Charmaine's face. "Oh, Pierre! What wonderful news you've brought me tonight!"

Most women were a horrible sight when they cried, but not his Charmaine. She was gorgeous!

"I've also brought you something else, ma cherie. I should make you wait—but I've not the heart to do it. So give me your hand, Charmaine."

She did as he requested, with a puzzled look on her tear-stained face as he reached into the pocket of his coat to take out the ring and slip it on her finger. The flashing brilliance of the pale yellow stone was enough to make her gasp, "Mon Dieu, Pierre!"

"It reminded me of that glorious flowing pale gold hair of yours, Charmaine, that first night I saw you there on the cliffs of the Channel Islands. With the moonlight shining down on you against the pale gold of your hair, you looked like some kind of goddess to me and now I know you are. You've made me a most happy man all these years and this is my way of telling you how I feel."

She was too overcome with emotion to speak and once again she could not stop the tears from flowing. So her deep blue eyes stared tenderly at him expressing the deep emotions that her lips were unable to utter.

Pierre sensed the depth of her emotions so she did not need to speak. He gathered her in his arms and held her close to him.

Tenderly he urged her, "Come, Charmaine—shall we go upstairs?" She slowly rose from her chair as his arm remained around her waist. As they mounted the steps of the winding stairway, he glanced her way to remark to her, "We've no reason to stay up to wait for our daughter to be coming home. I'm thinking that she won't."

She turned to look at him and she saw that devious twinkle in his eyes. A smile came to her face as she asked him, "So you do remember how it was with us when we were very young?"

"Like it was yesterday! But when a man is married to a sensuous and beautiful lady he never has to live with memories, Charmaine."

She squeezed his hand holding hers as she softly declared to him, "But it takes such a magnificent man as you for a lady to feel about her husband as I feel about you, Pierre Renaud! Don't you forget that!"

These two older lovers entered their bedroom chamber feeling as ardently romantic as they had some twenty-five years ago.

Tiffany could not believe that she had slept in Chad's arms for over ten hours. He was still asleep as she wiggled free and slipped out of bed. Quickly, she slipped into her lacy undergarments and helped herself to Chad's hairbrush to try to put some order to her tousled mass of black hair. To attempt to put it back in the style Magdelaine had created was an act of futility, so she just allowed it to hang loose and free down her back.

Chad was still sleeping so peacefully that she was reluctant to awaken him. What did it matter if another hour or two went by, she reasoned, since she'd not been home all night?

So she curled up in the chair, her legs tucked up under her, to gaze down at the quiet Paris street below. The light rains had ceased and the early morning sun was coming up.

Just sitting there silently by herself and thinking about the fury of their love-making made her blush now. Chad brought out a very wicked, wanton streak in her, she'd decided. She wondered if this was how it was with her handsome father and beautiful mother and the reason the romance was still so alive in their long marriage.

Chad's gray eyes had opened long before she was aware of it but he said nothing. He lay there just enjoying the enchanting sight of her sitting there in her white lace undergarments with her legs casually crossed and her black hair streaming around her shoulders.

He wanted to just lie there quietly, without her knowing that he was awake, to see if he could figure out what was going on in that pretty head of hers, for her expression told him nothing about what she was thinking. Was she happy as he was or was she having regrets?

But she happened to dart her blue eyes in his direction so hastily that he could not pretend to be asleep as he'd been doing. "Hello, sleepyhead!" she said and smiled at him.

"Good morning, love," he replied, rising up to prop himself against pillows with his bare broad chest exposed. His brown hair fell carelessly over one side of his forehead and he brushed it aside with his fingers.

She sat down on the side of the bed. "That's just it, Chad. It is morning and I've been away from home all

475

night long. Mon Dieu, I have probably given them a very restless night of wondering where I've been."

His arms snaked out to pull her to him. "I don't think so, Tiffany. But Noah would have surely told them that he left you with me in the park."

"But, Chad—"

He quickly interrupted anything she would have said, with his sensuous lips kissing hers. When he finally sought to release her, he had a serious expression on his rugged face as he asked her, "You are not ashamed of your love for me, are you, Tiffany? You see, I suspect that your mother and father are as ardent lovers as we are. I have no fear of facing them to declare how I feel about you."

"I am not ashamed, Chad," she declared.

"Good! Tell me that you are convinced beyond a shadow of doubt that you love me and no one else," he tested her.

A devious urge to taunt him ignited in her as she tilted her head to one side. With a provocative look in her eyes, she dared to purr, "Well, I think I am, Chad."

The little imp was teasing him and he knew it. A cunning grin creased his face as his strong arms reached out to grab her. "Well, I guess I just better convince you once and for all, Tiffany Renaud!" He proceeded to do just that.

Tiffany was convinced that he was the only man she could ever love with all her heart and soul!

Epilogue

A lavish, spectacular event was not what Tiffany or Chad had wanted when they were married, and Pierre and Charmaine respected their wishes by making it a very simple ceremony in their parlor with only the family gathered there. But Tiffany had insisted that two people be included besides her brothers and Grand-père. Magdelaine and Noah were there. Grand-père never went anywhere without Etienne by his side anymore, so Etienne was also there.

Grand-père's wedding gift to Tiffany was one he'd saved for this special occasion for many years since his wife had died. He presented her with her grandmother's magnificent collection of gems. When he'd kissed her on the cheek, he whispered his plans for the future: "I think I will have to take little Magdelaine into my household now, for you will be leaving for London and she'll have no mistress to serve."

She knew exactly what he was talking about. She agreed that it would be a magnificent idea.

The gathering might have been small, but the gala festivities taking place in the Renauds' mansion that night lasted until dawn. It was a wonderful night Tiffany would always cherish.

True to his vow to Delphia and Simon, Chad took Tiffany to England for the holiday season so they might enjoy their first Christmas in his townhouse.

A flurry of light snowflakes was falling as they left the carriage in front of Chad's townhouse, and Tiffany felt the warmth of his home even before Simon had greeted them at the door. The house was ablaze with lights as though Chad had been expected to arrive.

The bald-headed Simon had only to open the door that night and see the stunning young lady standing by Chad's side to understand his anxiety to get to Paris. She looked like something on an old masterpiece canvas with her hooded cape around her shoulders and that lovely face framed in her ermine-trimmed deep blue wool cape.

Delphia was elated that her Christmas goose and plum puddings were going to be enjoyed by Chad and his new bride. Like Simon, she was immediately entranced by the new little mistress of Chad's townhouse.

Tiffany did not feel the depths of despair to leave her beloved France and the city of Paris as she had when she left to go to New Madrid. She loved London and her dear Sabrina lived here. So she felt like no stranger in these parts.

The moment she'd walked into the entrance of the townhouse, there was no feeling of unfamiliarity. A warmth surrounded her and she felt she was home!

Chad sensed this feeling, for it showed on her radiant face, and he could not have been more pleased.

It was a grand homecoming for him to share with his lovely bride the delicious dinner Delphia had prepared and later give Tiffany a tour of her new home.

"I love it, Chad," she exclaimed. Privately, she was already planning how easily the small guest room next to their bedroom could be turned into a nursery. She had not mentioned anything about this to Chad yet.

All evening Chad also had indulged in his private

478

musings about old Cat Morrow and how pleased he would have been to know that the woman he'd truly loved would be sharing something very dear and precious with him. They would be sharing a grandchild. Someday, he would let Tiffany read those old yellowed journals so she might get to know the man who was his father.

When they finally climbed the steps to Chad's bedroom, the hour was late but Tiffany was not tired. Chad confessed to her that she had given him the most wonderful holiday he'd ever had. "I think I must have bought this townhouse with you in mind, Tiffany. I'm so happy that you like it. I was concerned about that."

Tiffany wondered how she'd ever imagined that he was an unfeeling man. She assured him that she loved her new home.

He reached into his coat pocket to take out the black opal ring—for he felt this was the right time to give her this special wedding gift as he'd told Madame St. Clair he intended to do. He took her dainty hand in his and slipped the exquisite ring on her finger as he told her, "This was my mother's and now it's yours, Tiffany. But I pray it will bring you more happiness than it did to her."

She stared at the rare gem mounted in its gold setting. "It will, Chad. I can't imagine I could possibly be happier. The only thing that will make me happier is when we have a young Chad Morrow running around this townhouse."

She held her breath to see what his response would be to this remark. She had to know for she'd delayed this so long now. Would he be repulsed by it?

"We shall have ourselves a son or daughter before 1836 is over, love. I will see to that, my darling Tiffany."

"Now how can you be so sure of that?" she giggled.

"I'll tell you why I say that, love. If you aren't carrying my child now then I'm going to work damned hard in making it happen."

She gave a soft gale of laughter. "Save yourself the effort, Chad. I feel sure that this has already happened some two months ago."

"You mean—you mean—," Chad stammered.

For the first time she found the silken tongue of Chad Morrow unable to speak. But he soon found it and declared to her, "Well, let's just make sure, love."

There was no doubt about that as far as Tiffany was concerned, but it was so wonderful to surrender to Chad's overwhelming ardor when he sought to make love to her.

There was no reason to deceive herself any longer, so all she had to do was give herself up to the wild, wonderful desires he always stirred in her.

No other man had ever made her feel as Chad Morrow had from the first moment they met. No other man ever would!

Forever, she would love him!